TERRAPIN SKY TANGO

Michael Warren Lucas

Copyright Information

Terrapin Sky Tango
Copyright 2019 by Michael Warren Lucas. All rights reserved, including the right of reproduction, in whole or in part in any form. Published in 2019 by Tilted Windmill Press.

Cover photo © 2016 baona | iStockPhoto

Editor: Zig Zag Claybourne
Copy Editor: Amanda Robinson
Book design by Tilted Windmill Press.

Paperback ISBN-13: 978-1-64235-026-5
Hardcover ISBN-13: 978-1-64235-027-2

This book is a work of fiction. Names, characters, places, and incidents either are products of the author's imagination or used fictionally. Any resemblance to actual events or locales or persons, living or dead, is entirely coincidental. This book is licensed for your personal enjoyment only.

Tilted Windmill Press
https://www.tiltedwindmillpress.com

For what it's worth, the people of Scottsdale, Arizona are lovely and charming despite living in a hellscape every summer. The UK is amazing and deserves better than Beaks gives it. The Detroit city block that contains two prisons and a police station is real, but I encourage you to visit one of the Motor City's delightful restaurants or live music venues instead.

My thanks to all the folks who demanded, wheedled, begged, and pleaded for more Beaks. I must single out Bob Beck and Kristof Provost for appreciation, for reasons that they'll be delighted to ~~rant about~~ explain should you see fit to inquire. Robert Watson provided helpful photographic evidence of the existence of Tesco coffee machines. Julianna Powell can be inexpensively bribed into discussing logistics. Especially copious and heartfelt thanks, regards, and offers of undisclosed services of dubious legality go to Brigid Collins, Zig Zag Claybourne, Bonnie Koenig, Brian Powell, Amanda Robinson, and Lucy Snyder.

Those who threatened to lock me in a room and feed me via the gap under the door until I finished writing this book are specifically excluded from this declaration of gratitude.

For Liz.

1

I need to scrub the blood off my reputation.

Yes, "mess with Beaks and she will utterly destroy everything you love" is a useful addition to it. And a rep should grow with you, developing fine notes and subtleties, so that it becomes worthy of a connoisseur's attention and a higher billing rate.

But a reputation is your best advertising. I can't put up billboards to broadcast my services. What would they say? *Beaks: She Steals, so You Don't Have To?* Maybe *Six Feet of Skinny Sneakiness?* Or *Limber. Lethal. Lawless.*

No, the only way people learn about me is by word of mouth.

Or the bulletin board at the local Interpol office.

Plus, I'm told there's an FBI agent that has my picture in his office, my smiling Mediterranean face over my real name: Billie Carrie Salton. And that he uses it as a dart board. But the person who told me that is kind of a suck-up, so who knows?

If it's true, it's adorable.

I've worked hard on the core of my rep: "They'll never know Beaks was there, until they realize something's missing." If you're a bloated rich bastard, you can hire me to rob some other bloated rich bastard. None of my clients think they're bloated rich bastards, of course, but here's a hint:

If you can afford me, you're bloated rich.

If you're thinking of hiring me, you're a bastard.

The one who hired me for this gig? Even more of a bastard. And not because of the thievery.

First: Arizona. No, not the nice cool mountains, but—ugh—Phoenix. North of Scottsdale, more precisely.

In August.

Even early in the day, before the sun's poked its head up above the mountains lining the valley, it seems the locals replaced the sky with an open-air incinerator. It's seven AM and I need another gallon of sunscreen. The light's bright enough to threaten my scalp beneath my inch-long hair. Four nights in this hellhole and I'm so dry my eyeballs hurt and the inside of my nose has cracked like I'm in close solar orbit. I can smell the dried-up traces of my own nosebleeds. I've already drunk a gallon of water just trying to keep the headache to a distant thud.

The few bushes and scrub trees scattered across the flat, dead ground have gone into some kind of weird summer hibernation. Even the cacti look shriveled. A couple of them have a sturdy wooden cage supporting them. I hear these particular cacti are a protected species, because the world doesn't have enough thorns.

We're standing at the east side of this useless intersection. A bunch of developers convinced the city council that the boom would never end and got them to approve this network of main roads in the desert. Four lane roads, of course, because everything grows forever and you want your city infrastructure to support all that growth, right? One square mile sections, so you can allocate chunks one after the other. And you'll want underground utilities, because they're storm-resistant and they cost more to install. Think of the tax base you'll get from all these homes and businesses! Oh, wait, there's an economic crash? Economies don't grow forever? Sorry, we'll take our fees for pouring all this concrete and shut up now.

The only thing traveling this road is blown sand.

The only sound: the faint grumble of traffic, thousands of gas-guzzlers and the shouts of frustrated drivers blended by distance.

Our rental car lurks behind us. It's a great big Old Rich People sedan, silver. The trunk is shut, but both front doors are open so we can leap in if we need to. I had to knock out the rear window when the bullet holes made the safety glass opaque.

We won't even have air conditioning until we get the hell out of this Hell.

A mile west I can make out the white line of the brick wall separating the cozy upper-middle-class condos from the wilderness. The limey reek of hot concrete already fills the air and it's not even proper daytime.

But if you want to exchange stolen goods for a suitcase of cash, and you don't want anyone sneaking up on you, this desolate intersection is perfect. The only man-made things in miles are the roads and a gray utility box sitting on the opposite corner like an abandoned bedroom dresser.

Next to me, Lou shifts uneasily.

Lou is the second problem. He's got to be twenty years older than me, at least mid-forties and probably pushing fifty, but in this business he's a newborn. Give him coveralls and a pipe wrench and he'd look like a Nintendo plumber. Maybe an older version, with the bits of gray salting his mustache.

I have no idea why Lou wants to be in the business. He'd tried to tell me, that first night, but I'd put him straight. Me knowing wouldn't help me and might hurt him. We freelance because we literally can't fit in anywhere else.

If you have a happy childhood, you don't do this kind of work.

Every one of us is a unique freak.

But we're in good company.

"Relax," I say. Lou is so nervous he looks like he's about to have his first prostate exam and fears he might enjoy it. "You did well so far."

"Well?" A voice that deep shouldn't crack quite that badly. "How many people shot at us last night?"

"Part of the job, sometimes." I study his outfit one last time. Three days ago he'd arrived in denim shorts, T-shirt, and baseball cap, but on our first day he'd swapped the cap for a floppy flow-through hat with a brim just short of sombrero. We'd spent most of the days afterwards posing as hikers to research our target. For the trade, I'd had him add sturdy slacks and a polo shirt, plus some sunglasses tougher than they looked. No, not darker—tougher.

Today called for unbreakable sunglasses. "The men after us last night, they worked for the man we robbed."

"We think." I've seen federal prosecutors look more trusting than Lou right now.

"Don't trust anything anyone says at gunpoint," I say. "Here, we're meeting our customer. Rules are, you don't bring a gun to the swap."

Lou glances up the south road. "Even if it wasn't the customer that was after us last night—are they going to follow that?"

"They'll have guns in their car." My lips tingle as I speak—they're a chapped ruin. Once we escape this level of Hell, I'm bathing in moisturizer for a week. "But they won't want to damage the goods. That's the whole point of this little game."

The breeze picks up, flowing through my outfit. My pants and shirt are a tough synthetic, breathable but difficult to cut through. It'll stop a knife slash. Won't do any good against a bullet, of course, but hopefully the shooting's done.

Until I say so, at least.

Plus, my pants have *pockets*. Screw you, fashion tycoons.

My earpiece buzzes. "Incoming," Deke says from his hidden nest. "White van, from the north."

"Thanks," I say. I've left my throat mic on—Lou and I won't be saying anything Deke can't hear. My Deke can hear anything I ever say. Last time I doubted Deke, he was tortured within an inch of his life.

That's when the blood got all over my reputation.

"Are we really going to return the car?" Lou says.

"When we're done."

"Won't the bullet holes make them—"

"That's what I bought all that rental insurance for." I raise a hand to shield the side of my face as I look north. I can't see anything yet, but a white van against the distant line of houses would disappear at half a mile. "Seriously, this isn't the time. It won't be an issue, I promise. We have to stay chill. Focus completely on the moment."

My phone buzzes with a text message.

Not my regular phone—the special one I wear on gigs. Maybe a dozen people in the world have that number.

I glance at the display on my wrist.

My brother Will.

Annoyance tightens my gut. Then I read the text.

FATHER IS DEAD.

2

I freeze like a tiny bug pinned to an endless beige display board.

The back of my neck flashes with heat as the first edge of the sun cracks the rounded mountains.

The text message's three words crank my headache up to eleven to thud in my temples. My parched eyes should tear up from the thunderous pounding. No, I probably have tears, but the ridiculous dry heat is sucking it away before they can run. My mouth is somehow even more arid, though.

How could Dad be dead?

I hadn't seen him since I started college, fourteen years ago. He'd tried to see me when I graduated with the triple bachelor's, but it hadn't gone well. And Father had been well on his way down Cirrhosis Highway back then, racing pedal-down towards Lung Cancer Junction.

I'd always imagined Cirrhosis Highway looked a lot like this barren desert, with straggly shrubs barely hanging on and a few grains of loose sand skittering across the hardpack. Father's road had Jack Daniels bottles instead of useless storm drains, though, and ditches full of Marlboro stubs.

Okay, I know perfectly well how he can be dead. Dumb question.

If he was that sick, though, why hadn't William let me know earlier? The idiot was supposed to be watching over Father.

"What's wrong?" Lou says.

I feel dizzy.

Breathe. I need to breathe.

Father's death had to be an accident.

Or slow alcohol-and-tobacco suicide.

I push the air out of my frozen lungs and deliberately pull in a deep breath. "Nothing." Another breath. The flat smell of drought-scorched earth fills my nose. "Nothing."

"Billie?" Deke says in my ear.

"Later," I hiss.

For Father, there is no later. There's only never.

A voice in the back of my head screams that I should have taken a chance to 'set things right' between us. But there wasn't anything to set right. Father is, *was* a drunk. He'd chased Mom off the Christmas I was ten, and she hadn't taken anything but her remaining teeth. Without Uncle Carl and Aunt Pat, his drinking would have taken me down with him.

I could have changed nothing.

I should have changed everything.

"Beaks!" Lou hisses.

I jerk.

A cargo van slows as it approaches the intersection, its pristine windowless white flanks glaring with early sunlight. The words TERRAPIN TRANSPORT gleam in bright blue on the flank, atop a grinning green turtle. A tinted windshield conceals the driver, but that's not suspicious. Scottsdale's in the running for Tinted Glass Capital of the United States.

I will myself to breathe. Inflating my paralyzed lungs takes concentration.

A couple yards short of the stop sign, the van pulls to the side, blocking my view of the drab gray utility box sticking out of the opposite lot.

The exchange is on.

Focus, woman! I fumble at my pants. The radio beacon makes a thin rectangular shape in my pocket. I push the "on" button through the smooth cloth and hear a low-pitched beep.

We're ready.

I deliberately relax my shoulders and unclench my hands. Father isn't a problem anymore. Hell, now that I'm not supporting him, I can keep all the money from this gig.

The thought doesn't help the voiceless burn in my heart.

Besides, there'll be funeral expenses. It's not like my brother has that kind of money. Or any money.

The van driver opens his door and hops out.

He's a stubby man, with baby-smooth skin above a harsh black five o'clock shadow, broad muscular shoulders, and a ghastly pale complexion that almost mirrors the sizzling sunlight. Dressed for the office, complete with a ridiculous short-sleeved white button-up shirt and fire-engine-red tie, he steps towards me with an incredibly well-balanced stride. It's like he expects an earthquake, but doesn't want it to knock the invisible ledger off of his head. His hands are open, relaxed, and empty. A bright red baseball cap with a white eagle-head logo on the front casts a vital line of shade over his naked eyes.

Basically, he's the exact opposite of Father.

Focus, focus, focus. "Stabinowitz." I raise my voice to carry the words across the intersection. "I thought I'd see you."

His toothy white grin reflects the sunrise almost as well as a mirror. "We've been around too long to stand on formalities, Miss Beaks. Please call me Joe. And what was your first hint?" He sounds like he's been awake for hours, and waiting all of them for a chance to strike up a conversation with a pretty blonde.

Fortunately, I'm a brunette today. "Joe it is, then. And it's just Beaks. Last night we came across a gentleman who'd had a butter knife inserted into his brain through his eye socket, and I asked myself 'who could do that?'"

Joe raised his shoulders and spread his hands. "Guilty. To be fair, he was trying to shoot me."

"I assumed as much." Stabbity Joe's skill with knives is both legendary, and his weakness. He's faster than me, and he practices with knives the way Father practiced with Pabst—*no, no, no. You just yelled at Lou to stay in the moment. Take your own advice.*

Stabbity Joe's hands are empty. He's wearing short sleeves, so the most obvious knife cache is gone. They've got to be in his pockets, or maybe down the back of his collar—no, that collar looks tight underneath his tie.

A gust of wind skitters sand past us. Joe's tie doesn't flutter.

That's one knife, then. He'll have a bunch more, hidden somewhere nastily clever.

Not as nasty as when Father got mad at the neighbor and—*no, stop it stop it stop it.*

"Who's your friend?" Stabbity Joe says.

I don't look at Lou, but he doesn't answer. Just like I told him.

"My problem," I say.

"Nice to meet you, My Problem." Stabbity Joe grins like that's funny.

"If you want to banter, Joe, then let's get this deal done and go to a bar," I say. "Ten minutes from now, this place is going to be even more of a hellhole."

His grin grows. "Don't tell me our desert is too much for you?"

Our? He's from a desert—maybe this desert. Or is he playing at leaking information? "You and I both know Phoenix was founded because this is where the settlers' last camel died. We stand here twenty minutes, we join it."

I need to seem impatient, but not too impatient.

This conversation needs to stretch until I get Deke's signal.

"Indeed." Joe slowly rotates on his axis to scan the horizon, pointedly spreading his arms farther as he turns his back to me. "I do believe we are quite alone, Beaks."

"Then bring it out." Those stupid verbal games would remind me of family any day, not just today, but my voice is still harder than it should be.

Cool, girl.

Collected.

Present. In the moment.

"Candy!" Stabbity Joe calls.

The van clanks.

I sense Lou's weight shift and suppress a wince. If Lou freaks out and starts anything, I'll have to put him down before Joe gets a chance to go all stabbity.

The side of Joe's van slides smoothly open, the sound of its motion barely audible above the breeze. I'm watching the dark interior, but also keeping an eye on the edges of the van and trying to peer into the shadowed space beneath it. Deke will warn us about another car coming in, but if Joe had seen Cape Fear one too many times and arrived with a shooter dangling from the undercarriage, this would be a good moment for him to strike.

Stabbity Joe was mostly honorable. In this business, freelancers who are willing to blow up the exchange pick up the kind of nasty stink that's real hard to get rid of. Don't get me wrong, he'd kill you if that was the job, but he'd do it properly. From behind, when you weren't expecting it.

But still, I had to be as watchful as when I'd been a kid and—

No.

That was petty shit. It's done. I'm the best in my business now, and Father's a lump of meat.

The hammering heat-headache threatens to knock my noggin off my neck. Better to think of that. Better still to watch the van. Just because Stabbity Joe was known to be basically okay didn't mean that he couldn't be offered enough to mow me down.

And Lou, yeah.

But mostly me.

Someone faintly says *oof*.

A scrawny woman with a tangle of dark hair flowing down past her shoulders clambers out of the van's dim interior. She turns her back to us, reaches inside, and heaves out a cardboard box plastered with the Amazon logo.

I hear good things about Amazon, but I'm never home to get packages.

Maybe Deke and I should steal a home one day.

"Prime Pantry," Stabbity Joe says. "The greatest boxes made today."

What? "The box is fine. What's in the box is the question."

Stabbity Joe steps aside, leaving room for Candy to pass.

She looks too scared to be a professional freelancer. Those denim shorts are too short, and the Arizona State T-shirt is way too tight. And any double-D needs to be wearing a bra—

Realization slaps me. "Joe, I thought we were professionals."

Joe gives that annoying pick-up smile. "She is a professional."

How *dare* he bring some random civilian into this? Is he really that stupid? "Not that sort of pro and you know it."

"It's an easy job," Joe says. "I'll eat my second-best Bowie if Mister My Problem there is any less green than my Miss Candy. And don't worry, she's being very well-compensated for her time."

Candy squints against the light at my back, and I feel like an asshole. Yes, I'd chosen to put the sun at my back as an advantage during the exchange, but a pro would have brought eye protection. She only has an arch of purple above each eye, making the sockets seem huge. At each sun-pained blink, glitter flashes on her darkened eyelids. Her lips are a tight line of fire engine red.

Candy's pretty clearly accustomed to working nights, when the artificial light and pancake makeup can hide the bruise on her left cheek. There's another on her left temple.

I'm not one of those moralizing assholes who thinks that women shouldn't do whatever they must to survive.

I'm one of those moralizing assholes who thinks you shouldn't beat people who are willing to sleep with you, even if they do it for money.

Mom covered up her bruises like that.

Fury blazes.

No, not now.

Survive the swap.

An hour from now, you can break down and scream and cry and whatever you need to do.

But right now, survive the swap.

Candy's slow pace doesn't come from her ghastly do-me glitter heels. She's terrified.

"You can't tell me she wants to be here," I say.

Stabbity Joe says, "You remember the gentleman with the butter knife?"

Candy flinches.

Stabbity Joe says, "He incapacitated my partner. I was forced to find a substitute, at short notice. That's far enough, Miss Candy."

Candy finishes her step and halts, square in the middle of the intersection. A racing car coming from any direction could mow her down.

Fortunately, the endless empty road stretching in all four directions would give her plenty of warning.

I wave Lou forward, into the intersection.

Candy hands Lou the box.

Lou sits on his heels so he can inspect the contents of the box. Counting should take between four and five minutes, but his impressively deft fingers finish leafing through the Panamanian bearer bonds in maybe three and a half. I hope it's because he's good, not because his attention slipped partway through. He folds the top of the box shut and stands to give me a nod.

"Good," I say. "The Duke's in the trunk."

3

Once the action starts, Lou's great at following directions. That's not enough to join this business, but it's sure a prerequisite. Lou retreats from the neutral intersection and heads to the bullet-scarred rental car behind me. I hear a click as he pops the trunk, then a huff as he heaves the Grand Duke out.

We'd had to drop the rear seats to get the Duke's case into the trunk.

Cellos are *not* small.

And better Lou looks towards the sun than me. My sinuses are so dry they ache, and sunscreen or no, I'm pretty sure this gig is going to scorch my olive skin to red. It's not only the sun—even the *sky* is brutal. Lou's mustache and his big hat would give him more protection than my sunglasses.

Besides, experience has its privileges. Let the new guy get the sunburn.

Stabbity Joe's still standing back by his van, about thirty feet away, with battered Candy at the halfway point. All nice and proper.

"You know, Joe," I say loudly, "since we've both been around a while, I think I should tell you that this gig hasn't gone well."

"Oh?" Stabbity Joe grins. "I'd love to hear about it some time."

"The thing is, this is the third time I've stolen this same cello. Each time it's been better guarded than the time before."

"It's a special one, I hear."

Lou comes up past me, humping the most ridiculously sturdy cello case I've ever seen. It's nearly as big as he is, the steel trim shining white over black bulletproof polymer. James Bond once rode an open cello case down a mountain, with a girl in his lap and the cello in hers. It's not an instrument you'd want to try to squeeze through an air duct.

Plus, the protective case is damn heavy.

"Stradivarius' Grand Duke," I say. "Commissioned in the summer of 1723 by the Grand Duke of Tuscany, but not completed until 1724 after the Duke was dead. One of his finest instruments."

Stabbity Joe purses his lips. "You sure read a lot."

I flashback to Father snatching *Surely you're Joking, Mister Feynman* out of my hands and screaming at me to get the goddamn dishes done. I was nine. My throat catches, and a little shudder traverses my spine.

I can't let any of that leak into my voice—we're already in enough danger.

"Here's the thing," I say. "That first time, I stole it from Colin Baywater. Last night, I stole it from him again."

Stabbity Joe laughs. "Really? That's fucking hilarious."

"I'm glad you think so. But the number of people who really care about cellos, and who have the wherewithal to hire me, is pretty small. I'm guessing there's only two."

Stabbity Joe laughs even louder. "I was wrong. *That's* fucking hilarious. You think our employer had you *re*-steal it."

"I'm a contractor. You're the employee." The last time someone offered me employment I blew up his home, his boat, and his private prison. "And I don't know that."

Lou's got the black cello case all the way into the intersection, about three feet from Candy. He kneels. Brass latches click, barely audible above the grumble of millions of frustrated commuters on the miles-distant freeway.

I say, "The point is, if you could do me a favor? Tell your boss that if I'm right, the next time he calls me, I'm going to have to tack on a stupidity tax."

Lou flips the case open.

"Don't tell me you wouldn't take the job?" Stabbity Joe says in mock surprise.

Lou reaches into the case and hoists the Grand Duke up for inspection, holding it by the slender curved neck.

The varnished wood gleams brown and red. The steel tuning keys are painfully bright in the sunlight. Lou hasn't put the end pin in, of course, so the base rests inside the heavy padded case. He spins the front towards Stabbity Joe, displaying the raised frets and the F holes.

"Check it," Stabbity Joe says.

Candy jumps.

The faded memory of my mom leaping before Father could throw a slap echoes up from the dusty bottom of my mind. My teeth clench.

"Quickly, now!" Stabbity Joe says. He's not angry, but my memories dance.

Candy takes a couple steps to cross in front of the Grand Duke. Her hands flutter as if she's going to touch it, but she yanks them back to her sides. She's been told not to touch the merchandise. She kneels and studies the front.

The Grand Duke has a little notch next to the fret, where Angelo Stucci's bow slipped during an especially frenetic performance in 1881. And the left-hand F-hole has a strangely curved edge of unknown provenance. Scholars' best guess is that some ham-fisted carpenter attempted "repairs" sometime between 1821 and 1823.

Candy stands. She offers Stabbity Joe two thumbs up.

"Beaks," Stabbity Joe says. "Could you ask My Problem there to turn the Duke around for us?"

I told Lou to expect the request. He obliges.

Candy crouches. The X grain should show up near the neck, and there's three parallel scrapes off to the right-hand side. Old Stucci was rough on his instruments.

This instrument is remarkable. I imagine it sounds glorious.

Not that I listen to classical music. Give me some Savages or Screaming Females and I'm good all day.

Candy hops back up and offers another two thumbs up. Even through the makeup, I can see her face has lost even more color. She's too afraid to shake.

Her terror is too familiar, and right now it's too raw. "Miss Candy," I say.

Stabbity Joe says, "Any instructions you want to give her, you tell me."

"It's not an instruction." I turn my attention back to Candy. "Anything you say, it can leak information. If Joe was going to kill you, he wouldn't have told you to be silent. Stay calm, follow instructions, and you'll make it home just fine."

Candy's face stills. Have I reassured her?

Or is she now so scared she's completely shut down?

"Pep talks for my people?" Stabbity Joe says. The light is so harsh, his five-o-clock shadow stands out like black paint on his pallid face.

"I want everyone here to get home alive and with a few extra dollars in their pocket," I say.

Joe's eyes stay hard, but his lips flirt with a teasing smile. "The rumors are right. You're a softy."

"Incoming," Deke whispers in my ear. "One west, one north, both at high speed."

His words give me a warm thrill of satisfaction. We're running out of time. I'm at my best when I'm out of time.

My pulse picks up a notch, pushing my headache back. "I believe in punching up. Punching up hard. Satisfied?"

"Oh, yes."

To Lou I say, "Hand over the cello and grab my bearer bonds."

Right on schedule, the cello's neck shatters into a billion pieces.

The sound of the gunshot arrives a quarter-second later.

4

Countless tiny splinters shatter through the air. Lou still clenches the cello's scroll, the curvy bit right above the tuning keys, in one hand. By the time the cello hits the ground, he's already flung himself to the side, arms outstretched to protect his face from slamming into that baked concrete.

Across the intersection, Stabbity Joe's already hit the ground and is rolling beneath the van. His face could go in the dictionary next to "Surprised."

Bet he wishes he carried a gun right about now.

I'm moving too, running back towards the car's dubious shelter.

This gig had gone wrong the moment Lou and I got the Duke.

More violence means everything has gone wrong again.

But this time, it's gone wrong in our favor.

Colin Baywater's goons had been chasing us since we grabbed the Grand Duke. The first gunfight was unavoidable. When we evaded the second, I searched for and deactivated the tracking beacon they'd stuffed into the cello.

That button I'd hit, right as Stabbity Joe pulled up? It turned the beacon back on.

Hey, Baywater's goons would have tracked me down anyway. This way, I get to control when and where they attack. If I absolutely must fight I choose my ground, hide a spotter in the desert, and put the rising sun at my back.

I dash back to my rental sedan. The sun-heated metal of the door burns my hand as I lean into the driver's space.

A distant gunshot splits the morning.

I snatch my .38 semi-auto off the driver's seat. It's a little clunky, because I've jammed a 20-round extended magazine into it.

Four more range-softened gunshots follow in quick succession.

"North car down," Deke whispers in my earpiece.

Deke's not just my spotter.

He's my sniper.

He's not Marine-grade, but against a target coming straight at him, he's good enough.

"Thanks." He doesn't have to spell out that he can't possibly get the car coming from the west—it's moving perpendicular to him, and each shot that misses will angle into that line of homes on the horizon.

I glance back west, raising the .38.

A distant red dot races right at us, maybe half a mile away.

Lou has dropped the cello's carcass and rolled to the side of the road, scrabbling for his feet, hands clawing at the concrete to get distance as he tries to run and rise simultaneously.

But Candy—

She's curled up like a pillbug, hands over her head, right where she was when the shooting started.

Straight in the middle of the crossroads.

"Candy!" I scream. "Move!"

That car's roaring in like they'll plow through her, through me, and straight on into the sun.

Or they'll pull up short and fill the obvious target full of bullets.

I need to put my car between the intruders and myself. It won't stop them, but it's cover.

But my feet freeze for a beat.

More than once, I'd seen Mom cowering like Candy.

My brain knows the smart thing to do.

But my feet are already running towards her.

Besides, I tell myself, she's right next to the box of bearer bonds.

My bearer bonds.

Hey, I brought the cello to the exchange, right?

That's *my* goddamn money.

But no amount of money is worth a head-on collision with an oncoming car.

The car is getting closer. It's a minivan or a little SUV, bright red.

"Candy!" I scream. "Run!"

Damn Stabbity Joe for bringing an amateur.

Lou's bent over at the waist, running for our car.

I taste bright adrenaline and hot dust.

The car's getting closer.

Candy can't even look at me.

The minivan's racing in. I can make out the windshield as a discrete rectangle and the curve of the grill.

Someone's leaning out of the passenger window.

The gunshot sounds quiet, the *bang* smothered by the minivan's racing engine—but it won't be for long.

I ignore the shot. Shooting while hanging out the passenger window of a moving car is a great way to waste ammo.

Candy's facing the ground. Her hands are clamped over her head.

I'm almost close enough to touch her.

That minivan is going to flatten us both in seconds.

The scream of its engine rushes closer.

"Move you stupid bitch!" I shriek.

The minivan's grill has the Chevy bent-cross logo in pristine gold.

Candy flinches.

Looks towards the minivan's noise.

I'm reaching for her when she spasms and throws herself backwards, hands and feet kicking at the pavement in a panicked crabwalk, her mouth flapping open and shut like a storm door caught in a hurricane. Her feet throw up little clouds of silvery sand.

The minivan's charging right at me.

I'm sidestepping, bringing up the .38, dancing across the pavement as I pull off a single shot.

It misses.

But it gets their attention.

Yards from the intersection, the minivan's brakes squeal.

It sluices sideways—yes, it's a mom-mobile, complete with a *Baby on Board* plaque and a cute little rainbow sticker on the passenger side window, meant for rolling to and from school and the Kroger, but now there's a goon with a gun sticking his head out the passenger window, the car's motion bringing him around to face me even as the driver fights to straighten the spin.

I take another step sideways, barely avoiding my cardboard box of bearer bonds.

The minivan's skidding to a halt.

I have the .38's sight lined up with the passenger window and pull the trigger, not really expecting to hit anything but wanting to keep their attention.

The minivan sluices to a stop, the sliding passenger door flying open.

The sun behind me illuminates the minivan's interior.

The guy in the back seat sure looks like he knows how to use that automatic rifle. The deft way he swings it up against his shoulder tells me that he's practiced.

I'm in the middle of the intersection. My car is yards behind me.

The only cover around?

A beheaded cello lying in the dust.

An open cello case right next to it.

I dive for the cello case as the gunbunny opens fire.

Bullets split the air behind me.

My feet scrabble on sandy pavement as I snatch the cello case, yank it upright, and crouch down tight to squeeze my six-feet-plus into its shadow, balancing my weight on the balls of my feet.

The automatic rifle thunders.

Bullets slam the case.

5

Yes, I'm an idiot.

But not because I'm using a cello case as body armor.

I'm an idiot because the cello case should have been my first warning it'd end in gunfire.

Say you have an incredibly valuable musical instrument, arguably the finest of its sort in the whole world. Perhaps even the finest of its kind ever made. And say you're a bloated rich bastard. That instrument is going to have the most protective custom case in the world.

Cellos aren't very heavy. Less than fifteen pounds.

Lou had trouble hauling this one because of that case.

Near as I can tell, it's made of layered carbon fiber with a Kevlar outer sheath. It's as if someone told the case builder, "This thing has been stolen twice in recent memory. The next time it's snatched, there's gonna be a whole bunch of blood and bullets. I want a case that'll stand up to military-grade gunfire. Hell, I want a cello case that can survive a United flight."

Half a dozen rounds hammer the cello case.

Crouching on the balls of my feet and sitting on my heels, I wobble with the impact—but the case, it shudders and slides an inch to one side.

The inside of the case doesn't have any handles. I'm supporting it by pressing my fingers against the sides.

All I can do is press harder.

I crouch lower, trying to drop my center of gravity.

The case's open lid bounces against my shoulder, making me wobble again.

A cello case is a misshapen suitcase. The upper part where the neck goes is narrower than my shoulders, narrower than my head, so I've got to damn near curl up into a ball. The dusty white concrete underfoot has already picked up the sun's August heat and started casting it back up.

I don't dare stick even a finger around the outside—the gunbunny might be really good with that rifle.

Another three-round burst pounds the case.

The concussion echoes in each knuckle, but I don't drop the case. "Deke."

"Shooting blind into the minivan," my Deke says in my ear.

I glance back towards my rental car.

Lou is kneeling behind the car. A car's body can't stop a bullet, but the engine block might.

More rifle shots.

The case's lid bounces back, knocking into my butt, pushing me forward. I have to shift a foot forward—are my toes sticking out from the case now? No, wait—how about my butt? That's all I need, one round straight through the cheeks and out the other side. I'd never live that down.

Lou rises a couple inches, pulls off two quick shots, and ducks back.

Deke says in my earpiece, "Can you lure him out?"

What am I supposed to do, hold up a white flag and ask for terms? They made it clear all night that this wasn't up for discussion.

Another three-round burst. The cello case shakes once.

The guy might have been a decent shot, but his aim is degrading. Firing a rifle on full auto is tiring. The gunbunny needs to lift more—

My money!

The box of bearer bonds is about eight feet back, but a couple of feet to my side. Well within the stray bullet field.

Banks don't accept bearer bonds full of bullet holes. Or bloodstains. Trust me, I've tried.

I try to look up, but I don't dare raise my head enough to see the top of the cello case. Do I have an inch of clearance? Or a hair?

Three rifle shots. All go astray.

Dammit.

I have to take a chance.

I quickly work one hand down towards the bottom of the case. The massive case wobbles with the unbalanced support, but I get my hand anchored before it topples. I rely on that ballast to hold the case long enough to reach up and press the side of my hand against the case's top, where the cello's body would end and the neck begin.

Sweat greases my forehead, but the heat's so bad that it turns to sludge and evaporates before it can hit my eyes. The summer desert sun hammers my back almost as forcefully as the next three-round burst from the automatic rifle.

I shout, "Don't suppose we can talk about this?"

My only answer is another six rounds, all punching straight into the cello case.

My shoulders are really beginning to ache.

Now the tricky part. I don't dare raise my head. If I turn a knee out from behind the cello case, it'll catch a bullet.

Teeth gritted, I ignore my screaming instincts and scoot the cello case farther away.

Another inch.

I push the case maybe three or four inches when I hit the limit of my reach. I could get more distance, if I wasn't holding the case's bottom and top firmly enough to balance it against the intermittent gunshots.

Then I shift my weight to the hand on the bottom of the case and start working my feet backwards.

The whole thing takes me maybe fifteen seconds. Each second feels like an hour.

The gunbunny stops shooting. Magazine change?

I hear Lou fire, one-two-three-four quick shots.

The gunbunny opens up.

Keeping my weight on the hand, I ease up on one foot. Careful—don't raise my head. Don't raise my butt above the top of the cello case. Stay perfectly in the case's shadow. Hardly daring to breathe, I stretch that leg behind me. Countless needles stab my blood-starved calf, but seconds later I have that knee on the scalding concrete. Pebbles barely larger than grains of sand gouge craters into my kneecap.

It's tempting to rush, but no. Just as carefully, I ease the other leg behind me, only exhaling when I have both shins firmly planted on the pavement.

Kneeling on the concrete gives me far more balance and mobility than balancing on the balls of my feet. I can concentrate more on keeping the cello case pinned upright and less on keeping myself upright.

It also lets me scoot an inch to the side.

New pebbles introduce themselves to my patella.

"Hey!" I shout. "How much is Baywater paying you? Not enough, I bet. Wouldn't a cut of the take be a better deal for you?"

Another burst hammers the cello case. Guess they know I don't pay my way out of problems.

Well, not in money.

"They're not coming out," Deke says in my ear.

"I noticed," I hiss, scooting a few more inches.

My foot bumps the edge of the cardboard box. My heart gives a little trill.

Someone shouts indistinctly from in front of me.

I quickly scoot my knees, an inch at a time, until the box is behind me, in the cello case's shadow. My knees are hamburger, but the money's safe.

Knee pads are standard gear during an infiltration. I guess I need to wear them during exchanges too. But then some dickbag would ask me if I'd also brought mouthwash and I'd have to kill him and the whole deal would go sideways.

"Beaks!" someone beyond the cello case shouts.

Why doesn't he mention Stabbity Joe? Or Candy?

If Candy's dead, I'll kill the gunmen. And probably Joe, for shanghaiing a civilian. "Yeah?"

He sounds like he's barely stopped himself from laughing. "I'm a-guessing that box has the payoff in it?"

Who calls it a payoff? Someone who's watched too many Mafia movies. "So what?" I shout. "It's *my* money."

The guy has an annoying choked-up laugh, like he wants to be an evil mastermind but can't quite get his full lungs into the Villain Guffaw. "You know you can't get out of this."

"I know the cops will be here soon." With the break in the gunfire, my headache demands a tribute of cool water or it will trample my brainstem. My mouth tastes like hot iron. "I can hang out here until they arrive."

Another gunshot, this one distant. "People coming from the north car," Deke says in my ear. "Handling it."

"The cops aren't coming," Failed Villain shouts. "We've handled them."

Crap. Not that I want the police involved, but a siren would shuffle all the cards.

"So how about it?" I say. "Take a few bills and say you couldn't find me?"

"Sorry," he shouts. "Mister Baywater doesn't want anyone messing with his niece's cello."

"You know she can't play worth a damn. The silly girl can't even hold her bow right. I saw the video on YouTube."

"Mine is not to reason why," he shouts. "Mine is to take your fool head back to my Boss. Thanks for keeping our bullets out of it, though."

Typical.

"I'm running around for a better angle," Deke says in my ear.

That'll take time. I have to keep Failed Villain talking.

"Listen." My mind churns desperately. "There's more money than what's in the box."

Failed Villain calls back "I'll take tha—"

His voice cuts off in a gurgle.

There's more gunfire, but it's not aimed at me.

Beyond the cello case, someone screams.

6

Sometimes, you have to go with instinct.

I get a knee up, and sprint forward.

Sprinting while holding a cello case isn't easy, but I manage.

I've got my fingers wrapped around the edges of the case—if I'm wrong, the gunbunny will shoot out my legs, not my fingers. The bouncing bobbling lid makes the cello case unwieldy, but I can peer through the gap between the lid and the case and still get some protection.

The inside of the van looks almost pitch black against the blazing desert hard-pack and the sunlight reflecting from the white concrete road, but I can make out struggling figures inside.

A shot. Close.

But not at me.

The stink of gunpowder grows stronger with each step.

I need speed more than anything now.

Good-bye, cello case. It hits the pavement with a heavy thud, and I'm suddenly light as a balloon.

My feet dance across the dusty pavement.

Another scream from inside the van.

A scrawny woman in knock-off desert camo topples out from the open front passenger door. The hilt of a knife protrudes from her throat.

Her hands scrabble at the bloody haft.

Bright red blood sizzles on hot white concrete.

I'd bought time for Deke—

—but Stabbity Joe had claimed it as well.

I can make out the gunbunny. He's still in the van's back seat with his big assault rifle, right where he'd planted himself to shoot at me. With the passenger out of the way he's got the rifle wrenched most of the way around towards Stabbity Joe.

Failed Villain must have been driving. I'm guessing Stabbity Joe took him out, then the woman in the front passenger seat.

In some ways, letting the gunbunny fill Stabbity Joe with bullets would simplify my future.

But it wouldn't be professional.

I pull my .38 and start shooting.

My first shot goes wide, but the gunbunny jerks his attention back towards me.

His rifle starts swinging back towards me.

Idiot. Always shoot the enemy you're aiming at, *then* switch targets.

I pull off another shot.

Miss again.

It's hard to hit a target while running, but my shots keep the gunbunny's attention long enough for a knife handle to sprout from his ear.

I don't like throwing knives. Each knife has its own unique weight and balance. Each is suitable only for certain targets. I don't even like fighting hand-to-hand with a knife. It's too easy to make the sort of mistake that increases funeral expenses.

Knives are a real pain to master.

Somehow, Stabbity Joe had thrown a knife from outside the driver's side door, between the seats, and hit a tiny, tiny target. No, not the gunbunny's brain—his ear, *then* into the brain.

The gunbunny spasms. His hand clenches. A quick burst sprays off into nowhere, then his seizing arm wrenches the hand further back and the rifle slips from his death grip.

Today seems like a good day for other people to die.

The gunbunny's body slumps. His rifle clatters against the edge of the van's door and out onto the ground.

I get to the van's gaping door, .38 in two hands in front of my face, and glance inside. This close, I get a good view of the driver's body draped over the blood-drenched steering wheel. More blood spatters the dashboard, the seats, the doors. The van only had three people inside, and they've all died with their hearts pumping their life blood out around stab wounds. The stink turns to copper glue in my sinuses, and my throat threatens to close in self-defense.

For a vital second, the only sound is my hammering heartbeat and the distant roar of a million oblivious drivers on the distant freeway.

Looking at the carnage, I wish I was with them.

Don't get me wrong—if it's them or me, it's gonna be them. But I really would have rather gotten away clean. My favorite gigs are those where nobody knows I've been there until they open the safe.

At least I don't know any of them. Killing strangers leaves me less sad.

This gig had gone bloody the moment Lou and I laid our hands on the Grand Duke. We were lucky to get this far unscathed.

Through the open window of the driver's door Stabbity Joe says, "Looks all clear."

"All clear here," I say.

"Got it," Deke says in my earpiece.

On the hot pavement next to me, the dying woman's delicate, gold-ringed fingers stop dancing around the knife blade protruding from her neck and collapse into the spreading pool of blood. The red looks absurdly bright in the quick-rising sun.

Search the minivan? No, no time. We need to finish this.

"Beaks," Stabbity Joe says. "Check out my problem."

What? I look over at Stabbity Joe. He's got his head tilted so that the bright red baseball cap shields his eyes from the sun, and he can barely peer at me under the brim.

But there's enough visibility to see his eyes fixed on me.

"Your man," Stabbity Joe says. "My Problem?"

Lou.

I whirl.

Another impossibly bright red pool is spreading from the far side of my sedan.

7

It's too late.

Lou is lying on his back, his feet right beneath the big sedan's front bumper.

One of the gunbunny's rounds cut through his neck, right where it meets the body. The hole is big enough for a golf ball and glints with shards of shattered collarbone.

I didn't even notice he'd been shot.

That ridiculous hat lies a few feet away.

His wide pupils can stare at the sun all they want now.

Thanks to the sun-heated concrete, the pool of red blood is already drying at the edges.

Despair crashes in on me.

Father was dead. Probably stupidly.

I couldn't have changed that—but I'd never know, because I hadn't been there.

Never mind that he probably would have killed me if I'd stayed.

But Lou. Lou was my responsibility. My problem.

Behind me, Stabbity Joe says something.

The job broker had asked me to take Lou along. See if the guy could hack it. He must have seen potential in the guy. And Lou had done okay for his first time out. Not great, but decent.

He'd tried to tell me his last name.

And I didn't even have time to arrange a burial. Someone would find him lying here and report him to the Scottsdale police. The machinery of state would take over. He'd go into a pauper's grave.

Anywhere else, my eyes would have misted up a little. In Infernal Scottsdale, tears evaporate before they can hit my eye.

"Beaks?" Deke says in my earpiece.

"Yeah?" My voice shakes a little. I need to shake the rest of myself. This little act isn't over. "Lou—he's out. Permanently."

"Shit," Deke says. "You okay, babe?"

"Yeah."

The pause tells me Deke can hear the lie. A breath later he says, "Finish this up, babe, and y'all can tell me all about it."

That sounds like the best offer I'm going to get.

But I can't leave Lou staring at the sun.

His ridiculous hat has fallen a few feet away.

I gently place it over his face. *Sorry. It's the best I've got right now.*

Then I turn to face Stabbity Joe.

Joe's standing near his pristine white van. He has a knife in each hand. An ignorant observer would think that he's amusing himself by flipping them end-over-end and catching them by the handle.

He's not showing off.

It's a threat.

The box of bearer bonds is gone.

Candy's rear end and legs are disappearing into the white van.

Stabbity Joe tosses the knife in his left hand up. It does one and a half spins on its way up and the same as it comes back down, sunlight flashing off the blade at every turn. He catches the blade between thumb and forefinger.

Now he's showing off.

And he's telling me he's ready to use it. Not a threat, a statement. He's got the money.

His right thumb and forefinger keep their relaxed grip on his other knife.

My breath comes smooth. I'll break down and have a good sob later, but I need to take charge of this right now.

Stabbity Joe must see my expression as I approach. "Sorry, Beaks. Losing people is never easy."

The unexpected sympathy softens something inside. I compensate by hardening my voice. "He knew the risks. And we're not done."

Stabbity Joe shakes his head. "I fear these bastards shot the Duke before we did the exchange. That's how it goes sometimes."

"*They* didn't shoot the cello," I say. "*My* sniper did."

8

I'm right at the edge of the desolate intersection. Stabbity Joe's on the other side by his van. Thirty feet or so should be plenty of distance against a guy armed with knives, but I'd seen him fling a knife through a car window into someone's ear. The space between my shoulder blades has this sudden, ferocious itch.

Stabbity Joe is holding a knife by the tip of the blade. I'm pretty sure he could put it in my eye, even at this range. But he's frozen up. He's got his head tilted so the brim of his baseball cap blocks the sun rising over my head. The shade beneath the brim is deep enough that I can't see his eyes. His lips turn straight and hard, though.

The only sound is the distant drone of the freeway.

I hold myself still, weight on the balls of my feet and my attention on Stabbity Joe's shoulders. If he so much as twitches I'll need to throw myself to the side. But if I let him think for a moment—

"This better be good," Stabbity Joe says. All that sympathy I'd heard from him before? Evaporated like my fresh sweat in the desert's appallingly dry heat.

"It is," I say. "The important thing first. Can you ask Candy to go over to the utility box?"

"Utility box?"

And that's why Stabbity Joe will always be in the minor leagues. He'd surely *looked* everywhere as he drove up, but he didn't *remember*. "Other side of the van. Gray utility box. It's not locked." I raise my voice so she can hear me. "Be careful, it's hot."

"Candy," Stabbity Joe says. "Do it."

"I have him," Deke says in my ear.

I don't answer. I don't even nod. Stabbity Joe looks ready to earn his name all over again. Sure, Deke can shoot him, but not before he throws those knives into me.

Minor league pitchers sometimes strike out major league batters.

The van quivers. A rectangle of light shines through it—Candy's opened the far door.

I let myself blink. If we stand in this dry heat much longer, my eyeballs are going to dry into powder and blow away. The sun is at my back, but the wind on my face feels like foundry exhaust.

Joe looks both perfectly relaxed and perfectly unhappy.

Something clangs beyond the van.

"Careful!" I say. "It's heavy."

"What is it?" Joe shouts.

The van and the distance muffles Candy's voice, but I can make out the words. "It's another of those big black cases. It's stuck in there."

I raise my voice. "You have to turn it a little."

Stabbity Joe's shoulder tenses a little. "Talk."

"We got into that museum Baywater calls a home," I say. "The cello's there in a display case, all set out for us to admire. It might as well have had a sign on it saying *Free to a good home*."

"So you did," Stabbity Joe says.

"Nope," I say. "It's a fake."

"We checked," Stabbity Joe snaps.

"It was a great fake," I say. "It was a fake meant to fool us. You'd turn the fake in to your boss, I'd take the money, and Baywater would hide the original or expose that we'd been had. I don't know about you, but I'd never work again."

Another clang. Candy shouts, "I've got it!"

"Bring it out!" Stabbity Joe's mouth is twisted downward. To me he says, "You had best be able to prove this."

I risk shrugging. "That's what YouTube is for. You do have signal out here, don't you? Tell me you don't have Verizon."

Candy appears around the van. I know for a fact that this cello case is as heavy as the first one, but she hauls it more easily than Lou had managed.

Fresh sorrow flashes through me again. I breathe deeply through my nose to soothe myself, but the heat scalds my sinuses and burns its way into my lungs.

I should have changed things for Lou.

I should have changed things for Father.

I can't change anything for anyone.

Stabbity Joe says, "Bring it around in front of me."

Candy hurries, dropping the case in front of Stabbity Joe.

I can't help wincing.

"Easy!" Stabbity Joe snaps. "That might be valuable."

Candy flinches at his tone.

I want to tell her to stand up for herself, that it's going to be okay, and to not hurt the merchandise all at once. I settle for, "It's worth something. It's worth a whole box of bearer bonds."

"We'll see." Stabbity Joe's attention doesn't leave me.

Candy fumbles with the case, eventually heaving it right side up and snapping the latches. "It's another one."

"Check it," Stabbity Joe snaps.

She hoists the cello, turning it around. "It looks exactly the same."

"Exactly?" Stabbity Joe says.

"Everything you said to look for!" she says. "It's there."

I say, "Candy, do you have a cell phone?"

"In the van," she says.

"You talk to me," Stabbity Joe snaps at me. To Candy he snarls "And right now, you don't talk at all."

Candy withers.

I want to slap Joe. Instead, I say "Then *you* ask her to check. Do a YouTube search on Felicity, Baywater, cello. There's a video from two weeks ago. We want three minutes and twenty-six seconds in."

"Do it!" Stabbity Joe says.

Candy scurries off.

"Baywater left the fake for me to find," I say. "He had it laid out for me, buffet style. The real one was in the conservatory. Locked in a closet."

"So you stole two cellos," Stabbity Joe says.

"The fake really was a work of art," I say. "You don't see that kind of craftsmanship in forgery these days. It's a shame."

"Then *why did you shoot it*?" Stabbity Joe snarls.

That's the heart of what's going on. All the pieces of the exchange are here, but our little game had confused Stabbity Joe. He's scared, and angry, and searching for an excuse to earn his name.

"They knew I was coming," I say. "Baywater had armed men waiting for me to leave. Somebody told him."

Joe's chin raises a notch. "You think it was me?"

"Nope." I spread my open hands. "When we shot the fake? You're not that good an actor, Joe." Use his name. Connect. "You had no clue there even was a fake." I lower my hands. "But someone told Baywater. And it sure wasn't me or Deke."

Joe's chin drops back down. It's the second half of a slow-motion nod. "And My Problem?"

"Had no idea what the gig was until go time."

Candy hops out of the van, holding a tiny cellphone in one outstretched hand.

"Over here," Stabbity Joe says.

Candy trots towards him. She's way past the "peeing herself in terror" stage and on to "stunned automaton."

"What am I looking for?" Joe says.

I smile. "The spot where a very nervous Miss Felicity Baywater slips with her bow during her first public performance and gouges the hell out of a priceless Stradivarius cello."

Stabbity Joe snorts. He watches Candy's upheld phone for all of two seconds, then his eyes glance down to the exposed Grand Duke.

There's a fresh white scrape in the front, right by the right-hand F hole. Nothing an instrument specialist couldn't sort out, but it'd need a few months in the shop. And the performance had been two weeks ago.

"What makes you think she played the real one and not the fake?" Stabbity Joe says.

"Baywater showed it off," I say. "You and I, we learned the markers to identify it. But there were actual musicologists at that show. Specialists who'd shown up just to see a teenage girl play a Strad. That girl had to mop their drool off the Duke before she could play. They'd know if it was fake."

Joe studies me.

I fight to not hold my breath.

"So you involved us in your little fight," Stabbity Joe says.

I fight down a sigh of relief. He believes me. One problem down. "Your boss wanted the Grand Duke. Baywater's thugs wanted it back. Someone told them I was coming. It could have been you." Now sweeten things a little. "And seriously? I'd *much* rather have you inside stabbing out than outside stabbing in."

Stabbity Joe's frown breaks into a smirk. I can see him decide to swallow the sugar.

I let myself relax a touch. It could all go bad still, but he wasn't ready to slice me right now.

"So," I say. "How about those bearer bonds?"

9

I crouch on the road with the box between my knees and count the bonds myself, the growing heat reflecting from the concrete encouraging me to hurry. Maybe Baywater's men had paid off the police, but the longer we stay in this wasteland the more likely it is someone will drive past. Stabbity Joe watches insouciantly. He must know that Deke has a sniper rifle trained on him, but he doesn't seem to give a damn.

Candy moves to retreat to the van, but Stabbity Joe tells her to close up the cello and wait.

A couple moments later I stand. My shins almost feel burned by a few moments on the road. "Everything seems good. Satisfied?"

Stabbity Joe relaxes a hair. "Yeah. Good enough." His lips tighten. "I don't like being drawn into a fight, y'know."

"I get it. I had to know you weren't the leak, though. I agreed to hand this over to your boss, not back to Baywater. But—" I let my lips hint at a smile. "I have to admit it. That last throw? In the guy's *ear*? That was pretty sweet."

Stabbity Joe huffs out a breath. "You think flattery solves things?"

"If it gets me out of here without a knife in my sinuses?"

He coughs a laugh.

"Besides," I say, "that *was* a real good throw."

Stabbity Joe gives a nod. "And nobody cowers behind a cello case like you do."

I roll my eyes. "Thanks." I heft the box.

Beside Stabbity Joe, Candy shifts her weight from one foot to another. Her big eyes study me. She's still got her weight on the balls of her feet, ready to leap aside when the bullets start flying.

I meet her gaze. "You did good too."

She licks her lips. For half a second her lipstick blooms fire engine red, then fades as the heat pillages its moisture.

I hate that she's terrified.

If things with Father had worked out differently, if I hadn't escaped my childhood home at fifteen, I could have been her: what Pratchett called a "lady of negotiable affection," working the nighttime streets with makeup caked over my bruises.

I glance over at Stabbity Joe. He's put his knives away. He can get them quickly, but he's not going to reflexively spear my pineal gland if I twitch wrong, so I fumble at the top of the box. "Here," I say, taking a step towards her.

Stabbity Joe's eyes raise.

I pull the top two bearer bonds from the box. They're printed on heavy linen paper, with gold illumination and ink so black that it could have been squeezed from the soul of a corporate pirate at the end of a long happy life hijacking widows' pensions. "I don't know what kind of trouble you have." I hold the bonds out towards her. "But maybe this can get you out. Go back home. You've got to have family somewhere? Old friends?"

Candy looks at the papers. Her brow furrows. "What are those?"

"Bearer bonds."

Her lips turn down in puzzled fear.

"Sign them," I say. "You can turn them into cash at any bank."

Her eyes grow wide at *bank*, and she retreats half a step. "Uh, thank you, but—I mean—like—"

Maybe she has too many warrants out? "It's okay." I tuck the bonds away. Stabbity Joe's got this calm, curious look on his face, so I sigh and set the box between my feet. "Look." I fumble in my pocket for my tiny wallet. "Here's… five, six…six hundred and twenty…seven dollars."

Candy looks at the outstretched money and glances over at Stabbity Joe.

Stabbity Joe's face has that careful arrangement that says he's trying not to laugh. "Fine with me. I'll still pay you."

"Just take care of yourself," I say. "Get yourself out. That's a bus ticket, it's gas, it's something."

Candy's shoulders shake a little, then her hand snaps out to snatch the money. The bills disappear into her generous cleavage.

Maybe I can't change what happened with Father. Or with Lou.

But perhaps, just perhaps, I can change Candy's life.

Probably not.

But I'm going to hang tight to "perhaps."

"You *are* a softy," Stabbity Joe says, but without rancor.

"Only when it matters," I say.

He looks at my face, glances at Candy, then studies me another minute. "Fine." One hand extracts his wallet. "Here's the money I owe you." He offers Candy a sheaf of bills. "And here's an extra…" He flips bills with a calloused thumb. "Four hundred and ninety-one. Call it hazard pay. And yeah, get out. You have human rights and all that shit. Use them."

"Careful, Joe," I say as Candy snags the bills. She doesn't quite have enough cleavage to store the loot, so she stuffs the rest into one of those tiny pockets in her shorts. "People will think you're going soft."

"Hardy har har." His eyes grow hard. "If they do, I'll know who blabbed."

I crouch to hoist the box. "Won't hear it from me."

"I believe we're done." Joe takes a step back towards the car.

My lips are scorched. I want to lick them, but my tongue is almost as parched. "Before you go."

Joe pauses to raise his eyebrows.

I glance back at my destroyed rental car, then at the miles of desolate undeveloped desert between us and the distant white wall that marks the edge of civilization. "Any chance of a lift?"

10

Joe doesn't have much choice. Eventually someone will drive by, and even a teenager busy texting and driving as he cranks up the stereo and chugs his energy drinks will notice the blood sizzling in the sun. If that happens while Deke and I are hitching into town, everything falls apart.

And "Dear Lyft: pick me up at the heap of corpses" won't end well.

Besides, I'm not sure I *can* walk to civilization. The heat is almost as debilitating as getting shot. Yes, we had half a case of bottled water in the car, but it's full of bullet holes.

Joe grumbles again when we pick up Deke. Deke locked the sniper rifle in a case, but that doesn't make Joe any happier.

But soon enough Joe drops Candy at a corner party store. She flashes me this look full of fear and hope and what-the-hell-just-happened, then vanishes inside. Deke and I get dropped a couple miles further on.

It's another hour until the taxi gets us back to our five-star hotel. Travel tip: Scottsdale in August is really cheap. We'd claimed a three-room suite decorated in Cheerless Luxury, complete with Gold™-framed paintings by that famed artist Tasteless Mass Production and a television slightly under IMAX size, all for less than I've paid for a Detroit fleabag. The air smells metallic and stale, like it's been breathed too many times because the air conditioner can't handle sucking in fresh from the foundry outside. Everything is glossy and smooth and as artificial as the inside of a space station.

Which is pretty much how everyone in Phoenix lives in the summer.

After a night of thievery and gunfights and car chases, I'm exhausted and dehydrated. The first bottle of chilled water evaporates in my mouth. The second steams away halfway down my throat. The third hits my stomach like a block of melting ice and gives me the strength to plop down in the hideously uncomfortable padded chair. It's not only that the seat has this weirdly hard padding, but the cloth has the nasty texture of a tightly stretched plastic bag yet still somehow snags at my parched skin.

Plus, the seat's too long. I'm over six feet, and I can't rest against the back without putting my feet up on the rock-hard settee.

I keep my feet on the floor. I might as well be perched on a wooden stool.

The overworked air conditioner mounted beneath the window groans to a stop.

The air becomes as still as I feel.

Usually after a gig, I'd be all over Deke. Even when someone dies—it's important to celebrate life. Right now, I feel detached from everything. I can feel the seat cushion beneath me and condensation from the water bottle on my hands. I pull air into my lungs. All of it feels distant. The blare of a car horn outside? It might as well be through cheap headphones.

An invisible wall has sprung up between my soul and everything else.

Deke finishes his fourth bottle and sinks into the desk chair. His massive frame makes the chair look like it belongs in a fourth-grade classroom. Lay a lever over those muscular shoulders and you could tip a bus. Those shoulders hang loose now. We're all-on when the action's happening, but once the fight passes both of us fall over.

He licks his lips to get some moisture into them. "Nice work, Billie babe."

Deke's face has a dull red scar shaped like a twisted X where a bullet had passed through his cheek. We're going to get that polished off one day, but he's been busy getting his teeth fixed and doing physical therapy so he can have a normal life again.

His body's nice, don't get me wrong, but what really matters is that he instinctively knows my heart feels cracked.

And he knows me well enough to not push.

The empty water bottle feels clammy as I rotate it in my hands. I'd wiped out that nervous fidget years ago.

I'm regressing. My childhood is rising, uglier than I remember.

Deke bends to open the little fridge, tosses me a full bottle of water, cracks another for himself. "Y'need more to drink."

Part of me wouldn't mind something stronger to drink, but Father's shadow feels like a quilt right now. If I start drinking to blot away those ripped-open memories, I might never stop. I don't really want more water yet, but cracking the seal and draining a mouthful buys me a few seconds where I don't have to say anything. When I sigh and collapse back into the chair, my waterlogged stomach rocks heavily back and forth like unmoored cargo on a freight plane.

"Ah'm sorry about Lou," Deke says. The more we travel the world, the harder he hangs on to his Southern drawl. His slow words encourage other people to underestimate him.

I nod. "Me, too." But that's not it. I study the nearly Mandelbrotian pattern of red flecks in the heavy navy blue drapes protecting us from the barren sky outside. I've always taken comfort in math and physics.

If it wasn't for Father, maybe I would have chosen a different university. Instead of defending my life from my doctoral advisor, I might have defended my thesis. I might be in a lab now, exposing the secrets of the universe.

And making arrangements for a quick trip home.

At least in my life, I don't have to worry about the company bereavement policy.

The air conditioner clicks back on with a roar. Sixty seconds of silence is about all you get before the temperature climbs enough to trigger the thermostat. Deke and I are probably radiating enough heat to set it off.

Deke knows how to wait.

I'd rather he talked about something. Anything.

But he knows there's something I need to say.

I can't drink any more. Not yet. Before I can think too much, I open my mouth and say "My father is dead."

Deke winces. He knows a bunch about Father. Not everything—even I don't remember everything about Father. But I've told Deke enough that he has a good idea how messed up everything is. "I'm sorry," he says. "No matter what, that sucks. What happened?"

"Yeah." Condensation sheathes the bottom two-thirds of the water bottle and slicks my hands. I set the bottle on the little bedside table. That's the advantage of hotels, nobody ever screams at you to use a coaster on Grandma's beat-up end table.

"What happened?" Deke repeats.

I shake my head. "No idea. I got a text right when Joe pulled up."

"No wonder you sounded off." Deke walks the office chair forward on its wheels. I still feel like there's a barrier between me and him, between me and everyone, me and every *thing*, but when he reaches for my hand I don't have the energy to push him away.

His oven-hot hand feels softer than mine. "Yeah." I lick my lips, but they're so chapped they can't absorb the moisture. Didn't have time for lip balm last night, what with the random running gunfights. I mean to take another drink, but drain the bottle. "I have to go back."

Deke nods. "You have to say goodbye."

I shake my head. "It's not even that. It's…" When did my fists clench so tight? I deliberately open them, laying the palms flat on the nasty scratchy fabric arms of the Inquisition Armchair. "I…I don't even know what it is. I just know I have to go back. I don't, don't even know when things happen." I snatch my phone and answer Will's text message. *Arrangements?*

Deke lets me finish. "That's fine. Whatever you need, we'll go."

"I'm going alone." The words fly out of me without consulting my brain, but when they appear I fully agree with them.

"Like hell you are," Deke says.

This time my head shake is slower and more definite. "There is no way I'm taking you with me."

Deke's jaw sets and his eyes narrow. "You aren't going alone."

My phone buzzes. I snatch it up. "The visitation's *tomorrow*?" Funeral the next day? Arranging a funeral takes time. How long has Father been dead? "What the hell is going on up there?"

"You ashamed of me or something?" Deke says.

"What?" I recoil. "No! No, that's not it at all!"

Deke takes a deep breath. "Billie. Talk to me."

"It's—" I don't know what to say. "I can't—I just can't have you with me." The invisible wall between me and everything feels thicker. "Not there."

Deke makes an obvious effort to still himself. "You don't sound like yourself. Are you thinkin' straight?"

"No I am not thinking straight!" I shout. The empty water bottle thocks off the tacky wallpaper before I realize I've thrown it. And I've wrenched my hand out of his grip. "I just know you're the best thing in my life and I'm not taking you anywhere near my goddamn fucked-up family!"

I recognize the invisible wall now. I'd built it during my childhood. I'd reinforced it in college, when I'd been stuck among kids three years older than me. The wall had stood intact until starting on my doctorate knocked a couple of holes in it.

It wasn't until I'd fallen in love with Deke that I'd been able to tear it down.

Now it's returned, higher and thicker and more impenetrable than ever.

Deke opens his mouth to speak, but I plow right over him. "It's not just Father. My cousins? My aunts and uncles? My *brother*? Uncle Carl, Aunt Pat, they're okay, but the rest of them, they are all just as messed up and I'm not having you anywhere near them." I'm quivering now, vibrating right up against my invisible wall. "I don't—" I've got to calm down somehow cause I'm out of air and I can't talk anymore but the hurt feels ready to rupture my chest and head and everything.

I am *over* this crap.

I've been over this crap for years now.

Or I've been lying to myself for years now.

Inhale. Or pass out.

My breath shudders. My heart hammers harder than it did when I was ducking bullets.

Another.

Deke gets an appraising look on his face when he's studying a situation, like when we find a bomb ticking down or the night vision goggles have picked up bonus guards.

He hasn't looked at me that way since the first night we met.

Until right now.

Fear quivers through me. If this makes Deke even *reconsider* us, I'm going to kill every one of my cousins.

The wall feels thick. Impenetrable.

I pull my hands back into my lap, then punch through the barrier to seize his hand between both of mine. Even his fingers feel hot. "I don't want you to see, see who I was around them."

Deke draws a deep breath. "I only care that you're okay."

The extra flatness of his voice wrenches at my heart. "I know that." Dammit, am I crying now? "I know that."

He gives me a nod. "Then let's compromise. You go to the funeral alone, but—" Deke's other hand covers mine. "I fly to Detroit with you."

My breath is a little steadier now. I don't even want Deke in Michigan with me. I need my mental armor to survive.

But I appreciate Deke more than ever.

I force my heart out through a crack in that wall and squeeze his hand. "Okay."

"And I'm driving you to the funeral home," Deke drawls. "Because if one of them cousins needs killin', you're gonna need a getaway driver."

11

Fortunately, the morning rush hour just ended. Deke calls the equipment contact to have her buy back the sniper rifle and the rest of our gear. By the time she gets to the hotel room, we have packed carry-on bags parked by the door and all the equipment laid out on the bed for inspection. I'm almost dancing with impatience as I let her in, but we can't abandon night vision goggles and lock-hacking gear and all the other toys in a hotel room. The maids would ask questions.

Deke has worked with this equipment dealer before. Usually they bicker and haggle over the buyback price, but this time Deke tells her to name a figure. She says something about needing to inspect for damage. Deke nods and hands her the key cards. "The room's paid until three PM. Put the cash in my account."

We're still incredibly short on time, but inside my barrier, gratitude fills me.

Deke really is the best.

The broker's stunned face is our only farewell. We grab the hotel shuttle to one of our banks to deliver the bearer bonds. The shuttle driver doesn't have anything better to do than wait for us, so takes us to the airport after and saves us the time to find a taxi.

Phoenix's Sky Harbor International Airport's main terminal tries to cram all of Arizona into one building. Skylights expose endless scorched blue. The air smells of peppers and frying eggs and the bus exhaust blown through the sliding doors. The escalator takes us through a billion years of rock strata replicated in plastic. There's about a million tons of air conditioner on the roof keeping the place at a constant seventy-two degrees, but stand too close to the wrong window and the sunlight will scorch your bones.

I let Deke plant me in an empty chair across from the ticket counters. Getting home—no, not home, *never* home. Reaching *Detroit* today demands the right kind of persistence. If I try it, I'm likely to open discussions by shooting a ticket agent just to show the survivors I'm serious.

Deke warns me I might not like the flight.

I nod. "Whatever you can get."

Flying long hauls east across the United States is a pain. Flights start leaving the East Coast in the morning and touch down out West in the morning. The time shift works in their favor. Going the other way, the time shift works against you. If we can snag empty seats, thanks to the time shift we won't arrive in Detroit until early evening at best.

If we can't catch a flight until tomorrow morning, I won't make the visitation.

And I really want the visitation.

I need to walk in and see Father's body.

Part of me needs to know he's really dead. Part of me wants to spit in his face. Part of me wishes he'd been a different father.

And yes, part of me wishes I'd been able to make things better.

Problem is, Father wasn't a thing. He was a people.

You can't change people. You live with them, or you walk away.

I'd walked.

The airport is nearly quiet. Nobody flies to Phoenix in August if they have a choice. A businessman in a custom-cut linen jacket, pristine white designer slacks, and five-thousand-dollar silk tie scurries past, staring at a phone that probably cost him a thousand dollars yesterday. Come October, I'll pay a hundred for that same phone and use it as a burner. His gleaming blue metal rolley carryon bag won't come down in price until someone invents something that screams Rich Asshole even more loudly. Maybe with rhinestones.

Manly rhinestones, of course.

A chain of five children holding each others' hands bobble the other way, ranging in age from Carefree Kindergarten to Serious High School. You can almost trace how each threadbare overnight bag, nearly translucent T-shirt, and repeatedly-patched pair of jeans fell branch by branch down the family tree. The harried-looking forty-something guy leading them has the sagging face and bulging gut of someone who struggles to get enough nutrition out of too much lousy food, but his eyes constantly flicker back to the child convoy as they traipse towards the security checkpoint.

That dad gives a damn.

Whatever brings them to the airport, he's doing his best to cope with it.

When stress and his crappy diet do him in, those kids will bawl their eyes out.

And that businessman's Testosterone Phone probably cost more than that dad made last month.

My guts knot with an urge to follow the rich wastrel to a quiet spot and arrange a private wealth transfer to someone who truly needs it. By the time I can get my breathing back under control, they've all vanished into the bowels of the airport.

Yes, it's best that Deke gets us tickets.

Ticket agents don't deserve to have me shoot them.

Unless they don't have tickets.

No, no—not even then.

My every muscle feels wound tight as a harp. I need to stretch, but the tough tile floor right inside the airport entrance is no place to claim territory. And stretching requires relaxing. Put a plane ticket in my hand, and maybe my muscles will unclench enough to let me drop into the splits for a few minutes.

Or maybe not. Maybe I'll only curl up tighter until I rip myself in half.

And mugging the businessman for his phone will only delay my trip.

Even if he deserves it.

I close my eyes and breathe.

Moments later Deke says, "Hey."

He's right in front of me, face worried and watchful. I want to reach out to take his hand, to reassure him, but reaching through my wall would take too much work right now. I'd explode or cry or something, and we don't have time for that.

He's holding a narrow ticket envelope.

I stop breathing.

"Flight out in forty minutes," he says. "Lousy seats, though."

"Back middle?" I say.

"First class."

"Fine." It's not fine. I loathe sitting up with the greedy bastards.

I haven't even seen my family yet, and already I'm compromising my morals.

The TSA checkpoint isn't a problem. Every ID I buy comes on the government's list of most trusted pre-approved passengers. The gate staff damn near push the peasants out of our way so we can board and the stewardess can dedicate her life to our creature comforts. I can't stand that kind of obsequious attention. My idea of a peaceful flight is reading comics, but I can't make myself even think about this week's new Iron Man. I flip through my language lesson—I'm studying Parauk, used in certain Myanmar highlands—but the words bounce off my brain.

I salve my conscience by napping until we're on the final approach to Detroit.

12

Detroit: the American dream gone belly-up. Once our country's fourth largest city, ripped apart by greedy businesses and granite racism and corrupt unions, and abandoned for jackals to gnaw the meat off her bones. Desperate families shelter in hollow-windowed half-burned homes that any civilized country would plow under. The city center only bustles because rich outsiders have taken advantage of the cheap real estate, and the only decent roads are the ones those rich outsiders take to their expensive private enclaves. The heat isn't as horrid as Phoenix, but it comes with humidity so thick the air seems solid. Walking to the car rental feels like trudging through hot gelatin.

I'm groggy from the time zone shift and from a sleepless night. The three-hour nap on the flight made things worse. My mouth tastes of cotton and my eyes feel sandy.

Plus, I have to decide what to wear. My family will judge me by my clothes, and while I want to say I don't give a damn what they think, I also don't want to listen to their sniping. I have a black outfit in my rolley bag, but if I go to the funeral home dressed as Catwoman they'll think *sexpot* not *thief*, so that's a nope. But how do I want to come across? I'm doing better than you so fuck off?

No, I'm not going to compromise myself any more than I already have. But I'm sure not going in dressed in Third-Hand Redneck.

Deke solves that by stopping at a mall right by the freeway and guiding me into an upper-middle-class place I've shopped at before. He knows they can fit me, and while it's only a few notches above Old Navy it's far more expensive than most of my kin can afford. Yes, Deke's as tired as I am, but he hasn't just lost a parent. His brain is still ticking over. He tells the clerk that my father died and I need a funeral outfit, and lets the system take over. Loose black flouncy blouse, fine. Shoes? Yeah, the sneakers won't do, okay. No, not heels—flats. You can't run in heels.

I push back on the fancy designer slacks, though. Elastic fabric is the best thing to happen to women's pants since ever. And what good is a pair of slacks so tight that they keep you from kicking someone in the head?

I don't plan to kick anyone in the head. But odds are I'll get to.

Have to.

Whatever.

We crash in a hotel room at the northern edge of the suburbs. I let Deke kiss me goodnight, but that's about all the intimacy I can handle. I get eleven hours of blissful unconsciousness, then it's ninety minutes up to the town I was born in.

Malacaster's burned smell penetrates the car before we even see the town.

The village is barely a dot on the map. The only reason it exists is because of the Conestoga Sugar processing plant, a vital link in the economic chain that converts Michigan sugar beets to belly flab. The whole place reeks of caramelization. It's like plunging face first into a running cotton candy machine. My stomach wants to cramp around the coffee I'd drained for breakfast.

I'm pretty sure "my health" is not why I avoid sugar.

Grocery store? Yeah, sort of. There's a party store with delusions of grandeur. Pharmacy? No, but there's a Ben Franklin general store with everything from a whole nine types of candy to pliers to an impressive three dozen bolts of fabric and forty shades of thread.

The library is even smaller than I remembered. I'd lived and died by that library. Seeing the bright blue plastic tarps nailed over patches of the sharply sloped roof sends sorrow bubbling up through my slowly seething anger.

It's stupid. It's insane. But part of me wants to know how Father dared to die and drag me back here. I know it's ridiculous.

Father wouldn't choose to die.

Not even to spite his ungrateful daughter.

Also, I need to remember to send the library some cash.

The funeral home is just as I remember it: a one-story ranch house converted to commercial property. The white siding has seen better decades, but they've hosed the dirt off it lately. A somber-suited teenager is standing behind the mercilessly cubed green hedge with a broom, sweeping the perennial spider webs from under the eaves. No place on Earth has as many spiders as Malacaster in August. The sign has been freshly painted with PINKERTON'S, the letters gleaming under the washed-out blue of Michigan's August sky.

Sometime in the last ten years, they asphalted the parking lot.

And right now, it's full of twenty-year-old road-salt-rotted pickup trucks and two-door sedans with busted-up fenders attached with duct tape. I see three trunks held shut with bungee cords and half a dozen windows replaced with taped-on clear plastic.

The best-looking car is the 1963 Buick sedan, its sea-green body gleaming with fresh wax and the chrome meticulously polished. I guess Uncle Mick is here. Unless he's dead, too, and Darryl inherited the car.

Deke pulls up right in front of the fire hydrant. "I'd really like to be going in with you."

"I know you would." I have a lump the size of a brick in my throat. "I'm sorry."

Deke pulls in a deep breath. He's struggling for control. "I've never introduced you to my family either. There's…reasons."

I nod. "Yeah."

"Lot's pretty full," he says. "How's about I wait across there, in that park?"

The park's a big sprawling hillside, rolling down to the river, with a mostly empty dirt parking lot. He can pull in, turn around, and point the car at the open road.

Not that I intend to come running out pursued by angry relatives baying for my blood, but you never know.

Maybe I should have stopped to get a handgun. No, that's still a bad idea. Some of those relatives need shooting, but this isn't the place and a gun might be too tempting. If there's trouble, the stiletto in my pocket will have to do.

"That works." I try to swallow the lump, and reach out for his hand.

Deke gently squeezes my fingers.

My throat tightens. "Thank you."

"You'd do the same for me."

"Yeah." I am not going to cry. I refuse to cry.

"You check in every hour now." His voice sounds tight. One of the hardest things anyone can do is stand back and let the person they love face their demons. Deke's job is harder than mine.

"I don't think I'll be that long," I say.

"You might be surprised."

"Will you be okay?"

"Sure. I got me some reading."

I glance into the back seat. Deke likes his magazines in paper. He's grabbed *The Economist*, *Forbes*, *MIT Technology Review*, and *Soldier of Fortune*. He loves the classified ads in that last one. He'll laugh the whole way through and read the most bogus bits to me.

I let go of his hand. The wall between me and the world feels thicker than ever. "When we get out of here…let's take a couple days. You and me. Someplace quiet." Where had we had real peace? "Maybe back in Poissey?"

Deke's lips twitch. "There's nothing in Poissey but that really good restaurant and acres of French countryside."

"And that hotel with the really nice beds."

Deke has a great laugh. It comes up from the bottom of his chest and fills the car. Hearing it lights a little hope inside my walls.

I'll see Dad buried.

Then I'll walk away and never think of this place again.

Deke and I will go back to our perfect life of making rich bastards pay us to pillage other rich bastards.

We finish this, and Deke's laugh will blow that wall around my heart to flinders.

Deke's smile makes his eyes bright. He can't stop looking at me, right into my eyes. Like he can see through flesh and into soul. "You're on."

"Stay here and fill your brain," I say.

Then I climb out of the car and head up the funeral home's cracked walkway, willing the wall around my heart to harden.

13

Funeral homes all smell the same. The air conditioner scrubs every drop of moisture and aroma from the air and replaces it with a carefully synthesized perfume designed to overwhelm mediocre embalming. They use dark carpeting so nothing shows, and it's stain-resistant so nothing stays. It's got good traction, though, so I won't slide if (when) I decide to run. I don't know where they get those awful chaises and chairs, but they're clearly designed to remain pristine by being so uncomfortable nobody can sit in them for long. The somber stripe-and-flower wallpaper looks painted on, but it's so glossy it's probably washable.

It's probably in *Funeral Homes for Dummies*: People have all sorts of drama at visitations, so remember you'll need to regularly hose the snot off the wall.

A massive television hangs across from the dark fireplace, showing pallbearers chosen from the Twenty-Something White Male section of the model agency catalog carrying—is that a canoe-shaped coffin? No, it's a real canoe. Do they offer Viking funerals now?

A balding man too stooped for his forty or so years, groomed and manicured within an inch of his death, greets me right inside the door. I'm pretty sure his severe black suit is available exclusively through discreet ads in the back of *Undertaker Monthly*. "May I help you?"

No you can't, I want to say. *You have two rooms. The door to the back room is closed. Father is in the front. And I can hear people talking up that way.* Instead, I say "Salton."

The attendant's chin dips and comes back up. His name badge reads FRANK CAVELL. "Are you family?"

My heart starts pounding even harder. "Daughter." The pallbearers on the TV don't look serious enough. Maybe the commercial's trying to sell funerals as parties?

Cavell's somber expression edges towards a frown. "Is your name Billie?"

The suspicious question slows my heart—it's still pounding, but the familiar hint of danger steadies me. My first thought is that Will left a group of his drinking buddies—assuming he's managed to keep any—in the back room, ready to rough me up and throw me out. He's known about the funeral for how long? And he texted me yesterday just to screw me up. The possibility of a real threat eases my back and relaxes my shoulders. "Yeah."

Cavell reaches for a breast pocket. "I have a letter for you."

"Who's it from?"

Cavell holds a business envelope in one hand. "The gentleman did not leave a name."

On the television, the camera veers to show a cremation urn in the canoe. They did the Viking funeral backwards—no. Not now. "Is he here now?"

Cavell says, "No, ma'am. He asked me to deliver this letter to you as soon as you walked in the door."

The lobby tightens around me. Some old school friend that I haven't seen since high school? No, ridiculously precocious me had utterly failed at making friends among kids in her grade or of her own age.

I'm too keyed up. There's a perfectly rational explanation.

Frank's holding the envelope with bare hands, so it's probably not covered in contact poison.

I snatch the envelope. He doesn't deserve my anger, but it doesn't have anywhere else to go.

"This way, please," Frank says, holding a hand to the front of the building.

"I know the way."

His chin dips again. "Yes, ma'am."

I pivot and walk away from the way Frank pointed. The tiny one-toilet restroom is right where I remember it, wallpapered in fake-charming climbing roses and so heavily perfumed that it transcends any particular smell. I fight down my gagging, push the button lock, and study the envelope. Where the address should be there's a single line of laser printing, all in the default Microsoft Word font: BILLIE SALTON. The flap is meticulously glued and then sealed with a strip of transparent tape, as if the sender wanted no chance of a snooping attendant steaming it open. It's nearly flat, without any bulge that might indicate unpleasant surprises, and can't hold more than a single sheet of paper.

I hold it up to the light. The envelope's a uniform shade of gray.

If this is a commiseration note from the fourth grade teacher who got me skipped ahead to sixth, I'm gonna feel like an idiot.

An unexpected knot forms in my throat. Maybe I should look up a few teachers? No, that's not just sentimental, it's stupid. What would I tell them?

I tug my stiletto out of my pocket, flick it open, slice the envelope open, and use the blade to tug the single sheet of paper out. It's also laser-printed, in the default Microsoft font.

Beaks,
You've worked for your father's murderer.

14

The tiny bathroom's sickening floral perfume turns both hot and solid. My stomach shrinks to a pinpoint. Sweat erupts along my back. I can feel the whole funeral home, the whole world, twisting around me like my mind is suddenly the Earth's axis of rotation.

Father was murdered?

I knew the murderer? Worked for them?

And *Beaks*.

Nobody in Malacaster knows that name. I'd only adopted it after I started freelancing.

The switchblade is sticking out the other side of my fist. I don't remember switching it to fighting position.

Who knew enough to find me here?

Laser-printed envelope and letter. No handwriting that I might recognize. I hold the sheet up to the light, but there's no watermark. It could have come from any printer in the world.

I force myself to breathe deeply and slowly, commanding my drum-line pulse to slow before I black out. I've performed the same exercise while crammed in a ventilation shaft hanging upside down over a dozen thugs with machine pistols, but disciplining my body feels more difficult than ever.

In a minute or three, my pulse no longer thrums in my eyes.

Keeping my breath slow and relaxed, I study the paper one more time. Seven words.

The question is, who sent them? And why?

I'd always thought that if anyone was going to kill my father, it was gonna be me. He was the kind of man someone would eventually shoot just to shut him up.

I should have checked the news sites. A murder would be huge news in Malacaster.

I carefully fold the letter back into the envelope, splash cold water on my face and march back to the lobby. Attendant Cavell is still there, looking a little more relaxed. I stomp right up to him and say, "Who gave you this letter?"

Cavell flinches. "He didn't leave his name."

I deliberately widen my eyes and relax my jaw, trying to downshift my expression from *murderous* to merely *do not fuck with me*. "He didn't sign it either. Describe him."

"Tall." Cavell swallows. "Maybe as tall as you, miss."

I'm twenty-eight. No longer 'miss' anything.

I let Cavell live. "That's it?"

"A good dark suit."

I let my eyes narrow a little.

Cavell hurries to say "He was very serious. As if he didn't have a sense of humor."

"White?" I snap. "Black? Asian, what?"

"Mostly white? Little darker than you?"

I look Mediterranean, so *darker than me* includes most of the planet. "He didn't leave a card? Anything?"

Cavell shakes his head. Judging from his face, I've held revolvers to people's heads without worrying them this much. "He—he gave me a hundred dollars to deliver that."

"And he just trusted you?"

Cavell's voice is thinner. "He said he'd know if I didn't."

"And you believed him?"

Cavell jerks his head in a single petrified nod.

Suddenly I'm disgusted with myself. Cavell's just a shmuck working a job. A job I wouldn't ever want to do.

Discipline.

I close my eyes. Empty my lungs. Draw a deep breath.

That anonymous note set fire to my soul. I'm dancing with madness.

A second breath. I consciously relax my features. Before opening my eyes, I say, "Thank you, Mister Cavell." The words taste bitter, but I push them out. "You have been very helpful. I apologize."

"We all react to grief differently," Cavell says quietly.

I open my eyes.

He's taken a step back.

Control. Discipline.

I give him a nod, step well around him, and start down the hall towards the front parlor. Everything looks too bright. The deliberately somber high-gloss wallpaper scratches my nerves.

Cry if you have to. Kill someone if they need killing.

But do it because you're in charge. Because you decide they need to die. Not because you're angry and want to kill someone, anyone.

I follow the turn of the hall, and am immediately caught.

"Uncle" Tommy was one of Father's cousins. I haven't seen him for over a decade, and even though his hair has faded to a bleached-out gray and his face has picked up a few extra lines and sags, I recognize him immediately. He's got to be, what, fifty years old? The bodybuilder physique I remember has dissolved into a water balloon. He's standing outside the door to the front parlor, face slack with fatigue and posture slumped, wearing a cheap dark blue suit meant for a man twenty years younger and whose pecs hadn't yet slipped down around his middle. When I'd last seen him he had a couple inches on me, but now I can peer over his head.

Seeing Uncle Tommy drives home just how intensely I don't want to be here. He's a symptom of everything I fled. Bile surges up the back of my throat.

Uncle Tommy peers at me curiously, then his face brightens and he takes a couple steps towards me. "Billie? Hey, little Billie, is that you?"

Memories erupt from half a lifetime ago: cousin Carol bawling in my arms. The impotent anger of that moment rises with it, buried for over a decade but somehow even fiercer.

I'm not going to give him the satisfaction of seeing it. "Tom Cartmill."

"Oh, you're too old to call me Uncle Tommy now?" He's got his arms open to pull me into a hug.

I walk forward, hand extended for a handshake, keeping my face carefully neutral. Here's a moment I've considered for years, usually at those dark empty hours in a strange city when I'm alone and I can't help hauling out old regrets to gnaw on them and make the night even more hollow.

More things I should have done.

Things a twelve-year-old couldn't have done.

Uncle Tommy sees my hand outstretched, and I know damn well what he's going to do—take my palm and pull me in close. Squeeze me up against him.

When his flabby, dust-dry palm closes on mine, though, I offer him my own surprise.

My rage hasn't diminished. But it's no longer impotent.

I instantly clamp my other hand over his.

Uncle Tommy hasn't been in a real fight for decades.

I fight for my life whenever things go horribly wrong. Call it monthly.

He doesn't have a chance.

I twist my grip and step aside, spinning his wrist around and turning his own momentum against him. Suddenly he's on one knee, his overextended arm pinning him to a kneeling position. I'm standing with my feet braced against each other, both hands close to my solar plexus and clamped tight around his hand so I can lean my weight against his wrist and keep him in place.

His hammy mitt tries to twitch in my double clench.

I dig my fingers in a little harder than necessary.

All my frustration, all the confusion of the last twenty-four hours has poured into this moment. Part of me wants to shriek with focused rage.

But my heart slows a touch.

The whirlpool in my mind crystalizes to ice.

Uncle Tommy shifts his weight off his knee to try to stand, but I have his arm hyperextended. He can't rise without snapping his own elbow.

I'd be okay with that.

He could fall down and roll out, but he's not smart enough.

He can barely twist his head enough to peer at me with astonished eyes.

"Listen carefully." I'm amazed I can keep my voice this cold. I should be screaming. "Carol told me what you did to her."

His eyes get a little wider. His jaw opens like he's going to say something.

You can keep someone from screaming, if you know when and where to apply pressure.

His words dissolve into a pained intake of breath.

He's about to exhale when I say, "I believe her." The urge to scream is building, but I channel it into a fierce whisper. "I'm not twelve anymore." I lean in a little closer, easing a few extra ounces of my weight onto his wrist.

This is a bad idea. It's a horrible idea.

It's the only idea.

His jaw clangs back together. Breath hisses between his teeth.

The ancient memory of cousin Carol's teary words and her impassioned warnings screech at me to shatter his arm. No matter how richly this monster deserves it, though, an ambulance visit will lead to police. Instead, I whisper, "You come within arm's reach, I will make you watch while I chop off your dick and feed it to the pigs."

We're in the hallway. Cavell could come around the corner any moment. My brother could wander out of the parlor.

Or worse, Carol.

I don't want Carol to see her father kneel before me.

Even if it is for her.

Cousin Carol needs to kill her own demons. I can't do that for her.

Besides. After the funeral?

Maybe I'll come back for one last visit.

Tommy's face screams that he can't believe this is happening.

Did he really think we didn't know? Aunt Beth covered up for him, she had to know, but it was a family secret and what a man does with his family is his business, don't you know that?

But his pain gives me savage satisfaction. It's not for Carol. Not really. Nobody did anything about Father when he smacked Mom around. Nobody did anything for me once Mom fled.

I ease up a quarter-ounce.

Uncle Tommy opens his mouth.

I put the pressure back on, and a little more.

A thin agonized wheeze escapes through his teeth.

"I'm going to ease up," I say quietly. "If you say anything other than 'yes, ma'am,' I will shatter your arm. Then I'll come back for you. Not now. But one day."

Uncle Tommy squeezes his eyes shut.

"If you understand, nod."

He raises his chin defiantly.

His hand is getting damp with sweat. I need to finish this before he gets too slippery.

A touch more pressure. Bones grind. His face turns almost purple.

"Nod if you understand," I whisper. "Or I'll break your wrist. Maybe your elbow and shoulder with it."

Uncle Tommy's defiance dissolves. He gives a desperate nod.

I'd always thought he was a coward.

But it feels so good to prove it.

"Remember," I say. "It's 'yes, ma'am' or you're in the hospital."

I release my grip. The funeral home air cools his sweat from my palms.

Uncle Tommy wobbles.

I step aside.

Tommy helplessly topples forward, right where I was standing. He tries to catch himself and lets out this mewling cry when his abused hand touches the carpet. He plummets right down, gasping when his face smacks the coarse industrial carpet.

He's close enough that if I swing my feet it'll break his jaw.

Not that I'd do that.

Here. Now.

For a second, nobody moves. Uncle Tommy's gasping figure is my world.

"Tommy?" someone says from the parlor.

I glance up.

An incredibly overweight woman wearing an enveloping black dress covered in irritatingly cute tiny white dots stands right outside the parlor door. She's looking at Uncle Tommy. "Are you okay?"

"He tripped," I say. "Isn't that right?"

Uncle Tommy licks his lips. "Yes, ma'am." His eyes are murderous muddy brown pits.

I'm not satisfied, but passing my teenage impotence to him soothes me a little.

"Did you take your medicine today?" The woman waddles towards him on legs surgically transplanted from an elephant. I have the feeling I should know her, but nobody in my family's that big. Was that big.

"I'm fine, Beth!" Uncle Tommy spasms away from her touch and flings himself to his feet.

"Aunt Beth?" I say. Eleven years ago, she'd been supermodel gaunt. Now you could fit a dozen supermodels in her and still have room for a handsy politician.

She cocks her head to the side and looks up at me. "Oh my Lord. Little Billie?"

Aunt Beth had always been kind to me, bringing me books and slipping me cookies and playing board games with me. No, not like Monopoly, more like *Ticket to Ride* or *Civilization*. Not that she ever had time to finish a game of Civ, but she'd tried.

But she also hadn't done anything to help her own daughter.

Far as I could tell, Aunt Beth moved through life by nailing a smile to her face.

All that fury that I'd felt on seeing Uncle Tommy suddenly gets tangled up with the painful knot in my throat. I don't think I can speak. Instead, I give a nod.

She moves to give me a hug.

I find myself reaching an arm around her to pat the back of her shoulders, all the while watching Uncle Tommy fume. I stare at him hard, trying to telepathically transmit *fuck off* by sheer willpower.

Aunt Beth clutches me like she's drowning and I'm one of the hunks on the old Baywatch show. "I'm so sorry. This was such a shock. To all of us."

I let go of Aunt Beth. "I know."

She hangs on for another half second, then reluctantly releases me. "Will told us not to expect you."

"I almost didn't make it." I don't see the point in saying that Will only texted me yesterday. She's not the one to have that fight with.

"We're so glad you did," Aunt Beth says. "Come on in. Everyone will be delighted to see you!"

I want to escape. Back in the car. Let Deke sweep me away to France. Forget Father, murder or no.

Instead, I'm going to walk in and face my family.

15

There's a dozen people in the garishly overdone funeral hall.

One way or another, I'm related to all of them.

I have no idea how I climbed out of this shallow gene pool. I only know I'm not diving back into it.

My quick glance picks out Uncle Carl and Aunt Pat at the back of the room, sitting side by side on one of the Torquemada couches. I can already see that Uncle Carl's eyes aren't so good anymore, and the way Aunt Pat clutches his hand tells me she has her own problems. They must be, what, in their sixties now?

Without Carl and Pat, I never would have made it to college. I'd be standing there like Cousin Molly, who must have carved a fresh hole in the ozone layer to get her hair that big. She'd been in a Goth phase when I'd seen her last, but that dress looks like she'd had to scrounge for something dark enough for a funeral. She's only a few years older than me, but she's got too many wrinkles around her eyes. And there's Cousin Carol, almost as big as her mother but in a meticulously hand-sewn black-and-gray jumper that hides her shape, perched demurely on the edge of a corner chair, silently watching everything, hands clasped in a textbook photo of propriety.

Opposite the door, someone's put a tripod supporting a poster board straight from a junior high science fair. Photographs cover it, ranging from faded Kodachromes to blurry inkjet prints of cellphone shots. Shaky printing across the top in broad-tip marker declares this IN MEMORY OF WILLIAM SALTON.

Yes, Father's name was William.

My brother is Will.

My name is Billie.

Father damn well meant for us to be his.

Just seeing his name like that sends triumph surging through me.

I'd escaped.

Standing next to the photo display, my cousins Darryl and Young Mack turn to face me. Darryl's turned out like I guessed, working hard to win the world record for Biggest Beer Belly. Young Mack? He'd inherited brains from his mom's side of the family and I'd hoped he'd gotten out. But he's already got the alcoholic's broken-veined nose and his white button-down shirt has seen half a dozen owners.

Will is with them.

Will is six years older than me, in his thirties now. His face is a flabby boozy flush beneath a carefully sculpted tangle of hair. His nose was broken when I left, and from the crook someone has busted it again since. His spare tire could support a pickup. Even from the doorway, I picked up a whiff of the cheap leather-and-spice cologne he bought by the quart back in high school.

Will's bloodshot eyes freeze at seeing me. His jaw drops open half an inch.

Will does most of his thinking with his little brain. My appearance has obviously made his big brain lock up from disuse.

Next to me, Aunt Beth announces, "Look everyone! Billie made it!"

At least Will recognized me before he had to be told.

The tension I felt negotiating the cello swap with Stabbity Joe is nothing next to how my every nerve sparks here. If someone moves wrong, I'll snatch that crystal dish of individually packaged oversized peppermint Life Savers off the end table and brain everyone with it.

Coming here was a mistake.

A mistake I couldn't *not* make.

I've left all this behind. I've made myself better than this.

"Billie!" Aunt Pat stares at me in joyful disbelief. "Dear Billie, come over here."

The words break my paralysis.

I might brain someone else, but not Aunt Pat.

When Dad had been so drunk he'd collapsed halfway down the stairs, Aunt Pat had gone to Parent-Teacher conferences for me. She'd persuaded the principal to send me to the gifted classes up in Midland. She'd helped me apply to colleges and get scholarships. She'd told me how to prove I was exceptional, so that the University of Michigan would offer me a full ride scholarship despite my youth.

That first night of university, when I'd broken down sobbing, she'd answered the phone at three in the morning and told me I could do this.

She told me I deserved better than Father—but that if I wanted better, I had to *take* it.

And she'd told me to call her any time I needed her.

Uncle Carl hadn't said so much to me, but after Mom left he'd taken Father out onto the back porch and talked to him a whole bunch of times. After each of those talks, Father had tried to treat me better. It only lasted until Father cracked his next can of Pabst, but Carl had done more to help me with Father than anyone else managed.

Uncle Carl had driven me and my lone suitcase down to Ann Arbor in his ancient pickup truck and walked me into the Dean's office.

When he left, he told me I was "the smartest people he knew."

I can't help smiling at Pat and Carl. I take two steps towards her before I falter.

What am I going to tell them?

I'm a thief?

I kill people—but only when they're trying to kill me?

Or if they really, really deserve it?

No, that's silly.

I'd told Will a cover. I'll use it.

That indecision only costs me half a second, but that's enough time for Will to arrive in a cloud of bourbon. "Billie." His voice is flat, but he stops far enough away that he can't touch me, so that's okay.

"Will." I stop walking. "Thank you for letting me know about today." I can't help adding, "A little more warning would have been good."

"I *ree*-spected your wishes." Will has picked up Father's drawl, and apparently booze makes it worse. "You said 'the next time you call, someone best be dead.'"

Anger flashes through me. "You wouldn't stop calling that time, and I was really busy."

"Yeah, your job as a big-shot company troubleshooter, right?" he sneers. "What, you were making slides for some big meeting?"

I'd been dangling in an air shaft, hiding from three infuriated security goons with large-bore automatic shotguns. Will's incessant drunken calls had blocked Deke's signal for me to move out. He'd almost killed Deke. "Your calls weren't urgent."

"Oh, urgent?" Will takes half a step towards me, far enough away that I can't punch him. I could drive stiffened fingers into his eyes, though. "What's more urgent than Dad having pneumonia?"

"You got him in the hospital. What was I supposed to do from—" Wasn't that the UAE Treasury gig? Or was it the Saudi solar research firm? Maybe the Georgian agricultural genetics lab? "—from, the other side of the world?"

"He could have died," Will says.

"He didn't," I say.

"You said someone better be dead. So he is." Will lashes a hand out towards the front of the room. "Hope you're fucking happy."

I can't help but follow Will's accusing hand.

Father's laid out in the front of the room.

His coffin's longer than most—it would have to be, I get my height from Father like I got my brains from Mom. The gleam doesn't look like wood; it's probably cheap laminate. Cheap doesn't surprise me. I sent Dad enough money to live on, but also enough to drive in grand style all the way to the end of Cirrhosis Highway if that's what he chose to do.

My throat grows tight. My pulse thuds in my ears.

I'd walked away from Father, but I hadn't been able to leave him behind.

Did the money I send bring this on more quickly?

The room is silent. Even Will has shut up. Everyone's watching the prodigal daughter.

Waiting for me to explode.

16

Cheesy frilly silk pillows prop Father's head in place, the pancake makeup insufficient to conceal an apocalypse of busted veins. Morticians can only do so much, but Father looks like they barely tried. Maybe Father had feuded with the mortician, like he had with half the town. At least they didn't put Father in a suit—a tie around his quadruple chin would have been a sick joke. He's in his tattered, beloved Black Sabbath tour T-shirt, hands folded on top of his potbelly. There's way too much powder on his face, his hands, everywhere. The shroud is pulled up a little more above the waist than you'd usually see, probably because that tormented shirt can't really cover his bellybutton.

Standing by the coffin, my shoulders tremble.

I don't know how many times Dad spanked me. Slapped me. And how often had he shrieked in anger because I dared to *read* rather than make his supper? Never mind that when I did crack open a can of Chef Boy-ar-dee, he'd yell because it wasn't a steak.

If you can't guess, we didn't have steak in the house.

But sometimes, he'd bring me books. I'd been eight when he'd got me a box of Buffy on DVD, and he even watched a whole bunch of it with me. I can hear his voice now: *rather you watch this than that pansy shit with rainbow ponies.*

Well, he'd started to watch it. A couple hours in and he was passed out on the couch.

My body stands before the coffin. My lungs are paralyzed.

My soul is lost in time.

It was—eleventh grade, wasn't it? No, tenth. The posse of high school girls who'd taken exception to a little girl rocketing up into their grade three years ahead of schedule. Father had taken me out into the backyard on Thanksgiving and showed me how to make a fist. When he'd tried to throw a slow-motion punch it was way too high, so he got on his knees in the damp grass. *You don't need to learn to dodge a big guy. Your trouble's those little bitches.*

They weren't that little, except next to Father.

We'd gone out for all four days of the long holiday, even in the rain. When I'd gone back to school, those girls weren't a problem anymore. Not where I could hear.

When the high school principal had called to complain, Father had told him to make the other girls leave his daughter alone or he'd bust his face. Then he'd sent me to my room without supper because I hadn't done the laundry, even though he hadn't picked up the soap on his beer run.

And he'd been a damn sight better to me than Uncle Tommy had been to his daughter.

Low bar, yeah.

What the hell am I supposed to do here? Make peace?

Remind myself that no matter how far I run, I carry a bit of him with me?

I wouldn't bust an elementary school principal's face. No matter how much he deserved it.

Shoot him in the face, sure.

That doesn't make me a better person.

Father would bitch—I don't use that word, not like that, but he sure did—he'd sit on the couch and *bitch* about the Conestoga Sugar owners squeezing the balls of the poor bastards who worked the line, the ovens, the bagging machines.

I rob rich people.

No—rich people pay me to rob rich people. I get those bastards coming and going.

Maybe I'm more Father than Father ever was.

I study Father's face. A bubble of dried glue sticks up into his eyelashes. Sloppy mortuary work, but nobody outside the family's going to put any effort into

William Salton's funeral. He's lucky the mortician didn't just industrial staple his eyelids shut and put a Pabst in his hand. Father's face is kind of puffy, his neck bulging between the sagging chin and the T-shirt neck—

I peer closer.

Father carried a lot of weight. He'd earned the quadruple chin.

But I've seen folds like those in his neck before.

The anonymous words *you've worked for your father's murderer* burn through me.

I whirl to face Will. "What did he die from?"

Will rolls his eyes. "Like you care." His every word stinks of bourbon.

My confused emotions still churn like a storm-tossed ocean, but the sight of Father's neck acts as a sea anchor. For this moment, my heart has something to seize hold of. "Are you going to tell me what he died of, or am I going to beat it out of you?"

My voice is a lot harsher than I intended. I don't care.

Cousin Carol says, "My Lord, Billie!"

I jump. Carol is three times my size, how did I not see her?

Carol says, "He broke his neck, falling at work."

"Work?" I say. "What was he working for?"

Will says, "How the hell was he supposed to make a living? Dad wouldn't take no government handout."

I'd sent Father enough money to pay cash for any house in Malacaster and fill it with empties. What had he done with it? The mystery doesn't slow me down, though. "Working at the plant?"

"He'd moved down to Detroit," Will says.

Translation: he'd burned through every manager at the Conestoga plant.

"Night watchman at the trainyard," Will says.

"Fine." I turn back to the coffin. Reach out.

"Hey," Will says, "what are you—"

I want to rip the pillow away, but my atavistic respect for human bodies makes me tug it instead.

Father's chin tips loosely towards me.

"Jesus fuck, Billie!" Will shouts.

I drop the little pillow.

Will yanks my shoulder back.

I go with the motion, letting him turn my shoulders so I can reach out with the other hand and gently press against the side of Father's cool head.

Rigor mortis passed days ago.

But still, his head moves too easily.

There are a couple of ways to break your neck. A mild break can kill you and leave your neck almost locked in place.

For his head to wobble like that?

That's not any kind of normal break.

And that gouge around his neck sure looks like the crease left by a noose.

Suddenly I know who killed Father.

Ayaka.

17

I'd been freelancing for about four months when the Ayaka call came in.

Deke and I had just finished our fourth job together, but he was out of touch for two weeks on a gig that didn't involve me. I was hanging around this tedious New Jersey casino town, aimlessly losing myself in cheesy entertainment. Once you've learned to pillage banks, stage magic gets lame. I can only stretch so long, read so many comics, and watch so many movies before that urge for excitement overpowers my good sense.

And—I admit it. I wanted to show Deke how much I'd learned. Prove I was ready to work on my own.

The job broker said he needed someone who could slither through a building's crawlspaces and render the security system harmless—not disable it, that would set off alarms, but make it keep reporting everything was normal even though the rest of the crew would be busy pillaging the safe. I'd done exactly that before.

And robbing a diamond company? Those bastards have dug up millions of those stupid little rocks and hoard them to keep the price obscenely inflated. Left to me, I'd steal everything and give the whole heap away, bring the whole filthy business down. Toddlers need three-carat binkies too!

Four days, including travel.

I'd be back before Deke. With a great big paycheck.

I didn't even think before saying yes.

Crew boss Ayaka impressed me. An older black woman, maybe five feet three, whose every motion seemed precise and practiced. Three other experienced professionals, each as hard as Deke but cheerless.

I neutered the alarm. The main crew came in.

It turned out that a dozen people worked that Saturday.

Deke and I cow civilians with a firm glare and a glint of gunmetal. If you don't make a fuss, you'll go home fine. A bullet in the leg settles down most anyone.

Ayaka's starting move? Hanging a man from the balcony. She left his corpse dangling over the hostages while her lackeys pillaged the safe.

What did I do?

I helped carry the crates out the door.

I'd told myself that if I'd said anything, I would have been hanging right next to that poor bastard. Truth is…I was terrified.

I went back to Jersey, locked myself in my hotel room, and cried.

Deke blamed himself. He said he should have guessed I'd fly on my own. He said he should have named people to avoid. He hadn't expected me to try so soon, though.

I didn't let him have the blame.

The money I made on that gig? I cashed it out and shoved it under the door of a rattletrap storefront church. Another year passed before I accepted a second solo gig.

It's not only that Ayaka started out by hanging a bystander.

It's how her eyes laughed.

I've never enjoyed killing. If I must kill, I've screwed up.

Ayaka calls death her "indulgence."

18

Will shouts at me. I hear his voice, but not his words.

Cousin Carol speaks.

But the wall between me and the funeral home is impregnable. The gears of my brain turn as I stare at Father's body and imagine what happened after he died.

Someone found the night watchman dead.

The local coroner pronounced him dead at a glance and shipped him off to the closest relatives.

The Malacaster mortician surely noticed the broken neck. But nobody in town would care if that troublemaker William Salton busted anything, including his neck. Father had spent a whole bunch of summer nights on the sagging porch of our ramshackle home, drinking and smoking and shouting at anyone passing by. Father attracted enemies like our house attracted ants.

I hand-select my enemies. I curate who to piss off, and how badly.

Father went for quantity, not quality. As far as Malacaster went, he'd earned the high score.

I'm confident he hadn't done any better in Detroit.

My heart trumpets that I should have done something to make things better with Father before he died.

My brain knows there was no *something* to be done.

But my heart and brain agree: if someone killed Father, I really, really want to find the killer. My tangled passions are a supersaturated solution that gets one particle too many; everything crystalizes into rock-hard purpose.

The kind of purpose I'm really, really good at.

The wall between me and the universe shatters.

"—come in here and disree-spect your father like that?" Will shouts. He's clenching my shoulders, shaking my limp body like a floppy doll.

"You're right," I say.

"You stupid—" Will's mouth flaps shut. "What?"

"You bury him." I bring my hands up in front of my chest and snap them out, knocking his grip off my shoulders. "I have more important things to do."

Carol gasps in shock.

I storm out of the funeral parlor and down the hall, leaving baffled shouts and exclamations in my wake. I don't care. I'm never returning to Malacaster. I'm never seeing any of these people again. I'm leaving them behind forever—

"Hey!" Will shouts.

I don't slow, but I can hear his feet pounding up behind me. "Billie, you miserable bitch! You can't just come in here and fuck everyone up like that!"

"Fuck. Off." Dammit, I'm better than that, but nothing else feels like the right thing to say. Snarl. Whatever.

Poor Cavell retreats into a corner as I storm through the lobby and out. Michigan's August wet heat drapes itself around me. My first breath tastes like I'm inhaling straight from a bodybuilder's armpit. The air conditioning had sucked my clothes dry, but in three steps new sweat makes everything cling to me. The low fluffy clouds crossing the burnished blue sky promise to rain away the stickiness and ease the browning grass, but they lie. The sun hurts my eyes, and the heat makes my innards even more unsteady.

And my soul is on fire.

The last day has been a disaster. I have to talk to Deke. Straighten my head. Shut down the whirling in my head and my heart and my gut.

I had dibs on killing Father.

I get one foot on the asphalt parking lot before Will's ham-hock hand snatches my shoulder. "You really want to hurt Uncle Tommy and Aunt Beth like that? Uncle Carl?"

Uncle Carl. Aunt Pat. I might have given a heart attack to the only relatives I give a crap about. My pace involuntarily slows.

Will takes advantage of my pause to jerk me around to face him. He shouldn't be able to make me shift my stance so easily, but I'm off balance. I've been treating this as a family funeral, not as a gig, and as of sixty seconds ago it's a job.

Perhaps the most important job I've ever been on.

"You get your skinny ass back in there and apologize," Will snarls into my face.

"Not a chance." I'm not thinking, only reacting. My self-control has evaporated. I'm sure Deke is watching.

I need to leave before my love puts a bullet in my brother.

I have dibs on killing Will, too.

Will says "If this is what a fancy liberal degree does to you, I'm glad I don't have one. You can't even show ree-spect when your own father dies."

"Astrophysics is *not* a liberal degree." I spit the words into Will's face. "And he didn't die. He was killed."

Shit. I shouldn't have said that.

Will's jaw drops. "What bullshit is this?"

"Never mind, I'm full of shit." That's not going to work.

"Bullshit." Will shakes my shoulders again.

"Get your hands off me." Breaking my brother's neck would raise too many questions.

"Talk!"

"Fine. Get your hands off me."

Will's face is a mask of rage, but he yanks his hands back. "Well!"

I lower my voice. "His neck's broken right at the C2 vertebrae. It's called a hangman's break. You don't get that falling to the floor."

"So what?"

"And he's got a wound from a noose around his neck." I shouldn't be telling him this. I *know* I shouldn't be telling him this. But right now, nothing's more important than smacking the outrage off his smug face.

"Bullshit."

"There are other kinds of shit," I say. "And it's there."

"That doesn't happen," Will says.

"Do you watch the news?"

He scowls. "Hanging stretches your neck."

"And how many people have you seen hanged?"

"Neither have you."

I glance around. Rusting cars fill the parking lot, but nobody's close enough to hear. Nobody's even walking by. Across the road, our rented SUV is ready to rocket away.

I lower my voice. "If you hang them right? Cut the person down right away? The neck snaps at the fall. A properly adjusted noose doesn't even leave much rope burn. And that one crease in his neck? It's too straight, wa-a-ay too straight."

I spent years getting Father's weird drawl out of my mouth, and ten minutes with Will has it right back. My fingers straighten and stiffen, ready to crack their own straight line right across my brother's throat.

"How the fuck do you know that?" Will says.

An unwanted memory flashes through me: a middle manager dangling from a balcony, feet kicking as he plunged. "I've seen it."

Will's face softens a little. Maybe he can see the memory in my expression.

"Someone killed him," I say. "And I'm going to find out who."

"They would have noticed," Will says.

"Who?" I bark a laugh. "The coroner? You think an overworked Detroit coroner gives a short shit about a night watchman? One look at Father and he'd say *fall* just to make his list shorter. They'd box him up and ship him off."

"Fuck me," Will breathes, his gaze distant.

"So you bury him," I say. "And I'm going to find out who did it."

"How you think you're doing that?"

"Check his home. Check his work. See where they take me."

Will snaps "Not a chance."

"I'm not calling the police," I say.

"Course not." Will's lips tighten. "But I'm coming with you."

19

Bring my brother on a gig?

"Not a chance." I wouldn't care if the funeral home parking lot was full of people, I'm gonna say it loudly enough that even Will gets it.

There is no way I'm taking Will. He's a drunk. I can smell the bourbon seeping through his skin. He's carrying an extra fifty, eighty pounds. If you can't drink it or sleep with it, he pisses on it.

I'm angry, yes. Furious. I need Deke to settle me down enough to think, and think hard, about how to find Father's killer and figure out who left the note, but I don't need Will elephanting around behind me.

"What are you going to do?" Will sneers. "Use them fancy corporate troubleshooter skills? Come in and tell the workers to lift with their backs? Hire a private dee-tective?"

My mouth opens to shout out what I do, what I really do, but I clamp my teeth back together. Tell Will I'm a high-class professional thief? I'd be better off taking out a full-page ad in the Washington Post. At least there, prospective clients might see it.

But I've got to be careful. Anger made me say too much already. Somehow, I've got to defuse Will without sending him shouting about murder. "I have skills."

Will rolls his eyes. "Because astro-o-physics covers finding killers?"

I tighten my lips. "The same way I've seen hangings before."

"What the *hell* kind of corporate do you troubleshoot?"

"I can't talk about it."

"You're still full of shit."

"But I know people," I say.

"Really, what are you gonna do?" Will sneers. "Say you're right. Say someone killed Dad, say you find them. You can't fight your way out of a pile of puppies."

I haven't thought about 'Uncle Tom's puppies' in years. Learning how Tom Cartmill had destroyed cousin Carol had scoured the joy right out of that memory. "I didn't want out of that pile!"

"High school girls aren't a real fight."

Knife hand to the throat. Palm strike to the groin. Stomp kick to the knee, rising knee to the face.

Oblivious, he says "That fancy job, you ain't never been in a real fight, where someone's swinging a beer bottle at your skull and his buddy's behind you with a chair. You'll break in two shakes. If you're right, I have to go."

I can't argue without telling him the truth. "You're not coming." I cross my arms. "You'll only be in the way."

"Oh?" Will raises his chin, daring me to punch it. "I know where Dad lived. Where he worked. How are you going to find that without me?"

"William Jefferson Davis Salton," I say. "Social security number 681-93-6437. One phone call and I'll have everything."

"You do that," Will sneers. "I'm going down to his place. See what I can find without you. You still drive like you're afraid of the pedal?"

The scream of rage and frustration I've been chaining back?

It finally explodes. Rips right through my bowels and out my throat.

My reverse punch slams straight into Will's gut, right above his bellybutton, and he'd gasp but the palm of my other hand crashes against his breastbone to stun his lungs and repel him a vital inch so that hand can slide up and grab his shoulder while my other hand grabs his wrist, then I'm taking a giant step and sweeping his leg.

Will hits the asphalt like a three-hundred-pound bag of cement. His face bulges with the effort to draw breath.

I drop to a knee.

The other knee? Right into his belly, beneath his ribs.

What little air he's managed to pull gushes away. Confusion glazes his eyes. A satisfied glow soothes my soul. "Keep away, you dumb asshole."

I turn from my family and go to avenge my family.

20

I slam the SUV door shut behind me and snarl "Drive." After the funeral home's sickening perfume, the rental car's air conditioning with hints of plastic tastes delicious.

Deke knows better than to ask if I'm okay.

Gravel crunches.

I don't look back at Will. I didn't black him out, but he isn't exactly conscious.

The SUV's motor purrs, and we're back on what Malacaster calls Main Street.

I'm desperately struggling not to think.

Battered homes converted to shaky businesses line the neglected macadam. The funeral home is in the best condition, because people die no matter what and the locals would rather spend their children's future than have their neighbors think they couldn't afford to bury their parents.

Besides, the funeral home offers the slow painful death of easy payment plans.

For a moment I think: *Forget all these idiots*.

Forget someone murdered Father.

Someone was always going to murder him.

Walk away.

Those rich bastards have it right. Stupid, foolish people like Father and Will don't deserve shit.

Even as furious and useless as I feel, though, I know that's all wrong.

It's not their fault they grow up believing the American Pipe Dream: *work hard, get ahead, make your life better. The rich are rich because they deserve to be rich. Because they earned it, and you can earn it too.* Every single television vomits that lie straight down their throats. Never mind that the rich earned their wealth by deciding to be born to wealthy parents, or by figuring out a way to claw an extra buck from people who didn't have it to spare, or by breaking any fingers that dared poke out of the poverty cage.

The desolate town I'd been taken to after Mom left, even more impoverished now but still reeking of sickly-sweet burned sugar, is the end state of the American Drug Dream.

But everyone needs hope to live.

Even if the hope is a lie.

Even if they *know* it's a lie.

And the park across the road is still nice, because it's *theirs*. The locals care for that rolling lawn that slopes down to the river, even if the river is probably so full of lead that nobody dares swim in it. The wooden benches beneath the trees have all gotten a coat of paint in the last couple years. Some vandal had sprayed graffiti on the side of the park's blockhouse bathroom, but someone else cared enough to try to clean it off. They'd left behind a fog of black and red, because paint is an absolute pain to clean, but the vandal's tags are gone.

Because the local families care.

They work hard.

They play by the rules.

I threw out most of the rules a long time ago.

If someone really murdered Father, I'll throw out the rest.

No, that's not right. Someone would eventually shoot him for being an asshole.

But was his murder about me?

Most freelancers adopt trade names, but it's not that hard to figure out their birth names. No, not legal names—I have a dozen names that are all legally mine, bought and paid for. Some of them don't even have arrest warrants. If another professional wanted my name, they could get it. They could find Father and try to hold him hostage for my behavior. Ten minutes in, they'd shoot him out of pure frustration—but they could try.

A thumping bass note rises through the small-town murmur. A rusty subcompact, the Chevette's spiritual successor, races up behind us. I count five or six teenagers crammed inside, arms hanging outside windows and waving with the beat. Kids with nothing better to do, but since there's no such thing as global warming they might as well kill time by burning up some of that infinite fossil fuel.

Listening to rap. In the wilds of Michigan. Because they're so tough and urban.

No, that's all distraction.

Maybe Father swallowed the American drug dream. But he was also a drunk. My feelings don't have to make sense.

Father was *mine*.

And someone took him.

The teenmobile is out of earshot when I'm finally still enough to say, "I got a note."

Deke's attention seems to be all on the road and the two ten-year-olds bicycling down the irregular sidewalk, but the way he says "From who?" tells me he's actively listening.

"I don't know." I need to steel myself before I can say, "It said Father had been murdered. That I—Beaks—I'd worked for his killer."

"What do you think happened?" His voice is tranquil. I'm sure Deke's already forming opinions. He's human. He can't help it. But he won't do anything to rile me up further, and won't act until I give him all the facts I have. Even then: *my* father. He'll do what I say.

Sometimes, love only listens.

"His neck was broken."

The car wobbles for an instant, then straightens. Anyone else would think Deke had swerved around a pothole. "How bad?"

"Right at C2. The coroner said a fall. I'd swear he had a noose wound around his neck, if anyone bothered to look. It's textbook. Professional."

After a breath he says, "Ayaka?"

"Or someone who wants me to think it's her," I say. "Someone who's trying to point me at her."

He takes his own deep breath.

"I completed that contract," I say quickly. "She's got no reason to go after Father, not on my account."

"But if someone hired her…" Deke says.

I don't say anything.

"We need to know more," he says, and I could kiss him if he wouldn't drive us into the ditch. "Where did it happen?"

"Detroit. He was working as a night watchman."

"With all you've sent him?" Deke gives a tight-lipped smile. "He ought to be on the beach in Florida."

"Yeah," I say. "You get us to Detroit. I'll get us some answers."

21

We get out of Malacaster and onto the two-lane highway through endless fields of head-high juvenile corn stalks, all rippling in the irregular August breeze. The SUV's finally getting comfortable, and with distance the stink of the sugar plant is finally starting to recede. We settle in behind a monstrously oversized beet sugar syrup tanker.

Deke pulls onto the five lanes of I-75 and heads south. We drive the speed limit, like any self-respecting criminal couple. Normally I'd take perverse glee in all the upstanding citizens ignoring the law and rocketing past us, but right now I want to tell Deke to floor it.

This is not the time to get stopped.

When I think I can hold a professional conversation, I raise my phone and punch in a memorized number. The phone rings twice, then an electronic voice declares that I should leave a message. Instead, I punch another seven-digit code.

The phone rings twice more, then a sleepy-sounding voice says, "Hello." It's not a question or a greeting. More of a flat *decorum declares you make this noise when you answer the phone, so that's what I'm doing*. If she was in a good mood, her answer would be totally different.

"Sister Silence," I say. "Beaks."

"Beaks!" Her voice gets all animated. "Darling! Blown up any Evil Overlords lately?"

"It was only the one overlord." The routine banter is weirdly soothing. "How are you?"

"I'm grand." Sister Silence yawns. "Sorry. Hacker's hours. What can I break for you?"

"I'm calling in my favor."

Sister Silence gets serious. "Got it."

I recite Father's name and social security number. "I have reason to believe he worked in or near a Detroit trainyard."

Sister Silence repeats the information. When she finishes—correctly, of course—I say, "I want his life. Employer. IRS. Friends. Debts. Legal. Financial. Everything."

"Easy enough," Sister Silence says. "Give me an hour, you'll know if he does boxers or briefs and which way he hangs his naughties."

I flinch. *Jockeys so old they're brown, and I don't want to know*. "There's more."

"There better be. Your favor's worth more than that."

"Salton's bank account received regular transfers from…" Which shell was it? "From the Magpie Mayhem Corporation. Last year, well over six figures. Find out where that money went."

"What else?"

"I'll have more, I'm sure," I say.

"You better," Sister Silence says. "Don't you dare underestimate that favor."

I lick my lips. Sister Silence is the most tight-lipped information retrieval specialist I know, but she doesn't need to know I have a family. "This one's… important."

"Speed. Discretion. Got it. You want anything on this Magpie corporation?"

"I have that information." I better have it, I set up that shell specifically to support Father. Just because I ran doesn't mean I forgot my responsibilities.

"You waiting for the full report?" Sister Silence says. "Or do you need facts as I get them?"

"As you get them," I say.

"Addresses first, eh?" She chuckles. "And I'm guessing more is coming."

"I'm sure. It'll probably be hot."

"I don't have anything else hot right now," Sister Silence says. "I'm on it. And you call back with more, right?"

"Of course." My chest is tight. I force a deep breath against rigid muscles. "Thank you."

"You're welcome, darling." The call dies.

The second call is quicker and less chipper. While Sister Silence is friendliness personified, at least with me, the man called Mall wants everything businesslike. I order a bag the same as I ordered last October for the Taiwan job, but for rush delivery in Metro Detroit. Mall lists everything, then declares that a couple specific tools are locally unavailable and suggests replacements. I agree.

He gives me a price.

I don't have the energy to haggle.

Mall sounds slightly perplexed. I'm not usually so accommodating. "It'll be ready tomorrow."

"Really rush delivery," I say.

"How rushed?" he says.

"How soon?"

A keyboard clatters in the background. "I can do ninety minutes if you can do Waterford."

Waterford is northwest of Detroit, but I-75 rolls right past it. "Done."

"An extra fifty."

Mall expects me to come back with ten thousand, and we'll agree on twenty-five. Instead I say "Done, but everything is top-notch and ready to go. I'm paying for perfection. Plus, this is wire, not cash. Transfer to the usual place?"

Mall pauses. "Yes?" I might as well have screamed *something is going on*. Laundering a wire transfer is worth an extra five, not twenty-five. I've shocked him, but his voice returns to normal when he offers an address. "Behind there. Blue van with a black stripe, near the green dumpster. Clock's on. Ninety minutes."

I hang up.

Maybe I'm overreacting.

But if someone really did murder my father?

Maybe Ayaka murdered my father. Maybe it was someone else.

Whoever it is: in ninety-one minutes, I'll be ready for war.

22

It's not three minutes before Sister Silence sends Father's home and work addresses, both inside Detroit.

We detour into Waterford long enough to pick up three heavy bags of professional-grade death from a pimple-faced boy, who clearly hopes the income from delivering illicit weapons will help him attract girls despite his truly astonishing halitosis. We stuff the bags into the hatchback, under the cargo cover, and head straight to Father's Detroit address.

The south side of Eight Mile Road, with Detroit's hopeless, windowless brick bars and eighty-year-old hotels peppered with bright, hopeful medical marijuana dispensaries, looks more blighted than the north side, but only because the north has more open fields where the City of Warren already plowed the most decrepit buildings under. I've seen better roads in Beirut. Abandoned men in shapeless thrift store clothing shamble down the sidewalks or gather in little clumps to share smokes or paper bags with protruding glass bottlenecks. A teenager with impressive dreads has his skinny rear planted on the thigh-high cinderblock wall separating a decrepit hotel's parking lot from the sidewalk, so he can stare at his phone. The women are either herding flocks of children or "gossiping" on street corners, dressed far too skimpily for even this torrid August.

Back in Scottsdale, I'd helped Candy with a few hundred dollars.

I'd sent Father enough for a rocket car down Cirrhosis Highway.

But I don't have near enough cash to help all these women find better lives.

The only way to help them is to burn the entire system down.

Deke pulls onto Father's street and slows down so we can spy for Father's apartment. The buildings date from the early 1900s, three and four stories of brown brick with enough space between them for a fleeing toddler to fall and break a leg but not enough for an adult to rescue them. The brilliant sunlight makes the homes look exhausted, with brick in desperate need of tuck-pointing and rotten double-hung windows that probably haven't opened in my lifetime. A bunch of those windows have cardboard or plywood nailed up over them. Every door has a barred outer door. Every roof sags. A trio of black women, two heavy-set and one as thin as myself, sit on the stoop of the nicest building, hands waving as they talk. Gossip? Planning? Exchanging the news?

It's the Motor City, so cars line the street. It's the hood, so they're one rusty wheeze from the junkyard. I suspect those engines have more repurposed nylons than proper belts.

Father's apartment building is four stories of rheumatically-twisted brick. The first-floor windows are high off the ground, the concrete sills clearly designed to repel intruders by crumbling under any weight. Deke pulls around the corner onto a little dead-end court, rolls past a cluster of men sitting silently on a stoop, and comes back around. He pulls to the curb in front of a fire plug that someone painted bright purple with cheerful yellow polka dots.

That's the thing about Detroit. You can kick folks in the teeth, deny generations real education and do your damnedest to starve the diehards out, and someone will paint fire plugs to cheer up the kids and someone else will scrounge up asphalt to fill the potholes.

Deke frees the wheel, flexes his hands and rolls those massive shoulders, and says "You know I should be the one to search his apartment."

He's right. I'm way too close to this. "And you know I have to do it."

Deke says, "We can't leave the car unguarded."

He's right. A carload of illegal ordinance bears a certain responsibility. That means I have to go in alone.

I give a single sober nod.

Deke takes my hand. He's one of the few people I've ever met with hands bigger than mine. His fingers, wrapped around mine, feel like safety and shelter and all the things my father never offered. "You need to be cool."

I choke my annoyance. Searching Father's apartment requires dispassionate attention, and I've been anything but dispassionate for the last day. I'll need to focus on what's present, not how it's different from our home fifteen years ago—or, worse, how it's the same.

I can only stay furious for so long, though. The drive down from Malacaster and the routine work of gathering equipment gave me time for the tumultuous rage to burn away, leaving me with the dull suppressed anger so familiar from my teenage years. That, the time change from Scottsdale, and jumping between the SUV's air conditioning and the breathable swamp of a Michigan summer has ignited a persistent throb right across the back of my skull.

But I've had worse. I open a bottle of water and swig half of it. "I'm okay."

Deke studies my face with those deep brown eyes. "Message me if there's trouble."

"What are you gonna do?" I smile. "Run up the stairs with a machine pistol?"

The unscarred side of his face bends up. That's the only time I notice his scar, when it blocks half his smile. "In one hand. Auto shotgun in the other."

"If someone comes flying out a top window, they gave me trouble." My smile doesn't feel forced at all. "Feel free to shoot anything that hits the ground."

"Hits the ground?" He squeezes my hand. "Do you doubt me, woman? I'll put a few rounds in them before they get *near* the ground."

He can, too. "I'll be fine. Quiet, in and out."

The men on the stoop watch with bored interest as I climb out of the SUV and march briskly around the corner to the front of Father's apartment building. The concrete steps were probably replaced as recently as the 1950s and barely wobble underfoot. Exposure and neglect have gutted the door buzzer, leaving only a holed plate that promises tetanus at a touch. My nose catches cabbage and garlic and cumin, underlaid with decades of dead rats.

The door itself is set well in the frame, and features one of the best key locks civilians can buy. It withstands my lockpicks for a whole eight seconds or so.

The sagging wooden stairs stink of pee and groan at every step. The landlord should be ashamed to demand rent. Apartment 402 is on the top floor, at the back of the building. The pathetic door lock surrenders with a single rake of my pick.

The door swings open.

To my shock, Will is already there.

And from everything I see, I'm stuck with him for a good long time.

23

Father was never a tidy drunk.

But he didn't rip holes in the wall.

Walls. Plural.

Someone had methodically crushed moldering plaster to powder and shattered tinder-dry lath to expose the gaps between century-old wooden studs. The indirect afternoon sunlight through the grime-coated double windows reveals ancient ball-and-tube wiring, dusty veins never intended to see light again. It's a methodical violation.

No air conditioning. This fourth-floor apartment has been storing up summer heat for days. The sticky-humid air is as still as a mausoleum, but opening the door stirs up enough plaster dust to coat my throat. The apartment reeks of decades of cheap cooking and insufficiently-bathed bachelor.

The bile-green couch sits inverted, legs in the air. Chunks of age-browned foam padding from the gutted cushions lay heaped between the couch and the 1970s-vintage wire-and-plywood TV stand. Overcomplicated wires hang loose from the old tube TV's ruptured case. Third-hand clothing sits in a ransacked pile next to the heap of overturned drawers next to the water-warped dresser.

Father might have trashed something in a fit of rage. He wouldn't stay angry long enough to inflict this much damage, though.

Someone had methodically searched Father's apartment.

My uncertainty about Father being murdered evaporates.

But Will is right there, leaning with one hand on the kitchenette counter and the other across his gut. He's still seeping bourbon through his skin. I picked the door so quick, he hasn't had a chance to hide that stupid surprised expression.

"What are you doing here?" I could have said something more idiotic, but only with a scriptwriter's help. Deke and I detoured for equipment. We obeyed the speed limit. Will had plenty of time to get himself up off the ground, drag his carcass to the truck, and race down here at fifteen over the speed limit like any self-respecting Michigander.

He hasn't been here very long, though. His cheap funeral suit is barely dusted with plaster dust.

"I have a key," Will says. "How the hell did *you* get in?"

Frustration flares. I take a deep breath, forcing it away. Now that Will has seen this destruction, there's no way he'll believe that Father wasn't involved in something. Will knows "angry drunk" even better than I do.

Deke was right. Finding my father's killer demands dispassion.

And blunt refusal won't get rid of Will.

"Well?" Will snaps.

"You left the door unlocked," I say.

"Down here? Bullshit."

I shrug. "It opened."

"And what the hell did you hit me for?"

"Because you're stubborn as hell and won't listen to me." No, that's too sharp. Cool. Collected. Dispassionate.

Will's bitter eyes study me.

I want to tell him he's utterly unqualified. He makes poor dead Lou look like an expert. Instead, I only glare at him.

An endless second later he grunts, "Not right to sucker punch your own brother," and turns back towards the sink.

It's not right to ignore your sister. "Don't touch anything."

"Just wanted a drink of water," he says. "The fuckers took the faucet out."

"They wanted to see if he was hiding it there." No, that's wrong too. He already knows you're smart. Say what will get rid of him, what will get him out of your way.

"Hiding what?" Will demands. "Dad didn't have shit."

I sent him piles of money. "Someone heard he was dead and took their time clearing out the place."

"This ain't a robbery," Will says. "This is…Someone really wanted to find something."

Why couldn't the beer have pickled his brain faster? "Whatever it was, it's gone." I keep my feet clear of the detritus as I move in.

I should have worn my throat mic and earbud, so Deke could hear all this. I'd never make that mistake on contract, but that first text from Will drowned all my habits in resentment.

Will steps toward the couch. Plaster crunches.

"Watch where you're walking!" I snap.

"Why? It's already trashed."

I force another deep breath. "Do you want your footprints at a crime scene?"

"If the police show up down here," Will says, "they'll be a SWAT unit."

"And anything *we* find won't do us a bit of good if you crush it under those clodhoppers."

"Like you know evidence."

This *is* the time to tell him how much I know. "I found this apartment, didn't I? I have where he worked. By the time I'm finished here I'll have his medical records and his Internet searches. This is what I do." Usually in reverse, but still. "Don't touch anything."

"I still beat you here."

"There's this thing called a speed limit." I can't believe I'm saying this with a straight face. "Maybe you've heard of it?"

"Fine," Will snarls.

He can be as mad as he wants, so long as he stops stirring up the dust. Or crushing evidence.

"Check under that counter," I say. "See if anything's left." Standing in place, I start a methodical scan of the room.

The upper kitchen cupboards hang open. It looks like everything's been flung out of them. Next to the kitchen, through the bathroom door, the sink's off the wall. Water isn't shooting out, so the intruder must have turned off the wall valve. The toilet's been dismantled, the tank and bowl lying on their sides. I can't suppress a faint smirk.

"What's so damn funny?" Will says.

"Father couldn't clean a toilet if he had a gallon of kerosene and a blowtorch." I nod towards the bathroom. "Whoever dismantled the bathroom had a nasty surprise."

Will coughs something like a laugh. "Not near nasty enough."

My smirk drains away.

What had Father gotten himself into?

24

Deliberately staring away from my estranged brother in the nearly bombed-out detritus of Father's pillaged apartment, I can't help wondering: What secrets could an old drunk trainyard watchman carry home?

There's only one way to know. "Listen."

"Yeah?" Will's face has a fresh flush of anger and his hands keep flexing into fists. Staring at the busted-up side table has his mad back up. He's breathing too quickly, on the verge of hyperventilating.

I say, "I need you to tell me what's not here."

"How am I supposed to know that?"

I turn to face him. "Listen to me."

Will jerks his attention away from the wreckage to snarl into my face.

I deliberately lower my voice. "Listen. This pisses me off too. But getting mad isn't gonna help. You want to figure out what happened? You need to calm down." *Pot. Kettle. Black.*

"You were right." Anger twists his lips. "Someone fucking killed Dad."

Shit. "Yes."

"They came here and tore the place apart. These neighbors wouldn't say shit about the noise."

"They wouldn't dare. The asshole landlord wouldn't do anything if they did. Listen to me." I steel myself. I haven't spoken his name in years. "Will." It's harder and easier than I expected. "We need to think."

"I'm thinking!" His teeth are clenched.

"No, you're *feeling*. Whoever did this, they're gone now. There's nobody for you to hit."

"So what the fuck are we supposed to do, call the police?"

"They won't do shit and you know it."

"Then *what*?"

"Close your eyes. Take a deep breath."

"How the hell are you so calm?"

I show my teeth. "I'm saving it. For when it'll do some good. But to get to that we have to find them. Doing that starts with you closing your eyes and taking a couple slow deep breaths."

"But—"

"No more," I say. "Close them."

Will glares at me. His head looks ready to pop.

For a heartbeat, I think he's going to take a swing at me.

Don't get me wrong—I'd put him down again, hard. But if his clumsy footsteps amplified the mess, Will's body flying through the air and crashing onto a pile of busted lumber and rusty nails would be worse.

And I don't want to listen to him whine about it.

Maybe lockjaw would improve—no. Tetanus takes too long.

Fortunately, he squishes his eyes shut and takes an exaggerated breath. It's not deep—he's inhaled without exhaling. But it's a start.

"That's it," I say. "Now exhale."

He lets out half a lungful.

"No, all the way out. Pretend I'm giving you a Heimlich."

One eye starts to open.

"Keep them closed. All the way out. Good. All the way in."

I get three deep breaths into Will before he opens his eyes. But the bright red choler has faded.

"Good," I say, even though it's pretty pathetic. I'd learned to breathe properly in Yoga Club my first year at U of M, and it saved my education. How had Will made it this far through life? No—I knew that answer. Make him mad, he punched you. "Now think. What isn't here? What did they take?"

"I gotta look around."

I nod. "Stay in the clear spaces."

Will deliberately stares at the floor and steps towards the dresser. His feet raise little clouds of dust, but he manages to not crush any more plaster beneath his cheap leather dress shoes.

I'll take it.

I turn away as if I'm looking inside the television. It gives me another twenty-year flashback: me with a multitester and a tube TV, tracing circuits and figuring out how it worked. I'd already learned to pick all the locks in the house, my homework was done, and Father didn't care so long as I'd come out of my bedroom when he bellowed for another beer.

No time for that. I slip my phone off my belt and send BROTHER HERE to Deke.

I walk over to the white-glazed metal kitchen counter beneath the tiny window. With a little work it would gleam, but years of hard use have left it dimpled. Scratches through the finish have become lines of rust. Father was exactly as good at cleaning a kitchen as he was a toilet. Plaster dust has caked into swirls of badly-wiped grease. The windowsill has its own layer of dust, but at least it's not so grimy.

Something green in the sink grabs my attention.

A heavy vine and familiar heart-shaped leaves lie tumbled in scattered dirt. It's a basil plant.

Was. The basil's roots have been ripped from the vine and shredded where someone fingered through its soil. It's not dead yet, only doomed.

My heart beats faster.

I'd grown basil, once, for a biology project my senior year of high school. I'd adjusted the soil chemistry for three plants to see the effects on both growth and taste. Won the school prize, of course, which really tonked off a whole bunch of the "brainy" older kids who thought I shouldn't have even been in their high school. The school troublemakers had congratulated me, mostly for showing up the older children.

One of the plants had done really well.

I'd brought it home. Put it in the kitchen window.

By the time I'd left for college it was over a foot tall.

I'd been proud of that basil plant.

Whenever I'd tried cooking something that didn't come out of a can, I'd tried adding a couple of finely-chopped basil leaves to it. Sometimes it tasted great. Sometimes it was awful. Father ate it anyway.

I wasn't sure if I could have a plant at college, so I'd asked Father to take care of it for me. I'd told myself he'd keep it watered, because that's what you do when you're fifteen and heading off to college years early and the world threatens to overwhelm you every day.

It couldn't be the same basil plant. I'd put it in a—

—coffee mug.

Lying on its side. The cheap orange dye has faded to beige. It's lying on its side right up against the world's most neglected toaster, obscuring half the words, but I know perfectly well the letters spell out WORLD'S GREATEST DAD. The handle's broken off.

I'd forgotten about that stupid plant.

Except I hadn't.

You never really forget the things you choose to abandon.

Somehow, Father had kept that little sprig of basil alive for all these years.

Then someone had murdered Father. Searched his apartment. Ripped the basil's roots from the dirt. Crushed the soil to find something Father had hidden.

Even if I took the basil with me, even if I put it in fresh dirt and watered it religiously, it was dead. There's no coming back from this kind of abuse.

On the sill sits a clear plastic half-pint eyedropper bottle of plant vitamins, saved by its transparency.

The basil hits me in a way that Father's death hadn't. Or maybe it was that it was easier to be angry with him if I forgot the kindness. If he'd been a wholehearted monster, if he hadn't desperately needed to preserve the lie that he was the WORLD'S GREATEST DAD, that plant would have been shriveled and crunchy a decade ago.

I grab the cool metal edge of the unclean sink. The plaster dust and scattered potting soil give it traction despite the greasy finish. My brain feels loose in my skull.

I don't want to care. I don't want to hurt.

But I'm still shaking and biting back tears.

Maybe a minute later—surely not longer, I'm not that messed up, I can't be—Will says, "Hey. Billie."

Crap—are my eyes wet? "Yeah."

My voice is harsh, but Will's seems less angry. He must be trying to not shout. "Dad didn't keep much. They left his checkbook and the hundred bucks he had stashed in the soup can, but took his laptop."

"Laptop. Fine." He's standing to my side, but I don't turn to look at him. "Anything you want?"

"A picture. And I'm not leaving the money for the landlord."

"Damn straight." Whoever let Father live like this deserves to lose their security deposit. And a couple fingers. "They got what they wanted. We're done here."

I make sure to keep my back to Will and walk out first.

So he can't see my face.

25

I leave Father's unspeakably decrepit apartment building like a summer storm, full of churning blackness and threatening lightning with every yard I cover, stretching my pace but refusing to run. Inexorable. I want to make good time. It's not that I want to make Will struggle to haul his flabby carcass down the busted-up sidewalk.

Unlike a real storm, I can't clear the cloying summer humidity out of the air. A suggestion of a breeze taunts with the implication that it could be strong enough to refresh me if only I deserved it. The sun glares down like a heat lamp.

I wipe my face like I'm brushing away sweat, not treacherous tears.

The three women are still gossiping on the stoop of the tenement a dozen yards away, but the brownstone past theirs has attracted four underfed teenage boys who watch us with the kind of mild interest that says we're the most unusual thing to happen all day. Maybe not the most exciting. You might get a turf fight or some woman coming to her senses and throwing her sperm donor out the door, but two white people around here is pretty unusual.

Deke's standing by our rented SUV twenty feet in the other direction. I finally notice that he's wearing the dark pants and white button-down shirt he calls his Respectable Mask, and since we got to Father's apartment he's dug out the dark blue tie. He'd worn that so he could come into the funeral home, if he had to.

If I needed him.

How did I get so lucky?

We'll check out the switchyard where Father worked, then decide on our next move. But first, ditch my brother.

I stop on a freakishly level section of sidewalk and turn to Will. "You've never done anything with crime, have you?"

Will huffs from trying to pace me. "You calling me a criminal?"

Laughter threatens to bray out of my gut, but I choke it down. "If I hadn't showed up, you would have tromped all over Father's apartment. You didn't know to look for the laptop, did you?"

"You're not cutting me out."

"You're an impediment to the job." My voice is cold and flat.

"I have more of a right to find this asshole than you do."

Maybe he does. I sent Father money so he didn't have to live in squalor, but never checked to be sure he got it. Will not only stayed, he followed Father straight down Cirrhosis Highway. "You're not capable."

Will's chin comes up, making it an even better target for an uppercut. "What are you gonna do if it gets rough?"

"I put you down."

"You sucker punched me! I wasn't ready!"

I'm always ready. I'm always aware. First rule of freelancing—always be ready to defend against an ambush.

"Is there a problem?" Deke says from behind me.

I manage to not show my surprise.

"Who the hell are you?" Will snarls.

"Will," I say. "This is Deke, my—" *partner? lover?* "—bodyguard. Deke, this…" My stomach knots. I'm soiling my bloody, criminal adulthood with my childhood. "This is my brother. Will."

"Hi," Will says sullenly.

Deke's voice is as cold as the gap between galaxies. "Hello." He glances at me. "I have made the arrangements you requested, ma'am."

My heart trembles. Deke only calls me *ma'am* like that when he's pissed. He's given me more support than I have any right to over the last couple days, and it's starting to get to him. I have no idea what arrangements he's made, but say "Good" as businesslike as I can manage. To Will I say, "This is where we part."

"I'm going to Dad's trainyard," Will says.

I keep my face straight, hiding the inner clench of guts. "If you want to waste your time."

Will gives a victory smile that desperately needs slapping away. "You said, right before you sucker-punched me. You're checking out his apartment, his job."

Dammit. I was pissed, but that's not any kind of excuse. There's no such thing as an excuse. There's only success and failure, and I failed. Hard. "Do you even know what to ask?"

"What he was doing, what he was up to," Will says.

"You want to go along?" My jaw aches to clench. Preferably with Will's throat in my teeth. I don't let it. This is all my own fault. I've got this great big brain that can devour astrophysics like cornflakes, and my gut and heart keep trampling it.

"You can go along with me," Will says. "It ain't five minutes from here."

Punch him again? No, there's about a dozen onlookers now, all having their own conversations but keeping a wary eye on the crazy white people throwing down in their hood. With this many witnesses, even Will can make an assault charge stick.

Helplessness makes my stomach burn.

Maybe there'll be more privacy at the switchyard.

Maybe Deke will have an idea.

"Fine." I whirl towards our rental SUV.

My feet want to run. I'm not going to let Will think I'm racing him to the switchyard. Even though I totally am. I feel Deke's mass behind me, easily pacing me as he imposes himself between me and my brother. I itch to seize the driver's seat, but I'm so agitated I'm likely to plow through lesser vehicles, like eighteen-wheelers, and run every red light I can find. I make myself go around to the passenger door.

Deke's getting in when I say, "Switchyard."

Deke slams his door and reaches for his seat belt. "Do you want him tracked, or disabled?"

I blink. "What?" My pulse thuds in my ears. Will's mere presence shredded every bit of calm I had scraped up on the drive down.

Deke sighs. "Your brother. His truck. Do you want it tracked, or disabled?"

"You…" I blink. "Disabled?"

Deke tugs a tiny remote from his pocket and hands it to me. "It'll fry his electrical." I barely have it in my fingers before he starts the SUV and pulls us forward.

My anger doesn't dissolve, but my massive love for Deke plunges onto it. The sudden knot in my throat makes it hard to say, "I don't deserve you."

The scar on his cheek twists, and he turns just enough that I can see his toothy grin. "I'm glad you know that."

The remote has one button.

I hit it.

I know the kind of electrical sabotage gear we use. If Will's truck was running, it isn't now. The electrical system needs a thousand dollars of work before it will start again. My heartbeat immediately slows.

Part of me itches to look around to see Will's disabled truck, but I resist the urge. I'd rather have the plausible deniability.

"How did you know which one was his?" I ask.

Deke's grin somehow gets bigger. "I rolled through the funeral home parking lot. Copied all the license plate numbers."

Of course he did. I reach out and squeeze his thigh. "Thank you."

"Turns out," Deke says, "I could have just looked for the truck with the testicles hanging from the trailer hitch."

I roll my eyes and focus on calming myself.

Once Will has transport he'll show up at the switchyard. We'll have finished questioning Father's coworkers by then. The nasty part of my brain whispers that this has worked out well. Will has all the subtlety of a rabid badger. When I start making progress in finding Father's killer, anyone who looks back will first see Will's blundersome interrogation.

The thought discomfits me.

It's not that I'm throwing my older brother to the wolves. He's throwing himself to them. He's *insisting* on it. I shouldn't feel bad about that.

I pay attention to my breath, trying to ignore that nibbling unease.

26

Back in the last century global firms snatched up choice bits of Detroit, built giant manufacturing plants that bled unnamed poisons into the ground, and walked away, leaving the city stuck with mile after mile of useless toxic land. These days the factories have more rats than employees, and you can't walk into one of those places without your nose squeezing itself shut in revulsion.

Father worked in one, until Mom left and he exploded. Imploded.

A few plants still make car parts, though, and some car manufacturers even assemble vehicles near downtown. Detroit still has countless miles of vestigial train track to support that handful of plants. The Mound Road trainyard is one of those.

The train tracks run conveniently past the Detroit Detention Center. If you're going to clang boxcars around at three AM, of course you want to do it where the only people you wake up are condemned to lifelong imprisonment for three ounces of weed. Stand at Mound and Davison, right by the north side of the Sacred Heart of Saint Mary Cemetery, and you'll see the two tracks that run cater-corner through the intersection open up into a bewildering maze of tracks and abandoned boxcars and titanic train engines missing, well, engines. If you leave a locomotive in the trainyard long enough it'll rust away and save the company the expense of disposing of it properly, right? Not to mention the paperwork.

For added security, the trainyard backs up onto the dump. Every major city has active landfills downtown, right? Next door to rows of single-story square tract homes, because why wouldn't you?

Deke has the rented SUV's air conditioning cranked up to Screw Global Warming. After the muggy heat and the stewed aroma of Father's old apartment, the SUV's over-filtered air smells heavenly and promises to ease the cold clamminess of my funeral clothes.

I take advantage of his meticulous adherence to the speed limit and traffic signals to intentionally relax my every muscle in turn. Everything aches, and not with the familiar stretching soreness. I still haven't caught up on sleep lost during the Scottsdale robbery. I've been crammed into an airliner, got in not one but two fights at the funeral home—though they weren't really fights, to be a fight the other person has to throw a punch or kick or something—ridden back down to Detroit on the same day, and searched my father's ransacked apartment while somehow not beating the crap out of my brother. Again.

The side street goes straight into the switchyard's entrance. Deke pulls through a cyclone fence gate that hasn't been shut since Nixon resigned, judging by the tree growing through the mesh, and stops

in front of a brick building the size of a two-car garage. I can barely read the MOUND SERVICE YARD sign engraved in the concrete over the door through the decades of smoke and grease ground into the brickwork. I'm reaching for my seat belt when Deke says, "Hold on a minute."

He's been beyond patient with me. I squash my ungrateful hastiness and turn to face him.

My love's eyes are full of concern, but his jaw is decisively set. "How are you feeling?"

"A lot better for losing Will." I draw a breath. "Thank you. Thank you so much."

His lips quirk up on the unscarred side of his face. "This once, I read your mind."

"I'm glad." I settle my hand over his.

"I'm worried about you." The intensity of his gaze puts lie to the lightness of his tone.

I nod. "I know."

Deke's face gets a hint of mischief. "I know you can play bereaved daughter a hell of a lot better than I can." He loses the smile. "But when this is done, we're finding a hotel room and stopping. We need to assess what we know. Nail down what we don't know. Make a plan."

My gut screams that we need to grab the first clue we find and chase it all-out, but I know that Deke's right. Besides: I'm not just tired, but full-out weary. We were up early, and evening rush hour is well underway. I need a solid night of uninterrupted sleep.

My muscles feel so stiff they're almost paralyzed. Before I can sleep I need to exercise so I can stretch them all, then exercise properly, and then stretch everything again.

I need a meal, not too heavy but healthy and tasty, to let my body and soul alike start to heal. I lost a partner—Lou was green as hell but still, a partner—yesterday, and haven't even had a chance to raise the traditional glass. Plus Father, and Will, and my criminally perv uncle whose name I want to scrub from my mind.

Young Billie Carrie Salton made a wreck of her life before she knew better. She knew more about multivariable differential equations than how to stand up for herself or her friends. Beaks did her best to abandon every scrap of it.

But now, Beaks has to clean up little Billie's life.

The thought isn't merely exhausting, it's dispiriting.

Deke is right. I say, "How about fish for dinner?"

"Blackened? Broiled?"

"I'm thinking sashimi."

"Seaweed salad?"

"How else?" I say.

"I'm thinking we splurge on some decent sake."

"In Detroit?"

Deke laughs. "Every liquor store has four hundred different craft beers. I'm sure we can find something."

I lean closer. "It's a date."

His quick kiss makes my whole face tingle. Maybe tonight, my Deke can relax me enough so I can stretch properly.

I'm reaching for the door handle when the steady rhythmic buzz-thud of a car with a subwoofer too mighty for its frame rises from behind. I shift my body so I can use the passenger side mirror. A tiny four-door coupe, body held together with red duct tape a brighter red than the faded body panels, is shooting up the road straight towards the switchyard entrance.

Our weapons are still bagged up in the back of the SUV. We should have stopped at some hot sheet joint to at least get the handguns ready. Not that this blouse has any place to hide a .38.

I'm too worn out to be digging into Father's death today.

Too emotionally involved to do it any day.

I brace myself to throw the door open and fling myself out.

The coupe slows as it approaches the gate, coming to a stop maybe ten feet behind us.

If someone climbs out with a weapon, I'll have to make the run. The office building's at an angle, if I can get around the corner I'll have a little wedge of safety. The gunmen will have to divide their attention between Deke and I—

The coupe's passenger door swings open.

Will climbs out.

27

My heart wants to plunge straight out of my body and down into the ground like a miniature black hole, right there in the train switchyard parking lot.

Will raises a hand to the driver and mouths thanks over the monstrous subwoofer before slamming the door and marching across the cinder parking lot towards our SUV looking like someone just shot his dog.

Or, maybe, blown up his truck.

I need to be calm. Cool. In control.

Anything that happens is my responsibility.

Poor Little Hurt Billie needs to go back in her bedroom and let grown-up, mercilessly logical Beaks handle things.

Deke says "Here." Before I can look he thrusts my earpiece and throat mic at me. He must have gotten them out of my rolley bag. I quickly stuff the earpiece in and wrap the mic around my throat, almost strangling myself in my rush. Will is almost at the SUV when I swing the door open.

The August air hits like a soggy, hot blanket. The afternoon sun burns against the side of my face and forces me to narrow an eye. The throat mic is light-absorbing black and designed to look like a choker to the unaware, but the snug strap is already burning a strip of warmth around my neck.

Cool. Collected.

I say, "Uber is exploitative."

"What the hell did you do to my truck?" Will looks ready to punch me, and doesn't even slow.

I raise my hands defensively. "Your truck?"

"I got in it and the engine caught fire!"

Crap. The truck probably had some kind of leak, oil or gas or something. A stray spark from frying a neglected electrical system could have set it off. "You think I firebombed your truck?"

"Who else?" He's still coming. Hands still up, I shift my weight to the balls of my feet.

"We got to the apartment, I went straight up." True. "And I have no idea which truck was yours." Also true.

Will stops, again just barely out of punching range. "I've had that truck for years."

"I haven't been home for twice that, you idiot." Oops.

"You got all Dad's info. You could have got mine."

"Why would I ask for it?" I say. "You were supposed to have the brains to stay home after I beat the crap out of you."

"Sucker punch don't count. Maybe it was your man there."

"You think your little sister carries around firebombs with her?"

Will rolls his eyes. "Please."

A punch to the throat would shut him up permanent.

So would a tour of the SUV's cargo space.

I swallow both thoughts as Will says, "I don't know how you did it, but you did. I had to pay one of Dad's neighbors twenty bucks to run me down here, and I had to leave it burning."

I blink. "You left your truck burning?"

"They're calling the fire crew. And I told you, I got more right to find out what happened to Dad than you do."

My dumbass brother abandoned his burning truck out of sheer unwillingness to be shown up by his kid sister. The cops are going to love this.

His teeth clench. "And now you owe me a truck, you stupid bitch."

I need to control the situation. I must control *him*.

Whatever that takes.

"I owe you a truck?" I stare flat at him. "How many miles were on it?"

His eyes narrow. "Only two-twenty k."

Probably twice that, but I'm not gonna argue. It's time to put the Monty Python foot down. "You got a bank app on your phone?"

"What does that have to do with anything?"

"You got an app that notifies you when someone sends you money or not? PayPal or something, maybe?"

"Sure, I got the bank app. Can't have the plant screwing up my pay, I got bills."

I hold up a finger and pluck my phone off my belt. Sister Silence's phone rings twice before the answerphone picks up, then I punch in my seven-digit code.

She answers on the second ring, a whole lot more chipper than when I called earlier. "Hello, I'd like to order a large pepperoni pizza."

I ignore her non-sequitur and don't even offer a greeting. "The subject of interest has a son, one William Salton."

"You have company," Sister Silence says. Keys clatter. "Got him."

All business, I say "I need a transfer from petty cash to the son's most active bank account."

"I'll fade you up to a million, no problem. How much?"

Will rolls his eyes. "This is bullshit."

I think back to the last time I bought a brand-new ten-cylinder pickup in a hurry, and then double the amount because—because shut the fuck up, that's why. It'll slash a big chunk out of my slush fund, but I give Sister Silence the total. "And I need it right now."

"Checking or savings?" Sister Silence says.

"Checking," I say. "He needs to buy a new ride this minute, so definitely checking."

Will rolls his eyes. "These things take a couple days." He's right; consumer banks delay transactions so they can earn a more little interest they're not entitled to. Only very specialized people know the levers to pull for instantaneous money transfers. "Don't try to bullshit—"

His phone erupts with the Homer Simpson *woo-hoo*.

Will's sneer crumples to surprise. "You're shitting me."

I don't let myself smile. "Please hold," I say to Sister Silence. Pulling the phone from my ear I tell Will, "Check your balance."

Will curses indecipherably as he tugs his phone from his belt and swipes the screen.

The way his eyes bug out warms my bitter soul.

I bring the phone to my mouth. "Transfer went fine. Expect reconciliation this evening."

"That quick?" Sister Silence says. "That favor's bigger than that, you know."

Hopefully the favor's big enough to cover rudeness. I close the phone without answering.

Will's continued silence is worth every penny.

"So," I say. "I categorically deny having anything to do with your truck catching fire. I also don't have time to argue with you about your rolling scrapheap."

"Right." He shakes his head. "Fine. Whatever."

I just gave you enough to buy the baddest truck in Malacaster, and the best you got is *whatever*? "I'm going in there to ask Father's coworkers about his last days. These people aren't going to hand out information freely. I interrogate people all the time. Let me do the talking."

"Yeah. Fine." I feel a surge of triumph. Will shakes his head, obviously trying to clear it. "If you do it right."

"No. I'm doing the talking. You stand there and look at new trucks on your phone."

"This ain't about money," he snaps. "Money isn't near the important thing here." Cinders crunch underfoot as he starts towards the office building.

How can he be so right and so wrong? I shift to block him off. "Promise me that you let me do the talking."

Will dances to the side. "Cut the bullshit!"

"Either I have your promise," I say, "or I will ask Deke—my bodyguard—to come out here and tie you in a knot. We'll drive out to Eight Mile, drop you at that Burger King, and come back."

Will snarls "Goddammit!"

"All right." I don't even raise my voice; that's why I'm wearing the sticky-hot throat mic. "Deke."

The SUV's driver's door slams shut.

Will's mouth twitches at the sound. "I have my rights!"

I jerk a chin towards Deke, coming around the front of the SUV. "Will. Take a look at Deke. My bodyguard." I keep my voice flat. "Do you have any doubt that we can put you anywhere I decide?"

Will snarls.

I stand silent.

Deke says, "Come along, sir" in his Butler Thug voice.

Will dances back. "Don't you touch me!"

I say, "Don't do any permanent damage."

Will glances around, looking for a way around Deke.

I say, "Unless you have to."

Will curses.

"Your promise," I say. "Or you're gone."

Will's face is brighter and brighter red as he jerks one step after another. Deke immediately blocks him. From Will's perspective, Deke's movements must seem near magical.

"He's stubborn," Deke says. "I might have to break a bone or two."

"It'll heal," I say.

"All right!" Will shouts. "All right! You do the talking!"

He mutters *bitch* at the end, but I decide I didn't hear that. Instead I say, "Promise."

Deke holds in place.

Will's shoulders sag, busted veins on his cheeks bright red. "I promise."

His sullen eyes promise that he'll have his turn.

28

The switchyard station seems ridiculously small in front of the triple train tracks. The dismal gray and brown cinder groundcover looks as barren as the Moon, lacking even weeds poking up between the coarse pebbles. Past the tracks, heaps of weed-covered dirt as big as houses must be an abandoned landfill or failed construction. A few boxcars and car haulers sit on sidings, most of them so rusty with neglect that you'd have to bring in WD-40 by the tanker to get the wheels to turn. Despite the clear blue sky and the late afternoon sunlight, no birds peck at the ground. Decades of oil and grunge are ground into the brickwork, so thick that even the air tastes of engine lubricant. Merely standing here means I'll need to shower in degreaser tonight.

My shiny leather funeral shoes aren't meant for crunching across the worn-out gravel parking lot, but that's okay. It's not like I was going to keep these shoes. Or this outfit.

I don't need funeral clothes. People in my career don't get funerals.

And I'm out of parents.

Will lumbers behind me. I can feel his fury with every step. He's not going to swing at my back, though. Not right now.

The handle on the station door is exactly as greasy as I expected. But at least the door opens easily.

Inside the station, someone's made a valiant effort against the grunge. Don't get me wrong—they lost, but they went down fighting. I smell bleach and cleanser, and the laminate counter running the length of the building has been scrubbed so much that its original pattern remains only as a faded speckled shadow. The wooden planks of the floor have soaked up more grease than your local oil change place, but they've been swept free of cinders. The windows are broad enough to watch the switchyard, but the century-old glass has started to slump. It distorts the view, but the overall effect is charming. This building has stood for decades, and sees no reason why it won't stand for decades more.

The space behind the counter looks arranged to best suit the skinny sixty-something black woman sitting at the ancient pine desk. An old-fashioned desktop fan with a heavy iron base sits in front of a half-open window, aimed where it can pass a breeze over her. While a phalanx of filing cabinets line one wall, two cabinets have been moved over next to her desk. A white dorm fridge perches atop another desk, arranged where she can easily spin her chair and reach in. She's set up her own private office amidst the desolation of a much larger operation. The air stinks of metal and grease, but there's also hints of sandalwood and cinnamon.

I have no idea how she accomplished that.

The woman looks up, shoulders back and eyes narrow behind tortoise-shell glasses.

Silence.

I'd rather she greeted us, but I'm not going to let Will jump in. "Hello," I say.

The woman gives us a single nod. "Can I help you?"

"Looking for someone who worked with William Salton."

She says, "Any inquiries must be sent to Human Resources downtown."

"That's not it at all," I say. "My name is Billie Salton. This is my…" *come on, you can say it* "my brother Will. We're looking for people who worked with our father."

The woman looks at us.

"What she said," Will says.

I flash Will a glare.

"Do you have ID?" the woman says.

I glance at Will. "Show her your driver's license."

"What," he says, "you didn't bring yours?"

"It's in the car." I always carry ID, but never with my correct name.

Will rolls his eyes.

Is my brother going to drive me to get a fake ID with my real name on it?

Will grumbles and tugs out his overloaded wallet. It takes him a moment, but he extracts his license without scattering his impressive collection of fast food loyalty cards across the floor.

The woman studies the card, then peers through the glasses at Will. When she turns her attention to me, it's like being at the wrong end of a telescope. Her faded brown eyes somehow seem to expose me in uncomfortable detail. Do I have the words *thief* and *killer* tattooed on my face in ink that only she can see?

The woman's eyes rise with her decision. "My name is Bethel." Her voice isn't nearly so hard now. She still carries a concrete wall of reserve, but she's decided to open a slit and peer through. "I'm terribly sorry for your loss. That must have been a shock."

More of a shock than you know. "Thanks."

"Thank you, ma'am," Will says politely.

"We were hoping to talk to anyone who worked with Father." I'm accustomed to playing roles. Here I keep wanting to drop into Polite Investigator, but that's not the right voice for a bereaved child. I need less cheer, and much less good-natured annoyance. "Did you spend time with him?"

"I'm sorry, miss—Billie, was it?"

I nod.

"Billie." She looks to my brother. "Will."

I see the question form behind her eyes, and I see her decide not to ask. I say, "Father wasn't the most imaginative man."

"I see." Bethel straightens. "The man you want is Jake Skald, the other watchman. Your father spent a great deal of time with him." Her voice is carefully polite and respectful. I can't get any read on her feelings.

I say, "Could you tell me where I could find him?"

"He's scheduled for the night shift," Bethel says. "But he's usually around the yard."

"We can find him," Will says.

Before I can kick him in the ankle, Bethel's voice picks up fire. "You may *not* go traipsing around my switchyard, young man. You might not see trains so much these days, but the four-fifteen is due any moment and it will *flatten* you."

"I can watch out—" Will starts.

"Hang on" I say, ignoring Will's glare at being cut off. "Ma'am. Any chance you have Mister Skald's phone number?"

"I can't give that out."

I'm about to ask Bethel to ask him to call us when she hoists a radio handset left over from the Korean War. "Jake? You out there?" She turns up the volume. The radio hums and chirps.

A tired voice says, "Yeah, Beth. Wha' up?"

"Come by the office," Bethel says. "You've got company."

The radio buzzes like a cloud of angry hornets, then "Tell the boss I'm not on the clock."

"Not the boss." Bethel eyes me, but doesn't deign to look at Will. "It's personal."

The radio hums for too long. I can imagine Skald's confusion at the other end. Watchmen don't get personal visitors at work. "On m'way."

Bethel gives us a reserved nod. "If you're not on train business, probably best you wait outside the office."

I offer her a tight smile. "Thank you so much."

Will nods. "You have a good day, ma'am."

Bethel watches us walk out of her empire.

Scraggly switchgrass, stirred by the gentle breeze from the west, somehow survives on the dirt heaps of the landfill across the track. The stenches of lubricant and rusting steel oppress my sinuses. Did I remember my sinus spray this morning? This is not the time to start sneezing.

I take a few steps out of the door, across gravel somehow not too greasy to crunch. The sun hammers down out of the August sky.

Will steps past me. "Let's wait in the car."

I nod. "Go ahead. I'll wait here."

Will glares at me, looks at the air-conditioned SUV, and crosses his arms. "Fine. We'll wait here. And you didn't need to cut me off in there."

"You promised I could do the talking." I keep my tone light, refusing to feed his anger. "And I'm holding you to that."

"You've been gone for years," Will says. "You can't just swoop in and take over."

"And you think you're qualified just because you're older?" I say. "I make my living learning things." *And stealing them.*

Will's shoulders get a little broader. Does he want to fight? What the hell does he want? Acknowledgement and obeisance as the sovereign patriarch now that Father's gone? "Dad's been my problem for years now."

I get a sudden flash of Stabbity Joe saying *My Problem*, and Lou's bloody corpse sprawled in the unforgiving sun. "And what are you going to do now? Demand people tell us what they know out of, of…respect?"

"Why wouldn't they, if I ask polite-like?"

"You wouldn't know *polite* if I tied it around a brick and threw it through your front teeth."

"When Mister Jake gets here, I'll show you just how far polite gets me," Will says.

"You start talking," I say, "and you can walk home."

Fury freezes Will's face. "You have to be the smart one."

"I *am* the smart one. And there's a million things that can go wrong. Leave this to a professional."

Will glances at the SUV.

Behind the windshield, Deke meets Will's gaze like he's bored enough to study a beetle.

I owe Deke big for this one. I don't want Deke around my family, but I'd be even more lost without him.

Will looks back to me. His mouth twists, but he falls silent.

From Will, I like silence.

It's maybe five minutes before a drooping figure appears around a decaying boxcar. He walks like he's spent his whole life dragging a tarp full of busted bricks, and he expects to spend the rest of his life doing the same, so there's no need to hurry. His shoulders are broad, but he's got an oddly thin torso, like he's a big man on a starvation diet. His hair is dark and cut close. He's close enough for me to see his unlined face when he raises a hand. "Y'all looking for me?"

"Would you be Jake Skald?" I say.

He raises his stride to cross the last chunk of track and approach. "Tha's me."

I nod. "My name's Billie Salton. This is my brother, Will."

My words stop him as cold as if he'd run into an invisible wall. Blood drains from his pale brown face. "Billie and Willie," he breathes, almost too faint to hear.

I wince. I'd gone many years without Father calling us that, and I could have happily lived the rest of my life without hearing it again. "Yes, sir. We'd like to talk with you about our father."

Skald's face twitches. He's trying to hide his reactions, but he's not quick enough. I suspect he's a terrible poker player.

Skald knows something.

29

Skald leads us away from the switchyard office into a long, low warehouse built over a train track that clearly hasn't seen use since before I was born. An arthritic multi-ton winch sits on a concrete base right beside the tracks, brown rust leaking through too many layers of sloppy yellow paint and its gears corroded beyond repair. Part of the train tracks run over an open pit, deep enough that people could stand comfortably underneath and look up at a train car's belly. Do train engines need oil changes? Tiny brown-and-white sparrows joyfully flit between age-stained splintering rafters and dive through the yawning sliding doors, dancing in the slanting light filtering through the filthy windows high up against the ceiling.

The plutocracy claimed the territory to build all this. Drained every drop of value from it. Then abandoned their trash for the rest of us to clean up, to live with. Or in.

In the middle of the cracked concrete floor, Skald has set up a little cluster of home. Old shipping crates form a half-dozen seats, polished smooth by years of rear ends. A slightly higher crate between them holds an old-fashioned semicircle-topped lunchbox of gleaming black aluminum. A well-read but tidy paperback copy of Smith's *Wealth of Nations* sits open and face-down beside it. I'm surprised to see he's two-thirds of the way through it—most people just read the free market part and skip the bits about regulation and taxation. A rusted-through steel barrel serves as a centerpiece, the sides above the irregular gaps stained by smoke. Old charcoal lingers on the still air. Despite the two open doors, the air here is a little cooler than outside, the August mugginess downgraded to clamminess. Some freak of construction or a function of slow rot cools this space.

It's pretty posh, if you're living in a Mad Max movie.

Skald waves a hand. "Please, rest your feet."

I don't want to surrender the advantage of standing. "I've been sitting all day. But thank you."

Will promptly plants his butt on one of the crates. "Don't be rude, Billie."

Skald shifts to stand near one of the crates. The man doesn't look tired—he looks exhausted. His eyes are red pits. His mouth droops at the edges. He might be anywhere from twenty-five to forty-five, but his obvious fatigue adds another twenty years to his every motion.

And clearly, stupid masculine chivalry is keeping him on his feet.

I grimace. "Only if you'll sit with us."

Skald nods.

I lower myself to a crate. It's a little short for me, raising my knees above my hips. My thigh muscles complain and my lower back aches.

I have got to stretch, and *soon*, or I'll outright petrify.

Skald sits with a groan. His shoulders slump even more. When he turns his exhausted gaze to me, he seems to pick up a nervous jitter. He's hiding something. "What can I do for you?"

Will says, "We wanted to talk with you before the service. Wanted to say somethin' about his job here."

I glare poisoned darts at Will.

Will pretends not to notice.

It's not a bad approach, but that's not the point.

"There ain't much to say." Skald's jaw works silently as he stares off into the rafters over the door. The jitter gets worse for a breath, then recedes. Maybe Skald has a neurological disorder? "We worked twelve-hour shifts. I did Sunday-Monday-Tuesday, he did Wednesday-Thursday-Friday. We traded Saturday night back and forth."

"So you worked alone?" I say.

Skald nods. "That's what we got paid for."

I open my mouth to ask about their duties just in time for Will to say, "You have a nice setup here for just one person."

Shut up, I'm doing this!

"Well," Skald says. He's looking at the far wall, like he doesn't want to face us. "You know how it is."

Will's about to speak, so I jump in with "Not really."

Will closes his mouth to glare at me.

"When you work this kind of job," Skald says, "you get used to sleeping days and being up nights. And there's nobody else around at three in the morning."

"So you'd hang out here," I say. "Even on your days off."

"Hang out and gab," Skald says. "Your dad, he was real proud of you two. You know that?"

The words hit like a bucket of ice water over the head.

"You went off to college and got your doctor," Skald says to me. "And you, young man. Following in your dad's footsteps. It's like he got everything a man ever hopes for in you two. I know he was right proud of you both."

My tongue feels as heavy and uncontrollable as the bricks in the walls around us, but I make myself say "Thank you." I don't want to hear that Father was proud of me. The words dredge up a stinking knot of emotions I don't want to name, feelings that I'd rather have stay at the bottom of my soul.

Will doesn't say anything. Is he just as stunned?

I've got to think. I've got to say something before Will does. I've got to get control of this conversation, and myself, but Skald's words threw tar into my mental gears. I lick my lips. They're still chapped after Phoenix. I've been in Detroit's awful summer humidity two days, how can they still be such a ruin—no, that's a distraction. Stop shying away and *think*.

"Did Father say anything about friends down here?" I make myself say. "Or hobbies? What he did in his off time?"

Skald snorts. "You've never worked nights, have you?"

If only you knew.

"The job owns you," Skald says distantly. His nervous jitter has receded a touch. "You start off thinking 'ah, I've got four days off, I'll do something during daylight,' but your body's all switched around to stay awake all night and you wind up sleeping until the alarm goes off at five and the rush hour's got everything stopped dead and you might as well hang around home till it clears, but then everything's shut. Maybe you see a midnight movie. Or drive out to the suburbs and hit the Meijer for groceries. The only folks you see are those that live your life." He shakes his head. "You sign up, it's your life."

I can't help but remember nights I've worked. Hanging on the side of a building, or crammed into an air shaft, or delicately cross-connecting alligator clips to an electronic lock inside an elevator. "I can understand that."

"So he'd hang here," Will says.

I catch Skald's flinch, but before I can frame the question he says, "Sometimes some of the others, too. We've got the best setup here, leastwise in the summer." He waves a hand at the boxes. "Come winter it's a mite chilly, but we'll ha—" His face twists. "Stay at the Mount Elliott yard then."

My brain catches Skald's stutter.

The word he'd stopped himself from using: *hang*.

I still my face against my flash of certainty.

"That place," Skald says, "it's as hot as the dickens right now, though. Pardon my language, miss."

What language? No, don't get distracted. "So Father would be here when he wasn't home," I say.

Skald shrugs with one shoulder. He's decidedly not looking at us. With his poker face, or lack thereof, I wouldn't look at us either. That nervous jitter has returned.

"So," Will starts.

Shut up shut up shut up! "We found some strange things with Father." Smooth, Billie. Real smooth. "The death certificate said he broke his neck in a fall, but I don't think that was it."

Skald freezes.

All those nervous twitches evaporate.

Will is glaring at me.

I keep my attention on the petrified Skald.

"I'm sorry!" Skald explodes. Tears pour down his face. "I couldn't stop it! I couldn't stand anymore! I'm sorry!"

30

Skald's desperate bawling is worse than heartbreak. It's not the soul-shattering devastation of losing your beloved spouse or child. He's having the kind of breakdown you get in combat vets who created all those orphans thinking it was to save their country, but figured out too late it was really about boosting stock prices. I wind up with the guy sobbing into my stomach, one arm around his back and one stroking his bristly hair, murmuring meaningless comforting words that eventually degenerate into soothing coos and hums.

At least he's had a bath in the last day. The switchyard grease and grime has kind of sunk into the guy, but that's okay. I don't like the smells of rust and oil, but they're honest stinks from honest work. I'll take them over perfumed ancestral wealth any day.

Will stands there, watching the burned-out walls like someone's projected the latest Hollywood guns-and-gore spectacle up there. He stares at the dead railroad tracks as if he needs to count the old wooden ties. The sparrows playing their games between the dust motes slipping through the sunlight slanting through the high windows fascinate him. He looks anywhere but at Skald's implosion. Confronted with honest human pain from another man, my brother has no idea what to do or how to act. He's carved that macho "shake it off" attitude into his bones.

Or maybe Father carved it there.

Part of me wants Skald to quit sobbing into my gut, but another part is grateful for the distraction. Father'd told Skald he was proud of me? Father had had fifteen years to say it to my face and had spent them serving up complaints and commands, seasoned with recreational slaps and served on a platter of belittlement. How the hell was he proud of me? He had no goddamn *right* to be proud of me.

I went to college at fifteen. Uncle Carl got Father to sign the legal authorization granting the university *in loco parentis*. From that point on, everything I'd done, everything I'd accomplished, was mine and all mine. My triple bachelor's at eighteen? *I* did that. Father did jack for it, for me.

He *had* shown up at my graduation.

Drunk.

No, maybe he had been proud. Aunt Pat told me that when the underpaid security goons dragged him out of the stadium partway through the graduation ceremony, he'd been shouting *That's my girl!*

Maybe if I'd left the stadium to talk to him after graduation, he'd have slurred how proud he was before he did his parking lot face-plant.

Teenagers are embarrassed enough of their parents.

But right then, there wasn't a chance I would have claimed him.

Instead, I'd gone to graduation parties. I had invites from all three of my schools: physics, math, and biochemistry. My classmates were still three years older than me, but at eighteen you can be sort-of-friends with twenty-one-year-olds. Maybe not great friends, but it beats the hell out of ten and thirteen.

The next day, I'd started reading for my astrophysics master's.

And I'd never seen Father again. We spoke on the phone every few months. Christmas. Birthdays.

Right now, I regret that.

Maybe I wasn't the only one who wished things could have been better.

Skald needs five minutes to reduce his sobs to tears, and another few moments to get his breathing back under control.

Will spends the whole time pretending he's on a solitary exploration of the switchyard warehouse. That's okay. I might be soothing Skald, but part of my brain is still digesting and repackaging Skald's words. I make myself repeat them again and again, until *I know he was right proud of you both* doesn't make me shudder.

Both of us? Will works in the sugar factory, doing his part for the United States obesity epidemic. I'm top in my field—yes, okay, I'd lied to my family about what that field was, but I'd sent Father enough money to live his dream. Even if his dream was boozes, floozies, and all-you-can-devour cruises.

But Father hadn't actually lived on that money.

From the looks of his apartment, he'd never touched it.

I knew he'd received it. He told me so.

Messed-up childhood or not, he'd been family.

I'd thought of that cash as taking care of him, of living up to my responsibilities. But now that I know he didn't do anything with it, guilt crashes in on me. I'd sent him cash to cover my own guilty conscience.

I should have done something.

Nothing could be done.

Dammit. I'm a lame-ass stereotypical adult child of an alcoholic.

I silently repeat *nothing could be done* until Skald tugs himself away from me. I instantly let him go.

Skald's face is bright red, both from the irritation of the tears and his own embarrassment. "I'm sorry, Miss Billie." He pulls in a quivering breath. "I got no right."

The hunt is back on. I shove my introspection back under my brain's carpeting, right next to some other suspicious-looking psychological lumps I don't want to look at (ever) right now. "That's okay. You're human. It's okay."

He sniffs and looks away, but from shame rather than his earlier secrecy.

Will stares at us, emotional discomfort twisting his face. It's obvious that the last thing he wants to deal with is another man's icky-squishy abmasculine feelings.

I give him my best glare.

Will freezes.

"Still." Skald didn't notice that little drama. "You're the one who's lost her pa."

"But you spent the most time with him," I say.

Skald nods. "It's not—it's not like we were best buds, you know? But life, it put us together."

I've been part of many teams, each assembled for a specific gig. We bond tightly. We struggle together. We might have different politics and different beliefs, but for a short time we share common goals and incredible adversity.

We succeed.

We break up.

We move on.

And then I run into people like Liza Bradley, or Burke and Hare, or Rob Fender, and all the time we've spent apart evaporates.

"I get it," I say. "You wouldn't know how well I get it." I let the silence sit for another couple of breaths before I say, "I know it was rough. But we really do need to know."

Skald nods.

"And," I say slowly, "I think you're the only one who can tell us what really happened."

"I'll do better than tell you," Skald says, voice heavy. "I'll show you."

31

Skald leads us back out into the switchyard. It doesn't look quite so vast now, with the sun inching towards the towering mounds of swill just inside the landfill's border. Down the twin pairs of tracks, the steel fence of the Detroit Detention Center glistens in the sun, the coils of razor wire sparkling like it's trying to convince you that Prison Is The Place To Be Seen. Past that the prison itself looms, a white concrete monument containing countless wrecked lives. American Calvinism, carved in bone and tattooed in flesh.

Gravel and cinders crunch beneath my torturous flats, and the August sun burns straight into my black funeral outfit. I'm a skinny sausage steaming in a polyester bun.

The ground shudders. The roots of my teeth ache at a distant squeal of metal on metal.

A step ahead of me Skald says, "That's just the four-fifteen pickup. Follow me, you'll be fine."

I've sat on a road watching a train cut off traffic in front of me, but that's a whole different experience than standing a few yards from the train tracks and having a million tons of metal rush into your personal space like a horizontal landslide. I catch a glint that makes me think the big black locomotive has its running lights on even though the brilliant sunlight makes actually seeing them impossible. The vibration passes up my legs and through my spine, vibrating my teeth against my jawbone.

Behind me, Will mutters "Damn."

Up near the brick switchyard office, Deke's watching me from the driver's seat of our rented generic SUV. I give him a solid, slow nod to tell him everything's okay. He taps his ear and returns the nod.

I hope he has the engine running. Without air conditioning, he'll be miserable.

Skald raises his voice to be heard over the train. "A train pulled in about two that morning." His jaw is tight and his burning red eyes pull almost closed against the sunlight.

"Is that normal?" I say.

"Sure, but—it stopped," Skald says.

I look around. There's a couple brick warehouses here, but for many years they've only housed vermin and debris. "Isn't that what a switchyard is for?"

"Service yard." Skald's head bobbles in a nod. "They don't change here, we do repairs and they drop off up at the factories. But we know about all that beforehand. Bethel makes sure the repairs happen. Have to arrange space for cars. Nobody does that here, not at two in the morning."

I fumble through old memories. "They track trains, don't they? Say exactly when they can stop?"

"You know it, Miss." Skald nods fiercely enough to make a less attached head fall off. "You mess with the schedule, there's all kinds of questions, all the way up to Washington. You don't jus' decide to stop the train."

So whoever stopped that train had power. They had contacts. Part of my soul bares rabid teeth, but I force myself to focus on every detail Skald offers. "What did you do?"

"Old William, he was on the job."

Old William? I suppose if Father called me Billie and my brother Will, he needed a way to differentiate himself. Besides, he looked pretty old last time I'd seen him.

"I went along because, well…" Skald gets a distant look. "I thought he might need another body. You help each other out."

Today's train raises a low cloud of dust, pulverized earth and stone and microscopic flecks of rail tie. I can't help coughing as I say "Right."

"There's people out there," he says. "There's no light, but there's people." He raises a hand. "Right there, where the four-fifteen is, the train's stopped. A couple of delivery trucks, they're parked there." He shakes his head. "That's a couple dozen rules busted right there. You just don't *do* that. You load and unload at a station, a cargo yard. Not a service yard."

He glances at me. Skald has cried himself out, but fear makes his eyes tremble.

"You did what you thought was right," I say.

Skald nods. "Old William, he raises his light. Walks right up there and starts raising seven kinds of devils, pardon my language miss. And they just…" He takes a deep breath. "They had guns. Big guns. And those funny goggles that let you see in the dark. Clubs. I still got the bruises."

I can imagine the scene. I can see Father coming out to raise his voice, relying on his height and weight and attitude and absolute moral certitude to take control of the situation. Skald might have serious shoulders, but the rest of him isn't a big man in any sense of the phrase.

The part of my soul that's baring its teeth grins more fiercely.

Having a train stop off schedule means power.

Armed thugs equipped with night vision means money.

I don't yet know for certain who murdered Father. But I have the feeling I've hated them since *way* before Father even set foot in this trainyard.

Skald's leading us towards this rickety steel gantry that looms over a siding. In an earlier age it might have been used to load coal into an engine or cargo into a tanker. Now it's a Tinkertoy tower of corrosion, standing only because it had originally been built to hoist chunks of trains and even half rusted away it has more structural integrity than most brand-new skyscrapers. Skald's pace is irregular, though. He gathers his will and plunges forward for a few steps, then falters and slows, only to clench his fists and march another few steps.

The train continues its slow progress, boxcar after boxcar grumbling past. Here in the open air, I can't help realizing how powerful that little locomotive has to be to haul this kind of cargo. There's a reason earlier generations loved trains.

Like Father.

When I was tiny, Mom had arranged more than one picnic out near the Malacaster train tracks, so Father could have a beer and a sandwich and watch the train. I remember sitting on his broad lap, one giant arm around me, Father's other arm raised to point out details of each car as it grumbled past.

I bite my lip and swallow bile.

I don't remember any of the specifics, any of the parts he pointed out, any of the fancy names for train wheels and types of cars.

But every part of me remembers the hair on his arm and how safe his lap felt. I am not going to cry. Not here.

Skald lurches to a stop. He lurches between staring up at the gantry and squeezing his eyes shut. He wraps his arms around his chest and hugs himself.

I wait to let him collect himself.

Will glances over at me, shifting from foot to foot in embarrassment at Skald's blatant distress. His mouth opens, closes, opens again. Finally he says, "You all right, buddy?"

"Right there." The train's grumble almost drowns Skald's words.

My stomach knots. Despite the oppressive heat, the sweat on my spine runs cold. I make myself say, "What happened?"

Skald shakes his head. "I couldn't stand. Not anymore. I tried, Heaven knows I tried, but…Old William, he was a big guy. I told him to pray."

My gut squeezes so tight I can't hardly breathe. *Tell me it's not what I'm thinking. Tell me it's not* her. But that's the first rule of interrogation—don't lead the witness. And anything I do to make things easier for Skald might nudge him from the truth.

"They said," Skald chokes out, "they said, if I tell anyone, they'll be back. I have kids. But…" He shakes his head.

The words want to come out. "I swear to you," I make myself say. "You tell me what happened, and I will make sure those people can't do anything to your kids. Or you."

Skald nods. I don't know if he believes me or not, but I can see his irresistible need to confess. "They ran a rope." He points up at the crossbeams. "They'd punched me a bunch. Old William, he got zapped." His eyes close. "They pulled up a car. Got…got the rope around his neck."

His voice drops further. I have to lean in closer to pick his words out from the constant shifting grumble of the train's turgid passage. My heart is jackhammering against my ribs, fighting to carve an escape path.

Father was killed in a very specific way. Not just hung, but hung without a rope burn.

That takes rare skill.

I learned the hard way that Ayaka has that skill.

"I stood much as I could," Skald says.

I dread what he's about to say. "It's okay."

It's not okay.

It might never be okay again.

I'm about to reassure Skald more when Will snaps, "What the hell did you stand?"

Skald jerks to stare at Will. His face blossoms in anger. "They put him on my shoulders!" he shouts. "They made Old William stand on my shoulders with a rope around his neck, so when I couldn't hold that fat bastard up anymore he'd fall and break his neck! And that crazy little black lady watched and laughed!"

My guts spiral into a tighter knot.

A crazy little black woman.

Ayaka.

"Last thing he said," Skald sobs. "Last thing your pa said before I fell down was to tell his kids he loved them."

32

The shaking in the ground isn't only the train's countless wheels receding from the switchyard. It's coming from inside me, a blow to my soul and a matching blow to my mind.

Father's last words were that he loved me?

And he'd been killed by one of the most maniacal freelancers I'd ever known?

You don't go into this business if you're normal. You don't stay in this business if you're insane. But Ayaka gleefully dances along the line between crazy and competent. She has decades of experience and completes her contracts with chilling precision, yes, but takes an unholy joy in hurting people on the way.

I could too-easily imagine Father's death. Hands tied behind his back. Noose snug around his neck. Knot precisely placed behind his ear. Forced to balance his big feet on Skald's shoulders.

Skald gasping at the burden. His shoulders are big, but not that big. He has muscles, yes, but they're the wiry sort, meant for quick, short burdens.

Father's bulk would have broken him in minutes.

Ayaka always overstaffs her contracts. She has plenty of people to handle the work, and then time left over. If whatever project had brought her to the switchyard had given her time, she would have done this.

Because it wasn't just about murdering Father.

It was about hurting Skald. In a way he'd never get over.

It didn't *have* to be Ayaka.

But Skald's words *crazy little black woman* narrowed the suspect list way down.

And Father's last words were that he fucking *loved* me?

Skald is sobbing piteously, but I can't care. My whole life is doing a slow-motion Big Bang inside my skull. My feet stand on the switchyard's crunchy gravel and greasy cinders, but my mind is a billion light-years away.

Did my father stumble into Ayaka's work?

Or had she come to the Mound switchyard specifically *because* my father worked here?

Had Ayaka killed Father because of me?

The answer didn't change what I was going to do. Only *how* I did it.

Never mind that Ayaka had decades more experience and resources than I did.

Put Father's final words aside for now—forever.

And forget the cost.

If anyone was going to murder Father, it should have been *me*.

Ayaka was going to die.

Whoever she was working for?

Them too.

Her flunkies? A pile of smoking bones.

"Hey," Will says.

His voice jerks me back into the world.

Will offers Skald one of those manly shoulder-to-shoulder-but-keep-the-balls-widely-separated hugs, but Skald seizes my brother the same way he grabbed me and is bawling into Will's shoulder and hugging him like a giant teddy bear. Will's giving Skald that macho back-pounding hug, like he wants to say *we're being affectionate but beating each other up at the same time so it's still manly*, but his blows are gentle enough to almost be pats. Will's face is contorted, bright red with blended embarrassment and grief. "Hey," he repeats. "It's…" Will's lips pull back in a grimace. "It's not your fault." Will pulls in a breath, trying not to break down crying himself.

Let Will do some emotional labor for a change. See how he likes it.

My heart hasn't stopped rattling against my ribs, and my breaths are short and sharp. My every muscle has clenched. My fury has paralyzed me.

I need to control myself.

I need to be calm. Cold. Dispassionate, even while my passions burn white-hot.

If I go after Ayaka with my mind shattered, she'll eat me alive.

"Skald," I say.

He keeps sobbing.

"Jake Skald!" I snap.

Skald's face jerks up off Will's shoulder.

"Have they been back?" I say.

Skald closes his eyes and nods.

"When?" I say.

"Every." His breath catches. "Every night since."

I nod. "Were they here last night?"

Skald's crying too hard to speak, but manages to nod his head.

"Dammit, Billie!" Will is crying too. "Give the man a minute."

"We don't have a minute." My voice is too hard, my boundless fury ready to erupt. "Jake." No, still too angry. I push all the air out of my lungs and draw a deep breath. "Is it always two AM?" Better.

Skald jerks a nod. He's fighting to control himself.

"Listen," I say. "The next time you hear the train stop—"

"I don't go out," he gasps. "I stay in the warehouse."

"Next time," I say. "That hole under the train tracks? In your warehouse? Like for an oil change?"

"Service pit." Skald is starting to get his breath under control.

"Go down in that pit," I say. "You want to be down there before the shooting starts."

Skald's red face pales.

"Christ," Will says. "Take it easy on the guy."

"I am," I say. "Easy is not taking a bullet."

Skald nods desperately.

"And…" My stomach tightens, and somehow my fists become even tighter. "That crazy little woman? She was…" *You should have stood there forever. You should have stood until Father lived.* "She was going to kill one of you anyway. If you'd stood too long, she would have busted your knee so you fell. It's…" My tongue feels like lead and tastes bitter. "It's not your fault."

I know I'm telling the truth.

But I still feel like I'm lying.

Saying those words loosens a knot in my chest.

Skald closes his eyes.

Will hammers Skald's back forcefully. "It's okay, Jake."

Skald takes the hint. He draws a shaky breath and releases Will. "Sorry, Mister Salton."

"Call me Will."

I nod. "Billie."

"Will." Skald tries to straighten. "Miss Billie. I'm…I'm sorry."

The words come more easily this time. "It's not your fault." It's the truth, but not in any way that matters.

Deke mutters in my earpiece. "Company."

I glance over my shoulder.

A cheap four-door sedan has pulled sideways in front of the switchyard gate, right where cratered asphalt meets gravel. It's not long enough to fully block the entrance, but there's no way we'd get the SUV through the gaps without doing serious body damage to both cars.

My body wants to tense further. It can't. There's no way I could wind myself any tighter.

The sedan's door opens.

I know the man who steps out.

He has my picture hanging in his office at Chicago's FBI building. He uses it as a dart board.

33

Special Agent Brody Tan looks like he should be a cover model for *Amazing FBI Monthly*. He's maybe six feet one of lean marathoner muscle. His thick brown hair has enough of a curl to advertise that if he wouldn't cut it so professionally short it would become long, flowing locks. I suspect that little cheap sedan he's driving comes with its own steam press, because despite the merciless sun baking decades of oil out of the gravel parking lot, the creases in his dark blue suit look machined. Black-lensed wireframe sunglasses above a chin you could mount on a ship and use to break Arctic ice complete the portrait.

I'd seen Tan a couple times before. The first time, I'd been thieving.

The second time, he'd recognized me from the first time.

His partner told me that after that encounter, Tan taped my photo to his office wall. And started throwing darts at it.

My reputation needs the blood polished off it, yes.

But the FBI knows all about me.

Our rented SUV sits pointed right at Tan, idling. Deke looks utterly relaxed, but I'm sure he has both hands on the wheel. The brake lights are barely visible in the August sunshine.

If Deke guns the motor, he's got a good chance of squashing the agent against his own sedan.

Except Tan will leap aside. Deke will T-bone the sedan and might total both cars. And then it's all over but the blood and bullets.

Tan's perfectly relaxed. His chin twitches as he looks between the SUV and me.

He shouldn't be here. Not without backup. Not without a surrounding cordon of snipers and dogs and helicopters and men with giant nets to scoop Deke and I up like wiggling fish.

Seeing Tan brushes away all the confusion Skald dumped on me. Nothing focuses the mind like the prospect of life without parole. The Ryan Correctional Facility, looming behind a dozen lines of train rails and a heavy-duty fence, only drives that deeper. "Jake."

Skald nods.

"Those people?" Tan is the kind of overachiever that would pick up lip reading in his spare time, so I turn my head to face Skald and lower my voice. "They have to have contacts inside the government to stop a train like that."

Skald closes his eyes and gives another short, sharp nod.

"That guy? He's FBI."

Skald glances past my shoulder at Tan.

"Thank God," Will says, shifting his weight. "We gotta tell them."

I catch Will's arm before he can take a step. "You tell the FBI, and the people who killed Father will find out."

"Good!" Will says.

"And the first thing they'll do is come back for Jake."

Will recoils like I'd slapped him.

Jake's face loses its flush as his blood drains away.

I keep my voice flat. "You want Jake's death on your conscience?"

"We can't just do nothing!" Will says.

"Oh, we'll do something." I'm talking too loud. I need to take a deep breath and slow down, but there's no time. "But I know him. An FBI special agent."

"How the hell d'you know an FBI agent?"

"We've worked the same gig a couple times." Technically true.

Will jerks his arm, but not hard enough to rip free of my grip. "So let's tell him to keep it secret."

"He'll talk to me," I say.

"This is bullshit," Will says.

"Oh?" I turn and raise my voice loud enough to carry to the gate. "Hi there! How are you today?"

Tan calls back, "I am having a lovely day, ma'am. No names please. When you finish talking to your brother and the watchman, however, I could use a moment of your time."

If Will's scowl gets any more sour, he'll turn into a lemon.

My gut keeps screaming that something is very wrong. Whatever Tan is doing, it's not official. And he believes in the law like he saw it die for his sins and rise again.

He doesn't want me to use any names? This is all kinds of wrong.

"Listen." I glare at Skald. "When he asks—and he will—you tell him just that we were here to talk about Father. You tell what happened that night, and Aya—that crazy lady? She'll be back for you."

Skald looks like he might faint. "I…I think I believe you."

I turn the glare on Will. "You get in the SUV. We might have to bail quick."

Will jerks his arm back, freeing himself from my grip. "Fine. This is still bullshit."

"You wanted to come along." I try to soften my glare when I turn to Skald, but I don't think it's working. "Jake. Thank you. Thank you so much."

Jake manages to nod. The day's hot enough for him to sweat, but the poor bastard has picked up the fresh stink of fear.

"I know you did everything you could." I pat his shoulder. "It's hot, go get something to drink." I turn the glare back up. "Will. In the car."

Will snarls and spits, but marches past me towards Deke.

I'll take my Deke anywhere, to Rome or a robbery, but I'm gonna owe him for tolerating Will.

I consciously relax my shoulders and assemble a fake but passable smile.

Then I casually saunter towards Very Special Agent Tan.

Tan doesn't watch. He *assesses*. His eyes suck in everything and his brain sorts it all by the charges he can bring.

As I pass the SUV, I glance at Deke without turning my head. He's got the SUV in gear, and I'm pretty sure whatever handgun he's picked up is near at hand. He looks focused on Agent Tan, but I'm confident he's completely aware of everything that happens anywhere on the switchyard's grimy gravel and burned-out cinders.

Talking to the FBI sounds better than talking to my brother.

34

"Beaks." I've never heard Agent Tan speak before. Shout, sure, but not *speak*. His deep voice sounds cultured, nearly English. I suspect he watched too much Doctor Who as a kid, or maybe British murder mysteries. He keeps his hands loose at his sides. Doesn't offer to shake.

Which is best, because I wouldn't accept his hand.

The FBI will never lay hands on me.

Worse, despite the sun pounding down and the torrid heat radiating up from the potholed black asphalt under his feet, he doesn't seem to be sweating at all.

My heart pounds with a different kind of tension. Tan was at the Dallas depository robbery I'd barely escaped. (Yes, *with* the contents of the safe deposit box, thank you very much.) He'd seen me at the Heisenbug gig in New York City, and I still didn't know how the FBI uncovered that one so quickly. My brain flips through possibilities like a fanned deck of cards. I have to focus on keeping my breath deep and regular.

I've killed to complete a job. Who hasn't?

And I'm not going to let anything as trivial as the United States Federal Government stop me from finding the "crazy little woman" who murdered Father.

But killing an FBI agent would make my life a lot more difficult.

Calm.

Tan didn't swoop in here with a platoon of agents, nets, and tear gas.

That means he wants something from me.

Something I can give only of my own free will.

I stop just inside the switchyard's gate. The actual gate was last opened sometime in the twentieth century, judging from the couple of scrub trees that have grown up through it, but that's not the point. There's an *implied* fence. I'm on one side of it, standing on gravel parking lot. Agent Tan is on the other side, on pavement. His four-door sedan is parked sideways to block the opening, but I'm pretty sure that my SUV could clip the back bumper and knock it out of the way.

"Agent Tan." I keep my words slow. "I'm sorry. It's Special Agent, isn't it?"

"Indeed." The black lenses of his sunglasses shield his eyes, but he's positioned so he can watch both myself and Deke. "I wanted to compliment you on your technique."

My technique? No, he wants you to ask, so don't. Cold and polite. "Thank you."

"While I don't normally approve of violence," Tan says, "my research indicates that Tom Cartmill certainly deserved the treatment you gave him."

Tom Cartmill—*Uncle Tommy.*

Tan had seen me put Uncle Tommy on the ground at the funeral home.

I would have noticed a stray FBI agent in that hall.

They'd put *surveillance* in the funeral home?

All my anger at Uncle Tommy flares right back up, intermixed with a profound sense of intimate violation. "You can't even let me bury my father?"

"I'm not inhuman," Tan says mildly. "I would have let you attend the service. But what happened instead is far more…interesting."

My blood rises towards a boil. "A man's murder is *interesting*?"

Tan picks up a faint smile. "What could possibly be more interesting than life and death? And certainly you didn't expect me to not notice your father's demise?"

I want to slap myself. I should have expected the FBI to monitor every member of my family—maybe not the cousins, sure, but my father? My brother? Any life event that might have brought me back home?

But I hadn't. The FBI is badly underfunded, and there's far worse people out there than me.

I underestimated how badly Agent Tan really wants me in a cell.

I shift my balance to the balls of my feet, but keep my shoulders and arms relaxed. "So is this the part where you try to take me in and I have to break your neck?"

"That's scheduled for tomorrow." Tan's mild tone inflames my anger. "After the funeral. But I don't think you'll be there."

"And where do you think I'll be?" I could close the distance in three steps. Grab his head with both hands. Give a sharp twist. Hearing his body hit the pavement would do me some good right now.

No. Don't kill the FBI agent. That would be bad.

Besides, then you'd have to move his car out of your way.

Skald's revelations unbalanced me. Time to get off defense. "Don't FBI agents normally travel in pairs? Where's your partner?"

"Deskovsky's not exactly dispassionate with you."

Both Tan and his partner want my ass, but for completely different reasons. I'm not sure if Tan's lust for jailing me or Deskovsky's old-fashioned lust is more annoying. "Still, you shouldn't be alone on the job."

"I'm on my lunch break."

"Great spot for a picnic," I say. "Get out of my way and you can eat before the time clock dings."

"It's lovely, if post-apocalyptic chic is your delight."

"What is it you want?"

"I have a gift for you." Tan sounds almost bored. "And an offer."

"Haven't you heard of cutouts? This is *not* the way to hire me."

One side of his mouth twitches up. "No. You won't make a penny off of this." He turns a hand over slowly, revealing a folded piece of paper.

I look at the paper.

"It's only an email address." Tan looks almost bored. "I had my chance to kill you at the funeral home."

I'm not going to let this guy think I'm afraid. I take two steps forward and snatch the paper from his fingers. Unfolding it reveals an email address, laser-printed in neat capitals: BEAKSNEEDSHELP at a free email provider.

"Help?" I don't pocket the paper. For all I know it has microscopic radioactive tracers in it. "You're going to get me off the watch list?"

"After that little escapade in Myanmar?" The other side of Tan's mouth twitches. It's almost a smile. "You're the talk of the Agency. Even if you get off our list, I'm certain the State Department has your picture on the wall. Probably the NSA and the Forestry Service as well. No, that's for when you hit a whole bunch of people you can't handle, but I can. Send me any evidence, and I'll nail them all."

Why is he wasting my time? I drop the paper. "Then you don't have anything I need."

"Keep going and you will." Tan's placid features hint at a smile. "Then there's the gift."

"I don't want a gift from you."

"It's surveillance footage." His growing smile feeds my impatience. "Of the last few minutes of your father's life."

35

Moments later, Special Agent Tan drives away.

I wait until his car vanishes around the corner back onto Davidson, then stomp back to where Deke and Will wait. The switchyard's greasy gravel and oil-steamy heat might as well be on a movie screen. The only thing that feels real is the flash drive clenched in my right fist.

Will is in the back seat. I can imagine the pissing contest over that.

The SUV's air conditioning hits me like a wall of ice, shattering my daze. Suddenly I realize how sweat has soaked through my cheap funeral clothes. My feet are dumplings steamed in shoddy leather, the small of my back a swamp as I sag into the seat. The stink of oil and grease still clog my sinuses and lungs. I didn't touch anything, but I'm going to need a long hot shower to clear them, then a long cold shower to reduce my temperature to something near normal.

"What was that?" Will demands.

I struggle to still my pounding heart. "He's using us."

Deke's eyes flicker to my face, then back to the terrain outside the SUV. "How?"

"He said…" I empty my lungs so I can inhale again. "If he gave me a hint, he wins no matter what."

The flash drive feels like a hot coal in my hand. It's all I can do to not snatch our disposable laptop from the cargo space. Will knows Father was murdered, but whatever really happened, assuming Tan's legit, I need to see the video first.

My brother is a drunken ass. Letting him watch our father's murder will only drive him to a bender. I don't have the spoons to blame him for being himself.

And if I shove him out of the SUV now, I'll have to worry what he'll do next. Better to have him close.

"What did he give you?" Will says.

"An email address."

"The other thing."

Deke says, "If she said she got an email address, she got an email address."

"Don't give me that," Will says. "I saw him give it to you."

"A flash drive," I say.

"What's on it?" Will's mouth is inches from my ear.

I won't turn to look at him. "Information. He said I'd want it."

"What kind of information?"

I let my annoyance drain into my face and corkscrew around to see my brother's red face. Cold air assaults my sweat-soaked back. "I don't know, because I haven't read it yet."

"Well, look at it!"

I grit my teeth. "Here's the plan. Deke, we need a hotel suite."

"Yes, ma'am." Anyone else would think he's merely formal, but I can hear his annoyance as he pokes at his phone.

"We need a base of operations." I fix Will's gaze with mine. "I need to review this. I need to make some calls. I need to figure out who to lean on next."

Will's scowl twists further.

"Look!" I say. "If an FBI agent gave me information, even off the record, I'd be a damn fool not to look at it before we go on."

"Fine." Will curls his lip.

I hold up a hand. "And give me a bottle of that water back there."

My real plan is a lot simpler. We get a hotel room. Tonight, Deke and I will go to the trainyard and see who shows up at two AM. When Will wakes up tomorrow morning, we'll be long gone. I don't want him to think we got taken by the people who killed Father, so I'll leave a note. Cash for a bus ticket.

After a few more hours, I don't have to see Will ever again.

Deke raises the phone to his ear. A tinny voice answers. He says "I'm looking for two adjoining rooms. Do you have any available?" A faint response. "We'll be there in twenty minutes. No, no credit card. You'll recognize me by the extra hundred."

Will rolls his eyes so hard they might knock off the top of his skull and throws himself back into his seat. "Do you just throw money at everything?"

If my heart keeps hammering, it's going to pop. "Do you have a better plan?"

Will flaps a hand. "Fine."

We're at the hotel in ten minutes of glowering silence. Leave it to Deke to remember every hotel we passed and choose the right one.

The Madrid Motel is two stories of dilapidated yellow brick. The only parts of the building that look maintained are the iron grills over each room's window. If they offer breakfast I wouldn't eat it because of the risk of lead poisoning from the decades of peeling paint, and the asphalt parking lot is smoother than the main road only because it's dissolved back into primordial gravel. Deke always checks the bedbug report before booking a place in the States, but I can't help wondering. The rickety mezzanine would collapse from the vibration of a fully loaded cement mixer grumbling past, but that's okay because it's clear none of the other buildings around have had any maintenance in decades either. This is the part of town that will be ignored until some wealthy developer can make a profit by destroying it.

Detroit is pretty much made up of those spaces.

And left-behind people, doing the best they can.

Deke ducks into the office to get us a room, leaving Will and I to steam silently at each other.

I'm not quite ready to murder my brother.

I am ready to leave him by the side of the road, hogtied and wearing nothing but his skivvies, but the afternoon sun is still high and the spawning-salmon-thick commuters on the four-lane road would rescue him too quickly. Besides, it would delay me from ripping open the USB drive gouging four corners into my clenched fist.

Deke comes back a century later and hands me a key. "Room eight. Mister Salton, room nine."

"So you're not just her driver," Will says.

Maybe I can find him some My Little Pony skivvies before I leave him by the road. "It's none of your business what he is."

Will leans back in his seat. "Figured."

As Deke drives us around the back of the building, I barrage Will with my psychic death ray. It doesn't work any better than when we were kids.

Our rooms are on the first floor in the middle of the row. Ground floor isn't ideal, but I trust Deke got us the best he could. The brand-new doors are unpainted wood straight from a big box hardware store, and the window's white fiberglass frame has only started to pick up dirt spots. I'm guessing the police battering-rammed the doors and windows only a few days ago. Two doors down, a decrepit man wearing only jeans and a doo rag sits in a rusty lawn chair, taking advantage of a narrow puddle of shade cast by an overgrown scrub tree looming over the rotting wood fence marking the far side of the lot. He watches us with eyes that have seen too much and don't care about any of it anymore, another victim of our country making disease and poverty profitable.

Will glances uneasily at the geezer.

If any black people mistakenly wandered into Malacaster, I'm pretty sure Will helped remind them that they weren't wanted. Just like Father.

If at any point Will drops the N-word I'll give him a lesson in manners. In the kneecap.

But Will only says, "Let's look at that there thumb drive."

"I'm not having you read over my shoulder," I say.

"Then get on it," Will says.

Deke focuses his attention on Will. "You need to chill out." His voice is flat and hard. "She'll look at the drive as soon as you stop poking at her. You have a room. Use it."

Deke's glare can make hardened criminals blink.

Will looks away in about half a second. "Just get on it."

"Room nine."

Will slams the SUV's door and the hotel door in quick succession. It's barely shut before I close my eyes. My chest hurts. I've been breathing wrong, too quick and too short. My nose burns, my eye sockets ache, and the muscles along my spine are trembling.

"Billie," Deke says.

I love that man, but right now I don't even want to talk to him. I am so incredibly frustrated with my brother. Maybe if I filled Will's hotel room with bullets he'd take me seriously.

No, if Will got shot he'd get even more noisy and demanding.

"It's been a shitty day," Deke says.

I drag my chin through a nod.

"Sit there a moment," Deke says. "Clear your head. I'll check the room and unload."

I give him the only answer I can, squeezing my diaphragm to shove every scrap of air out of my lungs. My ribs ache when I inhale, but it's a comforting ache that drags my attention back into my body.

Forget Will.

Forget Father.

Just be, right here.

My legs ache. My spine and shoulders burn. I desperately need to stretch.

The SUV wobbles with each equipment bag Deke heaves from the hatchback. I open my door to suck in Detroit's muggy, exhaust-choked air. It's not as smoggy as LA, but it's a heck of a lot more humid. When I feel Deke grab the third bag, I unwillingly open my eyes and follow him into the surprisingly large room.

The saggy queen-size bed looks like it retired after a long career hosting mating rhinoceroses, but the sheets have that stark gleam that means they were ferociously bleached no matter how much collateral damage the chlorine inflicted. Our three heavy duffel bags of equipment are a cruel burden atop the ragged gray bedspread. Deke's opened one of the bags and laid out a couple of tiny MP-7 pistols with perforated muzzles and extended clips, just to make the place feel more homey. The sight of still more tools of mayhem inside the open duffel comforts me.

The battered flat-screen television is mounted in a wire cage on the wall.

Decades of cigarette smoke, mingled with almost as much eau de burning marijuana and the bite-on-tinfoil scent of crack, give the place an ambiance I haven't felt since the last time everything went to hell. It's soaked into the building's bones.

But the walls are freshly painted that agreeable shade of gray that's widely used to cover any number of crime scenes. I pick up of hints of bleach beneath the old smoke, and someone's recently scrubbed the woodwork.

Some enterprising person got the rights to this heap and decided they could do better than running a shooting joint. Someone without much money, but with dreams of pulling themselves up out of their hole. Maybe they can't afford to replace all the walls and carpet yet, but they scraped up enough to cover up whatever home decorating horrors marked up the walls and they'd gone through a crate of deodorizer trying to make it smell less awful.

This is a place that's been all the way down and is trying to get back up.

I'm lowering the tone just walking in the door.

An interior door leads to Will's room. When I test the knob it doesn't turn, but the door would come apart at a kick. My brother is locked out.

My thrumming tension eases a hair.

The air conditioner mounted high on the wall clatters and groans, then starts oozing vaguely cooler air at us.

The round Formica table is so cigarette-pocked and drug-scored that it might be a map of the Moon, but it's been well-cleaned. I smell scouring powder. Deke has already opened our burner laptop. It's heavily used, completely disposable, and—most important—never connected to the Internet. I wedge myself into one of the two mismatched garage-sale-reject plastic chairs, force my hand open, and meticulously squeeze the thumb drive into the USB slot.

The drive has a text file and a video file.

Deke leans over my shoulder to watch.

I'm so tense I can barely work the mouse, but on the second try I successfully double-click the video.

36

Surveillance footage fills the laptop's tiny screen. The date, time, and longitude/latitude stamps along the side tell me this is either official United States Government video, or it was taken by someone who follows government standards.

The camera must have been mounted on one of the switchyard's light poles, about fifteen feet off the ground, probably right next to one of those radio transponders. The illumination comes from pools of glare from irregular pole lamps. The camera's pointed at empty gravel, but there's a cluster of people over to the left.

Skald's testimony tells me what's going on before my eyes comprehend the picture.

Four people in dark green tight-fitting outfits stand watching one of the rusty gantry cranes. I've worn clothes like them before. Black clothing stands out against the night, but dark green wraps the darkness around you. Dark streaks on their faces obscure their exposed skin. These people do not want to be observed, but they're standing near one of the lights.

Two men stand stacked directly beneath the gantry.

The one on the bottom is Jake Skald. He's got his feet a little wider than his shoulders and he's hugging his own chest.

Standing on his shoulders...

Father.

My heart stops.

Seeing Father from the side really makes his gut stand out. Had he somehow gotten even bigger? Or is it the bad angle?

His hands are behind his back. He's trying to pull them apart, but I already know that they're handcuffed together.

I've been sucked into the screen. I might as well be perched on top of the lamp pole myself, peering the few yards to the grisly display.

A tinny train whistle hoots from the laptop's speakers. There's audio, but nobody's talking. I crank the volume all the way up.

An off-camera grunt of pain blossoms into a cry. It's like someone stubbed a toe, grunted, and got stabbed for making noise.

The video's resolution is so high, I can see Skald's legs tremble and his teeth clench. Blood oozes from his forehead into his eyes. Two night-black rivers ooze from his nose and over his chin.

Dad bobs to one side, ready to fall. The noose catches his neck. He grunts as the rope tightens. He wobbles back, almost upright, but still partially supported by that horrific rope.

113

Five seconds in, and my bowels are petrified.

"Hey." The noose hasn't quite choked off Father's voice yet. "Jakey." Part of my brain realizes that the FBI must have cleaned up the audio to make his words audible, but mostly I'm sucking everything in.

I don't want to see this.

I have to watch.

Skald doesn't answer. His chest is moving too quickly. He's hyperventilating. He's going to pass out any moment. The little guy is giving everything to stay upright, but Father's way too heavy for him.

"Jakey!" Father's trying to shout, but that awful rope must have his airway squeezed down to the size of a thumb. "Not your fault. Remember. Not your fault. Tell Will. Billie. Tell them. I'm proud. Of them. Love them."

The image blurs with my sudden rush of tears.

I frantically wipe my eyes.

I can't cry. Not yet.

No matter how fiercely my eyes burn and my heart pounds.

"Hey!" Father's somehow squeezing a little more volume out of his strangled voice. "Psycho bitch lady!"

"You called?"

I know the voice.

The green-suited figure who steps out is shorter than any of the others. My memory immediately fills in the details obscured by the night and her outfit.

Ayaka stands maybe five-three. Rumor has it she's been in the business for decades, but you couldn't tell it from her unlined face. She carries a few extra pounds around the middle, though, and moves with the thoughtless care of someone who's practiced grace for decades.

She's wearing a dark cap, but I can see the line of white beneath it. Ayaka keeps her stark white hair a short natural. I'd seen what happened to a Chatty Karen that made a flip comment about it.

"Did you want something, darling?" Her voice is pleasant. Chipper. Ayaka's always chipper.

Especially when she's doing something appalling.

When I need to polish my reputation, I perform a burglary so perfect that nobody knows I've been until I've spent the money.

Ayaka's reputation as "inhuman for hire" doesn't need polishing. She's not just willing to do terrible things for pay, she *enjoys* them. Polishing her rep would require new heights of outrageous horror.

Ayaka gazes up at my struggling father while he wheezes in a desperate breath. I can see half of her peaceful smile.

"Just so. You know," Father wheezes.

"Yes, my dear?"

I can hear Father desperately suck air.

Then he pushes it all out in a single, explosive cry.

"My daughter is going to fucking kill you."

Father leaps off Skald's shoulders.

I don't know if the snapping noise is the rope jerking tight or his neck breaking.

37

The cheap plastic chair won't turn with me so I half-spin and half-stumble out of it, staggering to my feet as the decrepit hotel room's walls shrink in. The bright copper of adrenaline saturates the back of my throat. My mouth is open but I'm not screaming, I don't have the air to scream. Gravity has come unhinged, and I'm wobbling one way and another to stay on my feet.

Deke grabs my shoulders. "Billie!"

Father's last words keep rupturing forth from my heart. His final jump is burned into my brain, somehow looping over and over and every frame frozen front and center in my mind, simultaneously leaping and dropping and snapping with his head ricocheting back as his spine breaks, limp body spinning away piñata-style, one moment alive and a flash fraction of a second later three hundred pounds of meat dangling from a butcher's line because Ayaka is a butcher and loves being a butcher if it means she gets to torture someone on their way out and that's one thing Dad got right because I am going to murder her until she's past death, until there's bloody gobbets of her meat scattered over half the planet and people dare their friends to look at my Instagram without puking their kidneys out—

The hotel rolls sideways. The worn-out carpet doesn't have enough tread for my feet to stick. The walls and ceiling throb in time with my sledgehammer heart. The universe is dissolving.

Deke is solid.

I let him pull me in. Let him guide my chin into his neck as his arms wrap around me. He's making nonsense noises, they're probably words but my brain has shut down.

I hate ugly crying.

And for Father? That makes me even more infuriated.

But Deke has me. The world can't harm me.

Even when my whole mind comes apart under three gasped phrases.

Proud of them.
Love them.
My daughter is going to kill you.

Eventually the world reassembles around me. I'm repulsive, with snot running down my chin and eyes burning from too many tears. Deke has one arm around my upper back and is tenderly stroking my hair with his other hand, murmuring *it's okay* over and over until it's meaningless except it isn't, it's the only sound that gives meaning to the world and that's only because it's Deke saying it.

My fingers ache as I deliberately unclench them from Deke's shoulder blades. My muscles still shake with echoes of those horrible sobs, but I demand a deep breath and my body obeys.

Ugh. My nose is so stuffed I can taste it.

Deke loosens his grip from save-me-from-falling-off-the-skyscraper to never-let-my-heart-go.

I force a second breath and close my eyes. Even my eye sockets hurt.

"I've got you," Deke murmurs. "We'll get her. I promise you, we'll get her."

I nod into his neck.

His arms gather my shards together while I reassemble myself.

Eventually, I slip from his comfort and into the bathroom to wash my face in the rust-stained sink. The water tastes bitter, but there's not a spot of mold or rust on the fixtures. The cracked, foggy mirror obscures my face enough to hide how broken I feel.

When I come back out, Deke's opened another duffel bag and extracted two dark green bodysuits. An automatic shotgun lies across one, while one of my empty Nerd Utility Belts is draped across the other. They're incongruously new and tidy against the decaying but brutally cleaned hotel room.

I barely get back in the room before Deke steps towards me. I put my arms around him this time, but gently, drawing him close with affection rather than desperation. "I'm sorry."

"Y'all don't have nothing to be sorry for." He's trying to make me smile with that awful Southern accent. My mouth twitches, but only because I ache to find something beyond the sea of rage.

"Been thinking." Deke turns his head a degree to put his lips near my ear. "We hit the trainyard tonight. See who shows up. Maybe we can end this."

"My plan, too."

He squeezes just enough to tell me I'm loved. "We need to chill out for a few."

The echo of what he said to Will tightens my spine.

Deke grunts. I've involuntarily squeezed the air out of him.

I loosen my arms. "I'm chill as I'm going to be."

Deke tightens his arms, then eases to pull back and look in my eyes. "I mean it, Billie babe. This was a shock. And ever since your brother showed up, you've been running hotter and hotter."

"Ayaka killed Father," I snap. "You think I should be calm?"

"I think your brother is pissing you off. More than he should."

"You have no idea how much he should piss me off!" I retreat a step and jab a finger into Deke's breastbone. "And *he* has no idea what he's doing here, other than shoving his opinions in my face. He's everything Father was and more, drunk and so goddamn sure that he knows the right way to do everything."

"Billie—" Deke starts.

"Don't *Billie* me!" I stomp the three paces to the bed and yank a duffel bag open. The gun bag? Fine. I jerk out a weapon and tug the flannel wrapping away. A grenade launcher, a few scratches showing it's used but a newer model. A couple grenades in the train's bridge—what do they call the place where you drive a train, anyway? I need to study before we go, but there's no way I can even study a web site now. Deke's right, I'm too angry to take on Ayaka, and him being right while I'm so wrong only makes me more angry.

I'm not so angry that I don't verify that the grenade launcher's chamber is clear and the safety set before tossing it onto the pillow. "Ayaka tortured and murdered my father, and I am going to see her fucking *die*." Deke starts to say *You are* but his tone's way too patronizing before he even breathes a word and I blow right over him. "I'm going to that switchyard tonight and when she shows up I'm going to blow it to hell and back." The next bundle has shotgun shells, incendiary ones. The heavy brick of ammo hits the pillow with a thud. "Her. Every flunky that's there. All of them." I yank more flannel, exposing another assault shotgun. "That place is going to burn and burn and burn."

Deke's voice is hard and flat. "You go in this hot and you'll be the one to die."

He's right. "I know what I'm doing!" Grenades. I'll need those. A whole bunch of those. I drop the satchel at my feet.

"I'm not going to let you kill yourself!" Deke snaps.

I whirl, another flannel-cocooned mystery weapon in my hand.

Deke's got his hands open at his sides, self-consciously defenseless and unthreatening and infuriating.

I shake the bundle like a club. Some of the wrapping falls away to expose a brutal carbine barrel. "Get in the way, and I'll dump you like I'm dumping Will."

"Holy shit."

Will's voice shatters my momentum.

The suite door is open.

My brother fills the doorframe.

He's staring at me, at Deke, and at the big pile of guns.

38

I'd double-checked that the suite's adjoining door was locked, but this hotel should have surrendered to the termites twenty years ago. The bathroom taps barely work. Only tsunamis of bleach have repelled the mold and mildew, adding a chlorine tang to the pervasive fug of old crack and weed and tobacco. The carpet is barely more than strings of canvas over abused concrete.

Of *course* the suite door jiggles open at a bump.

Will stands slack-jawed, eyes narrow, face red and hands open as he stares at me and the rifle in my hands. His five-o-clock shadow highlights his extra chin.

Deke freezes as well, but he's got his weight on the balls of his feet and his eyes ceaselessly scan Will, me, and the whole room. He's ready to fight.

My brother, so he's my problem.

My first impulse is to crack Will's skull with the half-wrapped carbine in my hands.

No, I don't really want to murder my brother.

Even if I want to kill him.

But in the half-second it takes for me to fight that impulse down, Will steps forward. "Kid, what are you doing? You're gonna hurt yourself."

He grabs the rifle barrel.

My muscle memory takes over.

I whirl my arms in a way I've practiced tens of thousands of times, shift my stance, and take half a step. The rifle slips out of Will's grasp, then I've got one arm around his head and a grip on his wrist.

Will instinctively jerks away.

I follow his motion. Add my own pivot.

Will faceplants in the nasty unpadded carpet, huffing out a shocked breath.

I keep my hold on his wrist and spin, planting my butt between his shoulder blades and tucking his arm over my thigh so that my whole body sits between his arm and freedom.

Will meeps.

In practice, on the mats, you can bring your feet close to your body to keep a little weight off your partner.

With him sprawled on the concrete, I put my feet all the way out.

My heart thrums at my ribs, and my mouth tastes of acid.

Will fights for a breath. "Dammit Bi—"

I bounce on his spine.

Air explodes from him.

Will tries to squirm. He's strong. He needs a lot of muscle to haul around all his weight, so he might get away if I let him.

I shift my thigh to crank his arm another quarter inch.

"Fuck!" Will chokes.

"Quit it or I tear your arm off." The room feels wobbly. Breathing. The first thing I'd learned in empty hand fighting was not to stop breathing during a fight, and here I'm making that newbie mistake. I force my lungs to empty and fill while Will tires himself out beneath me.

Finally he says "Uncle, damn you. Uncle!"

My voice feels steadier. "You're not going to grab my shotgun again?"

Will's clenched teeth flatten his voice. "No."

"Don't get up until I'm on my feet." I pull my feet in. Will tugs at his arm. "Don't move! I'd hate for you to tear your rotator cuff." On the mats I'd roll backwards to disengage, but here I'll probably catch some previously unstudied species of cootie from the carpet. Ungainly squirming gets me to my knees next to him.

Will starts to scramble up the second my weight's off him.

I hurry to gain my feet—there's no way I'm letting Will beat me up.

"You're still going to get yourself killed." Will is short of breath. "You been hanging out in the fancy corporations, and—all this stuff? Where did you get this? Didya rob a gun show?"

Most of the people at gun shows don't have weapons good enough to bother stealing. "That's none of your business."

"It is if my kid sister is going to shoot herself playing with this shit." He waves a hand at the bed. "This is serious hardware. You want to blow the hell out of the people who murdered Dad? Let's do it. But get something you can handle."

"Like the .22?" I snap.

"That was a good rifle."

"Ayaka is not a squirrel!"

"Better a .22 you know how to use than a, a…" He points. "What the hell is that?"

"That, my brother, is a computer-driven Mark 47 Model 1 automatic grenade launcher." I let the sneer fill my voice. "It damn near fires itself."

"You're getting in over your head again!" Will shouts. "This is just like the time with the go-kart."

"Will you shut up about the go-kart?" I shout. "I was fine! And who talked the cops out of taking you to juvie? Who fixed your carburetor on prom night?"

"That was just words. *You* made fucking thermite!"

How *dare* he? "It was in wet compost, nobody got hurt!"

"You almost burned your arm off!" Will screams. "I'm your brother! I'm not going to let you kill yourself playing Rambo!"

"I put you on the floor!"

"Luck."

The heat in my blood instantly turns to ice. "That's what you think?"

"I got twice the muscle you do," Will says. "You do okay when you sucker punch me, but face-to-face I'd whup you. That's just how it is."

"All right." I roll my neck, willing it to relax. "Hit me."

Will has the gall to roll his eyes at me.

"Stop," Deke says flatly.

I'm so coldly furious with Will, at all the stuff I'd made myself forget and that he'd dredged up, that I'd forgotten the love of my life was less than three feet away.

Sitting calmly in the horrible plastic chair by the laptop, Deke casually holds his automatic handgun. It's not aimed at anyone, but his whole body has that predator relaxation that says he's ready to spring when something tasty wanders close enough.

Will opens his mouth to retort, but Deke's gaze shuts him down.

Deke's going to tell me to knock this off, to chill out, to quit arguing and focus on the real problem. I brace to yell back at him but Deke says, "If you're gonna do this, there's more room on the other side of the bed."

Isn't he supposed to have my back?

"Don't be an ass," Will says. "I'm not fighting my kid sister."

Before the words even hit my conscious brain my hand flashes out, snapping the palm of my hand into Will's breastbone and knocking air out of him. "So now you get all gentlemanly?"

Will forces a breath. "Don't be an ass, Billie."

"No bone breakers." Deke could be refereeing the most boring MMA match ever. "No gouging an eye."

"So both eyes or neither," I say.

Will rolls his eyes. Again.

So I snap a backfist at his face. I pull the blow so it stings like crazy but doesn't break his nose.

Will's hands fly up. "What the hell!"

"You say it's luck," I say. "Put up or shut up."

"You want a fight?" Will snaps. "Fine. I won't hurt you."

I whirl and march around the foot of the bed.

Behind me, Will's feet thud closer and quicker.

I pause a beat, then whirl to merge into his two-handed push. Steer him towards the floor.

Will hits on his side, lets out an *oof*, and rolls to his back.

"Don't worry." I nod. "I won't hurt you."

That gets Will on his feet and coming at me.

I duck and drop him with a double-leg.

He's not so quick to get up again.

But he does.

I bounce him off the wall. I let him clip my shoulder with a punch so I can slip the haymaker and sweep his leg. Deke pulls the equipment bags off the bed, so I toss Will over my shoulder and let him bounce off the mattress and into my fist. I pull the strike, but he's still gonna have a bruised cheek tomorrow. Will lands a punch in my gut hard enough to huff some of my air out, but I counter with an elbow to his face that would put him down like a child. The expression on his face tells me he knows I pulled the blow, and that just makes him more angry.

My brother is as stubborn as my father.

The dumb bastard won't stay down.

A dozen clashes later, guilt starts niggling at me. Will's face is bright red, and he's gasping like some half-broken machine, but he's not smart enough to know he can't beat me.

Or he can't accept that his little sister can whip his ass.

Eventually, though, he can hardly stand. His last punch, a wild looping roundhouse thing too clumsy to hit a wall, leaves him staggering in a circle.

I give him a carefully-timed push.

Will faceplants into the side of the bed without all the guns

And stays there.

My heart beats so quickly that my vision seems to pulse. My sweat saturates my funeral clothes and mats my hair to my head. Short, ragged breaths burn in my throat. I had a harder workout a couple days ago and I've sparred for a few hours at a time, but a few minutes with my brother and I'm a stupid wreck.

Will groans, rolls onto his back, and lies spread-eagle to try for breath.

I have an urge to sit down next to him and gulp my own air.

"Now." Deke sets the handgun next to the laptop and stands. "If you two have burned off enough of your anger to act like adults for a few minutes, maybe we can talk about our next steps." His eyes meet mine. "And if you're still fired up, we can show your brother here how it's done."

Annoyance flashes through me, but I'm too tired for it to be anger.

Admiration leaks through after it.

Deke was right.

I'm still angry. I'm angry at Father for dying. I'm angry at Will for inviting himself. Hell, I'm angry at Will for being my brother, for excavating all the things I'd rather stay buried beneath years of concrete-hard memories.

But Will can't dominate me anymore.

I take another deep breath.

When I think I can walk without tripping, I pull a bottle of water out of my bag. And hand it to Will.

39

The hotel room's bathtub has hit that age where the mildew has conquered the grout more thoroughly than any amount of bleach and scrubbing can counter, but my two minutes in the shower still feel like heaven. I haven't had a bath since before getting my hands on the Grand Duke. I've been in Detroit's mugginess since this morning, but my nose still welcomes the steam after Arizona's appalling dryness.

The water washes away more than sweat.

It takes strain, and stress, and worry. These moments of caring for myself take away the irritation that Sister Silence hasn't called to tell me where the money I sent Father went. Maybe I don't have to sucker punch Will, but Ayaka? There's nothing to prove there. I'll shoot her from the back without a flinch. My doubts and uncertainty and fear swirl down the drain with the water.

The ragged towel is probably recycled from a vet's office for being too coarse, but it scrapes the water off so I can change back into my real clothes: soft, breathable dark green leggings and a matching shirt loose enough to not be indecent but snug enough to show I could get away with a bikini. The sweat-soaked polyester funeral clothes can stay heaped in the corner of the bathroom forever.

Deke has our equipment laid out all across the grungy hotel room. We prep out the equipment the same way each time: the dark matte metal of firearms to the left, ranked by size. Penetration gear on the right, ordered from the Lock-Release gun up to the digital-cracking microcomputers. Miscellaneous equipment like the rope and the night vision goggles go in the middle. The equipment adds the tang of plastic and oil to the room's pervasive drug-den stink.

Whatever plan we decide on, when I load up for tonight I'll put all of my equipment in the same places it always goes. Deke will do the same. If everything goes wrong and a gunshot puts me down, Deke won't have to fumble for the Israeli coagulant pads; he'll *know* that they're in my left thigh pocket. I'll know that his spare knife is at the small of his back.

It's called teamwork.

And Deke and I are more than a team.

Deke is sitting in one of those horrible chairs, sorting forty-millimeter grenades at the drug-scorched table. Seeing the laptop next to the row of white phosphorous grenades resurrects Father's last moments in my mind. My throat tightens, and I'm grateful that he's closed the laptop.

Seeing Deke's fingers deftly picking up one lethal little lump after another, I'm suddenly grateful for a lot of things.

Deke looks up and smiles at my approach.

Ignoring the sudden death pinned between his fingers, I put a hand on each of his cheeks and pull his face up. I haven't kissed him this hard since I heard about Father. It's only been a day, but his response tells me he's missed me.

An endless minute later I ease back a fraction of an inch. Enough to break the kiss, but close enough that when I murmur, "Thank you," my lips brush his.

Then I'm kissing him again. The twisted X scar on his cheek burns hot in my palm.

When I break off, I whisper "Sorry I'm such a bitch."

He starts to say something, but I cut him off again. His mouth tastes like old breakfast and I don't care.

When I come up for air I murmur, "I'll make this up to you."

My eyes are closed, but I feel his smile in my palms and under my mouth. His "Love you too" is barely a breath and a twist of his lips, but the words reach my heart through my skin instead of my ears. His fingertips delicately trace up my hip and my flank to my ribcage, leaving a trail of heat far beyond his warmth.

The bed's clear—no, the door to Will's room doesn't really lock. Dammit.

Eleven years after leaving home, and I'm worrying about my brother walking in on my lover and I? Could he be any more frustrating?

At least Will now knows I can put him down.

Hopefully I won't have to prove that I can shoot him.

I let the kiss deepen, making a promise I'll enjoy keeping, then reluctantly break off. Deke gives a little regretful sigh but doesn't pull me into his lap.

I'm a little disappointed. Deke can shrink our world to just the two of us.

Maybe I wouldn't even notice Will coming in.

No, no, no. Traumatizing my older brother with the sight of me thoroughly enjoying Deke sounds delightful, but it won't help.

I turn the other chair to face Deke. The plastic seat presses hard against my tailbone. What kind of butt was this injection-molded monstrosity designed for anyway? Deke watches me, more relaxed than he's looked in a while. He's still alert to my mood, but seems less concerned.

And really? Throwing Will around did me some good.

Maybe I should have come home to show him who's boss years ago.

No, that's bullshit. I'd never realized that part of me really wanted to smack Will around, true, but I could have happily lived another eighty years without lancing that boil. Not all wounds need purging.

I hear another shower through the cracked suite door. "Is Will cleaning up?" I say. "I didn't think he'd brought clothes."

"I loaned him my sweats and a tee," Deke says.

Deke's tall enough that sweatpants long enough to cover his shins leave enough space around his waist for a full set of Santa pillows, but Will's about that size. It's still going to be a treat for the eyes.

I open my mouth, but stop myself before speaking. Deke's been patiently listening to me rant and rave since Stabbity Joe ditched us yesterday morning. I study his face and say, "What do you think about this mess?"

Deke relaxes another notch. If I'm no longer too pissed off to consider his thoughts, he thinks I'm calm enough to plan with. Irrational anger flashes through me, and instantly evaporates. He's my lover. My friend. My partner in a whole bunch of crimes. He protects my back from our enemies.

Even when the enemy is me.

And I wouldn't have it any other way.

"I think you either need to send your brother home and get him to stay there, or tell him what's going on."

My gaze rolls around the neatly lined thievery gear and the row of weapons. "He knows I'm not a corporate troubleshooter."

"Sure we are." Deke folds his warm hand around mine. "Corporations are trouble. We shoot them."

The joke's so old it wouldn't even merit a groan, but I give Deke half a smile.

"If he stays," Deke says, "maybe we can use him. Depending on the plan."

"We have a plan." My smile evaporates. "Carve Ayaka into bacon."

"That's a goal," Deke starts.

We finish in smiling chorus, "Not a plan."

And plans start from facts. "What do we know?" I say.

Deke glances at the cracked door to Will's room. "First. If he's in, we should wait for him. If not, get rid of him."

I grimace, but Deke is right. We don't want Will walking in while we're figuring out exactly how we're going to napalm people. He might get the right idea. "Whatever we do, we need more clothes." Nothing tells people you're shady characters more quickly than wearing yesterday's clothes. Deke and I abandon more street clothes than we wash, either because we're unexpectedly moving or because people ask questions when you wash blood out at the laundromat.

"Clothes and dinner," Deke says. "You barely had breakfast. Or dinner last night."

My hollow stomach echoes his words. "I could go for that fish." Eating out would risk someone seeing us, but I'd really like to escape the hotel room's burnt-tinfoil stink of old crack.

Deke grins. "There's a you-buy-we-fry at the corner."

I grimace and bop his shoulder. Neither of us eats carbs if we can help it. I must be pretty hungry, though—a big plate of fried flounder sounds appetizing. "Maybe we can get you a big platter of grits."

"I'll have the grits, but you'll need to keep me company with some mac and cheese."

"I can't have cheese if you don't get any."

Deke grins. "Who eats dinner without greasy cheese sauce?"

"Health nuts," I say.

"Not at all our kinds a' folks," Deke drawls.

The silly game brightens my soul.

My brother's still in the shower.

He always took long showers.

I glance around the dismal hotel room. What I need dangles on the knob of the outside door.

Seeing me walk towards the door Deke says, "I brought everything in from the car."

"I'm an adult now." I pluck the DO NOT DISTURB placard off the doorknob. "And if I'm going to give Will a chance to hang around, he's going to have to get used to some things." Exaggerating the sway of my hips, I stride around the bed, open the suite door, and hang the placard on Will's side before closing it. "He can give us ten minutes."

"Ten minutes?" Deke leans back in his chair. "I am an *artist*, woman. What am I supposed to do with ten minutes?"

"Fine." I roll my eyes and tug at the bottom of my shirt. "Fifteen, and not a second more."

He shakes his head. "You drive a hard bargain."

Deke comes for me, eyes full of fire.

40

Those fifteen minutes last a joyful hour, blotting out broken necks and dead fathers and murderous mercenaries, but eventually Deke and I have to untangle ourselves.

The world has become a little better place. Even this awful hotel room, with its scorched-drug miasma and walls that are only clean because of brutally layered all-forgiving gray paint, isn't nearly as terrible as it had been. The *Jeopardy* theme blaring through the wall of Will's room drowns out the outside noises.

I pull my shirt on. "He's got that TV awful loud."

Deke's tying his boot laces. "Do you think we bothered him?"

"We were quiet. The bed didn't even break."

"Huh." He tugs his shirt over those caressable abs. Regret twinges in my chest. "I *was* trying to make you scream."

My belt clicks into place. "Me? You should have heard you, there at the end."

"Well. We'd best go apologize."

Deke's smile fades. What he's really saying is that it's time to get to work.

I hate that he's right.

"When this is over." I reach for the suite door, dropping my voice to a conspiratory whisper. "Poissey. French food. And we won't get breakfast until noon."

Will's room mirrors ours. He's sitting barefoot on the bed, leaning against the wall. Deke's sweats and shirt offer him the essentials of decency, but not much more. His bare feet look too white and too calloused—he doesn't take care of them. Alex Trebek booms answers to humanity's least important questions from the wire-caged television mounted on the opposite wall. The evening sunlight slants nearly vertical through gaps around the stained plastic-backed blackout curtain.

His room isn't full of weapons and tools, so it feels spacious.

Will fumbles for the remote chained to the bedframe. "You two finished scaring the neighborhood?"

"Not even close." I say cheerfully. Will grimaces and I add, "For now, though."

Deke follows me in, one of our injection-molded lawn chairs dangling from one hand. "We need to talk." He's all business.

"Damn right," Will says, rolling to his feet. "Where did you learn all that? And what's with all those guns?"

I look to Deke.

He raises his eyebrows.

My brother. My choice.

I take a deep breath and claim a seat at the table. The table in here is square, not round like ours, but the Formica is just as cratered. "Come on, let's talk."

Will tries to roll to his feet, but grabs his side before he's off the bed. He walks like he spent the afternoon in a tumble dryer.

Maybe I didn't pull all my punches as much as I thought. I hadn't wanted to hurt Will—well, no, I did, but only enough to make him pay attention. I'd wanted to slap him awake and make him realize that I wasn't the teen who'd gone off to University of Michigan. Not cripple him for a week.

Deke sets his chair to my right, leaving an empty seat facing me.

Will looks at Deke, looks at me, and tromps over. The chair's arms barely accommodate his bulk. He rests his elbows on the table and crosses his arms. "So talk."

Until yesterday I'd never imagined talking to my brother again, let alone talking to him about what I really do. "First." I need a breath to organize my thoughts. "All that gear in the next room?"

Will nods. His gaze burns holes in my face.

"I'm the kind of person who uses it. All of that."

"And whaddaya use it for?"

I glance over at Deke. Anyone else would think that he was utterly expressionless, but I can see he wants me to say very little.

"If I tell you." I take a deep breath. "No. The truth is, I'm not going to tell you everything."

Will's face twists in anger. "I am your brother. Your family deserves to know."

"It's for your own safety," I say.

"You still think you're better than the rest of us," he snarls.

I concentrate on my breath as he talks. "What you don't know can't be tortured out of you."

Will rolls his eyes.

Deke's voice is flat. "How many of your fingers do I need to break before you believe her?"

"That's just movie shit," Will says.

"We don't have time to persuade you by reason," Deke says.

Deke doesn't like breaking fingers, but he's done it on more than one gig to compel compliance from bystanders. Most civilians fold like a cheap paper plate when they see a pinky sticking straight up out of the back of someone's hand. It's kinder than a bullet, and a properly performed break heals fairly well.

"Hang on," I say. "Back in two seconds."

I don't let myself run to our room, but walking quickly it takes maybe a breath before I return with an AK-103 rifle in one hand, an AA-12 shotgun in the other. I thrust the shotgun at Will. "Here. Hold this."

Will reflexively raises his hands in surprise, and I dump the weapon in his fumbling grip.

I don't like firearms. When you have to pull a gun, the whole gig has gone horribly wrong. But when you need a gun, nothing else will do.

And if you need a tool, you best understand it and know how to use it well.

The AK-103 is the minimum viable rifle for the modern untrained soldier, and the manufacturer will happily sell them by the gross or license the plans to anyone willing to send hard currency to Russia. It's not terribly accurate, but you can drag it ten miles through a swamp and it'll still fire. My hands pull the clip, check that the chamber's empty, and start to strip the rifle down. "Even if you wanted to take that risk, you're not just taking it for you." I lay tiny metal parts on the tabletop, not bothering to be quiet. "You might keep your mouth shut for yourself, but what if someone starts in on Young Mack? Or Carol? The people I deal with…are not good people."

Will's brow furrows. I can see his mental image of me dissolve as my obviously practiced hands strip one part after another from the rifle. "Even if you were some kind of badass, nobody's going to look at me."

"If you stick around," Deke says, "they might."

My fingers brush an engraving under the stock. "This is a Saudi model."

Deke nods. "Mall buys a bunch of gear there."

My fingers set more parts on the table. "Good. Those 74Ms we got from Georgia were shit." The stock comes off. "Will, seriously. What are you going to do if someone starts to burn off Aunt Pat's face with a propane torch?"

"That doesn't happen here." Will's voice is strained.

I start reassembling the rifle. Normally I'd concentrate completely on this kind of task, but I'm doing this only so Will can see my hands working on their own while we talk. "Maybe you're willing to take that chance. I'm not." Will opens his mouth to argue but I roll over him. "What I am willing to tell you, though, is: we're the good guys."

"Never said you weren't," Will says.

"You thought it," I say.

"You were always a Girl Scout," Will says.

"Girl Scouts threw me out." Why does he have to remind me of all this crap?

"You mouthed off to the Scoutmaster."

"Girl Scouts don't have Scoutmasters."

Will shakes a hand. "Whatever. Point is—"

I sight down the reassembled rifle to the outside door, finger outside the trigger guard.

"Point is," Will says, "how the hell did you get involved in—in whatever this is?"

Progress. "I won't tell you that either." I set the rifle on the table and pluck the assault shotgun from his slack hands. The shotgun is Deke's. Its recoil would rip my shoulder off my torso after three shots, but we both know how to use and maintain every tool we select. "The point is, I know what I'm doing."

Will shakes his head. "I can't believe it." But his face shows the kind of disbelief that's just before acceptance. There's something extra real about a shotgun with a thirty-two round drum magazine.

Will might drink too much. He might have chosen to bury himself in Malacaster. But as I'd hoped, seeing me offhandedly field-stripping an assault rifle and starting on the automatic shotgun while arguing with him is starting to punch through his skepticism.

Deke speaks. "Would you believe your father?"

I jerk to Deke. "No."

"What about Dad?" Will says.

My hands stop unscrewing the shotgun's stock. "He doesn't need to see that." It's not anger driving my words. I'm feeling—protective? My surprise slews my thoughts.

I don't want Will to see Father's last moments.

Because I don't want Will to carry that memory.

And I haven't even really processed Father's last words. His real last words.

My daughter is going to kill you.

I'd hidden everything from my family.

But somehow, Father *knew*.

I don't know how to feel about that.

"Beaks." Deke's voice is gentle. "If he's in, he's in."

"What else aren't you telling me?" Will says.

I swallow a hard lump. "Deke. Go get it."

Deke rises.

"What is it?" Will demands.

"That FBI agent?" I look towards the front door. It's better than watching Will's face. "He gave me something."

"I knew it," Will says.

"It's a video."

Will's brow furrows.

I toss the shotgun on the bed, next to the automatic rifle. "It's bad."

My tone must have penetrated Will's thick skull. He sounds a little quieter. "Of what?"

I take a deep breath. The words don't want to come out. "Father. Being murdered."

Will's face loses three shades of pink.

"It's bad," I say again. "I mean—you don't want to see it."

Deke returns with the burner laptop, Agent Tan's flash drive sticking out of the side like the pommel of a buried knife.

"Doesn't matter," Will says. "He was killed. If we're going to get help, go to the police, we need to—" He runs out of air.

I take advantage of his breath to throw my words in. "We can't go to the police. The man who gave this to me? He's FBI. If he *could* do anything, he would. And anyone who can stop a freight train like that, unscheduled? They have contacts. The woman in charge of this? When Ayaka runs an op, she buys or blackmails or flat-out intimidates the cops."

"Who's Ayaka?" Will says.

Deke turns the laptop towards Will. "A mercenary."

I want to leave the room. But that video is the best hint we're going to get. I go stand behind Will, to watch over his shoulder.

41

Watching Father's death isn't easier the second time.

Even when hiding behind my older brother.

Will's shoulders shake when Father appears on screen. His hand squeezes the edge of the table when itty bitty Ayaka starts talking.

He freezes when Father shouts *My daughter is going to fucking kill you.*

His whole body shudders when Father leaps off Skald's shoulders.

The image freezes.

Will shoves his chair back, almost knocking me over. I open my mouth to complain, but he growls "'Scuse me" and staggers to the bathroom.

I shake my head as the door slams. Will had broken his arm jumping his bike off the riverbank the spring I was—what, nine? No, Mom had been gone by then, I must have been ten or eleven. The whole drive to the hospital, as Father told Will to *man up* and *men don't cry*, I'd just kept staring at the sliver of bone poking out of his bicep and trying not to cry myself because I didn't want to make it harder for Will to contain his own tears.

Has Will even cried since Father died?

"Well," Deke shook his head. "You all right, Billie?"

"Yeah." I rub my own eyes and pretend I don't hear gut-deep sobs through the flimsy bathroom door. "It's…still hard."

He nods. "I've gotta watch it a few more times."

I nod. "We both do."

Deke's voice softens. "I can handle it."

"No!" Too loud. I draw a deep breath. "This is a job. I'm the client, but still. I'm a professional."

Deke's face tightens. He had to offer. He hoped I'd let him study the footage alone. He knew my answer before he asked, though.

I pace around the table and kneel beside Deke's chair, wrapping my arms around him and being cradled in return.

After a few breaths Deke says, "Maybe we can use him to drive."

I shake my head into Deke's chest. "He's too pissed off."

"His anger," Deke murmurs. "It's armor."

I nod into his chest. I'd left Father, but packed all my issues along with my clothes and books. Will stayed and kept accumulating them.

"I think you broke through," Deke says.

"Maybe I can get him to go home." There's no chance.

Deke snorts a laugh. "He's almost as stubborn as you. It'll take a whole lot more than a snuff film to drive him off."

"I'm stubborn. He's pigheaded."

"Yes, ma'am." I can feel his smile.

I close my eyes and breathe Deke in deep.

He gives me time to think, but my brain is a jumble.

Really, that's all the information I need to make the most important decision.

I straighten to put my lips by his ear, "I'm biased. And I'm a mess. I need you to take charge."

Deke's arms tighten around me, just short of squeezing my air out. "I swear to you. We will get Ayaka. And whoever she's working for."

I squeeze him back.

I take a few moments of silent comfort, until the sound of water running into a sink comes through the bathroom door. By the time Will opens the door I'm back in my chair, my face towards Deke but my peripheral attention on my brother.

Will's fresh-washed face is still blotchy and red rings surround his eyes and nostrils. His—Deke's—shirt is wet where he's done hurried cleanup, and the straining cotton has enough translucent dampness to show off his hairy stomach.

But he's got his chin up and his shoulders back, like all the noise we heard was his glorious final victory in a brutal week-long battle with constipation.

Deke loses all trace of his good-old-boy drawl and his subservience. I asked him to take point, and he's already there. "Will there be any more stupidity about Beaks knowing what she's doing? Or can we get on with business?"

Will blinks in surprise at Deke's harsh tone, then shakes his head.

Deke points at the empty chair. "Time to figure out what we know."

"If we're not going to the cops," Will says, "then what *are* we doing?"

"Sit," Deke commands.

Will glances at me and takes the seat.

"Plans are built on facts," Deke says. "Once we pool our information, we can build a plan."

Will glares at Deke. "Who put you in charge, anyway?"

"Will," I say softly.

Will tries to glare at me, but his crying jag stole his driving fury.

"We need to be cold," I say. Will's lip curls but I plow over him. "These people took charge of the trainyard, night after night. They're professionals. That woman who," I swallow, "who killed Father? We know who she is."

Will's chair creaks as he learns back. "You said her name. Eye of something."

Deke says, "Ayaka."

"Yeah," Will says.

"There's no room for emotion here," I say. "And right now, we're both not making the best decisions."

"I'm fine," Will says.

Deke huffs a laugh. "Your estranged little sister shows up unexpectedly at your pa's funeral. She says he was murdered. She whups your ass."

"Hey!" Will says.

Deke doesn't slow. "Your father's apartment's pillaged, the old man in the trainyard saw him murdered and your sister knows an FBI agent. Plus, she just now whupped your ass again." Deke's voice has all the momentum of a speeding dump truck. "She put you on the floor dozens of times, then showed you she knows how to use an automatic shotgun and an assault rifle. Don't even try to bullshit me, your head is spinning like a washing machine. The only reason we're talking to you? One, you're her brother. Anyone else'd, I'd chain to the freeway median and leave there. And two?" Deke narrows his eyes and leans forward. "Anyone else your size, they'd stay down after two or three falls. I counted. You got up off that floor forty-one times. You're almost as pigheaded as your sister."

"Hey!" I say.

Deke doesn't slow for me either. "That's something we can use to nail Ayaka's head to the wall. So, either you're with the team and you listen to me, or I give you bus fare and we put Ayaka down ourselves."

Will's eyes, huge after Deke's declaration, glance over at me.

I lean towards him and keep my voice soft. "Deke is the reason I'm alive today. He's good at this. You can trust him."

Will's gaze bounces between Deke and I. An endless second later he says, "One question."

Deke's face is stone.

Will looks at me. "You know this woman. Is this payback? Did Father die because of you?"

42

The hotel's cheap plastic chair seems to wobble beneath me.

Will's question rattles around inside my brain and makes my breath catch. It's a good question.

Had I gotten Father killed?

Will's got his poker face on, but it's nothing compared to Deke's expressionless mask.

And I don't have the "no" answer I want to give.

I force myself to take a deep breath and look Will in the eye. "I haven't seen Ayaka for two years, and after last time I promised myself that I'd never wo—go near her again. As far as I know, she had no idea he was my father, and she had no reason to go after either Deke or me." I lick my chapped lips and make myself shrug. "If it turns out I did get Father killed, we'll deal with it then."

Will studies my face for an uncomfortable moment, then nods. "All right. For now."

We sit in silence for a breath, until Deke says, "Are you in? Knowing that I'm in charge?"

Will's face tightens. "Yeah. I'm in."

Deke relaxes. "Good. Let's start from the beginning. Will, what do you know?"

"Billie came in and started raising hell—"

Deke's helpless smile as he raises his hand warms my heart. "I'm sure she did. Before that. When did you hear about your father's death?"

Will has the storytelling skills of a toddler. Deke isn't an expert interrogator, but he slowly teases out the facts. The county sheriff's deputy came to the plant and pulled Will off the line. Will had been pissed because he hadn't done anything for the cops to be interested, but the deputy had said that Father was found dead at work. It had taken two days to get his body shipped up to Malacaster, then another three days before they could get a slot at the funeral home for the visitation.

Father had died the day before I arrived in Phoenix. I simultaneously felt annoyed that Will hadn't let me know sooner, and grateful that I'd been able to re-re-steal the Grand Duke with a peaceful soul.

"And then Billie showed up and started raising hell," Will says.

"Did they say anything about an autopsy?" I ask.

"Would they do one?" Will says.

I glance at Deke.

"Hey now," Will says. "If we're in this together, you gotta tell me."

Deke says. "Billie, how broken was his neck?"

Will barely flinches.

I can't help remembering Father's head rolling to the side. "The morgue van couldn't have missed it. Let alone the mortician."

"A fix, but not helpful," Deke says.

Will looks puzzled.

I say, "Someone got to the coroner."

"Detroit," Will snarls. "Even the damn mayor went to jail."

"There's different kind of neck breaks," I say. "Your typical trip-and-crack in an industrial yard doesn't leave you nearly so…"

Will's jaw tightened. "His head kind of fell over."

"Yeah." I swallow. "That's a violent break."

"And a coroner would know that," Deke says.

"Okay," Will says. "So the coroner covered up Dad's murder. We go find out how."

"We can ask." Deke is being deliberately, consciously patient. I both appreciate it, and want Deke to tell Will to keep up. "It was probably a sandwich-or-stick bribe, though."

I wait for Will to ask.

Instead, he grimaces. "So whoever this Ayaka is, she's got something going on at the switchyard. She gets her sick jollies with Dad. She tells the coroner it's money or a bullet. And you come home."

"Yeah." I'm a little surprised he put that together so quickly. I never thought Will was smart. Next to little Billie who started at University of Michigan at fifteen, though, there aren't many smart people. And maybe he's extra motivated right now.

Deke raises his eyebrows, but lets Will go on.

"What I wanna know," Will says, "is why the FBI guy gave you that. You sure as hell aren't with the government."

I can't help a laugh. "No. No, I'm not."

"It's a win-win for Agent Tan," Deke says.

"Either I take out Ayaka," I say, "or Ayaka takes me out."

Deke says, "No matter which, the FBI wins."

"The FBI doesn't like you," Will said.

Other than Agent Tan's creepy partner? "No."

"And the FBI can't touch this bitch?" Will says.

"She buys influence," Deke says.

"Agent Tan knew damn well when I saw—" my chest tightens so fiercely I have to push the word out "—*that*, he was aiming me right at Ayaka. And he gave me an email address, to call for help."

"Seems the least we can do," Will says, "as good citizens, is help him out."

I want to laugh and cry. My brother sounds utterly flippant. He has no idea what I do, what we're going to do, or how much the FBI hates me. The poor bastard thinks he's the new Punisher, but when the bullets start he's going to realize that we're all just walking meat waiting for someone to gut us.

And there's no way I can explain it. He won't get it until someone's blood splashes in his face.

The window shatters.

The thunder of gunfire fills the air.

43

When you're standing outside a hotel room and want to massacre everyone inside, but you can't see through the blackout curtain, don't just grab an automatic rifle and start spraying. Be methodical. Stand a couple yards from the window, far enough back that the shattering glass won't cut you up. Work from one side to the other, slowly enough to cover the whole room but fast enough that your ammo will last. With a little practice, a thirty-round clip gives decent coverage.

Bullets hammer the hotel room's left and right walls simultaneously.

Two coordinated gunmen.

Before the second shot I'm flinging myself to the ground, hugging the worn-out carpet's horrible canvas base like a long-lost lover. I know Deke's doing the same.

Just as I know my idiot brother is still sitting in his chair.

Maybe he's opened his mouth by now.

Without even looking, I lash my feet out and catch the flimsy plastic legs of Will's chair, yanking one towards me and the other away. The spindly plastic collapses, tumbling Will to the ground. He hasn't even had the time to shout his outrage about someone daring to shoot at a Real American like him before he thuds into the floor, chunky arms and legs and jowls rippling down as bullets punch the air above us.

If Will can't take that as a subtle hint to *get down and stay down*, he deserves to get shot.

Meanwhile, I'm slithering across the floor to the bed. It sounds like an angry god of thunder's pitched his tent right outside the hotel room, way too loud for only two gunmen.

They must be hitting the other room as well. Blow everything to hamburger and let the janitor Shop-Vac us up.

I use my fingers and toes to squirm right up against the bed, scraping my cheek on the carpet and trying not to choke on decades of feet and drugs and blood and who-knows-what that's soaked into the fibers. The unmistakable stink of gunfire doesn't help, especially when I don't have any kind of weapon.

Will hasn't stopped screaming. Has he even taken a breath? Is he hit? Do I need to slither back and wrap him up?

No—stop that.

Me worrying about Will will get us all killed. He can't be my dumbass brother right now. He needs to be just another bystander, an innocent cowed into obedience while Deke and I break into the vault or snip the wires, not the older brother who'd pissed me off every day since I'd realized he thought I was a pain in his ass. I can't even tell what kind of scream it is through the bombardment.

Seconds later the barrage stops.

Forget him.

I glance up. The abused mattress sags right above my head, like there's a heavy weight on top of it. Blown-out holes show where bullets punched through the mattress, and weightless tufts of abused memory foam drift through the air over my head.

I close my eyes and strain to sift sounds through Will's panicked screams.

The question is, how much collateral damage are the intruders willing to inflict? Throw a bundle of dynamite in the room and we're all greasy smoke—but that takes out the whole hotel. No city'll ignore that. Not even Detroit. A thud means a grenade, and the bed's flimsy wooden base isn't going to do anything against that, but a grenade means structural damage, but if I'm lucky they'll—

The door to the parking lot explodes.

The visiting god of thunder punches the air, sudden pressure squeezing my eardrums and pushing me into the floor. Light hammers my closed eyelids, and I feel splinters of destroyed door patter down on my back.

Just as I'd hoped.

My arm flashes up, body following as my hand snatches the stock of the AA-12 I'd set up there, eyes narrowing as I kneel and bring the weapon hard into my shoulder, thumbing the safety right as a cautious hand reaches around the door, holding a little black metallic lump.

I squeeze the trigger.

Thor hammers my shoulder. My own thunder rips the air.

The hand goes away.

No, the owner doesn't retreat. The hand is gone, a haze of bloody mist, ripping a scream from the victim.

I launch myself to my feet, hurtling myself forward just in time to see another dark green figure step into view.

I fire.

The AA-12 smashes into me. That shoulder's going to bruise like crazy. Gunsmoke fills my nose.

The figure crumples.

He wasn't using his head anyway. At least, not the front half.

I dash forward, hugging the wall separating Will's room from ours. Every step exposes more of the parking lot, the macadam gold-cast in the sun's dying rays. It's the time of day when innocent children are out getting their last round of kickball or tag or whatever it is they play these days, before their parents summon them in for baths and bed. The gunmen might not care how many walls their rounds punch through, or whose flesh they finally end up in, but I do. The rounds in this shotgun don't travel far, but they rip flesh from bone. The rotting wooden fence separating the parking lot from whatever's on the other side isn't going to stop a harsh sneeze, let alone these vicious loads.

That monster black SUV at the back of the lot, a Ford Behemoth or something—that wasn't there when we arrived.

And someone's leaning around the front.

I dance back two steps before flinging myself to the ground right under the window.

Bullets fill the space where I'd been, then start punching through the wall right at chest level as the gunman works his way back.

Will is shouting behind me.

A thunderous blast of gunfire erupts somewhere really close.

I can see only a narrow slice of parking lot.

Someone stumbles backwards through it, blood dripping from his head.

I grin. Deke must have slithered back to our room to grab a weapon.

If only Will would quit screaming that someone was still alive in here, we'd take care of this.

The hurt gunman is the distraction I need.

I roll to my knees. The decrepit blackout curtain has picked up a full set of bullet holes, but they're too small to quickly peer through. I know where the Ford Exorbitant is, though, and only need half a second to line up one of the curtain's old tears with the gunman hiding behind its bumper. I bring the AA-12 back up.

This is gonna hurt.

Him worse than me, yes. But I've got to live with my pains.

I lower the shotgun's aim a fraction of an inch.

Squeeze and hold the trigger for half a breath, exchanging two blasts for a double blow against my shoulder.

The split second the shotgun blasts through the curtain I'm flat against the carpet, a full-body hug. Even if I hit the gunman, someone's going to spray where I was with bullets.

There's an old-fashioned radiator under the window, squared-off ovals of iron pipe. I slide over, trying to take advantage of that narrow shield. Drywall and brick dust obscure my vision and tickle my throat. My lungs want to cough it all out, but there's no time. My heart's thunder isn't as loud as the shotgun's, but my vision quivers in time with it.

More gunfire from next door.

Across the parking lot, someone screams.

The curtain above me flutters, but only from the muggy breeze through the shattered window.

Either they're all down, or they're playing possum to lure me out.

Staying here until someone flings a bundle of dynamite into my lap isn't a choice. I draw myself to my feet, pull the shotgun into my protesting shoulder joint, and advance towards the door. Each step exposes another slice of parking lot. I really hope old guy who'd been sitting in front of a room isn't lying dead out there. Another step exposes a prone foot, I'm pretty sure it's from the man I shot in the head but I have to resist the urge to fire a round to make sure it's not a trick even though lying in front of the door would be a pretty stupid trick. At least Will's shut his mouth, but the guy I tried to double-tap's still shrieking nails into my ears.

That'll teach me to miss.

I barely catch a short, sharp whistle from outside. I ease my finger on the trigger as a tall figure darts across my field of view.

Deke.

Running for the shelter of a car.

We're advancing.

I give him two seconds to reach cover, then hurtle after him.

The sight of Deke crouching against our rented SUV eases my breathing. We wear wireless earpieces and throat mics on the job. I'd know if something happened to him—don't laugh, I would—but it's a lot easier to work together when you're, you know, *together*.

Best of all, he's carrying my MP-7. It's small enough to fit under a trench coat, even with the stock, but it should come in a box labeled "Death Hose" and has a world less recoil than this damn AA-12.

We've practiced this sort of advance I don't know how many times. I sink to a crouch beside him but facing the opposite way, covering my half of the parking lot. I'd shot two people, but there's three bodies sprawled out there, plus the half-headed man I dropped right outside the doorway.

Nobody moves.

I cast half an eye back at Deke. He's holding himself still.

My field of vision is clear.

Deke's MP-7 barks.

A thud.

Will has stopped screaming, but one of the gunmen is still shrieking.

A still breath.

Another.

I deliberately relax my shoulders, awaiting the next barrage.

44

The hotel had been painted and braced against the decrepit indignities of old age, and here we've violated its whole backside. Shattered windows line the tilted cement sidewalk—not only ours; incompetent stray shots blew out the neighbors as well. The geriatric brick walls are cratered and punctured, filling the air with century-old brick dust and probably a collection of mold spores safely tucked away since World War Two. The August air's warm and humid enough to sprout them. The bystanders are long gone. The geezer who'd been sitting out in front of his room has vanished, hopefully to somewhere with more than a couple brick walls between us.

Whoever'd painted and scrubbed up this place? We've destroyed their aspirations.

The shiny new rental SUV we're hiding behind? That's another vehicle we're not getting the security deposit back on.

It's a good thing we never use our own credit cards.

Not that anyone would give me a credit card, but still.

Ideally we'd wait for the surviving gunmen to move and pick them off, but Eight Mile road is a main cross-Detroit boulevard. My ringing ears can pick out the hoot of air brakes and the growl of expensive engines even with the two-story hotel in the way. The locals might ignore the occasional bark of gunfire, but these idiot gunmen must have gone through a hundred rounds in thirty seconds. And there's no way to mistake automatic shotgun fire for anything else.

The cops are on their way, following the gunsmoke rising through the humid heat. If they come from the east, the setting sun will even backlight the plume for them.

And all that screaming is abrading my nerves. Near the gunmen's shiny black Ford Behemoth at the back of the crumbling asphalt lot, one of the gunmen shrieks in agony. Probably literal mortal agony.

When nobody shoots at us for fifteen seconds, I cover Deke so he can scurry up to the Behemoth. He covers me while I search around the surrounding cars.

Deke and I are damned lucky. We killed five gunmen who had the drop on us. The sixth is lying on the ground by the Behemoth.

The gunman's jeans and heavy flannel shirt are totally wrong for the hundred-degree hundred-percent-humidity Detroit summer, but I can see the bulk of a bulletproof vest beneath the shirt. He'd stand out on the street, but more in a *what an idiot* way as opposed to *look at the gunbunny*. An AR-15 lies a couple feet away, close enough to grab if he wasn't clutching his blood-drenched thigh and writhing like a snake with a tire tread across its middle.

I'd fired two shotgun shells at him, aiming through a tiny slit in the blackout curtain. I should be impressed that I hit him even once.

Deke kicks the AR-15 away.

The clatter draws the gunman's attention. His eyes roll towards us and he draws a shuddering breath. "Please," he groans.

I hand Deke the AA-12. He puts the MP-7 in my hand. The familiar grip fits right into my palm and triggers an ache. Firing that shotgun pounded bruises right into my spine.

"Please what?" Deke sets the AA-12 into his shoulder, gaze scanning the parking lot.

"Ambulance," he groans.

"You ambush us and want help?" I snarl.

Behind me, footsteps scuff the asphalt.

I whirl, MP-7 set in my shoulder.

Will has gotten himself together. His face is still blanched and red, his hair pointing every which way, but he's on his feet. The idiot grabbed not one but two .38 semi-autos from the stash and clutches one in each hand. In Deke's sweats and T-shirt he looks straight from Quentin Tarantino Central Casting.

I roll my eyes and turn back to our prisoner.

The MP-7's shoulder stock is a little smaller than the AA-12's. The sting at its touch tells me that whole shoulder's going to be purple tomorrow.

"There's no time." Deke's voice is personified indifference. He practices that voice like he practices karate and shooting. "The police are on their way. Answer everything, quickly, and we'll see you get help. Who do you work for?"

The man grits his teeth.

"Ayaka?" I snarl.

He squeezes his eyes shut and nods.

Will is coming up behind me. He has both pistols raised and is scanning the parking lot like a fearful child in his first funhouse.

"You're part of her gig at the trainyard," Deke says.

He nods again, frantically.

I swallow bile. This little shit is part of the crew that murdered Father.

My heart hammers almost as hard as when this scrawny ass was shooting at me. "Tell me what she's doing."

The scrawny gunman's gaze meets mine. "Betray Ayaka?" His chin shakes back and forth like a kid denying he's got his hand in his little sister's bag of Halloween candy. "Not…a chance."

I lean my head forward to loom over him more. My hand moves of its own volition, arranging the pistol so he's looking straight down the black hole of the barrel. "Do you have any idea what we can do to you?"

The guy grimaces. "You're Beaks," he coughs out. "The worst you'll do is shoot me."

I grit my teeth in frustration.

The hell of it is, he's right.

Ayaka would torture him for spilling his guts.

The police are on their way.

We have no time.

For prisoners. Or anyone.

I squeeze the trigger.

45

"Billie!" Will shouts. "What the fuck!"

I turn from the dead man. The gunsmoke is clearing, but the residue is soaking into my fresh sweat. I had a shower not two hours ago and I'm *already* filthy. "What?"

"You just—" He tries to point at the gunman's body with the tidy red pit of blood above and between his eyes, but only waggles his .38. "He—he was helpless!"

"He helped kill Father." I lower my automatic and start back towards the hotel room.

"You can't just—"

Deke cuts him off. "The police are on their way." His eyes don't leave Will. "Beaks, wheels. I'll get our gear. And you?" His voice tightens. "That man was more afraid of Ayaka than of your sister holding a gun in his face. Ayaka is a monster. Getting her will be bloody and violent and awful. Want off this train? Wait here for the cops and tell them how your little sister shot that man. The FBI already knows about her, so you're not betraying her. Or you can help me load up the gear and get her out of here before the police arrive."

The look on Will's face screams his internal confusion. The pulse throbbing in his forehead and his gaping jaw show his realization that the foundations of his world have shifted like the San Andreas Fault. A drop of sweat carries drywall dust into his eye and he doesn't even blink.

I know that feeling. I had it once before.

As I was finishing my thesis during a coveted internship at the Large Hadron Collider, Doctor Kamp—my advisor—tried to steal my work, then tried to kill me when I caught him at it. The in-your-face revelation that the world isn't the soft, cozy place you always thought it was literally shatters your soul. I look at Will's face and remember the hollowness of my guts and how my thoughts ground to a painful halt. *Your father is a drunk* doesn't come close to preparing you for *people are soft and easily destroyed and someone you thought harmless will commit murder because it's convenient.*

When it happened to me, I'd had a whole six minutes and twenty-one seconds to reassemble myself and shut the collider down before it blew. No pressure.

The cops will arrive in much less than that.

Probably in full-on SWAT mode.

Will's face makes me feel horrible, and helpless, and weak.

And I don't have time to nurse him through a meltdown.

My heart can bleed all it wants, so long as we *move*.

I grit my teeth, cock my ears for sirens, and scan the parking lot.

Forget our rented SUV. The half-dozen bullet holes, including a couple big ones from the shotgun, might not disable it, but every rental car has a GPS tracker and the police would be right on us. Plus, Ayaka's team had unfettered access to it for who knows how long. They could have left all sorts of nasty presents. The gunmen's Behemoth, the same. There's a couple of little two-doors along the rotting fence, the sort of things the car dealer issues you when you graduate from college and get your first set of Lower Middle Class Slavery Shackles—er, I mean, *paycheck*. Even if they're not tracked, they won't hold our gear. We need something with a trunk—not the four-door pickup, the back's open and it's new enough to have its own tracker.

There, at the end.

That Cadillac's a wreck, but even at this distance the tires look excellent.

I don't have the strength to spare a glance at Will as I trot past him into the hotel room. Deke is stuffing gear into the duffel bags as quickly as he can without damaging anything, but I snatch a little gray pouch of tools from the mess and run back out to my target, three tons of authentic Detroit steel.

The Cadillac's chrome is corroded almost entirely away. The paint that survived terminal rust was once fire engine red, but faded from decades of exposure. Two bungee cords hold the trunk shut. Another anchors the hood. The passenger side windshield wiper is a stubby bladeless stick.

Cheating with the Lock-Release gun makes quick work of the driver's door.

The bench seat is newer than the body, but I don't have time to enjoy the plushness. I scrape a knife across the old wires under the dash and expose the copper. A touch. A spark.

The engine growls like some ancient road-beast prophesied to eat the world at its rising.

The brand-new MP3 player artlessly wedged into the dash lights up. A single skull-pounding beat erupts from a trunk speaker before I can slap the button to turn it off.

Whoever owns this car wanted it to look like crap and run like a demon.

I stomp the clutch and yank the shift into gear.

Deke's got the first bag out the door when I pull up. His eyebrows almost disappear into his hair.

I put the car in park and scurry out to pop the trunk so Deke can load. My biceps quiver to pull the bungees up. They're not that tough, but my post-combat shakes are starting to kick in. I need to get some water and calories in me and arrange a few minutes of stillness.

Will appears behind Deke.

He's got the other two duffel bags, one slung over each shoulder.

My heart breaks, just a little.

The idiot should have stayed for the cops. He should have walked to the bus station, called Uncle Carl or even Uncle Tommy for a ride home, gone to the nearest cathedral to confess his sins.

Anything, really, but stay with me.

Will has decided to destroy the person he was this morning.

And there's no way I can explain it to him, any more than I could have explained to my younger self what staying to fight my advisor would mean. After that horrible night, even if I'd had absolute proof that my advisor had tried to kill me, proof that would have convinced the police and Interpol and the CIA, what I did to that poor LHC aborted my career in astrophysics.

It's a fate I wouldn't wish on anyone. Not even my brother.

William Salton might return to Malacaster and the sugar factory.

He'll be the least innocent person there.

And I can only watch.

The bungee surrenders. The lid groans up.

The trunk's already full.

I blink.

There's a couple of AR-15s, magazines in place, just sitting there.

Right next to eight bricks of white powder wrapped in clear heavy plastic.

46

A classic Detroit Road Beast, with a trunk full of coke or heroin or whatever. We're living the cliché.

I don't handle drugs. Not only is the law brutal to traffickers, but drugs are yet another boot rich bastards use on the face of the poor. Folks escape an unbearable system any way they can, then the monsters who make that system unbearable get to lock them up and enslave them.

There's a scrap of cloth jammed up against one tirewell. I tug it out—an old T-shirt. That'll do. I wrap it around my hands as makeshift gloves and start flinging bricks across the potholed macadam.

I'd rather set the drugs on fire to keep the cops from putting them back on the street, but we have no damn time.

The AR-15s might come in useful, but the weapons we purchased are guaranteed clean and anything in this ride is almost guaranteed dirty. I don't throw them like the drugs, but haul them out so Deke can shove his duffel into the vacated trunk.

The good news is, these old Caddys have trunks big enough to stick a Subaru in. The bag's clank as it lands almost echoes.

Deke grabs another duffel bag from Will and crams it in as I yank the AR-15's magazines. Maybe I just killed a bunch of people, but I'm not leaving automatic rifles lying around loaded where some kid could pick them up.

Deke slams the trunk and stretches a bungee down. "Will. Back seat. Beaks. Drive."

I toss the two magazines into the back seat and slide into the driver's seat. My hair brushes the ceiling, triggering a shower of dust. The cloth head liner has been cut away, exposing the Caddy's metal roof and lingering shreds of crumbling foam padding still held up there by last century's glue. Scratches over the front seat show where someone tried to scrape the padding clean but couldn't get it all.

Deke has the trunk shut and is in the passenger seat pulling the door shut before Will has himself in the back seat. My brother's moving like a zombie. I adjust the mirrors as he gets his feet in. His door isn't even shut when I stomp the clutch and roll us out.

The rear-view mirror shows spent gunfire and shattered glass and scattered bodies. The hotel was already skirting survival. It probably won't even be able to reopen after this. Ayaka's goons destroyed some desperate person's last-ditch livelihood.

Maybe the cops will decide this is all a drug buy gone wrong. All that coke will probably give them a thrill.

The Caddy wants to eat the road—the trans is geared for accelerating quickly and swilling gasoline even faster. My pounding heart demands I unleash the motor and rocket away, but we need to be inconspicuous. The fence at the back of the parking lot might have cut down on witnesses, but back out on Eight Mile there's plenty of eyes. I merge into the evening traffic like an infirm grandmother who's afraid of breaking ten thousand miles on her twenty-year-old sedan.

I flip down the sun visor to shade my eyes from the setting sun. The overheated muggy air streaming through the open windows carries exhaust and dust. The Roadbeast predates air conditioning. It doesn't even have seat belts.

In the rear-view mirror, distant red and blue lights approach.

I watch as the hotel recedes behind us.

The cop cars stop at the hotel.

I let out a hard breath. My chest hurts, and not just from the shotgun.

Next to me, Deke's eyes are closed. He's clearly concentrating on his own breath. The cross-shaped scar on his cheek is flushed, and his dripping sweat leaves trails through the dust glued to his skin. When you think "firefight" you think about bullets and blood, but nobody tells you how dirty you get even when you escape unscathed.

We get maybe thirty seconds of silence before Will leans forward. "What. The. Literal. Fuck. Was that?"

I say, "That was Ayaka's people trying to kill us."

Will snarls, "How did they find us?"

I'm pretty sure Will isn't angry about how they found us. He's not angry that someone tried to kill him. He's probably not even sure what he's angry about.

I remember that anger all too well, though.

I was angry that my world had come apart.

"Someone told her," I say.

"Skald wouldn't do that!" Will snaps.

"Didn't have to be him," I say.

"Well, who then?"

I say, "My money's on the FBI."

Will coughs. "They weren't no FBI."

"Agent Tan gave me that video because he couldn't do anything," I say. "I suspect Ayaka has her fingers in his agency. We know the FBI has cameras in the switchyard. Someone sent Ayaka our faces and the rental's license plate."

"So they knew it's a rental, so what?" Will says.

The right lane where we're rolling is all red lights ahead, but a little disposable two-door just passed me on the left and there's lots of room behind it. I hit the blinker. There's an Audi coming up fast from behind in that second lane, but there's plenty of space and it's not like I'll be cutting it off.

The Caddy eases over like a graceful whale.

Next to me, Deke's eyes are still closed. He's breathing and thinking. If Will gets out of hand Deke'll jump in I'm sure, but he's my brother and my problem.

"Rentals carry GPS trackers." The little Audi coming up from behind races up straight to my bumper. *Go ahead, hit us. You'll bounce into the median and the Roadbeast won't even notice.* "Given the plate, she'd have a fix on our car in an hour. Another hour to assemble a strike team. Hell, we had lots of time, she was slow."

"But why?" Will demands. "This crazy bitch isn't shooting everyone who shows up at the switchyard, is she?"

Deke turns to face Will. The bench seat is so wide he can easily get a knee up without coming close to touching me. "You need to understand something." His voice is raised just enough to penetrate the road noise and the wind pouring through the open windows. "Your sister is dangerous. The FBI knows she's dangerous."

In my peripheral vision I see Will's mouth open.

Deke rolls right over him. "You need to think about what happened. Five men, armed with military-grade automatic weapons, opened fire on us through a hotel room window. We had no warning. She was on the ground before the second bullet hit. She dragged your pasty ass down after her. And if she hadn't?" Deke leans an inch towards Will. "You would be dead."

Will's jaw slams shut.

"All five of those men are dead, and she doesn't have a scratch." Deke's voice gets flat. "Think about the kind of person who can pull that off. Especially when you speak to her."

"She's—"

"I am sick of your feeble whining and complaining," Deke snaps. "So you don't get along? So you haven't seen her in years? You got shit to work out? Fine. Later. Right now, you will treat her with respect or I will tie you up in a little box and ship you off to people who make Ayaka look like the Cookie Monster."

Will says, "You got no right—"

"This isn't about right!" Deke thunders. "This is about life and death. This is about your father being murdered. Are you going to put your petty little shit away until we nail Ayaka? Or do I put one of those .38s up your ass and pull the trigger myself?"

I still myself, focusing on the road ahead. The entitled Audi behind me switches to the third lane without signaling and roars ahead a few yards, only to be righteously cut off by a lumbering overloaded pickup.

Will mumbles something.

"What was that?" Deke says.

"Fine!" Will snarls.

"I'll hold you to that," Deke says. "You should know that I love Beaks. Very much. I've killed to protect her. She'd be pretty pissed if I had to kill her brother to save her life, but she's worth it."

Will's face turns a little red.

Eight Mile Road goes on forever, but we don't dare drive it that far. Once we leave the hood and head into the suburbs, a cop will pull over the rusty Roadbeast on general principles. It doesn't even *have* seat belts. And we're dangerously close to Southfield.

Nobody says anything while I turn around and head back the other way.

"So what now?" Will finally says.

Deke draws a deep breath. "We need food. First we stop for carryout and switch license plates with some other clunker. We find a place on a side street to park and eat. You finish telling me all the details. We make our plan. And then…" His lips quirk up at me. "Then we get to the fun bit."

Only one phrase comes after *the fun bit*. I try to hide my answering smile.

"The fun bit?" Will says.

Deke and I answer in cheerful chanting chorus, "We're gonna rob the Walmart!"

47

The Roadbeast's decaying foam head liner creates a constant rain of fifty-year-old dust, so we park by an open field that had once been a row of houses and sit on the curb, in the shade of a broad-limbed maple that had graced the front yard of a now-bulldozed home. The sun's dancing with the treetops and an evening breeze promises cooler air tonight. It's quiet enough that I can hear kids playing on the next street over. Smoke from someone's unseen backyard grill sends out the delectable aroma of cooking pork, and the smell seems to carry barely audible Motown rhythms with it.

Over a bucket of steaming hot beer-breaded cod and a mountain of fresh-cut crinkle fries from the you-buy-we-fry, Will tells Deke his Switchyard Saga. Will has no idea how to debrief; he jumps forwards and backwards, one minute talking about the cool service house where Skald hangs out in his spare time and the next falling back to the old lady in the yardhouse. I focus on peeling batter to expose the succulent fish beneath. I eye the fresh-cut fries, but Deke says they didn't have any malt vinegar so I pass.

Yes, Detroit's city administration is kind of a wreck. But the food and the people are amazing.

When Will winds down I tell my own saga—in chronological order, thank you very much. I include the unmanly parts Will skipped, like how Skald bawled in Will's arms. Will busies himself with fries every time those details come up.

It's not that I want to embarrass my brother. Details are important.

Embarrassing Will is merely like malt vinegar on fries.

Will keeps downing fried fish like he hasn't eaten in days. Maybe he hasn't; Father's death and funeral might have put him off his feed. And nothing builds an appetite like the first time the other guy sprays bullets at your face and misses.

Deke and I quickly sketch out a plan, constantly interrupting each other. A bystander might think we're being rude, but my Deke and I have figured out so many incursions and infiltrations together that two words can carry a speech.

When our discussion slows, there's only a couple pieces of fish left in the bucket. Half the fries remain despite Will's valiant efforts. We stick the leftovers in the back seat and head for the Walmart on Van Dyke, a couple miles over the Detroit border into Warren.

I never feel bad about using bogus credit cards at Walmart. They skirt the edge of employment law in the name of treating employees horribly. Yeah, the company might bring the city tax dollars, but the government pays a whole bunch more in welfare for those workers.

Really, shafting them is a moral obligation.

Plus, the merchandise is shoddy crap built in a forgotten pesthole by the lowest bidder. I don't feel a twinge about disposing of it after a gig.

Deke waits in the car—we're not leaving the armory in our trunk unguarded. Will keeps wanting to ask questions, but I tell him not in public and dispatch him for item after item. Despite my best efforts, we only manage to do about six hundred dollars in damage. All the gear fits easily into the Caddy's back seat with Will, leaving room for only a clan of refugees or perhaps a pony. Deke hasn't been able to get the train schedule, so I grab one of the new burner phones. I'd like to roll up the window to cut down the road noise, but the window crank spins without even making a click or grinding noise. Who knows if this thing even has a window inside the door anymore? I resign myself to raising my voice over the wind and dial.

Sister Silence answers on the second ring, in her flat sleepy tone. "Hello."

"Beaks," I say.

"Hi! How are you doing?" Sister Silence is usually happy to hear from me. She might sound exhausted, or a little grumpy.

But she sounds…solicitous?

Unease shivers in my spine.

That's ridiculous. Sister Silence is as solid as they come. "I'm fine," I say. "Listen, I—"

"Before you ask," Sister Silence interrupts. "I'm still poking into William Salton, trying to figure out where that money went." She sounds weirdly hesitant.

Something's wrong.

I keep my voice confident. "You can find it."

"That's not it." Even through the road noise, I hear her deep breath. Unease tickles my gut. "I don't poke my nose anywhere it's not paid to go, and I never snoop into my clients' lives."

"What's going on?" I say.

The words spill out. "You mentioned one, but I've found two children."

I stop. *Oh.*

She's realized she's investigating my father, and it's pushing right up against her ethics. A trustworthy information dealer never digs deep into her clients.

"I know," I say. "It's okay. I—"

She sighs with relief.

I swallow. "I probably should have said something."

"Next time, yeah, I'd appreciate it."

I flinch. "There won't be a next time."

"I'm sorry," she says. "That was tacky, I mean…you know."

She doesn't want to spell everything out on mobile phone. "Yeah. I get it."

"I'm guessing…" Sister Silence pauses. "You called in a favor about this guy. I'm guessing this trip and fall isn't the whole story?"

I pause, but Sister Silence could have sold Deke and I out to the highest bidder long ago. "Far from it."

She holds quiet for a second. "That favor? You helped my family. You need my help, you call."

I can't help smiling. "Thanks, sweetie."

"Don't go telling everyone," she says. "You'll ruin my reputation for hard bargaining."

My laugh is a little bitter, but honest. "Deal."

"So," Sister Silence says in her usual chipper tone, "what can I dig up for you today?"

"There's a Mound Switchyard in Detroit," I say. "I'm told most nights a train comes through at two AM. Can you verify?"

"That's it?" I hear a flurry of typing—Sister Silence must use one of those keyboards with mechanical springs. "That's not even confidential."

"Sorry," I say. "I can't find it on the phone."

"No worries, darling. On *this* case, consider me your Duck Duck Go." More keys clatter. "There's no switchyard…here's a service yard?"

I vaguely remember those words. "Yeah, that's it."

A keyboard clatters. "It's on a spur."

"What's that?"

"A little dead-end track off the main line. Probably meant for factory deliveries. They'll do minor repairs there."

I nod. "Any deliveries at two AM?"

Sister Silence says, "Star Metals at four-fifteen and…yeah, two eleven AM, Monday through Friday morning. From Blount Island, Florida, up to…that's odd."

My breath catches. "Odd?"

"The data doesn't match." Sister Silence's keyboard rattles like a machine gun. I have no idea how she types so fast. "The Star Metals dock is not approved for nighttime delivery, as of a week ago. Those trains shouldn't be going there. Plus, boxcars slated to go over there contain assembled new cars. The train arrives at the Mount Elliot yard at one-thirty AM. Looks like they get unloaded for the GM plant there. The last five cars get put on a pup engine and hauled down to Star Metals."

I say "Okay" to let her know I'm paying attention.

"Finished cars, going to a metals plant? Why? And…they wait an hour and return." The fusillade of typing stops. "I don't know how long it takes to unload six boxcars of finished cars, but I think the answer's probably 'longer than an hour.'"

My spine tingles. "There's something there."

Sister Silence resumes typing. "Oh, this is delightful. The boxcars aren't unloaded. They're taken to the metals plant, sit for an hour, brought back, and attached to the train again?"

A feral smile stretches my cheeks. "That metals plant, is it anywhere near the switchya—uh, service yard?"

"A couple hundred yards past, looks like."

"It never makes it to the factory," I say. "It stops in the service yard."

"Let me check something." The phone goes silent for fifteen seconds. "The Mount Elliot substation's really for the GM plant. It's wide open. And…" They keyboard clatters anew. "It looks like GM security patrols it."

"Whatever they're doing," I say, "they don't want witnesses."

Behind me, Will leans forward and says something.

I shake my head and put my finger in my free ear. "So we have an officially purposeless side trip to a factory."

"Charming, isn't it? According to the private national logistics database, that's what's been happening."

I blink. "Isn't there a public schedule?"

Sister Silence laughs. "Where's the fun in that, darling? Besides," and her voice grows serious, "this is the data on where the trains really go. The public schedules don't show this little trip."

Deke eases the Caddy to a stop at a red light.

I say, "My understanding—" The road noise has stopped for a moment, and I don't want to shout this to the sneering suit in the brand-new Lexus next to me, so I lower my voice. "My understanding is, there's fines and stuff for messing with train schedules."

"Oh, believe it, darling. The NHTSA will put your tender morsels on a plate and serve them to you."

"If the train stops…" I ponder. "Who could stop it? How could they get away with it?"

"This is why you're my favorite customer," Sister Silence says. "I mean, aside from that bit where you helped me out. You ask the bestest questions."

I can't help smiling. "Happy to oblige."

"I don't have an answer, but I'll dig one up."

"Wonderful." If it's old fashioned cash-in-hand bribery she won't find a thing, but these days almost everything leaves electronic spoor. And nobody can find those leavings like Sister Silence. "Let me know."

"This number?"

"For now."

"Stay in touch, darling."

"I will, sweetie."

"And Beaks?" Sister Silence's voice hardens. "Whoever they are? Hit them hard."

"Planning to," I say.

Right after my nap.

48

No, I don't really nap. We spend a few hours in a dismal Downriver motel, though, and I finally have time to stretch. My legs won't quite sink into full splits—the last couple days have my muscles nineteen kinds of jacked up. The discipline of pulling my muscles until they burn and ache soothes me. Will lies down and closes his eyes, surprisingly without complaint, and a few minutes later he's snoring off the adrenaline jag.

Deke and I select tonight's equipment, then I catch a couple hours of shut-eye myself, not deeply asleep but solidly resting, fingers intertwined with Deke's.

It's gonna be a long night.

At midnight, we're off to the graveyard.

The sun went down a few hours ago, but the air's barely thinned from "rabidly muggy" to "ferally muggy." It's still pushing ninety degrees, and sweat glues my dark green cotton shirt to my skin. We pitched the dead bucket of fish and chips back at the no-tell motel, but the aroma of fried everything still wafts through the Roadbeast. The sky is clear, but ambient light from downtown and the suburbs blots out the stars. The road seems to run into the darkness towards the glittering cylindrical columns of downtown's Renaissance Center. The city's flagship office towers wear gaudy hoops of neon blue. Here, though, the only light comes from the brilliantly illuminated but grimly fenced Detroit

Detention Center. In moments, the Roadbeast grumbles across two sets of train tracks and leaves the jail's lights behind to cross into cemetery darkness.

The Sacred Heart of Saint Mary Cemetery runs for a good half mile along Mound Road, right next to the DDC—very convenient for the prison-industrial complex. Rows of nineteenth-century marble tombstones gleam like teeth in the darkness. The streetlights along Mound are dark; the city's either cut the power to save money, or nepotism and corruption exhausted their comprehensive federally-backed lighting renovations before they got this far. Mound Road is a boulevard down here, three unmarked lanes of cratered concrete each way separated by a stretch of weedy grass broad enough for ten more lanes.

Most of the homes opposite the cemetery are dark. I suspect a whole bunch of them don't have electricity. An insomniac's flickering television casts a forlorn square of light.

At McNichols Road I pull a quick right and immediately pull over, pushing the button to kill the Caddy's headlights. The forward-thinking drug dealer who previously owned the Roadbeast removed the interior light, so Deke hops right out. I can make out the cemetery entrance, a tidy brick arch with an iron gateway to protect the dead from the living.

Deke defeats the gate padlock in less than a minute. I take my foot off the brake and let the Caddy idle between the gates. In the rear-view mirror, I see Deke's shadowed shape swing the gates together before he rejoins us.

I'm calmer than I've felt since I learned of Father's death. Yes, we're about to do something ugly and brutal, but it's familiar. I don't know how to mourn Father. Impending vengeance sends a weirdly soothing rattle in my veins.

The cemetery road's in better shape than Mound Road, probably because it doesn't have corporate tractor-trailers hammering it twelve hours a day at taxpayer expense. Ambient light barely exposes the road. With every yard we pass my eyes adapt further to the darkness.

Behind me, Will draws in a nervous breath.

"Relax," I say. "We're not going far."

"I am relaxed," Will mutters.

I bite back my reply. This isn't the time to argue.

Like the satellite map says, the road makes a couple sharp turns but keeps heading up towards the glaring block of the DDC.

I stop the Roadbeast in deep shadows short of the circle of light marking the caretaker's building at the cemetery entrance. The engine purrs and silences itself.

Deke cracks his door. "Everybody out."

Standing feels good. Merely moving sends a little thrill down my spine all the way to my feet. Maybe revenge is a dish best served cold, but I'm pretty sure it's gonna be as tasty with a side of hot lead.

The loudest noise is the Roadbeast's back door squeaking through the rust as Will climbs out. I grimace. This car should be a classic. It needs an owner who would cherish it. Instead, it had drug dealers who probably wanted it to rust out…and us.

"Will," Deke says. "You remember the plan."

"Yes," he grumbles. "I take the car around and wait past that club we passed."

"Pandora's Boxx," Deke says. "Not too close."

"Far enough past that folks think I'm waiting, not close enough that people ask me if I want *company*." I can hear Will's grimace. I remember Father cursing men who were so useless they paid for "company," and it sounds like Will picked that up.

Besides, it's pretty clear that Will has no idea what kind of *company* he'd find outside that bright purple strip club. I'd hate to have to give him a lesson in manners for dropping the six-letter F-bomb.

Maybe not "hate." But there's no time.

"If there's trouble?" Deke says.

"I go down McNichols, and park under the hamburger sign."

I pull the bungees from the trunk, lift the lid, and start slipping gear into my pockets.

"Good." Deke doesn't normally praise flunkies for remembering basic instructions; he's being gentle for my benefit. "What do you do?"

Will has all the enthusiasm of an unwilling fourth-grader picked by the teacher. "I keep the earpiece in and wait for your call."

The foamed metal body armor fits perfectly over my torso. With no advance notice, Mall somehow came up with our sizes. I don't really mind that I overpaid him this time. Don't get me wrong, I'll try to squeeze it out of him next time, but the greedy bastard deserves every penny he makes.

"You stay awake," Deke says.

"I got that jumbo coffee when we filled up," Will says.

"That'll hold you a couple hours," Deke says. "Don't get out of the car to piss."

"What do you want me to do, get a Gatorade bottle?" Will says.

Thanks, Will. I did *not* need that image.

Deke says, "I put the empty lead additive bottle in the back seat. Use that."

"Opening's too narrow," Will says.

Maybe the car will have an electrical short and kill him right now. I can hope.

"It's plenty big enough," Deke says. "Unless they call you Tuna Can or something. When you hear us?"

"I listen," Will says.

"What for?"

"You or Billie to say 'extract.'" Will's voice picks up an annoyed singsong. "And you want me to not say anything while you're there, even if it's important."

"Good," Deke says. "When we ask for extraction?"

"Start the car. Pull up that road right here to the mission."

"And if we ask for the backup location?"

"Hump on around to that Star Machinery place on Nevada."

"And if not that?"

"Listen for you to tell me where to pick you up."

My fingers double-check the MP-7's safety without troubling my eyes.

"Good," Deke says. "And while you're waiting?"

Will sighs. "No radio."

"Turn down your phone screen."

Will extracts his cheap cellphone from a pocket, scrunches up his face, and fumbles. I resist the urge to take it away and fix it myself.

"Lower," Deke says. "There."

"I can barely see it!" Will says.

"And nobody can see you," Deke says. "You're not buying or selling anything. You're not live-tweeting this. And if the cops see you sitting in a Caddy like this with a phone light on your face, they'll bust you on suspicion."

"I'm not doing anything," Will says.

I say, "You don't have to do anything. The cops can hold you for forty-eight hours on a whim. Ask me how I know, but later."

"Fine!" Will says.

"Besides, the battery will last longer with it dark," I say. "And we might be a while."

"I thought she was coming in at two?" Will says.

"We're pretty sure she is," Deke says. "But nothing starts until we decide it starts."

"Sure, sure," Will says.

I'm kind of surprised Will remembers his instructions. We drilled him earlier, but I expected everything to fall out of his brain before now.

The only question I have now is, will my pigheaded brother *follow* those instructions?

Deke starts pulling his own gear from the trunk. He leans his overlong sniper rifle against the bumper and drapes a ratty hotel blanket over it to obscure the shape. "Check your radios."

In the ultra-light foamed metal body armor and with various implements of mayhem carefully arranged in a dozen different pockets, I feel more myself than I have since I learned of Father's death. The possibility of sneaky violence is more comfortable than talking to my brother.

I turn to Will's shadow. "We're counting on you."

"You just bring me that bitch's head," Will says.

Deke and I lope into the darkness.

49

There are worse places than this switchyard to stage a hit, but I can't think of any offhand.

Our research revealed a long, narrow block. The city jail, the Detroit Detention Center, dominates the east side. The Ryan Correctional Facility looms over the west.

Centered in the north side? A freaking police station.

It's Law And Order Central.

In between sits a bunch of factories to process oil and scrap metal and unspeakably toxic sludge that gives three out of four people explosive cancer and transforms the fourth into the Joker.

South of the tracks, struggling businesses and methadone clinics line McNichols, but between them and the tracks there's street after street of tract homes full of people doing their best to get by in a city stripped of resources by racism and decades of corporate rule.

Stray bullets will cost innocent lives.

And attract police attention.

In the middle of all this, right by the tracks?

What I'd thought was a landfill was really a line of building-sized heaps of waste dirt running along the tracks, full of who knows what pre-EPA industrial chemicals. Walking on that dirt's probably enough to make you grow a tail.

Oh, and Michigan's biggest soda syrup company. Because nothing says "cola" like PCBs.

We can't drive up to the switchyard—no, *service* yard. Ayaka knows we've been there. She's had one shot at us. If we're going to approach, it needs to be quiet and slow and very, very indirect.

Besides, we don't want to start in the service yard.

Ayaka knew we'd been there today.

Did Ayaka compromise the FBI's video surveillance along with the FBI? Does she have her own surveillance? Or did she slip a few bucks to Bethel at the switchyard office and ask her to call when strangers showed up?

We can't cut through the factories. You don't keep a factory running down here without investing in security—and not "geezer with a cellphone" security either. Those people have dogs and guns and inconveniently-placed electricity.

We could cut through the neighborhood and get through or over the ten-foot chain-link fence that separates the street from the tracks, but someone would see us.

So Deke and I hop over the cemetery fence, cross the darkened road, and walk towards the jail.

No, it's not as crazy as it sounds.

There's a bottleneck at the intersection, where the train tracks come within yards of the jail's fifteen-foot outer fence. Once we're past the intersection, the fence veers away. The night swallows the rails.

And us.

50

The night is perfect, and I shouldn't be so content.

The ambient light from downtown Detroit and the distant light from the jail combine to make the railbed a ghostly gray river of pebbles next to us. Switchgrass hisses against my shins. Guns normally mean failure, but for this gig the weight of the MP-7 over my shoulder reassures me. Familiar shapes in every pocket shift with every step. The uncomfortably warm air feels bloated with humidity and pollen and a hint of industrial smoke. Did I use my sinus spray today? I must have, or I'd be sneezing like a fiend. I have the night vision goggles ready, but they won't help me yet. The ground is still cooling from its long afternoon bake, and the goggles would only show a shifting sea of switchgrass. The only sound is the distant hum of traffic on the trench freeways, blended by distance into a grumbling hum. The goggles would probably hide the clouds of dancing fireflies, too, and what's an assassination without fireflies? Instead, my feet are my eyes, testing the uneven ground at each step. Walking the rails might be faster, but more dangerous and less stealthy.

Even the pressure of the mic around my throat and the earpiece inside my ear ease my heart.

Deke's angular shadow loping along next to me speeds my pulse right back up. How many people get to work with the love of their life? Bullets and scumbags and all, I am ridiculously lucky.

He's not only had my back through Father's death, he protected my fractured soul during all the revelations and headaches afterwards. He hasn't seen the worst of how I grew up, but he's seen enough that I'm starting to think that maybe I need to tell him the rest. I've always known that he'd love me despite everything Father had been, but I still never wanted him to know how I grew up.

It's not that he needs to know.

It's that maybe I need to tell him about it.

The good, yes. And the bad.

But this moment, sneaking through the night on the way to commit mayhem right in front of a prison and a jail *and* a cop shop, is perfect.

We traipse past a little copse of scrub trees. Something much larger than a raccoon shuffles in the brush. If I pulled on the night vision goggles I'd probably see whatever poor bastard calls that scrub home.

I leave that poor bastard whatever dignity the night offers and keep walking up the tracks.

Soon enough the service yard's fence cuts across our path, rusty iron somehow glittering against the darkness. The scents of oil and old smoke are stronger, and the service yard's half-dozen pole lights silhouette abandoned, looming boxcars.

My hand reaches out and meets Deke's. We simultaneously squeeze. My heart beats a little faster. I turn to face him, and he's already coming for me as if he read my mind.

We're getting in position to deal with Ayaka. This isn't the time for passion. In this perfect silent darkness, though, surrounded by fireflies and gunmetal sky and with the distant lights of the prison and the jail shining over the heaps of weed-festooned fill dirt, I can't help clutching him close for a second as his lips unerringly find mine.

My heart thrums.

Perfection.

Deke makes a little hungry noise deep in his throat.

I can't help responding.

And two seconds later my earpiece erupts with Will saying, "Was that you, Billie?"

I'm gonna *kill* my brother.

Pressed tight against me, Deke's chest twitches with laughter.

I just might kill Deke, too.

"At the outer fence," Deke mutters. His throat mic delivers the words to me more clearly than the air. "About to split up."

This is where I start to hate the plan. I agree it's the best plan we have to achieve my goals, but I don't like it.

Deke holds me close for another precious beat, then his hands slide out from around me. I open my arms and retreat half a step, letting my hands trail down his outstretched arms until our fingers entwine in the darkness.

And part.

Deke's smile flashes at our last touch. Heedless of Will's intrusive eavesdropping he says, "See you on the other side," as he always does. Two steps back, a hop across the tracks, and he dissolves into darkness.

I slip around the fence, study the hiding places, and claim a position behind a heap of rusted-out metal crates. Kneeling, I strap the night vision goggles over my eyes and survey the yard. A tiny digital display in the corner of the goggles tells me it's 12:37 AM. We're right on time. The top-of-the-line computerized goggles, complete with digital display and built-in camera, even out the widely spaced blurs of brightness from the yard's lights while exposing the sun-heated shapes looming in the shadows.

Nobody's here yet.

No, wait—there's one human figure glowing yellow-white near the brick office building. He's got broad shoulders but a thin body, and doesn't so much walk as trudge in the wake of a flashlight. I'm pretty sure I can guess who it is, but I won't be certain until I can see him in real light. In moments he steps beneath a pole light and yes, it's Jake Skald. The poor guy looks terrified as he scans the darkness. In this day of tiny LEDs he's carrying a big old-fashioned quadruple D cell flashlight with a heavy head. It's a legal bludgeon that happens to cast light.

I don't duck. The dark green streaks across my face break up my profile, and the matte night-vison goggles pretty much absorb light.

Jake scuttles from light to light, waving away the teeming insects attracted to the illumination. The poor guy is trying to do his job, all the while knowing that at some time real monsters are going to appear and all he'll be able to do is hide. Just showing up to work is bravery. He shows no inclination to go behind any of the drums or crates or even peek beneath the rust-paralyzed boxcars.

I relax and focus on my breath. The tough pants protect my knees well enough from the gravel-studded dirt, but I have at least another hour to wait.

Skald finishes his sketchy rounds and disappears into his service house. I can imagine him huddling down in the concrete trench meant for working on a locomotive's underbelly.

At least, I hope he's there. Once Ayaka's team arrives, it'll be the only safe place.

Moments later, Deke murmurs in my earpiece that he's scaled a one-story warehouse a block west and has an overview of the service yard.

I sit and breathe, letting the night flow through me.

The trouble that arrives is completely unexpected.

51

Lurking behind the rusted-out crates of the service yard, I have to shift my legs every few minutes to keep them from going numb and prevent the countless half-buried pebbles from drilling craters into my kneecaps and shins. I move those vital inches with complete mindfulness to avoid touching the heap of scrap metal parts right next to me. I must not violate the service yard's silence. The surrounding trees and houses and the heaped spoil across the tracks absorb the city's sounds, leaving the service yard to the grumble and surge of cicadas. Mosquitoes swirl and dance in the halos of light cast by the pole lamps, and fireflies trace curves over the glistening train tracks and out in the darkness. Countless crickets creak out their mating cries. The muggy air has me sweating, but my clothes live up to their branding and breathe like crazy. I'd leave them a good review, but I can't legitimately say they're worth the money. That's the problem with fake credit cards.

The freeways are over a mile away, but even at this hour there's enough traffic to create a constant underlying hum blended from hundreds or thousands of lives. From here, it's gasoline-powered white noise.

I need to absorb the service yard's corrosion-laced tranquility.

Ayaka might not show tonight. It could be tomorrow, or the next night. But if she does, I must remain calm.

I need to look at Father's killer without rage, and act.

I recite multiplication tables, then all the characters who've appeared in the Catwoman comics this century. My legs and back keep wanting to lock up, but I tense and relax each group of muscles one after the other. If the gravel wasn't so greasy and grimy, I'd do my neglected stretching right here.

It's about one-forty when Deke says in my earpiece, "Someone's coming up to the gate. On foot."

I frown. Surely Ayaka's people didn't hike in? No, Skald had said *delivery vans*. "How many?"

"One," he says. "Wearing shorts, pants and shirt. A bag over a shoulder, but no visible weapons."

I peer over the crate at the gate. "You sure he's coming here?"

Deke says, "No idea where else they'd be going."

Will says, "What the hell would someone be doing there now?"

"That is the problem, yes," I mutter. "Unless you have information to add, stay off the channel."

Will snarls "Fine."

Half a breath later, the night vision goggles illuminate a glowing figure scuttling through the gate. He's moving too fast for a walk, with the quick short steps of someone hurrying over unfamiliar ground. The goggles show the bright glow of bare skin over his lower arms and legs as well as their face. A satchel bounces clumsily against his side.

The intruder brushes against a pool of light, and the goggles automatically shift to color vision. It's a pale-skinned woman, tidily dressed, with a purse big enough to hold half a dozen bricks of plastic explosive slung over one shoulder. She can't be twenty-five. I'll be shocked if she's twenty-two. A cricket lets out an extra loud trill and she snaps her head to look. A braid as thick as my wrist and long enough to reach the small of her back lashes the space behind her.

No pro would wear their hair long enough for someone to strangle her with.

My gut says that she's not working with Ayaka, either. Anyone Ayaka sent would have a weapon. This woman's purse is so big and bulky that it'd make a mediocre blunt instrument.

What side she's on doesn't matter. I tap my temple, telling the goggles to snap a picture.

Whoever she is, she bounces away from the insect noise and back into the shadows.

Maybe she's a buyer, waiting for Ayaka? No, she can't be. One, this is a stupid place for a buy. And I have no idea why Ayaka's stopping this train here, but this woman moves like an inexperienced mouse at the Cat Convention.

She scurries behind a heap of pipes a dozen yards away. Something clanks and clatters. A distant "Darn it!" sifts through the night.

She can't even swear properly? Ayaka would wash a pro's mouth out with napalm for that.

My gut clenches. Skald would have said if someone else worked at the yard overnight. She's an intruder.

And her skin is way too pale to be a regular visitor to these acres of grease and rust. Detroit is insanely segregated, and she's so white the streetlights make her glow against the night.

So she drove.

Parked her car outside.

And walked in.

This woman hasn't wandered into the service yard on an insomniac stroll. She made the decision to dress like an office drone and visit an industrial wasteland after midnight. Maybe she dropped something earlier today? No, she would have waited for sunrise, driven to the gate, and searched the ground.

She stumbles around in front of the pipes, limping a little to favor her right side. The silly woman twisted her ankle? What did she *think* would happen if she went traipsing through a service yard at one AM wearing sneakers?

She stops and fumbles with the massive Purse of Doom. Seconds later, a tiny spot of light pricks the darkness. The LED flashlight isn't strong enough to penetrate too far, but it'll show her where not to step.

My blood runs cold.

The flashlight's halo is moving slowly around the service yard, pausing on each object it highlights.

She *is* looking for something.

A place to hide.

The light reaches my crates.

I resist the urge to duck under cover. She won't recognize a face through the goggles and the streaks of dark green camouflage, but if I move she won't mistake me for a raccoon wearing night vision goggles.

The circle of illumination drops to the ground.

I release a breath I hadn't known I was holding.

I don't have time to inhale before she scurries towards my hiding place.

52

I'm sure that the woman with the heavy-duty braid and the Purse of Doom thinks my crates are pretty isolated. The over-bright pools of light cast by the widely spaced pole lamps make the surrounding night feel even darker and cast her capering shadow across abandoned boxcars and the rickety gantry. Behind me, the heaped waste dirt separating the service yard from the prisons is as black as an investment banker's soul and nearly as impenetrable. If she claims my spot, she'll be nearly invisible.

She can't see me, so I must have a good spot.

My pulse thrums and air rattles through my chest too quickly.

I hate it when I'm predictable. Predictability is death.

The crunch of her steps on gravel blends into the chorus of August crickets. I feel a ridiculous urge to wait until she's close enough to touch and hiss *find your own hidey-hole, bitch*. This is not a night for amateurs.

The night vision goggles say it's 1:46 AM.

Ayaka's due any moment.

I bite my lip. Maybe she *is* Ayaka's scout. Or maybe she's innocent.

Can't let her see me. Can't shoot her in the head.

Dammit.

The woman slips on the gravel and looks down at her feet.

I duck my head out of her view and subvocalize "Moving."

"Ack," Deke says.

"What?" My brother has the gall to sound annoyed.

"Will," Deke says. "Stay off the channel."

"Yes, boss," Will grumbles.

I'm gonna slap him. Wearing brass knuckles.

But for now, I bend at the waist and scuttle into the darkness, getting behind a boxcar as Little Miss Unwanted slaloms into place behind my crate.

If she's one of Ayaka's thugs, I want to be behind her. A bullet between the cervical vertebrae cures all ills. Right now, all I can do is breathe deep and slow.

Tiny flashlight clenched between her teeth, she fumbles in her bag for a couple of minutes. I practice patience.

Eventually she straightens and turns off the flashlight. I can make out the shape she raises. It's a little bigger than my MP-7. An automatic? Something metallic and brutal?

My fingers twitch with the impulse to raise my own weapon.

No—it's a camera. A big one, with a lens like a snout. Maybe she's a reporter? She's not Ayaka's scout, she's a Girl Scout.

Fucking Nancy Drew is crashing my father's memorial massacre.

I subvocalize, "Bystander has a camera. Relocating."

"Ack," Deke says.

"Ack," Will sighs.

I want Ayaka in a crossfire, preferably without shooting Nancy Drew. Shooting Nancy would make me an ass. That really only leaves one area to hide. The thought turns my stomach to acid and knots my throat. Paying close attention to how and where I place each foot, I silently sneak around the yard to the corroded gantry.

The gantry where Ayaka murdered Father.

Each step twists a knife in my guts. My brain obstinately recalls the video footage I'd studied in the hotel. For a fraction of a second, a derrick's shadow becomes my father's dangling corpse.

Only the thought that Ayaka's going to die in a hail of bullets from beneath that same gantry soothes me.

A decaying forklift right behind the gantry looks like the best cover. I can see the whole parking lot, the overgrown gate, and the gap in the fence where the two-eleven train will appear. The ivy-saturated chain-link fence is a dozen yards behind me, but I see three fallen spans I can readily escape through.

Nancy Drew's hiding between me and the platform where they'll presumably offload the train's mysterious cargo. Ayaka will have to park her delivery van and walk across a dozen barren yards of cinders and stones to get to the train. The service yard office's brick walls will absorb any of my shots that miss. So long as Nancy doesn't panic and run straight into the bloodbath, she'll be fine. Hell, she's white and we're between two prisons and a police station. By the time she hits the ground, the cops will arrive with her complimentary teddy bear and a gift certificate to have a black man of her choice beaten to death. And I wish I were joking.

One fifty-nine AM.

I spend a moment testing how well my MP-7 rests on different parts of the forklift's corpse, and finally settle on the seat's steel shell. The decaying aluminum shell wouldn't stop a softball, let alone a bullet, but it'll hide my movement. The machine pistol's flash suppressor will obscure my shots.

As much as I'd like to see Ayaka's face before shooting it, I'll be perfectly content with seeing it afterwards.

Metal clangs over by the crates I'd abandoned. I grimace, waffling for half a heartbeat before triggering the throat mic. "Deke. The photographer's clumsy. If she provides a distraction, we—" no, Deke's in charge. I draw in a deep breath. "I suggest, if she draws attention, we strike."

"In the back is the best place to shoot people," Deke says.

"What?" Will says.

"Stay off the line," Deke and I say together.

Too loud. I clamp my teeth together, trying to pull the words back before someone hears them.

The cricket chorus doesn't even pause. From the underlying susurrus of distant freeway traffic, air brakes squeal. The cloudless streetlight-poisoned sky obscures the stars.

I'm holding my breath. Relax. Breathe.

Nancy doesn't stir. My hiss wasn't loud. Maybe she didn't hear.

I need to take the camera anyway. The last thing the world needs is a photo of me kicking Ayaka's broken corpse in the skull. My personal Very Special FBI Agent would probably put it up as a new dartboard.

Not that anybody's going to question what happened. I'm sure the FBI surveillance is still in place. Even without pictures, Agent Tan would report "information received" that the dark camouflaged figures that blew the hell out of Ayaka's posse were Deke and I. They'll treat it as a fight between criminal gangs.

I force myself to relax and breathe, willing my heart to slow. I must save my adrenaline.

Insectile silence swallows the night.

At two-ten AM, the distant freeway noise picks up a new note. A deep, grumbling tone that slowly rises from the chorus. It's a noise that could take on every muscle car's kitten growls and the mewling of tractor-trailers, and win.

A train.

Getting closer.

I glance towards the gap in the fence where the train should emerge.

Deke says, "Incoming."

Across the service yard, a van's twin headlights probe through the overgrown gate.

53

The sight of the cargo van pulling into the corroded service yard threatens to ignite the greasy air in my chest. The pole lamps cast twisted shadows through wrecked boxcars and abandoned machinery, forming nebulous jagged monsters guaranteed to terrify any six-year-old. My pulse ignores my wishes and climbs right back up. My hands—are they shaking? And I'm sweating. Dammit.

I deliberately empty my lungs and draw another deep breath, willing stillness and only partially succeeding.

This isn't normal pre-gig tension. I feel like an abused mastiff straining at the end of its backyard chain, obsessed with ripping out the savage mailman's bowels. Except this mailman murdered my father. The forty-round clip in my MP-7 isn't enough. I want a forty hundred round clip, forty million, enough to supplant Ayaka's entire body with hardened steel.

"Breathe, everyone," Deke says. "Relax. This is it."

Deke doesn't just love me. He understands.

And he made his encouragement a general announcement, trying to not embarrass me in front of Will.

My daughter is going to kill you.

Damn right.

A second cargo van pulls in behind the first. The first stops quickly enough to spray gravel. The second glides to a halt on the far side of the first.

Not to worry. Deke's sniper rifle can drill a round anywhere through both vans. My little MP-7 won't punch through an engine block, but otherwise it'll punch straight through both vans and anyone inside them.

My mind serves up a sudden flash of myself as the host of a craft show, declaring *Today we're going to convert these scumbags' cargo vans into useful kitchen colanders.*

Waiting for Deke to signal is perhaps the hardest work of my life.

The closest van's back doors swing open.

Dark-suited men hop out.

My hand aches to wrench the MP-7 up and start spraying death. Instead, I carefully brace the weapon on the forklift's seat and watch the van straight down the gunsight.

The van drivers climb out, carrying small boxy weapons—probably submachine guns. An over-muscled thug with shoulders broad enough to lug oxen and a complete absence of neck emerges from the back.

Then it's a chorus line of failed linebackers in dark green. Six? Eight, maybe?

I consciously ease the petrifying tension in my shoulders. With each thug that passes my gunsight, my index finger burns to twitch inside the trigger guard. A slip, a squeeze, and it's all on.

But there's no point in shooting until Ayaka appears. She'll stand out like an evil hobbit amidst all these wannabe orcs.

"Hold your fire," Deke whispers in my ear.

I want to snap that I know that, that I'm following his instructions, but if I speak right now I'm going to scream.

The way that one thug walks—he doesn't quite limp, but his subtly lopsided gait looks really familiar. Was he on the video? No, my brain's jumping. There's no evidence. I can't condemn someone to death because of an offhand detail from a video.

I *can* condemn him for murdering Father.

As soon as Ayaka appears.

The vans stop rocking. Everybody's out. Two men with firearms, another four with empty hands.

There's no Ayaka. My heart thrums, adding to the rolling thunder of the approaching train. Is that vibration in my fingers and spine from tons and tons of grinding iron or from my own adrenaline?

Deke better be able to see her. I trigger the throat mic. "Negative on Ayaka."

"Negative here," Deke says.

Thankfully Will keeps his mouth shut. Maybe he's asleep. Maybe he's figured out that Pandora's Boxx doesn't have women performers and he's fleeing at top speed for the safety of the straight white north.

The four unarmed thugs trudge towards the tracks. They're only halfway there when a single baleful headlamp blooms into view above the tracks and the engine lumbers into the yard. It's moving slowly, maybe two miles an hour, plowing unstoppably through the night. The vibration travels up my spine and echoes in my teeth. Steel wheels click and clang. The train's groaning, clattering effort to slow only makes its mass palpable even from my perch behind the forklift.

My skull feels ready to shatter from tension and frustration. Where is she?

But I already know the answer. Agent Tan gave me the video because he couldn't touch Ayaka. She's probably compromised the FBI. During our encounter Tan had stayed outside the service yard, probably to avoid the cameras.

"She's not going to show," I mutter.

"She could be in one of the vans," Deke says.

The locomotive's noise drops to a dull earthquake. I have to fight my natural tendency to raise my voice above that fierce grumble—the throat mic will filter out the train's belly-growl. "Someone at the FBI saw us this afternoon and tipped her off." We might as well see what we can learn from the thugs' steaming corpses.

"Prep the drone," Deke says.

My stomach somehow twists even tighter. "Fine."

I raise the goggles, releasing little clouds of trapped humidity from my eye sockets. It's not nearly the relief it should be, because I'm digging in my left thigh pocket for a hard plastic case the size of a paperback best-seller. The dark plastic shell seems to absorb light, but when I flip it open the matte black drone sits cradled within white foam.

I've practiced for hours with drones like this. Even the fractured needles of illumination slipping through the decaying equipment are enough for my fingers to gently tug the fragile plastic from its nest and unfold it, each section silently snapping into place. Expanded, it's a triangle no longer than the palm of my hand, including all three helicopter-style rotors.

I touch the control stud on the middle. A small red LED blinks three times, then falls dark.

Ignoring the decreasing vibration of the nearly stopped train, I pull my phone from its pocket. The screen is already turned down so far I can barely see the icons, but I know the drone control program is on the third screen, bottom left. I hold the drone in the palm of my outstretched hand and tap the button.

The tiny plastic toy buzzes in my hand. The locomotive's vibration should drown it entirely, but the drone has its own distinct note. I feel the rotors spin up, then the drone lifts free of my hand.

I burn to watch Ayaka's goons rather than pay attention to the drone, but the drone has only enough power for maybe three minutes of flight and I'll need every second. The drone's crappy camera transmits a terribly distorted fisheye image in stark black and white, making the service yard look even more hostile. It's visible light only, no infrared, and keeps pixelating as the signal fluctuates. The night swallows the drone only a yard or so up, though, so I have no choice but to maneuver via the phone's tiny screen. Fortunately, once I get it past the gantry there's nothing tall enough to obstruct the path to the vans.

I have the drone about halfway to the parking lot when the train finally hisses to a halt with the first three boxcars inside the service yard. Glancing up, I catch the dimly outlined shapes of more boxcars at the end of the train. Ayaka's thugs immediately tromp up to the boxcar right behind the engine, but I can't spare them more than a single murderous glance before turning back to my job.

The image is even choppier by the time I maneuver it over the closest van, but I manage to ease the drone down onto the roof. I touch a button and the app flashes green. The drone's magnetic base has struck metal.

"Uh oh," Deke mutters in my earpiece.

My head jerks up at those words, but I force myself to jerk back to the phone. If I don't plant the tracker, we lose Ayaka. I tap the last button.

The picture goes dark. With the train grumbling like a snoring dragon, there's no way anyone inside that van can hear the drone's rotors and flimsy flight superstructure detach. The drone isn't a drone anymore; it's a tiny transmitter, magnetically attached to the roof of a van, surrounded by plastic clutter that'll slip away the moment the van moves. It has only enough battery for ninety minutes of short-range transmission. We'll have to follow closely, but hopefully it'll lead us back to Goon HQ.

"Drone on van closest to me." I look up, and see what worried Deke.

What the thugs are offloading from the train?

People.

54

A line of people stagger from the train towards the vans. The service yard's stark lighting robs them of all color and transforms them into an undifferentiated mass of arms and legs and bent heads shifting against one another. At this distance it's hard at first glance to sort out how many people. It's straight out of a World War II newsreel of refugees.

One of the thugs stands back by the boxcar, watching the door smoothly slide shut. He's picked up a club somewhere—no, probably a collapsible baton.

I'm pretty sure the taller people in the crowd are the thugs. They loom over the others, raised batons reflecting lines of light. I try to parse out the shuffling figures, and finally guess it's maybe…a dozen victims? Fifteen? More than ten, less than twenty.

My pulse thrums in my throat and temples. My mouth is parched. Even my sweat seems to instantly evaporate.

Someone veers out of the crowd, their stumbling transforming into a shambling run. Towards me? No, he's bolting towards a dark gap between the rusting corpse of a boxcar and a half-collapsed brick shed.

I have no idea what's through that gap. Neither does the escapee.

The thug's snarl is barely audible over the train's grumble. He swings his baton right against the escapee's shin.

The victim tumbles to the ground.

I don't know how my MP-7 got braced on the forklift's seat, but it's there and my finger's already inside the trigger guard.

"Don't shoot until I say," Deke says.

I want to snarl and demand to know who he's watching, them or me? But he doesn't have to be watching me to know how I'll react.

I don't know who rides inside a boxcar, but my first guess is "nobody society considers important." I'm automatically on their side.

"We follow them," Deke says in my earpiece. "We follow them to Ayaka."

My loathing is hotter and heavier than the humid August night. I try to avoid killing people, but I've never been more certain that someone deserves death than I am right now. Treating humans as property, as merchandise, as *things* is filthy.

Another prisoner stumbles, and gets a baton across the back for it.

My finger trembles on the trigger.

I can't shoot. If we're going to find Ayaka, I need to let the thugs take their human merchandise another step towards their horrific fate. We follow, dispose of Ayaka and her goons, and let the prisoners run out the door.

I feel like an Old Testament prophet restraining herself from smiting the ungodly.

But if I shoot, the bullet will go right through the thug and probably into a prisoner. Those poor bastards have ridden who knows how far in a boxcar. They deserve better than they've gotten. That doesn't include a vigilante perforating them with high-quality hardened steel rounds.

Plus, we're right next to two prisons and a freaking police station.

That thought gives me the will to drag my finger back outside the trigger guard.

I shake my head, trying to dislodge my fury.

The boxcar door eases closed. The trailing thug turns to rejoin his fellows.

Something clangs, clatters, and echoes, the high-pitched tone clearly audible above the idling train.

I freeze.

The noise came right from the crate I surrendered to Nancy Drew.

My memory flashes back to the little heap of scrap metal behind the crates. I'd been careful not to touch it. Nancy probably didn't even notice it.

The trailing thug glances around the yard, then stomps over towards Nancy's lookout.

I bite my lower lip and remind myself to breathe. In the real world there'd be only one Nancy Drew mystery, called *Nancy Drew Gets Capped*. I don't want to watch that.

But the thug's going for a pile of broken bricks a few yards from Nancy. If she keeps her cool she'll be—

Nancy bursts from her cover and dashes towards the train. The girl doesn't even know how to run. Yeah, she's putting one foot in front of the other, really quickly, but her knees are going every which way and the huge flopping Purse of Doom throws her even further off balance so that she needs to wave the other hand to maintain balance and she's got the camera in that hand, flailing around as if she wants the world to know she's been taking candid snaps of very private people.

The thug is already running when he shouts "Hey! Stop!"

He knows how to move.

Nancy somehow picks up speed, her massive hair braid bouncing in her wake.

But the thug closes quickly. Before I can take another breath he thrusts his baton between her legs.

Nancy lets out a shriek and tumbles face-first into the gravel, bouncing and rolling. I glimpse the camera's doomed flight as it arcs into the darkness.

Nancy rolls twice before stopping, lying on her back in a pool of light.

The trailing thug takes two more steps to reach where Nancy lies face-up in the gravel.

I know what's coming. My stomach is a supernova. I have an urge to tug the night vision goggles back over my eyes just to obscure details.

The thug silently raises his baton and brings it down, hard, across Nancy's gut.

I can't hear her gasp from here, but she doubles up like cardboard. Anyone who says *darn* as if it's real profanity has never taken a proper beating.

Normally I'd plant a bullet between the thug's shoulders before he could swing his baton again. But I tell myself the horrible truth: I'd rather watch him beat this poor woman to death than risk my lead to the woman who murdered Father.

Why couldn't Father have simply drunk himself to death like a responsible alcoholic?

Nancy shouts, "I'm just—"

The baton comes down again.

Her thin, uncomprehending keen punches through the train's grumble.

They don't care about excuses, kid. Sorry.

Another thug tromps back towards Nancy—the broad-shouldered, no-necked goon who got out of the front of the van. He passes under a light and I see he's holding an MP-7 exactly like mine. I wouldn't be at all surprised if Ayaka uses my weapons broker. Our weapons probably were shipped to Detroit snuggled up next to one another. Like puppies in a litter, each sold to separate trainers before facing each other in an illegal ring.

The baton-wielding thug strikes a third time, straight across Nancy's flank. She thrashes, but must not have the air for another cry. "What do you think?" His voice is high and nasally. "Ship her back? Good price on redheads."

"We're done here." The gunman's voice is deeper and slower. "Not worth the trouble."

My finger's back on the trigger.

Nobody would show up to photograph Ayaka's operation if they weren't on our side. Maybe Nancy's an FBI analyst who's caught on that this case has been squashed, maybe she's a plucky newspaper reporter for the Daily Planet, I don't know.

If I shoot, the thugs might not return to their lair before the tracker's power runs out.

My mind flashes back to Lou. His heart had also been in the right place. I'd abandoned his bloody corpse on a baking road beneath a scalding sun.

Maybe if I hadn't been distracted by Father's death, Lou would still be alive.

And now someone else will die so I can avenge him. Bitterness burns my stomach.

But my body's lining up the MP-7.

The gunman raises his own weapon.

If I watch Nancy die, we'll find Ayaka.

My finger's inside the trigger guard.

I've told Deke that he's in charge. I gave him my trust.

A giant fist is squeezing my heart. My own hand squeezes in response.

Firing would betray my beloved Deke in favor of my loathed father.

A gunshot rips the night.

55

Did I shoot? No—no kick from my machine pistol.

But I'm so tense, the report almost makes me squeeze my own trigger.

The service yard looks like it's been ripped from an especially pretentious post-apocalyptic art film. Detroit's city lights cast a gray haze over the sky. Abandoned boxcars and shipping containers loom in the dark. The ground vibrates with the force of the locomotive's idling engine and its trailing boxcars form a glittering wall in the night. Everything stinks of old oil and decades of smoke.

Amidst this black and white tableau of rust, four pole lights cast pools of incongruous color. Nancy Drew's lying on her back in one of them, the no-necked thug standing over her with an MP-7 like mine.

And the thug's cheek fountains in a spray of red.

For half a second, nobody moves.

"Take half the gunmen," Deke says.

The giant fist around my heart eases its grip. Deke couldn't watch them shoot hapless Nancy either.

One of the thugs shouts "Holy fuck!"

A prisoner screams. Another bolts. Then they're all running, shrieking in mortal terror.

"Panic the gunmen," Deke says. "Make them run. I'm disabling the other van."

"What's happening?" Will shouts in my earpiece.

I set the sights on a thug who's whirling his head every which way, searching out their attacker. A single squeeze of my trigger and he stumbles back like he's been kicked in the breastbone. Fancy head shots are for folks with fancy sniper rifles. For a machine pistol, aim right square in the center of mass.

Two gunmen start shooting, vaguely off in Deke's direction but way too low to hit his rooftop nest.

The one who clubbed Nancy leaps over her and to shelter behind the crate she and I had both chosen. It really is a great place to snoop, provided you don't put your flank to a second shooter. Like me.

More gunshots shatter the night.

The first thug I shot is starting to get back up—he's wearing body armor, dammit. A three-round burst knocks him back down and hopefully takes a couple ribs with it.

Deke's rifle blasts three times in a single breath.

Take half the gunmen would be a hell of a lot easier without all these prisoners scattering every which way and men shouting and the train suddenly letting out a dull growl and groaning into reverse, tons and tons of rolling steel triggering a grumble in the Earth that sets the cinders underfoot crunching against each other.

I hold my MP-7 steady on the ruined forklift's seat, willing my hands to stay dry and my pulse to slow.

There—a thug stumbling for the train. The night vision goggles make his head brighter than his torso, thanks to the armor holding the heat and steam in, but there's enough light for me to put another three-round burst right into his back and send him stagger-toppling headfirst into a rusty drum. I have no idea what's in that drum, but the way it doesn't quiver when his head bounces off it tells me it's even heavier than water.

He hits not far from Nancy, who's holding her gut with one hand and scrabbling to her feet. The thug doesn't move, and she detours long enough to flail an ineffective but heartfelt kick in the general direction of his head before rolling to her knees. Another thug's coming for her. I try to plant three rounds in his chest, but the MP-7's kickback raises the barrel and the third round punches right through his jaw and out the side of his skull instead.

What's the opposite of *oops*?

We had the advantage of surprise, but the thugs are starting to get themselves together. One thug has his own machine pistol out and scans the darkness left and right.

I fire.

My rounds pummel his body armor right as Deke's sniper shot goes through his head.

I say "Perfect" exactly when Deke says "Nice."

"Is all that shooting you?" Will sounds really nervous.

"Hush," I say.

"Busy—got him!" Deke says. "That's it, let them run."

Three of the thugs are still on their feet. They've gotten themselves side by side, with their backs to the switchyard office. One scans the darkness with his machine pistol raised, as if he's going to shoot any of the escaped prisoners he can pick out of the darkness. A couple of the escapees cower behind a pile of pulled-up track off to my right, not only hugging the ground but trying to silently squirm deeper into the cinders and gravel.

The sudden silence feels hollow.

"Encourage," Deke says.

I point the MP-7 a few yards off to the thugs' flank and start walking bursts down the office brick wall towards them. One of the windows shatters—I'm making a hell of a mess for poor Bethel to clean up in the morning.

But nobody can watch gunfire approach, spraying ricochets and chunks of brick from every impact, and not take cover.

The survivors break for their wheels.

I grin.

They start for the wrong van, the one I haven't bugged, but one notices that the tires are flat and they scurry to the other. I send a couple rounds through the windshield to bid them farewell, then the van's spraying gravel and rocketing out of the service yard.

"Extract," Deke says.

Will doesn't answer.

My idiot brother can't even listen for his signal. "Will!" I shout.

"I'm here," Will says.

"Extract," Deke repeats.

"I'm starting the car now," Will says. "Meet at the mission."

The tension thrumming through me hasn't exactly eased. What had been blind fury has transformed into a sense of purpose, though.

The scattered bodies are a down payment.

It's vengeance. On the installment plan.

56

The service yard has achieved a new level of mess.

The supersaturated air is already starting to lay dew as the temperature dips to merely hot, and the haze of gunsmoke makes the clamminess feel soiled. The square office building is too heavily built to have suffered any real damage, but I see bright spots where ricocheting rounds chipped holes in the hundred-year-old brick. Both of the wide windows on this side of the office have only a few intact mullioned rectangles. All that beautiful century-old runny glass, ruined.

Fortunately, the most common building material here is abandoned industrial iron, and my rounds did nothing but ding divots in the rust.

Two prisoners lay nearby, face-down in the cinders, trying to make themselves shorter than the shallow heap of pulled-up iron tracks they used to hide from their captors. One raises his head to look around. The other hisses something in an unfamiliar but sort of Spanish-y language. The first drops his head back down.

The train has vanished, back up the line to the main switchyard. I doubt the engineer even heard the ruckus over the growl of the engine.

House-high mounds of dirt still form a backdrop on the far side of the tracks, casting shadows from the prisons beyond. Is that light a little brighter? Maybe the engineer didn't hear it, but I'm sure the cops and prison guards know the sounds of mayhem when they hear it.

It's time to get out.

Right now, Deke is climbing down from his perch and starting to run. Will is driving at a slow, steady pace towards the homeless shelter we chose as a rendezvous. I need to start jogging if I'm going to make it.

But Ayaka made a critical mistake here.

I mutter, "Deke. The prisoners. Nancy."

"Nancy?" Deke says.

I shake my head—I'd named her Nancy Drew only inside my head. "The photographer. And the prisoners." I remind myself Deke's in charge. "I'd like to grab the photographer and one of the prisoners. See what they can tell us. And any cleanup on my way out."

After a long breath, Will speaks up. "I'm on my way. Get out of there, Billie."

I ignore Will.

After an endless moment Deke says, "Car."

It's our shorthand for a whole bunch of instructions. The knot in my chest eases a tug. "Car. Ack."

I flip my night vision goggles back down, both to conceal my face and illuminate the darkness. Thugs and escaped prisoners alike become bright green blotches. The two prisoners hugging gravel don't even twitch as I blatantly march past them. I let the wretches think I missed them—they don't need any more terror tonight.

Someone's lying on their side, up next to the office building. It's a weird spot for a prisoner, but maybe one got tripped or shot in the mayhem. Two thugs lie broken on the ground, the goggles betraying the warmth of blood draining onto the cinders. The stink of gunfire burns my sinuses.

Nancy lays on her side, curled around her gut, sobbing piteously. I stop near her head, turned so I can keep an eye on the trainyard. "Hey. Miss Photographer."

"Don't," she chokes. "Don't shoot."

"I kept that guy from shooting you." Technically Deke, but Nancy doesn't need any complexity right now. "Can you walk?"

She only quivers.

That figure huddled against the building slowly starts to straighten. They're moving carefully. Is it fear, or are they hurt? If I didn't have the night vision goggles, I wouldn't even know they were there.

"Can you walk?" I repeat, letting a sliver of my frustration leak into my voice.

Nancy doesn't respond.

The figure reaches for a warm, boxy shape on the ground and starts to raise it.

I twitch my machine pistol and squeeze the trigger almost offhandedly. The sound suppressor is pretty much shot. There's no mistaking that three-round burst for anything except gunshots.

The glowing figure drops. A splash of brighter light in the middle of his forehead tells me it's forever. The only thing I feel is a touch of satisfaction.

Nancy curls up tighter and shrieks.

"I just saved your life again," I snap. "Those men who wanted to kill you? They're still around. More might show any second, and there's no time. Move or die. Lie there and you're dead. Come with me right this goddamn second and you get to live."

Nancy shudders.

I'm going to give her a count of three before abandoning her and running for the rendezvous.

I'm surprised when at two she gives this massive shake, raises her head, grabs the Purse of Doom, and starts lurching to her feet. She cradles the side of her belly where the thug beat her, but grits her teeth and keeps moving. That massive red braid flails as she thrashes herself upright.

I grab her arm to help her, holding the MP-7 ready in the other hand. "Where's your car?"

The night vision goggles make Nancy's face look even more flushed and blotchy. She's shaking like a chilled Chihuahua.

"I said, where's your car?"

Her voice is deeper than I'd expect, but thin with fear. "A block."

"Take me." I start her marching towards the service yard's permanently open gate, holding onto one arm. "Can it take three people?"

"Focus," Nancy gasps.

Why is she telling me to focus? "Can it take three people?"

Nancy stumbles on a stray brick, but nods frantically. I steer her away from a sprawled corpse, because if she trips on that her psyche will shatter and I'll never get her away. I spy the edge of someone crouching behind a tottering tower of half-rotten wooden pallets that's only a couple yards out of our way, and adjust our course to pass near it. Not too near, but near enough.

The cowering figure holds perfectly still as we approach. If they were a goon, they would have pulled a weapon by now. I let the MP-7 sweep past them as if I'm holding ready as I search, then swing it back and stop walking. "You. Behind the pallets."

Nancy takes another half step, but reels back with my grip.

The figure doesn't move.

"Do you speak English?" I say.

They don't respond.

I raise my MP-7. "I shoot on three. One. Two."

"Yes!" The desperate voice has an accent I should be able to place, but can't. "Yes."

"Walk in front of us," I say. "I need to ask you some questions."

He steps slowly out, hands raised.

He's wearing a polo shirt that color of yellow-brown that always makes me think of puke, denim pants that aren't too old, and cheap sneakers. His features are a little darker than mine, and he's not quite due for a haircut. Other than a smear of grease on his forehead and a swollen cheek that probably indicates a broken bone, he looks like a weary tourist.

"I won't hurt you." I immediately give lie by twitching the MP-7 towards the gate. "That way. Quickly!"

The man starts trudging forward.

"Quicker!" I snap, hauling Nancy by her arm.

He picks up the pace. I hold us about five feet behind him, out of easy punching range.

"What are you doing?" Nancy says.

"Asking questions." To the man I say, "What's your name?"

"Francis." Bitterness tints the desperation in his voice.

"Francis. Why were you in the train?"

"Oh," Nancy says. Maybe it's a groan, I'm not sure.

"They offer us work," Francis says.

I'm going to have to drag every word out of this man. But I don't have time to give him reason to trust me, and I don't need a lot of information. "What kind of work?" It's almost certainly sex work, even if he thinks it's something else.

"Nurse."

Yeah, it's sex work. "How did you get in the train?"

"They take our passports," Francis snarls. "Fly us from Butuan, take our passports and beat us, shove us in train, leave us there all night and all day."

"Those monsters didn't want you as a nurse," I say.

"We are all nurses!" Francis snaps. His anger is starting to overcome his intimidation, and the way his feet are starting to pick up energy tells me that he's about to do something stupid.

I can only force one person to go with me.

I want both. But one has something I *need*.

177

"Okay, Francis," I say. "You want to stay with your friends? Stay."

He whirls and hisses, "Do not play." His chin raises. "You want to shoot me? You face me."

I don't have time for this. He's about five feet away. I nudge Nancy to the side with my grip, keeping my weapon trained on Francis as I gather some distance. When I'm about fifteen feet from Francis, I turn and urge Nancy to walk faster.

Somewhere not too far off, police car sirens blare.

57

Nancy's parked around a corner only a block away, between darkened two-story homes that must date from the 1920s or 30s and haven't had a thorough overhaul for a good forty years. I can make out front porches augmented with cinderblocks and steps rebuilt from loose brick. The owners have done their best to rehabilitate their homes despite the pervasive poverty. The moonless night, light-polluted gray of the three AM sky, and the deep shadows surrounding everything makes them feel outright ancient. The air tastes a little cleaner, but my sinuses have absorbed the service yard's rust and grease and I feel like I'll never breathe cleanly again.

Homes in this neighborhood don't have central air, and I glimpse a whole bunch of windows that don't have any glassy reflection from the ambient light or the lone streetlight at the far end of the block, so they're almost certainly open. But there's no sound from televisions or computers. No music. No people talking.

No night owls. Only buzzing insects.

People that live down here know the sound of gunfire too well. They hear one shot, they probably freeze for a breath before carrying on. They hear a whole bunch of automatic weapons fire, they kill the lights and hide in the basement.

Do the two prisons and the cop shop right across the toxic landfill improve or hurt response times? We've gotten this far without seeing a single flashing blue light, even though I hear sirens in the distance, so I'm betting the cops will lock down the prisoners they have before going out for new ones.

The post-firefight aches are starting to kick in. My shoulder's bruised clear to the bone from Deke's automatic shotgun, and the ibuprofen is wearing off too fast thanks to all my adrenaline. My stomach is a burning pit and my tongue tastes bitter. My eye sockets and the back of my skull ache from the night vision goggles. And when did I smack my elbow?

I keep my left hand on Nancy Drew's bicep. She's quivering like she's never been in a gunfight before, or even had someone hold a gun to her head. I'd been there myself, once, years ago. Either she'll get used to it, or she'll collapse.

Either way, I need her car and her knowledge.

No suburban glow-in-the-dark white girl who doesn't even know how to swear properly gets her kicks by sneaking into a train service yard in the hood.

Nancy leads me to a little blue Ford Focus hatchback (she wasn't telling me to focus, she was trying to say her car's model) that can't be more than a year old. I've half-dragged her a little over a block at just short of a march, and she puts her hand on the back-roof pylon and pants like I've made her run a marathon at gunpoint.

Someone needs to teach this kid to breathe.

I let go of her arm and reach into my back pocket for my gloves. "Keys."

She gives me a puzzled look.

I keep my voice professional, as if I'm discussing a quote to snake a drain or fix a transmission. "You're in no shape to drive. Do you want to be here when those goons come back with their friends?"

Nancy shakes her head and fumbles in the Purse of Doom.

What she digs out isn't a key ring as much as a key chain that would shame any elementary school janitor. Janitor keyrings also don't have a fuzzy little white cat dangling from the end. I snatch the keys from her hand, and at her flinch I snap "Get in the car. We gotta go."

Opening the door reveals spotless leather seats and a gleaming dashboard. Nancy obviously takes care of her belongings. I'm gonna feel really bad about wrecking it—not that I know how that'll happen, I'm just fairly sure someone's going to show up and start shooting or throwing grenades or scattering caltrops or something. The gear in my pockets and the foamed metal body armor makes the seat utterly uncomfortable, but I get myself wedged behind the wheel and tuck the MP-7 between me and the door. By the time I work the lever to crank the seat all the way back, Nancy has closed the passenger door and belted herself in. She's flung that hair braid over her shoulder so she doesn't sit on it. It hangs nearly to her bellybutton. How many hours a day does she spend maintaining that monster?

The keychain cat bops my knee as I start the motor. The interior light flips off, the headlights automatically light, and someone starts singing from the speakers.

Nancy listens to Irish folk music? Of *course* she does.

Air starts trickling from the dashboard vents. It's as warm as the rest of the night but even the breeze on my face is a relief, with the promise of cooler air soon.

I fumble at the dimly lit buttons on the plastic steering wheel until I kill the caterwauling. "In the car," I say for Deke's benefit.

Nancy makes a small, confused noise, but she's breathing too hard to speak.

"West on McNichols," Deke says in my earpiece. "Will, I told you to go slow. Let her catch up."

I put the car into gear. "Small four-door blue sedan."

I keep the car at a steady fifteen miles per hour until we get back out to the main drag. Nancy's breathing way too hard. First Will, now her—I need to teach a class on Breathing In A Gunfight for Newbies. "Slow down. Deep breaths, exhale all the way." I can't keep calling her Nancy Drew. "Tell me your name."

Her lungs are already full, and she's trying to draw more.

"Exhale," I say. "Tell me your name."

"Nancy," she huffs.

"You're kidding me."

"Huh?"

"Never mind. Nancy what?"

"Nancy Edwards." The simple answer calms her.

"Okay, Nancy Edwards." I turn onto the three unpainted lanes of McNichols Highway, keeping our speed well below the limit. Her lungs aren't nearly empty enough to inhale like she's trying to do, but at least she's slowed down and won't pass out before I've grilled her.

"They're heading south on I-75," Deke says.

I want to say *stay in range of the tracker*, but that's like telling him to wear gloves while pillaging a safe deposit box. I press the accelerator a touch, holding right at the twenty-five mile an hour speed limit. "We'll catch up."

"On it," Will says.

"Going two-way, and manual," Deke says.

He's using the cellphone app to turn off Will's mic and radio. Good. Will doesn't need to hear me interrogate Nancy. Flipping the throat mic to manual means he'll have to touch a button on the mic to transmit. It'll save me from having to listen to him correct Will every thirty seconds.

I flip the mic switch. "Manual."

Nancy heaves a breath and wheezes, "Who the dickens are you?"

Even being shot at doesn't rate swearing? This woman has a positively neurotic commitment to decency. "Call me Beaks. I'm the one who kept you from getting shot."

"Who are you talking to? And what kind of name's Beaks?" Nancy's trying to put herself back together.

"My partner. And it's the kind of name that won't get ugly men with uglier guns showing up to ask you ugly questions."

Nancy closes her eyes, nodding. "Right, right."

A couple hundred yards ahead, two sets of flashing blue-and-red lights pull onto the road and start rocketing towards us.

"Police." Nancy says it like she's sighted the marathon finish line.

I lift my foot off the accelerator, letting the car coast. "Right now, you don't want to talk to them."

"Why not?" Nancy's looking at me in puzzlement, but there's alarm there too. I've worried her.

"Those cops are responding to gunfire. They're keyed up. Ready to shoot. You call 911 in a bit, talk to someone who's not looking to fill someone with bullets." The air vents are starting to blast coolness, sparking a nearly carnal pleasure across my sweaty arms. If only I could take off the body armor, I'd be in heaven.

Studying me seems to give Nancy impetus to control her own breath. If you're the sort who doesn't swear and who keeps their car pristine, unwillingness to talk to the police is automatically suspicious.

"I'm chasing the people who tried to kill you," I say.

"Chasing them where?" she says. "And how come?"

I try to hide my grimace. A dozen excuses come to mind, but right now I need to be asking the questions and the quickest path to controlling the situation is the truth. "They murdered my father." I touch the throat mic. "Deke."

"Here."

"The prisoner I talked to claimed that everyone in the train was a nurse. Is there a market, or is that a scam?" All over the world scumbags promise innocent folks employment in a foreign country, then trap them in sex work. It's pure filth.

"No idea."

"Right." Sister Silence would know, but I don't want to call her with Nancy in the car. "Okay, Nancy." McNichols is widening to eight lanes of paved freeway, and I let my foot get a little heavier. "Why the hell did you go down to the hood in the middle of the night?"

"Who's your partner?" Nancy says.

"You don't want to know. Why were you there?"

Nancy licks her lips. She's dehydrated. I'm parched too, but we're not stopping at a bodega any time soon. "The data was dirty."

"What data?"

"The logistics database."

I make myself take a deep breath, then another as I turn left onto the freeway on-ramp. "I know you've had a rough night. Start at the beginning. How did you get this data, and why do you care that it's dirty?"

As I pull onto the freeway Nancy tries to reach up for the handle above her door, but winces and grabs her gut instead. "I'm a database administrator for a logistics exchange. I handle the automotive shipping database, tracking all the parts for just-in-time and car delivery. There was this weird entry, and most of them I can track down, but this one I couldn't. And the conflict was happening right here."

"So you went sneaking around a trainyard at midnight?"

"Nobody could explain it!" She's starting to sound indignant. "I've put in all kinds of overtime cleaning up that data, calling all over the country. Most of it's just people being lazy, the usual one-off mistakes that we have to reconcile, but this keeps happening. Then Eric, he called me into his office and told me to stop poking at it."

I've known a whole bunch of computer types. Some of them are obsessive, but Nancy seems overly so. I signal and switch to the fast lane. "Why does it matter so much?"

"I've been out of school four years now."

Four years? She looks awful young for that. I can't throw stones there, though.

In my earpiece Deke says, "They've turned onto I-94 west."

I touch my mic. "Ack." To Nancy I say "Sorry, go on."

"All the men I got hired with have gotten promotions." Her voice gets bitter. "I did the work, and they got the credit. So I looked in the payroll system, and it turns out they even started at ten grand a year more than me."

I can't help asking, "You run the payroll database too?"

The car bounces with a pothole.

Nancy says, "Hey, I just had the alignment done!"

"Sorry." Just because I saved her life, that's no reason to recklessly trash her ride. Unless we get shot at, or I need to ram a building or something. "The payroll database. You run it?"

Nancy answers too quickly. "They didn't secure it. Not really."

A tiny smile threatens to break free. I kind of like this woman. "But what brings you down here?"

"None of those guys, Jerry and Paul or any of them, got the data half as clean as I did." Nancy sounds disgusted. "So I figured if I cleaned the database, truly cleaned it so every last thing matched up perfectly, they wouldn't have any choice but to promote me. I'm twice as good as any of those, those…jerks." Her tone tells me that's the strongest language she's ever let pass her lips. But now that she's started, the words pour out of her. "I made a couple more calls, and Eric called me back in. Here I am doing my job, and he's really angry. He was madder than the time Paul dropped the airfreight index table, and Paul got a promotion six months later. Told me to forget about this inconsistency or he'd fire me. So I said—I said I would, and I came to see what was really going on."

"What was this inconsistency?" I say.

"This train kept coming at night, even though the factory was closed!" Nancy says. "It didn't make sense."

I almost hear the facts click together.

The database that Sister Silence pillaged to get train information?

Nancy runs it, and knows the people who compromised it.

58

The raised interstate shoots past at a steady seventy miles an hour. I don't dare take my eyes off the concrete. It's August, and they still haven't filled the potholes. It's not like the Michigan state government deliberately tries to make Detroit uninhabitable; that's just a side effect of loathing the city. But the streetlights nicely illuminate the way, and the vents are blowing delightfully icy bone-dry air straight at me. I shift my arms a little, and successfully direct a touch of the blast behind the chest plate of my foamed metal body armor. My hands are starting to cool, even inside the driving gloves.

Cool air in a Michigan August is a joy.

I hold our speed on the I-94 interchange ramp until I feel the little car's wheels hint at slipping, then ease off.

Plunging from the elevated interstate down to the trench freeway resurrects memories of Father taking this same interchange at speeds his beat-up truck shouldn't have been able to handle. I was barely tall enough to see over the dashboard, and probably should have been in a booster seat except Father didn't hold with that.

Will was taller, and could grab onto the handle above the door to keep himself from sliding.

Centripetal force would push me right into Father's side. He would chuckle and say *you like that?* I would laugh.

I deliberately slow the car and crush the memory before merging into the sparse traffic.

I thought I-75 was bad? I-94 doesn't have potholes, it ranches them. Each join between slabs of concrete feels like a speed bump. Plus, the limit down here's 55 but the slowest car in sight is doing at least ten over that.

Over in the passenger seat, I-can't-believe-her-name-is-really-Nancy is starting to pull herself together. Her breath is slowing to something approaching normal, and the post-fight shakes are easing. Maybe she doesn't know how to use an f-bomb, but she's not an idiot. She went looking for a mysterious train, nearly got shot by a mysterious thug, was rescued by a mysterious woman, and is now en route to a mystery destination. In her car.

Oh, and the mystery woman is pretty good with a gun.

Nancy's thinking pretty damn hard right now. I need to get her thinking usefully and not about, say, jumping out of a car doing seventy down the freeway, or reaching across my body to grab my MP-7 to try and intimidate me and shooting her nose off instead.

"This train," I say. "It went where it shouldn't, for no purpose. So I'm guessing you wanted to know if it was really there?"

Nancy nods. "Right. And I brought my DSLR so I had proof." Her wince tells me she remembers a thug walloping her with his collapsible baton, and her DSLR sailing out of her hand.

And if the trains hadn't shown up, was she going to take pictures of an empty track and declare victory over the database?

"Did you expect the people?" I try to keep my voice light.

"No! Who would carry passengers like that?"

"Someone who thought they were cargo, not passengers."

"Those boxcars were full of luxury cars. People aren't supposed to be in them once they're sealed."

"Boxcars are sealed?"

"There's a freight seal," Nancy says. "It gets locked down at Blount, and it's only supposed to be unlocked when it gets officially offloaded."

"Do you know when they'd offload this?"

"Tomorrow morning." Nancy blinks. "This morning, I guess."

I try to respond and cough instead. Damn, I'm parched. A beat-up two-door coupe that's seen better decades rolls by us, doing a solid eighty-five in the passing lane. "Those pointless diversions. Were there always cars in those boxcars?"

Nancy nods. "From the same company. So they must "have a duplicate seal for that shipper. How would they get that?"

"You'd be surprised," I say, trying to keep the laugh out of my voice. "Deke, where are they going?"

"Still west." Deke's voice in my earpiece soothes me. "Just passed Telegraph Road. We're about a mile behind them, holding steady."

We're too far behind. I glance over my shoulder. The passing lane is clear, so I hit the accelerator and move over. I don't want to attract too much attention, though, so I hold distance from the coupe that just passed us and turn my eyes to avoiding the cavernous potholes. Hopefully, the cops will notice the coupe first and I'll have time to slow. "Catching up."

Nancy reaches for the Jesus bar above the passenger door. "Do we need to go so fast?"

"Those thugs aren't going to slow down for us."

"I see." Nancy's breath is getting shallow again. Before I can say anything, she bends and reaches into the giant purse stuffed between her feet.

I tense.

She draws an aluminum bottle from her bag. Even over the whirr and thud of tires on road I can hear water slosh within. I focus on the road while Nancy flips the top and swills. She lowers the bottle with a start. "Oh, I'm sorry. You must by dying over there. I don't have another bottle."

I make myself smile. "It's okay. You weren't expecting to be rescued."

"Here." She drains another mouthful, then holds the bottle towards me. "I'm done, finish it."

I feel surprisingly touched. Manners would tell me to refuse, but if I'd returned to the Roadbeast I would have downed two bottles before saying hello. From the heft, there's a good pint left. I remind myself to say "Thank you."

The water restores life to my mouth and clears the smoky post-firefight thickness from my throat. I have to turn my head to drain the last from the upturned bottle, keeping one eye on the road before us.

The coupe I'm following suddenly lights up with brake lights.

I lower the bottle and take my foot off the accelerator. Our car's speed immediately plunges to eighty-five, eighty, seventy.

Nancy visibly relaxes.

At sixty-five I touch the accelerator again. Following the speed limit down here probably rates a ticket for obstructing traffic.

I hand her the bottle. "Wow. That helps."

Blue lights flash ahead.

I move into the middle lane in time to see a police cruiser trail the speeding coupe.

Nancy heaves a breath. She's probably never been stopped by the police either.

But the flashing lights remind me of the service yard. Condescending words flash through my brain: *That's for when you hit a whole bunch of people you can't handle, but I can.* "Shit."

Nancy actually flinches.

What kind of weird-ass cuss-free world does she live in? "*That's* what he meant." Very Special Agent Tan wouldn't tell me to contact him to bust some skulls for me. He sincerely believes in the FBI's mission. He truly wants to *help* people, he just picked the worst possible career for it. "Those people. The prisoners. Email. Can you send an email?"

"I *do* have a phone." Nancy doesn't need to swear to tell me I'm an idiot.

"Any chance you have—" No, Nancy won't have a burner phone. Or a throwaway address. Plus, she showed up on the surveillance footage. The FBI might not be onto her now but any moment they'll knock on her door, tap her phone, and politely interrogate her cat. (With that keychain? She's got a cat.) "I need you to send an email."

"To who?"

"An FBI agent."

"Oh. Wouldn't it be better to call?"

"I don't know his number." True, but irrelevant. He said email. I have to assume an email from me will make his phone trumpet an alarm. He's probably waiting for that sound.

Nancy lifts her phone and taps a couple buttons. "Okay."

Reciting the BEAKSNEEDSHELP address knots my stomach. I'm not the one who needs help, but I'm not leaving a bunch of nurses who only wanted a job in the hands of random police or corrupted FBI agents or, worse, Customs and Border Patrol. Maybe Very Special Agent Tan can help them. Maybe he can't. "Write 'Human trafficking victims at switchyard.'"

Nancy's fingers dance. "Service yard?"

"Dammit, fine, service yard."

My mild language makes Nancy flinch, but her fingers dance over the touchscreen. "Any signature?"

"He knows who it's from."

Nancy frowns. "Drat." She taps the screen. "Sorry, typo. I'm tired, sorry. There, sent."

"Good." My shoulders unclench a little. "That's one problem solved."

In my ear Deke says, "Bad news. They're heading into the airport."

My heart seizes right back up.

I should have guessed.

How many flights leave Detroit each hour? Even if I can sneak inside without preparation, an airport's the worst place in the world for a fight. How many armed TSA officers are stationed there, even at four AM?

I scream in frustrated rage and pound the steering wheel.

59

The little car suddenly vibrates. The road noise goes from a buzz to a roar.

We've veered onto the rumble strip at the edge of the passing lane. Concrete barriers dividing eastbound from west flash past less than a foot from the side view mirror.

No, *we* haven't veered. *I* lost control, and *I* almost drove Nancy's little car into the wall. Broken glass and twisted bits of plastic along the base of the wall reflect the brilliant streetlights.

Nancy is cowering up against the passenger door, hanging onto her shoulder strap like it can keep her from flying through the windshield when I inevitably drive us head-first into an overpass.

I force myself to take a deep breath. Nothing, but *nothing*, makes me as livid as helplessness. That red rage won't help.

"I'm not done," I mutter to myself. "I am *not* done."

"Okay." Nancy's voice is firm but quiet—is she trying to *soothe* me?

Of course she is. I almost drove us into the wall.

I need another breath before I can double-check the car's speed. We're up to ninety. I ease back to seventy and tug my phone off my belt. "I need to drive. You dial."

"Sure."

"Code to unlock it is 15350609."

Nancy types. "One five three five…"

"Zero six zero nine."

"What the heck is that?"

"Frequency ratio of deuterium." It's burner phone two, so it has to be deuterium. "Hit the call button."

"Okay."

I give her Sister Silence's number as quickly as she can enter it. "When the voicemail picks up, I'll give you another code." The next words make my gut ache, but I'm still furious and I absolutely must keep both hands on the wheel if I have enough miracles left to *not* kill us. "Put it on speakerphone."

Sister Silence answers on the second ring. "ACME Incorporated, home of the rocket roller skate."

"It's Beaks," I snap. "Detroit Metro Airport. We're tracking her thugs to the airport."

"DTW, got it." There's a hum, then the familiar clattering of Sister Silence's keyboard.

"I need to know which flight they're on."

It's thin.

It's all we've got.

Hopefully Ayaka's thugs are rendezvousing with their mistress. Hopefully they're on a flight, and not just meeting in the parking lot. No, the parking structures are crazy monitored, she'd meet up anywhere else. They have to be on a flight.

The slopes along the highway are dropping, exposing the illuminated tops of warehouses.

"There's an awful lot of possible flights," Sister Silence says. "Can you help me narrow it down?"

"Slaves," I snarl. "She's taking fucking slaves."

"What kind?" Sister Silence says.

"What do you mean, what kind? Does it matter?"

"It changes the kinds of flight they can use," Sister Silence says.

I remind myself that Sister Silence is on my side. I don't have so many friends that I can afford to alienate one. "Sorry." I haul a deep breath. "She killed Father, and then…this."

"That's okay. Do you know if they were skilled labor?"

I lick my lips. "Nurses. The guy I talked to said they were all nurses."

"Then they were coming into the country. They'll be used as nurse's aides, that doesn't take licensing and they'll slash some nursing home's expenses." I don't hear Sister Silence's keyboard. "Your quarry is probably going back for more victims."

"Shit."

"It's most likely to be a poor country," Sister Silence Says. "But early morning commercial flights out of DTW, they could hit any of the big European cities and connect to anywhere."

I am not letting Ayaka get away.

But the only tool I have right now is rage, and passion can't leap through the air and scorch her no matter how much it burns. The road crawls by at a paltry seventy, and I ache to slam the pedal down and add a couple zeroes to that number.

I can probably get this little sedan up to ninety-five before the engine explodes.

A twenty-foot stretch of concrete so cratered it might have been bombed out dissuades me. I have to slow merely to keep my teeth in my head.

"Would they fly their victims commercial?" Nancy's voice is so quiet that I almost don't hear her.

"What was that?" Sister Silence says.

I spare a glance towards Nancy. She's still hugging the shoulder strap, but her eyebrows are narrowed in thought.

"They won't fly the victims out," I say.

"Coming into the country," Nancy says.

"Sister," I say. "Would the victims fly into the US commercial? Or a special flight?"

Sister Silence says, "If it's skilled labor, they need to be brought in quiet. Otherwise you need visas and paperwork."

An ugly thought hits me. "Sister…how do you know all this?"

The phone goes quiet. "You've met some of my family." Sister Silence's voice drips barely controlled anger. "They're common victims."

I clamp my teeth together. That favor I'd done for Sister Silence had hinted at her life. "I'm sorry. I'm—I'm pretty pissed right now. You don't deserve that."

Sister Silence says nothing for a beat, then calmly says, "Apology accepted."

I've got to make it up to her somehow.

"So it's private transport," Nancy says. "He was sealed in that boxcar on Blount Island three days ago."

"How do you know that?" I ask.

"Because that train never stopped until it reached Detroit," Nancy says.

"Who is this chick?" Sister Silence says. "I kind of like her."

"My name's—"

I cut Nancy off. "Call her Sue." To Nancy I say, "The fewer people know your name, the better."

"And he came from Boo-too-an?" Nancy says.

I would have sworn Nancy was stunned and shocked as I marched her out of the service yard and interrogated Francis. She'd been hurt, and trying to get her body to work, but her ears had passed all sorts of trivia up to her brain.

"Boo-too-an?" Sister Silence's keyboard clatters. "Butuan, maybe? Philippines?"

"Their language sounded kind of Spanish." Contributing makes me feel less helpless. My anger fades a little, barely in time to avoid yet another stretch of car-killing potholes.

"Chavacano, right." Sister Silence says. "A creole Spanish." How the hell does she know that?

"Blount Island is in Florida," Nancy says, "right next to Jacksonville International Airport."

I want to shout that knowing the start point doesn't help. But Sister Silence is the data expert. If she's following this trail, maybe there's a reason. Or maybe it's a dead end and she's grasping at anything. I force myself to concentrate on driving. The walls of the freeway trench are rapidly dropping, and suddenly we're out into an open industrial landscape. LED billboards, their brilliance obliterating my night vision and any hope of seeing anything in the darkness, advertise expensive engineering services and cheap auto components.

Sister Silence says. "They might have spread some money around to get people through customs, but they can't hide the plane." The sound of her keyboard clattering cheers me. Work is happening. Even if they can't track Ayaka—

No. Sister Silence is good. She'll find her.

"Got it!" Sister Silence says. "Boeing 777, owned by Global Transport Charters, flew into Jacksonville from Manila nine hours before that train left."

Nancy grits her teeth. "Drat. I hoped the owner—"

"Already on it." The typing on the far end of the phone becomes a torrent. Is she using two keyboards simultaneously? "Right. That flight was chartered by Tarot Twelve Solutions International."

I cough.

"Beaks?" Sister Silence says.

"I had a flaky roommate junior year," I say. "One of you, do a search on Tarot cards. By any chance, the twelfth big card…what's it called?"

There's silence for half a beat as Nancy's fingers dance on the phone. She and Sister Silence both answer simultaneously.

"The Hanged Man."

My sudden grin shatters my helplessness, taking the rage with it. The thugs suddenly don't matter as much. "Sister. Twelve Tarot Solutions. Rip that company open. Send me *everything*."

60

I turn off I-94 at the Merriman Road exit, but turn Nancy's little sedan away from Detroit Metro Airport. The clock's grinding towards four in the morning, and my energy from that lead on Ayaka was only temporary. Sister Silence is busy burrowing for data on Ayaka's organization. Next to me, Nancy has slumped in her seat. She keeps closing her eyes and deliberately unclenching her hands.

Nancy's phone rings, the Bluetooth setting off the car's speakers. A little screen near the top of the screen lights up with HOME, and a synthesized woman's voice declares "Call from. Home."

Nancy perks up.

"It'll wait," I say. "Just breathe right now. Empty your lungs first. Then fill them. It'll help."

How do people in this country get to their twenties without learning how to breathe? No, I shouldn't whine; I learned to breathe as a teenager, but the first time a man made me kill him, Deke still had to remind me to breathe.

My doctoral advisor had started the fight, yes. I'd been defending myself.

And his death had been ugly. What a hastily hotwired and rewired Large Hadron Collider can do to the human body is not pretty. But I hadn't hyperventilated until the panic was past, until the blood had been spilled and smeared and insta-baked on the wrong side of the observation room glass.

You would have stopped breathing too.

I feel a surge of sympathy for Nancy. No she hadn't had to pull a trigger, or even touch bare wires together to simultaneously engage two different radiation sources. But a man standing over her had been shot through the head. People had died all around her. When I'd first talked to Nancy, I'd detoured to fill someone with bullets.

I pull the car to a stop at the edge of a hotel parking lot, equidistant between two streetlights and far away from any other cars, and take my own deep breath before repeating the hotel name so Deke can hear it.

Nancy theatrically pushes out another lungful of air and sucks it back in. The dim streetlights rob most of the color from my vision, but her face looks less pallid.

I turn the car ignition off. Extract the keys.

And offer them to Nancy.

She blinks at me. "That's it?"

"That's it," I say. "I got you out of there before more thugs showed up. You told me what you knew. You even helped me find the next step. I'll get a ride from here."

Her breath rattles out. "Oh."

"Was there something else?"

"Well—you're..." Nancy pauses, then sucks in another deep breath to push the words out. "You're kind of scary, you know? And we're in an empty parking lot in the middle of the night, so I kind of thought this was where I fight for my life."

I can't help it. I laugh. It's the stress, ripping out of me all at once. Seconds later, Nancy's laughing too. It's not funny.

Maybe thirty seconds later I rein it back in. Nancy needs another moment before she can shudder air in and quiet herself.

I can't help asking, "How were you going to do that?"

Nancy's face gets tight. "I have pepper spray." Her far hand comes up, and she's got a little tube clenched in her hand.

Her finger's on the trigger.

I see the doubt in her face. Am I playing with her? She's seen me kill people. Is this the moment when I turn on her?

I give a single nod and put my hands on the useless steering wheel. "You got me, pardner."

Nancy studies me, then snorts and lowers her hand.

I say, "Can I offer some advice?"

"Don't play around service yards in the middle of the night, I know."

"That too." My throat tightens. "Call up the FBI. You want Very Special—I mean Special, just plain Special Agent Tan out of the Chicago office. Talk to him, and only him."

"What about all the police?"

My smile probably has too much pity in it. Nancy still believes the cops are on the side of Law and Order and Justice. "You think anyone can run slaves—I'm sorry, human trafficking, that's the genteel way to say it, right? *Human trafficking* through a place right next to two prisons without at least a few cops knowing?"

"Oh."

She doesn't look convinced. I'm not going to convince her tonight. I'd needed years of convincing. "I don't know that they're all dirty. I do know that Agent Tan wants these assh—er, bad guys, caught." I'm cleaning up my language for Nancy Drew? I'm way, *way* too tired. "You tell him the truth. Tell him everything I told you."

She frowns. "Don't you want me to not tell him about stuff like Tarot Twelve Solutions?"

"He knows." I sigh. I don't merely want a big thick mattress, my floppy muscles feel like they're transforming into one. "I'm the one that didn't know. And he's not going to do a thing to stop me." Not after he left a note at the funeral home and snuck me a video.

Tan's evading his coworkers.

He must believe Ayaka's turned someone, that his precious FBI can't touch Ayaka.

I'm kind of relieved that Tan wants Ayaka dead more than he wants me in prison. For someone like him, a crook achieving "less awful" is an achievement.

"You have his number?" Nancy says.

How has this woman survived to her twenties? "Could you really trust a phone number I gave you?"

"Oh. I guess not."

"Spill your guts to Tan," I say. "You've done nothing wrong. And make sure you tell him about your boss leaning on you to not clean up that data. He had a reason for it. I think there'll be some openings above you real soon."

Nancy grins.

"One last thing," I say.

Her eyebrows raise.

I let my voice get hard. "Never—*never*—tell anyone you've got a weapon. If I wanted to hurt you, now I'd know how you're armed."

She deflates. "I thought—I thought you were friendly. One of the good guys."

I lean an inch closer. "I am one of the good guys. I'm the absolute worst good guy you'll ever meet. You make people like me prove they're friends. I'm gonna prove it to you right now by getting out of this car and walking out of your life. Forever."

Nancy's eyes are big.

The damn phone rings again, and the car declares "Call from. Home."

I say, "You better get that. Don't say I'm here."

Nancy swipes at her phone. "Hello?"

I'm reaching for the door handle when the woman calling says, "Nancy!"

I know angry agony when I hear it.

61

Nancy's car feels even smaller. It's a cool little island in the nighttime heat, rapidly warming at the back of this parking lot. The only signs of life are the vehicles rolling down I-94 a couple hundred yards to the south, tractor-trailers and comparatively tiny cars distinguishable only by the distance between their headlights and tail lamps. I ache to stagger into the hotel, boots and body armor and MP-7 and all, and tell the desk clerk that if he wants to keep his spleen he'll give me three days in a quiet room with a soft bed, hot shower, and a really good lock on the door. Yes, I could use one of my credit cards, but remembering the fake name on the fake plastic feels like too much work.

But even under the streetlight illumination seeping through the window, Nancy's face has turned bone white.

"Nancy?" the caller sobs.

I flip the switch on my throat mic to make it constantly transmit.

Nancy stares at me. "It's me, Mia." She sounds as panicked as when I stuffed her in the passenger seat. "What's wrong? My heavens, what's going on?"

Mia lets out a choking gasp, then there's the low scrape of the handset being jerked out of her hand. A man with a deep, cigarette-ravaged voice says, "You Nancy Edwards?"

My gut tightens. There's no way to get to Nancy's home quick enough to stop this, this…whatever it is.

"Who are you?" Nancy says. "Leave her alone!"

"Your friend is fine," the man growls.

"Fucking liar!" Mia shouts in the background.

The man says "Shut your mouth or my friend'll punch you in the head till you pass out."

"Mia!" Nancy shouts.

"She's being smart," the man says. "My friend broke her arm, but it'll heal."

Nancy's staring at me with the biggest eyes I've seen. She's holding her massive braid in one hand and squeezing it so hard, if it was a neck it'd choke. I don't think she's breathing. "Please don't hurt her." Trickling tears reflect what little light we have, even as she's frantically shaking her head. "Please, please."

She'll sell me in an instant to save her friend.

I don't want to punch her in the throat to shut her up, or crack her head on the dashboard to buy my escape. But I might have to.

"You left with someone," the man says. "Put her on."

Nancy's jaw drops.

My brain's churning. How the hell did they—

The man says, "Put her on or we break her leg."

Mia shouts "You asshole cocksu—"

A thud of fist on flesh.

"No!" Nancy shouts. "She's here, she's here!"

The man's voice is a little quieter, as if he's holding the phone away from his mouth. "If she spits that out, break her jaw." Louder he says, "Say hello."

"I'm here," I say. "Leave these ladies out of it."

"You're hard to get hold of," the man says.

"Try my message drop next time."

"We did," the man says. "You didn't answer."

I grimace. I haven't checked my message drop since Scottsdale. "What do you want?"

"Got a message for you."

"Give it to me."

"It's a phone number. Got paper?"

I pull out my burner phone and open the note app. "Close enough. Go."

He recites me ten digits with an unfamiliar area code. "You call the bottom bitch in the next hour or so, maybe nobody gets hurt no more."

I hate, hate, *hate* being boxed in. "Who is that?"

"Lemme pop this lady's eardrums and I'll tell you."

"No!" Nancy shouts.

I quickly say "Never mind."

The man says "Nancy. That's your name, right?"

"Yeah," Nancy says.

"This foul-mouthed bitch an' you're friends, right?"

"My sister! Don't you dare hurt her!" Nancy shouts.

My throat tightens. A sibling is better leverage than a roommate. I should have told Nancy to never volunteer information.

"That's up to you." The man coughs like he's got lungs full of pond scum. "'Scuse me. You want to hide the next couple days. Don't talk to the cops or the feds or anyone, right? You get out of town. Get a hotel room. Room service, pay-per-view. Got it?"

"I don't…" Nancy trails off.

"It's real easy," the man says. "You vanish for a few, you and your sister never see us again. You come back before…let's call it Tuesday morning, we make sure neither of you ever talk to anyone again. Hide or die. Up to you."

My brain churns furiously. It'd be a heck of a lot easier to wait for Nancy to get home. Why are they doing this the hard way?

"Got it?" the man repeats.

"Got it." Nancy shudders. "I'll hide."

"Good," the man says. "Lose the car. The cops can track it. Lose the phone too—that's how we figured you're still with your friend."

I file that tidbit away.

"Don't use no credit cards either," the man says. "Or your real name."

Nancy says, "How can I get a hotel room without a credit card? Or a driver's license, or—"

"You ask your friend there," the man says. "She helps all the orphans."

Stabbity Joe talked? I'm gonna fly back to Phoenix to shove his own knives so far down his throat I can scrape off his athlete's foot.

The man continues, "Most every job, she bails out some idiot. If there's a high-profile robbery and the janitor got an art scholarship with his gag, that's her."

I clench my teeth. Okay, maybe Joe didn't talk.

And that's an exaggeration. It wasn't a *full* scholarship. Or for art school.

The man says, "She makes the call, you're okay. You hide, you're okay. Anyone don't behave, you're done."

I say, "How do I know you're not gonna put them down after?"

"Hey, we showing good faith here," the man says. "That call don't cost you nothing."

"That it?" I say.

"Yep."

"Then you put Mia back on the phone and walk out," I say.

His chuckle sounds like he's auditioning for Laughing Lung Cancer Patient. "Sure thing."

A second later, I hear a different cough. "You filthy cocksuckers. I'm gonna—"

"Mia!" Nancy and I both shout.

"—off your shitty head and use a strap-on to stump—"

I glare at Nancy and point at myself. "Mia! Pay attention."

"What?" Mia shouts.

"Where are you?" I say.

"Who the fuck are you?"

"She's a friend," Nancy says.

"What kind of *fucking* friends do you have?"

"Not now," I snap. "Where are those men?"

"They're shutting the back door. I'll fucking well back-door them! With a pole saw!"

My teeth clench. "Are they inside the house? Or outside?"

Something on the other end of the phone thuds and scrapes. Mia grunts and says, "Outside. They're leaving."

I say, "Do you see their car?"

There's a longer scrape. "Hang on." Scrape, groan, scrape. "Yeah. They're both getting into it."

"What kind of car?"

"A pickup. A little one."

"Make? Model?"

"Do I look like a fucking car ho?"

"Watch for it to come back," I say. "How bad are you hurt?"

"Cocksucker busted my arm. No bones poking out though."

"That's it?"

"Other than I'm tied to this goddamn chair by my fucked-up arm and have to drag it around to look out the goddamn window, yeah!"

Nancy sags in relief next to me.

Mia must have bruises as well, but she's probably not feeling those thanks to the arm. "Can you untie yourself?"

"Yeah, just not quick," Mia says.

"Good." I swallow. "Listen. I'm gonna set your sister up with a place to hide."

"You gonna make that damn phone call?"

Nancy's staring at me.

I stare right back at Nancy. "One thing at a time. Get yourself to the hospital. Take some clothes. Don't go home again till Tuesday."

"Gotta feed Shitfuzz."

"Sifu!" Nancy says. "His name is Sifu, you meanie!"

"Stop it!" I say. "Stop it or they kill you both!" Do Will and I sound this stupid when the pressure is off?

For a breath, the only sound is the distant surge and ebb of traffic down I-94.

I say, "You are *not* in the clear. Not yet."

"I'm sorry," Mia finally says.

Nancy lets out a choked sob. "Just be okay. He'll be fine on dry food for a few days. Can you get the bag open with one hand?"

"I can get that little bugger in the carrier with one hand." *Bugger* might be the closest thing Mia gets to an endearment.

"I'll let you know where I am," Nancy says.

"This bitch you're with," Mia says. "You trust her?"

Nancy looks at me. "She kept me from getting shot."

Mia says, "You take care of my big sister."

I say, "She'll be so safe she'll be bored silly."

"Get her to watch *Crashpad*. Some porn would be good for her."

"Hey!" Nancy blushes fiercely enough to see in this near-dark.

I say "We gotta go."

Nancy says, "Love you, sis."

"Yeah," Mia says. "I guess I do too."

I hit the button on the steering wheel to hang up.

A breath of silence.

"So," I say. "I guess I'm not walking out of your life forever. You're gonna have to trust me anyway."

62

Nancy's little car feels way too snug and too warm. My knees brush the bottom of the dashboard and my head sits too close to the roof. The phone call with Nancy's sister and the thug leaves me feeling even more wrung out.

At least Nancy's trying to breathe like I told her. She's over-inflating her stomach with each inhale and making a little hissing noise as she exhales, but that's okay if it keeps her calm.

I follow her example, but more quietly.

After another breath Nancy says, "I'm in trouble, aren't I?"

I nod. "Maybe not as much as you think."

She gives a bitter laugh. "They'll come back."

"I don't think they will." I try to make my smile reassuring. "Crooks don't work any harder than they have to. The easy thing for them to do would be to wait for you to come home and make sure you never talk to anyone again."

Realization cross her face.

"They want something. Something that I can give only if I decide to give it. And killing you would just piss me off even more."

"Why do you even care?" Nancy says.

"I don't like innocents getting hurt." I raise my voice. "Deke. You get all that?"

"Sure did," he says in my earpiece.

"Pickup for two."

"Thirty seconds."

I turn back to Nancy. "Your phone. Put it under the seat."

Her face tightens.

"You heard that thug," I say. "Even if you turn the location off, so long as it's got a battery in it the bad guys can track it."

Nancy sags, turns the phone off, and tucks it neatly in the glovebox.

"Any tablets?" I eye the Purse of Doom. "Laptop? Let me see that purse."

From the look on Nancy's face you'd think I'd asked to see her underwear, but she hauls it up. She's got a second phone in there, a thick wallet of credit cards and another of discount cards—both filed alphabetically—and a tablet. First aid kit. The tiny LED flashlight. A whole bunch of other stuff. The furry handcuffs change my image of her, but not by much.

The quad headlights of the Roadbeast swing into the driveway and head for us.

"We need to leave all this in the trunk," I say.

"But it'll get stolen," Nancy says.

"You were on camera at the switchyard," I say.

"Service yard."

No wonder her sister swears. "If the bad guys know who you are, the cops will know soon. They'll track your car by the satellite radio and impound it in nothing flat. So yeah, it'll get stolen, but by the cops. You'll know who to complain to."

If Nancy's face gets any tighter her skin will split.

"We'll get you some basics." Nothing that connects to the Internet or the phone network, but some pocket cash and a couple changes of clothes.

"Okay."

The 1960s Roadbeast pulls up as I toss the purse into the meticulously vacuumed trunk to join a gallon of windshield washer fluid propped in place by a premanufactured auto tool kit that looks like it's never even been opened.

Nancy clearly does not belong in my world.

"No last names," I tell Nancy as I close the trunk and hit the lock button on the keyless remote. "Don't volunteer anything." She's looking at me like I'm speaking Serbian. "Don't say anything unless Deke or I ask."

"Who's Deke?"

I jerk my head towards the Roadbeast. "Come on."

Deke's driving now. He looks alert but his eyes are tired. Will's in the back seat on the opposite side, not quite asleep but sure not awake.

I open the rear door behind Deke and wave Nancy in. "Deke. Nancy."

Deke nods politely. "Ma'am."

Nancy gets in the car like she's trying to not touch anything in it. Getting in the front passenger seat, I can't really blame her. While the roomy, plush front bench seat feels good after Nancy's tiny car, the vinyl feels gritty from the rest of the constant slow dusting of exposed ceiling padding.

I look over my shoulder at Nancy and jerk my head. "That's Will."

Will doesn't answer.

Nancy looks from Will to Deke to me. "A pleasure to meet you."

"What's the plan?" I say.

"We hunker down," Deke says. "See what Sister Silence has for us. Then you make a call."

63

It's times like this that I question my career choices.

No, the robbery part's great. Getting paid by rich bastards to steal from other rich bastards gets the oligarchy coming and going. But if I was a law-abiding civilian and I somehow figured out that Father had been murdered, I wouldn't have expected myself to do anything about it. Sure, I would have phoned the detective in charge every day until he blocked my number, but I wouldn't have expected myself to go all Punisher on the perpetrator.

But with my life, I know the police can't touch Ayaka.

And being an experienced criminal credited with dozens of high-value thefts means that even if I did call the police or the FBI or whoever and whined that my father had been murdered by some random crook, they'd play the recording at the Quantico Annual Picnic to give everyone a good laugh.

I didn't sign on to be a babysitter. We've got Will and Nancy in the back seat, ready to be filled with bullets and too ignorant to get out of the way.

We're right in a hotel parking lot, but if we check in, whoever finds us could rightfully claim we weren't even trying. Deke makes a couple calls, then drives the Roadbeast ten minutes to a little motel in Romulus. The place we wind up is like the Madrid we'd filled with bullets yesterday, but fifty years younger. Unlike the Madrid, though, the owners are riding the tail of previous renovations and don't feel any need to invest in their business. They don't quite rent rooms out for tricks and meth labs, but will soon. The reek of overused cooking oil from the low-end chain restaurant at the far end of the building only adds to its charm.

I prefer the Madrid. It was more run down, but the owners were trying.

Four people could get by fine with two double rooms, but we get three. I'm not putting Will with Nancy.

The approaching early summer dawn is brightening the eastern sky by the time we find our rooms. I tell Nancy to get some sleep. Will grabs his Walmart sack of toiletries and clothes from the trunk and staggers into his room with a grunt.

Deke backs the Roadbeast up to our room and we spend a couple minutes shuffling bags of destruction from the trunk to the room, then lock everything behind us. There's no time for a shower to get the service yard off of me, but washing my face in chlorine-tasting tap water makes me feel a little less soiled and gives me a touch of energy. I plop my butt in one of the undersized chairs and fidget on the nearly worn-through vinyl, waiting for Deke to finish his quick ablutions. The groaning air conditioner wafts chill air stinking of old, neglected refrigerator at me. A mediocre landscape painting hangs on the wall above the sagging bed, executed by someone with more enthusiasm than skill. Someone attempted to improve the art with tiny ballpoint graffiti of stick people and freakish genitals. It doesn't help, but it doesn't really hurt either.

In moments Deke steps out of the bathroom, face gleaming and clothes filthy. The body armor beneath his shirt makes him look even bigger than usual, but we might have to dash out of here in a minute.

Depends entirely on the phone call.

"Anything from the Sister?" Deke says.

I shake my head. "She'll call when she has anything."

"This phone message." Deke yawns. I've been running him way too hard. "What do you think?"

My lips tighten. "They went after Nancy's sister to get in touch with me. They have the surveillance feed from the switchyard, in pretty much real time."

"And they knew who Nancy was, so they have context." Deke rubs his shadowed eyes with the palms of his hands. "And you're going to call the number, because there's an innocent hostage."

"Mia's not exactly innocent" I say.

"Let me check the number first." Deke feeds the number into a search engine. "It's a free voice forwarder," he says a minute later. "Registered to—" he snorts—"Jane Bogus."

"Nice of them to tell us up front." These voice call forwarding services make their money by violating the call's privacy in any way they can conceive. The call recording and computer-driven transcription will be stored for eternity in the off chance it can be economically pillaged later. But it's already been thirty-five minutes. "Give me one of those bottles of water, and I'll make the call."

"Put it on speaker. I'll keep quiet."

Throat sated, I make the call. First I call my own phone forwarder, to disguise the number I'm calling from, then I enter the mystery number. All this forwarding will make the call a little laggy, but nobody wants anyone knowing where they are. On the third ring, someone picks up. "Speak."

"I was told to call this number."

"Who this?"

I grimace. "Beaks."

"Just a minute." The phone goes dead silent—we've been muted.

Deke glances at me, then back at the phone.

Seconds later a woman says, "So glad you could take time for me, kid."

My spine and guts tighten.

I'd only worked with Ayaka once, but I won't ever forget her voice.

64

Ayaka sounds like the grand dame of the yacht club greeting the newest member, a youngster who's the Right Kind of People but still has to serve for sixty years to earn anything beyond the barest courtesy. That patronizing tone ought to combust my bones.

My anger ices my marrow instead.

Deke's face is tight, pulling the cross-shaped scar on his cheek even more out of square. He nods at me.

I need to get on with this.

I keep my voice brisk and businesslike. "You rang?"

"I completely understand why you're doing this," Ayaka says.

"You're not an idiot," I say.

"If I'd known the troublemaker was your daddy, I would have picked another way."

Daddy? I'd never called Father "Daddy." No, she's trying to unbalance me. "If an old drunk night watchman gave you trouble, you've gotten soft."

Ayaka pauses half a breath. "You've forced me to roll up operations."

"Part of them," I say.

"Part of them." I can hear good humor at a quick student, and I have the sudden urge to punch through the phone. "A small part. And mere apologies are wholly inadequate."

I feel no urge to respond.

Deke's gaze steadies me.

Ayaka says, "Would you consider ten million dollars sufficient?"

"Why would you even think that?" I say.

"I remember being so righteous. So sure I was fighting the good fight. Making a difference. I was going to use the earnings to make some changes. You get a little older, you'll realize the revolution only changes who's on top."

"Get to the point," I say.

"You can't get me," Ayaka says.

"Anyone can be got," I say.

"You've already caused me trouble. Cost me."

"Good."

"And you didn't even like your daddy," Ayaka says.

"If I'd liked him, you'd be dead already." Too much. Pull it back. Don't lose control.

"King Solomon offers a solution."

"Saw you in half? Let's meet." That's *not* pulling it back.

Ayaka's voice loses any pretense of gentility. "The Parcells Senior Living Center in Brandon, Mississippi. They live under the name Jonas and Matilda Beaumont. Mom's got dementia, but Dad's still sharp as hell."

My breath stops.

Ayaka says, "I'm sure you have a data mole that can verify this."

She hangs up.

I stare at the phone and will my heart to slow. "Did she just say what I think she said?"

Deke nods. "Yep."

Not King Solomon. Hammurabi, and…Leviticus, I think?

An eye for an eye.

What kind of fucked-up person says *oops, my bad—here, kill my parents to make up for it*?

65

My bones feel full of lead, my head stuffed with burrs, my eyes hot glass orbs stuffed into my skull. My mouth tastes like gunsmoke and old panic, and my stomach's a puddle of acid.

I feel like this hotel room looks.

Deke's face is relaxed and blank. He only does that when he's worried that I'm going to blow.

Father gave Ayaka trouble.

And she killed him for it.

What would it mean, to kill her parents instead?

The coldness of the offer horrifies me.

"She's worried," I say.

"She should be," Deke says.

I shake my head. "We can't touch her parents."

Does Deke relax a hair?

I tense. He should know me better than that.

No, I need to chill. I got suspicious of Sister Silence, and she's had my back all along. Deke and I are both wiped out. Last time I got this angry, I blew up half a mountainside.

If Ayaka even offered up her real parents.

No, that's not important. Real parents or not, I'm not touching them.

I purse my lips, thinking. "What else did making us call her accomplice for her?"

"It got us another groupie," Deke says.

"She's smart." Maybe not as smart as me, but smart. And decades of experience plus decent brains beats the hell out of my great brain and a few years.

"She's buying time," Deke says.

Why didn't I think of that? I'm stupid tired, that's why. "I think you're right. Those thugs didn't wait for Nancy because they didn't have time to."

"And to show good faith." Deke's mouth tightens. "I bet she *would* pay the ten million to get you off her back."

"Yeah." This is the first chance I've had to really think since Deke and I split up outside the service yard, a few endless hours ago. I need to slow down my whirligig thoughts. Lay them out like jigsaw puzzle pieces. Test each to see what locks into what, and what only seems to. "If she's willing to pay that? It's more than smuggling a few slaves in."

"And her folks? She's cold, but—" Deke shakes his head, rests his elbow on the table, and puts his chin in his hand. "She's got a big stake in this."

I say, "Maybe she's not contracting. She might be running her own gig."

"Or someone's got serious leverage on her," Deke says.

"Or they're not really her family," I say.

"Or she really hates her folks," Deke says.

"I'm sure they've got protection," I say.

"Maybe not," Deke says. "Only way to tell is to go look."

"And waste time." I chew my lip. "The question is, how big is her operation? Would she seriously pay ten mil to protect it?"

The handful of prisoners we cut loose in the trainyard weren't worth ten million. "Sister Silence said the flight into Jacksonville was a Boeing 777."

Deke frowns. "Some of it mighta been cargo."

I'm too tired to be infuriated. "What's the profit on a slave these days?"

Deke shakes his head. "They provide ongoing labor, as long as they last, so maybe…ten grand each a year?"

It's a wild guess, but we have to start somewhere. "A 777 takes, what—three hundred people?" I pull out my burner phone and tap in a search. "Three hundred and five, in three-class configuration. How many could you stack in if you crammed all the seats together?"

"They rent the plane," Deke says. "It's not custom-built."

"So three hundred and five." My stomach is twisting, and it's not just fatigue. "You think she's got the whole plane?"

"Why would she rent it otherwise?" Deke says.

I studied too much math in college. My brain can't help automatically doing the math. One planeload of slaves nets three million dollars—in the first year. There would be expenses, but once you corrupt a customs officer or an FBI agent the ongoing cost is pretty low. The risk of blackmail keeps the officers from being too greedy.

"She knows who Nancy is," Deke says. "So she'll assume that Blount Island and—where was it? Jacksonville International?"

"Jacksonville," I confirm.

"That's all blown," Deke says. "She'll need to bring flights into LA, or Miami, or somewhere."

"Somewhere else with a distribution network."

Deke picks his head up off his hand and leans back to stretch. "A flight comes in. She breaks the people up into groups. Sends a dozen to Detroit, two dozen to New York, and so on."

"It's too big to roll up overnight," I say.

"If she's willing to pay to get us off her back," Deke says slowly, "she's not gonna roll the whole thing up. There's too much money."

"So she's buying time to rearrange everything," I say.

"How much everything is the question," Deke says.

"Sister Silence is digging," I say. "Let's see if she knows."

I put the phone on speaker. Sister Silence picks up half a ring after I enter the code. "I am actively researching for you right now. Asking when I'll be done only makes it take longer."

"I know," I say. "We've got one specific question, that's all."

The thundering keyboards on her end don't even slow. "Go."

"How many flights does Tarot Twelve Solutions charter in a year?"

Sister Silence speaks in a monotone. I only have a tiny sliver of her attention. "I'm still untangling all the parent and child companies. Incomplete data. And it's changing right now—they've started canceling every charter they have."

Ayaka's rearranging the paperwork. Hiding her tracks. I say, "She's thrown out some chaff to slow us down."

"She can chaff all she wants," Sister Silence says. "I'll find her."

"Seriously," I say, "even a low estimate will let us guess the size of this."

"Fine." Sister Silence hates giving incomplete information, a trait I usually admire. "Last calendar year I've found one hundred fifty-eight chartered flights, all big planes going every which way, but always transoceanic."

My throat tightens.

At three million dollars per flight, Ayaka's turning about half a billion dollars a year. No—slaves keep earning, she's increasing her *income* by half a billion a year.

Assuming Ayaka doesn't sell them straight off.

Assuming the profit's only ten grand a year each.

Assuming Sister Silence found them all.

My mouth is bone dry again. I struggle to say, "Thanks." I lick my lips. "Your research. Do we have time to get some shut-eye?"

"Please," Sister Silence says. "I'll wake you the moment I have anything."

"Thanks." I end the call and lean back in my chair.

Deke rubs his eyes. "Okay. As the leader of this little fiasco, I declare we're in downtime. Get your bones out of that body armor and throw the clothes in the trash."

"I said you're in charge on the job," I say. "This isn't the job."

Deke stands. "If you don't get out of them, I'll be in the shower by myself, and who's gonna scrub your back then?"

I give a tired smile. "I'm certain a high-quality place like this provides a loofah."

"You're a hard woman."

"I'm tired woman." I pull myself upright. "Too tired to work a loofah."

Deke's pulling his shirt off. "I thought you'd see reason."

We really ought to clean our equipment first. But right now, I'm more likely to shoot myself in the leg than properly disassemble my MP-7.

And when you're weary down to your bones nothing's better than tenderly caring for the one you love and being lovingly cared for in turn, then tumbling straight into bed and sleeping as long as you can before Hell shows up to party.

Hell lets us sleep until almost noon.

66

The knocking on the door disturbs my sleep, but not enough to make me actually wake up or turn over or even pull the lumpy pillow over my head. Timid rap-rap-rap knocks aren't for me. When someone wants my attention, they knock on the door with fists or rocket launchers or something.

Deke groaning and rolling out of bed does wake me.

There's half a second of disorientation. The musty air conditioning? No, I've smelled that in places from Boston to Bangkok. It's not unique. Nor is the mattress that aspires to be a hammock, the sheets working their way through Sandpaper School, or the sweaty stink of the body armor I've got to clean.

The drifting thought *half a billion dollars a year*, though?

I'm in a run-down hotel room outside Detroit. Hunting the woman who killed my father.

I fling the covers back, grab my .38 semi-auto off the chair, and a textbook two-hands firing position at the end of the bed, ready to fill the door with bullets.

"Who is it?" Deke never sounds that sleepy, unless he wants to fool someone.

The response is almost too faint to get through the door. "Nancy."

Deke steps aside and yanks the door open.

Eye-scorching sunlight pours into the hotel room. Brown carpet isn't supposed to show stains, but once it's so old that the stains outnumber the fibers they're pretty obvious. The muggy August hits our clammy air conditioning and throws up a few wisps of fog.

I need a beat to resolve the lone silhouette into Nancy.

"Come in," Deke says.

I lower the handgun as she steps timidly inside. "I'm sorry to bother you," she says. "I didn't dare go anywhere else, and housekeeping knocked."

Deke shuts the door and flicks the light switch. "It's okay. About time we were up." He keeps his .45 in his hand.

Nancy looks worn. She's taken a shower, but put her grimy clothes back on afterwards and they stink of the train service yard. Dark half-moons hang beneath her eyes. I've seen healthier and happier people on day two of a five-leg steerage-class intercontinental flight.

I'm achy and my mouth still tastes bad. The sleep has done me some good, though. Coffee and a meal will erase my headache, if we can get anything decent around here. The greasy stink of the chain diner attached to the hotel promised a side of dysentery with every sandwich, so I'm not hopeful.

I plop down on the edge of the bed. "Have a seat," I say, nodding to the worn-out vinyl chairs by the little square table.

"Thanks."

Deke lumbers back to the coffee maker. "Anyone want a cup?"

"Sure," I say.

"It's bad," Nancy says. "It's real bad."

Deke studies the foil coffee pouch. "This expired last year."

"You want me to go get us some?" I say.

"Nah, I'll go," Deke says. "Breakfast?"

"They're not serving breakfast anymore," Nancy says.

"What time is it?" I say.

"Noon," Nancy says. "Right after."

We needed the sleep, yeah, but it's been about seven hours and Sister Silence still hasn't called back. How much digging does she have to do? How big *is* Ayaka's operation?

"Then it's lunchtime," Deke says. "You must be starving, ma'am. I'll go to the diner. What can I get you?"

"I'm okay." Nancy's knuckles are tight around her massive red braid. "Your brother took care of me."

I stiffen. "He did?"

"He knocked on my door about ten, asked if I wanted to go get breakfast with him."

Deke says, "Did you?" His tone has that lightness that says he's not going to shout until he's absolutely certain there's a reason to.

Nancy says, "Didn't she tell you I'm hiding? I asked him to bring me an egg sandwich and a real coffee."

Deke relaxes. "Good."

So long as Will didn't mouth off to everyone in the diner, that is. But at least he hadn't creeped Nancy out.

"I feel like I could eat a pizza by myself," Nancy says, "but I really don't need that."

"It's the excitement," Deke says. "You can use a few extra calories today."

Nancy's face stills like she's a doctor about to tell a patient they have terminal cancer. "Will said something about chocolate cake."

I'm torn between laughing at her expression and demanding my own slice of chocolate cake, but I manage to keep my own face impassive.

"Chocolate cake it is," Deke says. He doesn't ask me what I want; I know he'll do the best he can. Probably eggs and bacon, maybe yogurt. I can't afford to pack on any weight. If I quit exercising discipline, in weeks I'll be heavier than Will.

"And another coffee?" Nancy says. "Black?"

"The only way to drink it, ma'am." Deke glances between Nancy and I, grabs a pair of jeans and a T-shirt from our bag, and strides into the bathroom. He needs maybe a breath to get changed and slip out of the room.

Nancy looks at me.

This is the closest thing to a quiet moment I've had in days. I didn't get enough sleep to feel good, but I no longer feel burned-out exhausted. My tender muscles, aching joints, and tired eyes remind me I've pushed myself beyond all sensible limits this time. A robbery turned bloodbath, a funeral home with dramatic family reunion and well-deserved beating, an ambush, and a bloody gunfight while trying to not hit any of the slaves burned up my energy. Awareness that we're waiting for Sister Silence's call itches at my soul, goading me to act even without a lead. I'd prefer to lounge in bed and read comics until the good Sister calls, but Nancy looks ready to patiently watch me until I can give her a hand out of her unexpectedly upended world. It's not like she has anywhere else to be.

I groan. "Two—three? No, two days non-stop. I have *got* to stretch."

"Sure," Nancy says. "I did my yoga this morning. It helped."

Years of abuse and equally abusive cleaning have left the carpet barely better than a rag, but it's been vacuumed recently and the patch of it right by the bed looks free of anything particularly repulsive so I sit near the bed, put my right leg out and lean towards my ankle. I'm tighter than I thought. I can wrap my hand around my foot no problem, but each joint in my spine grinds when I lean sideways and pull my head towards that foot. I should be able to put my toe almost in my ear, but there's a good six-inch gap and I'm panting with a familiar soft ache barely short of pain. "You're probably wondering," I gasp, "what's next."

"I've been busy checking my email, posting Fediverse updates, and updating my address with the post office. There hasn't been a spare moment to worry about the rest of my life."

I can see the worry sunk all the way to her bones, but the little bit of insolent mock cheer reassures me. If she has the strength to be sarcastic, she'll be okay. "I think the deal's legit."

"Why?"

I try to sink another half inch, drawing a hiss of discomfort from my gut. "I talked to the person behind everything we've been dealing with last night. They're rolling up the Detroit branch of their operation. By Tuesday, anything you tell the cops would be worthless."

"I watch Midsomer Murders," Nancy says. "Sometimes killers, they clean up loose ends."

"That's at small scale." My calf and thigh are starting to burn with my stretch, and from this close the carpet has a peculiar musty-boozy aroma I've never had the misfortune to encounter before. Maybe it's best I can't get my head much further down. "This is a huge operation. They don't have time to personally trebuchet every witness."

"That was a good episode." Nancy's thin smile disappears as quickly as it came. "So I stay here?"

"Nope." I ease up on the right leg, straighten the left, and sink down. Miss two days of stretching and my whole body petrifies. What's going to happen when I'm in my thirties? What about when I get hospitalized?

No, that's not helpful now. "Hotels, even hotels like this, have video cameras. We need to get you out of here and into a safe house. You lie low there for a few days. There's what, forty seasons of Midsomer?"

"About twenty," she says.

"So catch up on them. Sleep."

"My job," she says.

"Today's…" I think. "Saturday?"

"Yes."

"Do you work weekends?"

"No. Not really."

I disguise my sigh with a groan as I try to sink deeper. The carpet doesn't smell as bad as I'd expect; despite appearances, nobody's bled out on it. "You mean you check your email, and deal with any little problems that come up with the machines." The left side of my back is even tighter than the right. "They're your responsibility, and it doesn't take more than an hour or two a day, right?"

"Yeah."

"They're taking advantage of you." My spine's starting to tingle, the first hint that my muscles are starting to relax. My head's way too far from my feet, and I have a whole bunch of postures to practice before I can drop into the splits, but at least I've started again. "They tell you it's a forty-hour job, but you probably check your email for an hour each night. Four, five hours on the weekend. And all the times you get out late."

Nancy shrugs. "That's life on salary."

"Salary." I ease another inch down. "Another way to say they own you."

"I'm rented. Those wretches last night? *They're* owned."

Bad choice of words. "The point is, they can do without you for a day. We'll make a call on a burner before we leave here, let you leave a message with your boss."

Nancy reaches up to pinch the skin under her chin. "Uh..."

"Let me guess." I try to sink my leg deeper into the floor, straightening the knee and relaxing the hip in a perversely satisfying ache. "You don't know your boss's phone number."

"That's why we have Google."

"Another megacorp. Does Mia have the number?"

"She might. Yes, I think she does. I messaged her Eric's number, I bet she'll still have it."

"Do you know your sister's number?"

Nancy closes her eyelids. I see the eyes twitch beneath them, as if she's looking at a page printed inside the lids. "Yes. Yes, I do."

"Call her. You have a family emergency." I coax my ear another inch closer to my toes. My spine is a line of twitching muscles that would rather stubbornly complain than surrender, and a dull burn sparks around my hip sockets. "You can't come to work, you aren't answering calls."

"Eric is not going to like that."

"So screw him." She flinches. Come *on*, I didn't even use the F-bomb. "Not literally. But you give that company more than a third of your life, and now you're in trouble and you're worried about them?"

Nancy laughs. "Silly, isn't it? But I suppose they can't fire me. Who's going to do all the work? One of the boys?"

I sink a hair further and try to make my teeth a grin rather than a grimace. "Damn right. Worst case, you'll have to go to the police. Make Officer Friendly call your boss."

Nancy laughs at that. "Eric might think I did something dreadful."

"That's not a bad thing." I switch back to the right leg. "Worst case, hide behind the police. You pay taxes to the bastards, the least they can do is be an excuse. Do you have a lawyer?"

Nancy blinks. "Not really? There's the guy who did Mom's trust a few years back?"

"Tuesday morning, once this is all over. Call him." The second round of stretches on the right feels better. For a proper deep stretch I should go for a run first, but I don't have time before Deke comes back with breakfast. "Get his recommendation for a criminal defense attorney. Put him on retainer. Tell him what's happened. He can find out if the cops are looking for you."

I'm about to roll forward and ease myself towards the splits—not into them, I'm way too tight, but if I don't maintain I'll slip further—when there's two double raps on the door. "It's me," Deke says.

"That was quick." Nancy rises to get the door.

I spread my feet as far as I can get them and roll forward. My calves can rest on the floor, but my thighs don't even come close to touching the ground and my center aches like I'm about to pull myself in half. I gasp out a breath and rest my weight on my elbows and forearms.

Deke strides confidently in, carrying a big plastic bag bulging with the rectangular shapes of carryout containers and a cardboard drink caddy with huge disposable cups wedged into it. "Coffee."

I'm surprised to see Will following Deke. There's a bit of red beside his mouth—blood? No, it's got to be ketchup. Gross, he didn't even bother to look in the mirror after breakfast? What about brushing his teeth?

Will blinks as his eyes adjust to the relative dimness of the hotel room, and flinches when the spring-loaded door automatically thuds shut behind him. His eyebrows go up when he sees me with my legs stretched halfway across the floor. "Uh. Hi, Nancy." He gives that little half-flinch most men do when they realize I'm doing the splits. "Morning, Billie."

I kind of wish Will'd been surly. He doesn't even stink of bourbon anymore. I content myself with sinking further towards the splits, not letting the pelvis-splitting ache show on my face. "Sleep okay, Will?"

My brother doesn't just have black bags beneath his eyes, they're full-sized carry-on suitcases. The eyes themselves are bender-bloodshot. "Good enough."

Deke sets the coffee caddy on the little table and the bag on the bed. "Coffee for everyone." He's lowering my cup to the floor next to my hand when my burner phone rings.

Nancy's sitting, and Will's still standing uncertainly inside the door.

"Will," I say. "That phone, can you hand it to me? Kinda tied up here."

To my surprise, he doesn't even look annoyed. He must be too tired to be bitchy.

Without rising from the splits, I swipe the phone and raise it to my ear. "Yes."

"I got her," Sister Silence says.

67

My brain zings to full alertness, and the grungy hotel room snaps from a somewhat sleepy haze into high definition.

Unfortunately.

The coffee Deke's put by my head smells surprisingly good, but isn't potent enough to cover the years of hotel room grunge ground into the worn-out carpet. I'm not nearly all the way into the splits, but a sudden ripple of tension down my spine makes my pelvis go from aching to outright hurting, compelling me to ease up an inch. The walls desperately need painting any color except their current baby poop beige.

Really, the best-looking part of the room is the subtly graffitied landscape painting over the bed, and it's hung a few degrees off true.

Nancy's caught my tension. She barely keeps herself in her chair, knotting her fingers together instead. Will's busy trying not to gape at my contorted posture. I'm sure I'd done the splits before I was eight or so, but that was almost twenty years past. Deke busies himself distributing coffee and carryout containers, but only because we've got to fuel ourselves to act. I have his overwhelming attention.

"Sister Silence," I say.

Deke turns a hot iron glare at Will and raises a finger to his lips. The look Nancy gets is less intense, but Nancy's smarter than a brick.

"I don't have everything." Sister Silence is talking too quickly, but somehow her voice sounds like a drunken walk. Her tone wobbles up and down and the spaces between words are wrong. How long has she been awake? "Not close. To it. She's got a huge op, operation. Billions of dollars. Pounds. Euros."

"It had to be," I say. Holding the phone to my ear with the elbow on the ground to support my weight is more uncomfortable than holding my incomplete splits, but I don't want to spend the minute or two I'd need to properly ease myself out of them. I try to shift more weight to the other arm. The motion tries to drag a groan out of me, but I choke it to a hiss. "That many flights, it had to be."

"I could spend days on this," Sister Silence says. "Saw Deke's charge, so you're up. Tired."

She even knows what fake credit cards we're using? The stretching tension in my pelvis makes me ease a pained breath out through my nose. "I appreciate it. Seriously."

"I owe you. Canary Wharf."

I blink. "What?"

Her voice slows down and becomes more deliberate. "Ayaka's in Canary Wharf. You know. London? England? Crumpets and strumpets? Ogden in Scaffold Incorated, inporeeted, po*rated*, rents a floor in Thorntree. I got verification through the Met's cameras. Facial wreckage—recog." She coughs. "Re-cog-nit-ion."

My every muscle immediately clenches. My thighs and hips shriek at being overstretched, and I gasp as I involuntarily jerk my feet closer together to try to relieve the strain. My knees quiver, and I have no choice but to clumsily pull myself forward and collapse out of the splits with an undignified groan. I barely avoid dumping my coffee, but at least I don't tear any muscles.

"You okay?" Sister Silence says.

"Yeah." The carpet smells a lot worse with my nose pressed into it. "Sorry." Raising my head makes the tightness in my throat feel even bigger. "You sound all done in. Why don't you send me what you've got and go crash?"

"Gonna," Sister Silence says. "Not a report," Sister Silence says, "Just notes. DB extracts. Doc zips."

"Got it." I've read worse. "Not to worry."

She doesn't say goodbye before hanging up. I'm lucky she said anything but *Ayaka Canary Wharf* before starting to snore.

But it's enough.

I've barely pulled the phone from my ear when Will says, "What's going on?"

"A lead." I roll to a kneel and grab my coffee in one hand. For a place that smells of nasty grease from the outside, the coffee is surprisingly smooth and strong. "Right next door to Rob's party with Burke and Hare, and Ellsworth."

Deke gives me that two-thirds grin, the best he can do with his poor scarred cheek. "Road trip."

"Road trip," I say.

"What bullshit is this?" Will says.

"Bullshit?" I know what he means. I should deal with my brother like an adult, but I haven't drunk my coffee yet.

"You're hiding the next stop," Nancy says.

Deke nods at Nancy. "What you don't know can't be tortured out of you."

Nancy shudders. "Right. Right."

"And you," Deke says to Will. "You have your fake passport ready?"

"Passport?" Will says.

I want to sentence my brother to a real good slap for crimes against intelligence. But this is part of why I asked Deke to take point; he can shut Will down without screaming at him. Instead, I sip my coffee and let the heady aroma fill my sinuses.

Sinuses. Sinus spray. I gotta dose myself before I become the Amazing Phlegm-Woman.

Deke rolls his eyes. "Do you have a passport? For any country?"

"Got one of them enhanced drivers licenses," Will says. "Gets me into Canada."

"We aren't going to Canada," I say.

"You're not ditching me," Will says.

"You're welcome to come to the airport with us," Deke says. "You can even buy yourself a ticket. If it's got your real name on it, the TSA will grab you and hand you straight over to the FBI. Get to another country without a passport, they'll turn you right around and put you back on that plane."

Will's turning red and his jaw's working. "You know how this stuff works. You can get me around it."

I could. I really could.

But looking at my brother, I have a sudden flash of Lou lying dead on a desert road. For a fraction of a second, the brutal wound that had instantly dropped him and sent his lifeblood gushing out seems to be superimposed on Will's neck.

Wait—am I *worried* about Will?

I shove the thought away. "A rush job on a fake passport's a twenty-four-hour job," I lie. "And it won't hold up. You want to spend the rest of your life in some foreign prison?"

"And you, you're just gonna breeze in?" Will says.

"Our passports are good," Deke says.

"The best," I say.

"What am I supposed to do?" Will says.

"I've got a job for you," Deke says.

We do? I hide my surprise behind my coffee cup.

Will glares at Deke.

Deke looks impassively back. "If Nancy doesn't get to cover, she's dead."

Nancy flinches.

"She can't be seen," Deke says. "Not until Tuesday. Even when we get her to a safe house, she'll need someone to watch her back for a few days."

I'm kind of surprised. It's a shit job, yeah, but it's not made-up. Once we get her in a safe house I would have hired a couple of goons to watch over Nancy heel-and-toe. We can't go to a licensed bodyguard agency, so anyone I could get would be about Will's level.

"You want me to be a babysitter?" Will says.

"Look," Deke says. "Right now, the cops and the FBI and who knows who-all is crawling around that service yard. You went there with your sister yesterday.

They know who you are. The staties are probably staking out your house right now. You want Ayaka to go down? The best thing you can do now is lie low and not talk to the cops."

"Wouldn't tell them anything," Will says.

He'd fold like a New York pizza. "You wanted to go to the cops yesterday," I say.

"That was different," Will says.

"Everyone talks to the cops," Deke says. "That's why they're the cops. Come Tuesday, Nancy can spill her guts, but you need to lay low until you hear from us. Or you read about the explosions."

"I don't even know where you'll be," Will says.

That's when I know we've got him. "I'll leave you a burner phone," I say. "We'll get Sister Silence—one of my contacts—to warn you if the cops are on the way, so you can bail."

"You don't get along with your sister," Deke says. "I get it. My little sister's a total dumbass. Half the time I want to grab her ear and drag her out of whatever mess she's made for herself. Your sister, though? Last night should have shown you she can handle herself."

Will turns to me. His lips curl like he's tasted something awful. "Nancy told me 'bout last night," he says. "Guess you did okay."

The words *glad you finally got your head out of your ass* press against my teeth so hard I almost drop my coffee. My face probably looks as unhappy as Will's as I make myself say, "Thank you" instead.

"You might not be happy with Beaks," Deke says, "but do you think she'll run off and leave Nancy here alone and unprotected? You think she's that much of an asshole?"

"Beaks." Will shakes his head. "Silly name. You got that, right?"

"It's for business," I say.

"Oh, I got it all right," Will says. "It's your initials, B C S. You couldn't go with something a little harder to guess?" His voice hardens. "Is that why Dad got killed?"

"Ayaka didn't know who he was," I say.

"And how the hell do you know that?" Will says.

"Because I talked with her last night," I say.

Will recoils.

Nancy leans back. "Was that who…"

Deke nods. To Will's confused face he says, "Ayaka sent some thugs to Nancy's house. Beat her sister to make Billie call her."

The words taste bitter in my mouth. "She said she didn't know."

"Oh, right," Will sneers. "You gonna believe that bitch?"

Deke says, "She offered ten million dollars blood money."

"So?" Will says.

"When that didn't work," I say, "she told me where her parents live."

"Who cares where her parents—" Will freezes mid-snarl. "Oh."

"She knows she screwed up," I say. "But you know what? This isn't about Father anymore. I mean, it is, but—that train last night? It came from a flight of three hundred people, brought into this country as fucking slaves. And last year Ayaka had a hundred and fifty of those flights. That money she offered?" I shake my head. "It's doesn't hurt her near enough."

"Ayaka has professional defenses," Deke says. "This operation requires professionals. Where you can help?" Deke jerks a thumb at Nancy. "Take one worry away."

Nancy's cheeks are bright red spots in her blanched face. "I'd really like someone I know I can trust to stick around a few days."

I can't believe I'm about to ask this. "Do you trust Will?"

Nancy looks at Will and nods. "He was straight with me. And he got my breakfast right."

"They didn't have ham," Will says.

"As right as you could, then."

Deke's focus has never left Will. "You on board?"

Will grimaces. "Fine."

A knot I hadn't noticed before loosens around my heart. No matter if I live or die, Will will be out of it. I'm simultaneously relieved, and pissed with myself. I tell myself it's okay; much as with Father, if anyone kills Will it should be me.

"That's a plan," Deke says. "Eat up, everyone. Beaks, you're on transport and gear. I'll get a safe house. You two go back to your rooms."

Next stop: London.

Ayaka.

68

Deke somehow got mediocre smoked salmon and a fairly decent yogurt from the hotel restaurant. I'm glad it's not the good stuff, so I don't have to feel guilty about snarfing it in our dismal room while scanning flight information, trying to figure out the quickest landing in London Heathrow while still leaving time to get Nancy and Will to a safe house.

A lot depends on our equipment. I'd bought three bags of gear from Mall, and we'd only needed about half of it. I not only overpaid, I'd overbought. I'm tempted to ship the whole lot to England ahead of us. I know brokers that can almost guarantee a package will pass through Customs without inspection.

Almost.

And those three bags contain enough mayhem to level an airport.

I call Mall and inquire about the availability of gear in London and buying back our unused equipment. My call worries him at first, but once I start hemming and haggling like usual he settles down and we quickly get to an agreement. He can't deliver our fancy foamed metal body armor in the UK, so we're going to fly that in. He won't buy back the used weapons, not that I expected him to, but he'll take the explosives and grenades and other consumables at half. That's generous for him—but then, I'd overpaid him yesterday. Mall likes his money, but not as much as he likes stability. Uncertainty is for people who use weapons, not those who sell them.

I buy flight tickets. Early evening departure.

I hang up feeling more professional than I have since Scottsdale.

Deke's still on the phone hunting a safe house, so I start cleaning the body armor. Not only does it stink, it's probably got gunshot residue all over it. A good scrub with waterless cleaner, followed by soap and hot water in the bathtub, and it's clean enough to get through Customs. Then I wipe down and dismantle our used weapons. We'll throw parts of each in widely separated dumpsters. Even expensive firearms are as disposable as used Kleenex.

Deke drives us out into the wilds of Superior Township, most of the way to Ann Arbor, and pulls up in front of a sprawling farmhouse that's had so many additions and renovations over the decades that I have no idea where they'd tack on a fifth or sixth mother-in-law apartment. The nearest neighbor is a couple hundred yards away through chest-high grass gone brown and dormant under the scorching August sun. Scattered oaks and maples tower all around the property, a little too evenly spaced to be anything but a conscious, deliberate gift launched into the future fifty or eighty years ago. We're far enough from the freeway and the cities that the air smells fresh and clean.

There's even an old tire swing, positioned to glide out over a pristine man-made pond. At the opposite end of the pond, a fountain spews a two-foot-tall dome of water that casts joyful misty rainbows. The smothering muggy heat compels me to imagine riding the tire out over the pond, only to let go at the right moment and plunge.

It's the picture of tranquility. I wouldn't mind spending a few days here with Deke.

Safe houses are usually in the most dubious part of town and one good sneeze short of demolition. "How did you get this place?"

"The owner's working in India for two years," Deke says. "My contact knows the guy who manages the rentals. Not many people want it because there's no Internet."

"It's not what I imagined," Nancy says.

"Wonder if they stocked the pond," Will says.

Deke glances at his watch. "Let's check it out."

We don't have time for more than a cursory tour through unbearably country-cute rooms, but the house has four exits and a second driveway out the back that comes out on a different main road half a mile away.

We end on a shady screened-in porch with a comfortable-looking glider and two sturdy wooden Adirondack chairs that are probably as old as the trees but meticulously maintained. A breath of breeze drifts through the mesh and carries a touch of the heat away.

I could settle in here for a few weeks. One day, we're going to have to steal a house a whole lot like this. Maybe, when this is all over, we can even rent this place?

Deke's giving Will—and Nancy, but mostly Will—a whole bunch of instructions. Stay out of sight. No, don't use the pond, but this porch is okay. Here's some cash, go buy Nancy some clothes, she'll tell you what she needs. Here's a phone, don't make outgoing calls.

"It's not even a smartphone," Will says. He smells sweaty and somehow unhealthy, but at least I don't sniff any booze coming off him.

"You don't need a smartphone," I say. "You're laying low."

Nancy licks her lips. "What if someone shows up?"

"You run."

Deke says, "They'll deliver a burner car in an hour or two. The keys will be in it."

I look at Nancy. "Anyone who shows will be law enforcement and you want to stay out of their hands for a few days. Or they'll be Ayaka's crew and want to fill you full of bullets. Either way, you run." I glance at Will. "Deke gave you enough cash to get a hotel room up north somewhere. If they come after you hard enough, sleep in the car."

Nancy grimaces.

"Stay alert," Deke says. "No drugs, no drinking."

"We all could use a beer," Will says sullenly.

Oh, hell no. "You might have to run any time," I say. "Once this is over you can go swimming at the Pabst plant, but till then? Stay straight."

"Fine." Will doesn't quite roll his eyes, but he's sure got the tone that says he's gonna do what he wants.

"Ayaka said that your father gave her trouble," Deke says. "We don't know what sort of trouble. Until we figure out what happened there, you need to stay ready."

Will grumbles, "The old man always was a pain in the ass."

Agreeing with Will ticks me off. "I'm pretty sure being a pain in the ass is what got him killed," I say. "I don't want to see you get killed for the same thing." The words surprise me even as I'm speaking them, but you know what? They're not wrong.

My brother infuriates me by breathing, let alone when he talks.

I don't want him dead, though. Slapped every thirty seconds until he starts using his brain, sure. But not dead.

Lou thought he'd be okay on his first gig. Turns out he wasn't alert enough to duck a barrage of bullets. And he was in decent shape.

Will's carrying enough weight to build two healthy men, and he's worked too hard on his drinking. Ayaka's people wouldn't even notice killing him.

I don't want to give a shit about Will. I desperately crave indifference to his fate.

At least *I'd rather he didn't get shot* is a pretty low bar for caring.

Deke glances at his watch. "Flight's soon. Time to go."

Yesterday, I'd walked away from my brother twice, each time full of rage. This time, I'm almost relieved. Whatever happens, he'll live.

No matter what, Will is probably going to trash his life, but…maybe not.

I clutch *maybe not* and climb into the Roadbeast.

69

Deke and I hit Detroit Metro Airport in time to drop the body armor at a freight terminal, labeled "martial arts protective gear" to give the security flunkies an excuse to ignore it, and scurry to McNamara Terminal. While we're waiting for TSA inspection, I text Mall with the Roadbeast's location and photo so he can pillage the explosives, ammo, and assorted equipment from its trunk before some idiot kid finds it.

It's a public service, really.

We board so late the flight attendants give us a welcome with a side of Death Glare. The cabin door almost flattens me as it closes.

Getting a last-minute transatlantic flight isn't hard, so long as you have gobs of money to shovel at the problem and you don't care where you sit. I couldn't get two seats together, no matter which class of ticket I bought. And if I have to sit up in first class next to some supercilious colonizer returning to the Empire after popping across the pond for a jolly good Friday night party, the flight attendants would be too busy cleaning up all the blood to take care of the folks sitting in Peasant Class.

I got Deke a seat right behind the wing. It's the middle of the row, but a fairly smooth place to ride.

My seat is also in the middle of a five-person row.

The last row.

Right up against the bulkhead, so my seat can't tip back. The seat in front of me should be able to recline, but my legs are so long that getting my knees into place almost shoves it a row forward. I'm square in the middle of four college students who are too busy squeeing about England and Scotland to worry about little things like uncomfortable seats.

At least the male students have claimed the aisle seats. The women sitting next to me are a whole lot less likely to break their fingers by accidentally fondling me in my sleep.

There's no meal service back here in Serf Class, of course, but the aromas of Peasant Class and above waft our way so we know what we're missing. One whiff of microwaved carbs with a side of carbs covered in gooey sweet carb sauce and I'm happy to skip it. I have Sister Silence's massive data dump on my tablet, but this far back the plane bounces like a bucking bull. Even attempting to read gives me a horrid headache, so when they dim the lights I slip the tablet into my bag and close my eyes.

I return from my midnight mid-flight pee to find the passenger in front of me reclined his seat while I was away. I wind up with one of my knees sticking into one of the college girls' space, who puts her knee into her boyfriend's space, who grunts and sticks a leg into the aisle.

Everyone survives, including the snoring passenger right in front of me.

Even though he's in the perfect position for garroting.

Still beats the company up in Colonizer Class.

I manage a few hours of sleep, once we get over the Atlantic and the plane stops trying to buck me off.

Several hours later and five hours ahead in time, the lights flutter back on and the pilot announces that we're circling into London Heathrow and should land at the glorious hour of seven thirty AM. Another hour to crawl through Customs and collect yet another set of real stamps on these fake passports, and we're on the London train into Paddington Station.

Once again, my feet share the same soil as Ayaka's.

And with any luck, she doesn't know we're already here.

70

London always feels more homey than home.

Every time I step under the high arched glass ceilings of Paddington Station, I think it's the nicest shopping mall I've ever seen. Despite tens of thousands of people bustling around us, everyone trying to get everywhere, the crowd feels a whole lot more civil than Detroit or New York or anywhere in the States. I'm sure everyone's just as impatient, but there's not so many elbows and I smell a lot more fresh-baked bread and grilled sausage than I would at home. The sandwich vendors and travel accessory shops in the cubical stalls are all chains, but they're unfamiliar chains and brands so they feel like mom-and-pop places carrying local product.

The entire United Kingdom's a touch smaller than Michigan. Everything's a local product.

I have to keep reminding myself that despite how friendly everyone seems, this little island once conquered half the world and never quite got around to giving it all back.

Under each those smiling faces, there's a little bit of crazy.

Even in August, London temperatures only hit the mid-seventies and the nearly daily rain scrubs the humidity away. After spending the last few days in an active incinerator and then a steaming swamp, air that's not actively trying to murder me wipes away the worst of my fatigue.

We rent a car, find a room, and check out Sister Silence's latest data dump.

Early yesterday morning, London Metropolitan Police's all-pervasive camera system caught Ayaka entering the Thorntree. The Thorntree is London's newest and tallest skyscraper, eleven hundred feet of the latest technology engineered to show off one's egregious wealth in the most spectacular way possible.

With balconies on every floor, so you can literally piss on the people far beneath you.

The good Sister traced a chain of ownership from Twelve Tarot Solutions to a company called Ogden and Scaffold Incorporated. They rent half of the Thorntree's fifty-second floor, supervising a web of contracting firms in thirty-three countries.

Back in the 50s, the poet Maurice Ogden wrote a poem about a hangman and his ever-growing scaffold. What people name their companies tells buckets about them, so I look it up. It's vaguely familiar. Maybe I read it in high school, or U of M's "you will be well rounded dammit!" literature class. The Hangman is clearly meant to show the importance of standing up for those less fortunate for you—the sort of stuff elementary schools teach kids before life brutally instructs them in the supreme importance of serving the oligarchy.

If you turn it around, though? If you're selfish and psychopathic?

It's a tale of how you can do anything to anyone, so long as you rule by terror. I bet Ayaka loves it.

The same surveillance system says she hasn't left. And Sister Silence's hooks in the Met's facial recognition system haven't picked her up anywhere else in town.

Ayaka's gone to ground.

I didn't take the money and her parents are still alive, so she knows we're coming for her. If she'd hidden away in an isolated country house and surrounded herself with loyal goons, we could have arranged an air strike. I'd have to steal the Mona Lisa or something to pay for it—no, wait, we're in England, I should pillage the Big Box of Stolen Treasure instead. But still. Money is a solvable problem.

I can't blow up the Thorntree. It would hurt her human shields.

And she knows it.

Plus, I don't merely want her dead.

She's enslaved *people*. I want to know where those people are.

Who she's sold them to.

I want the whole world to know.

We get a tiny but private hotel room overlooking Hyde Park and settle in with our documents and our imaginations. Late on the first day, Sister Silence tells us she picked up FBI chatter pinpointing Nancy's location and moved her to another safe house. I thank her and run out for sandwiches and plasticine coffee from the Tesco Express on the corner.

I'm glad the Sister's on our side; she lets me concentrate on sleeping and eating and stretching and breaking and entering.

Ayaka is fiendishly competent. She's either built or taken over a billion-dollar business, and runs it with the same competence she displays robbing a diamond company. The three of us need two intense days of deep research and quiet surveillance to come up with a plan good enough to take Ayaka down without collateral damage.

As little collateral damage as possible, that is.

71

A little after ten o'clock PM, the security guard at the entrance to the Thorntree's underground parking lot stops our rented minivan. Deke's fake driving license gets us into the giant concrete corkscrew, and he deftly guides us downward.

Audis and Rolls-Royces and Lamborghinis occupy half the spaces on the top three loops, because what's the point of making the big bucks—sorry, the pretty pounds—if you don't spend it all displaying your status? A few of those cars probably belong to obsessive billionaires campaigning for comic book supervillain status, but most of them are probably high-level flunkies scrabbling for the next rung on the Ladder of Servitude. Why settle for being a mere vice president when a few more years of twenty-hour days can make you an *executive* vice president and get you the corner office, a prettier secretary, another serf to lick your boots while you lick your masters'?

I've seen dirtier walls in hospital operating rooms. The air smells fresh, filtered free of exhaust or grease or even body odor. The natural daylight spectrum LEDs cast shadow-free illumination into every corner. The elevators in the parking garage's central pillar look almost soft, with bronze doors surrounded by elegant pale wood trim and separate, gentler lighting. They promise luxury, decadence, and wealth.

You can't see the filth. You have to know it's there.

There's even cell signal down here, because Finance forbid a C-level need to quit shouting at peons while arriving for a hard day of abusing their lessers.

But the seamless signal lets Sister Silence whisper, "Third access door is clear," into my earpiece as we circle downward.

I'm wearing loose-fitting workman's khakis with big cargo pockets and high-traction boots, as if I'm about to patch a roof or silence that pesky toilet in the Chief Petulance Officer's private loo. We need to look innocuous until we penetrate the Thorntree's innards, and nothing's more innocent than workmen up too late.

By the third spiral around the garage, cars are rarer and the SPACE RESERVED FOR IMPORTANT DIPSHIT signs more obvious. We go another half-turn around and back the van into a spot near a plain metal door set into the central column, directly opposite the elevators.

Deke shuts off the engine.

Our eyes meet for that last moment of reassurance. Without looking away Deke says, "Sister. You ready?"

"You never showed up on camera," Sister Silence says in my earpiece. "The guard station never sent the notice that the gate opened for you."

"I'm doubling your pay," I say.

"You're not paying me," Sister Silence says.

"Then I owe you another one." I really do. The original favor I'd done for Sister Silence used a whole lot less time than she's spent for me.

"I knew you'd figure that out." I can hear the smile in her voice.

I hop out of the minivan and run straight into a pillow of silence.

A parking garage should have a rattle and hum of activity. The sound of motors should combine with people's voices and diffuse around all these corners, blending into a low growl of activity. Even if all the cars are off and nobody's down here, the ventilation fans should provide a base susurrus.

If nothing else, we're in the middle of London.

Instead, the almost oppressive quiet wraps itself around me. The architect claimed that the parking garage had been designed to dampen sound. I hear my boots hitting concrete, but even that feels muffled. This isn't a parking garage, it's a mausoleum.

I shake off the feeling and circle to the back of the minivan.

The unlabeled metal door leading into the central column has last year's high-security lock on it. There's no visible keypad or card reader, but Sister Silence assures me we'll need a key and a card to open it.

"At door," I murmur.

There's a double click from the door. "Electronic bolts withdrawn."

I release my breath, and a bunch of tension with it. Sister Silence had said that she'd fully compromised the Thorntree's systems. She'd gotten Deke's bogus ID in their system. She said she'd jinxed the surveillance system's central node so it would substitute the background for our images.

But my guts needed to hear the *thunk-thunk* of the bolts withdrawing at Sister Silence's command to believe rather than merely trust.

Deke's opening the minivan's rear doors, mostly concealing us from anyone who happens to drive past. Our law-enforcement-grade Lock-Release gun on the top of our gear snaps that obsolete lock right open.

I hold the door.

Deke lugs two bags through.

Then I close the van doors and follow, heart pounding but breath steady and smooth.

The tiny maintenance room we've found is entirely for the workers who support the Thorntree's luxury. There's a phone handset on the wall and a few metal shelves with primly arranged boxes of screws and bottles of brightly colored fluids. Whoever does the cleaning and repairs down here was clearly hired for obsessive tidiness. The double doors opposite our entrance feature a big DANGER sign and a distinct lack of handles, knobs, and visible hinges.

Deke drops the bags, and we both start scurrying into our gear. Select tidbits go into my pockets. I disdain body armor on a robbery, but I don't normally go in planning to steal lives so I strap it on. The armor consists of thin, overlapping plates of foamed metal within a lightweight synthetic cloth that folds over the front and back. It'll stop most civilian and even some military rounds. The knees and elbow pads were originally designed for motorcycle armor. The non-Newtonian material stiffens at impact but otherwise remains supple.

I strap on my pre-loaded utility belt with all its dangling tools, and pull on my ultra-thin protective gloves.

The outfit's heavy, but nicely distributed across my frame.

I can snatch the silenced .38 with my left hand, and the unsilenced one with my right.

Really, the most annoying part is the computerized night vision goggles. There's no way to share that weight with my shoulders or hips.

I slip a small backpack with a few more tools and weapons over my shoulders as Deke finishes dressing.

"Ready," I say.

"Door," Sister Silence says.

The double doors slide open, exposing the most dangerous part of any skyscraper.

72

The elevator shaft is utterly black, and the illumination through the maintenance room's service door doesn't come close to puncturing it. A thick haze of grease and overheated ozone pours out to clobber my nose and coat my tongue. Even my lungs feel greasy.

I can barely make out how the shaft drops another three floors onto the roof of a cab. Upward, the shaft dissolves into dark infinity. The shaft's broad enough for three elevators, each corner of each lane marked with its own columns of steel L-brackets to restrain the cabs.

Deke flips off the maintenance room's lighting, letting our night vision goggles switch to dark mode. It helps. A little.

I don't climb elevator shafts unless there's no other choice. Wiring shafts are far preferable—they have ladders, and air ducts, hand holds, and all the conveniences *Die Hard* trained people to expect in elevator shafts. Real elevator shafts are featureless, except for the deathtraps.

But the Thorntree has no wiring shafts. The prefabricated snap-together walls come riddled with built-in conduits. If a tenant wants to run fiber from the basement to their floor, the building owners cut a hole to expose a private conduit and up the rent.

Climbing an elevator shaft is the next thing to suicide.

Fortunately, we don't have to climb it.

We only have to wait.

Going after Ayaka is sufficiently suicidal.

My watch says ten forty-eight.

An elevator cab trundles from above in a wash of greasy air. From the back, we see only oily levers and warning labels. A series of heavy cables connect it to another cab a couple meters above it, and then a third. The Thorntree uses triple-stacked elevator cars to boost capacity.

Standing next to me, Deke's eyes are almost closed and he seems to be looking at nothing. His hands hang limp at his sides, and his gear doesn't seem to weigh on him. His on-demand napping cat impression always amazes me.

I catch myself smiling.

Deke taught me that tension is a limited resource, like adrenaline and concentration. I'm lucky to have him.

Closed eyes or no, the side of his mouth quirks up.

He feels the same.

I try to follow his example. I can't relax everywhere simultaneously the way he can, but I rotate my attention from each muscle to the next and focus on easing the tension. The ebb and flow of rising and falling elevators feels nearly meditative.

The elevator cab glides back up. It takes a slow count of *one thou-sand one* between the moment the top of the cab rises into view and the bottom disappears above.

"Your ride just got here," Sister Silence says. "It's Adeola Adebayo, floor fifty-one. Ride the uppermost car."

The promise of imminent action does what my attention couldn't and eases my whole body. We're going to be tired at the end of the night no matter what, and climbing fifty-some stories would exhaust us before the party even started.

It's much easier to let Sister Silence monitor the cars coming into the parking structure and find someone scheduled to start a conveniently timed shift on a nearby floor. Almost the whole Thorntree has surveillance cameras, except for Ayaka's floor 52, the hotel rooms on floors 70 through 81, and the penthouses above floor 90. Maybe there's no Urinal-Cams, but the bosses can sure track how long you spent in the restroom.

Bosses who want to spy on exactly who's wasting time in the potty by playing a game on their phone or sobbing piteously still have to install those cameras special. But I'm sure they're bribing legislation through Parliament to allow them to correct this heinous oversight.

The problem is, I'm certain Ayaka has access to the same surveillance that Sister Silence does. Ayaka wouldn't rent in a building she couldn't compromise. She'll have eyes and muscle in the lobby.

We couldn't walk in.

But the elevator shaft has no space for a watchman, and the building doesn't surveil it. Employees won't sneak into the elevator shaft for time-wasting activities like breathing, after all.

Sister Silence says, "She's parking."

Even the high and mighty have a pecking order. And anyone low enough to get stuck working the midnight shift is someone lowly enough to be told to park way down in the peasant level.

Which means they must board an elevator below us.

My pulse thrums with anticipation. We're about to sneak into a place we shouldn't be, nobody will know until it's too late, and I absolutely love it. I love being smart and sneaky and absolutely fucking over the bloated bastards ruining the world with their avariciousness.

I get to exult for a whole minute until Sister Silence says, "Your car is coming. Unoccupied."

The chitter of gears on grid grow louder.

We move to the edge of the door.

The bottom of a cab chitters into view, lowering a greasy wall of machinery.

I can't help tensing, ready to move.

A second cab crawls past.

The third seems to ooze downward.

Then the roof's visible, lowering towards us.

It's just above the floor of the maintenance room when Deke and I step forward to alight on the cab's flat roof.

Deke mutters so softly, his voice is louder in my earpiece than from his mouth. "On the cab."

The maintenance doors slide shut, trapping us in the elevator shaft.

73

The Thorntree might be Europe's tallest skyscraper this year, but the elevator cab's roof feels like the top of every other elevator. Winches and cable mounts crowd the surface, and the whole roof vibrates far more than you'd expect from inside. The oppressive heat makes each greasy breath feel like I'm a turkey being deep-fried for Christmas.

Father tried deep-frying a Christmas turkey the year Mom left. He'd left some water on the skin. The fire department lost the big tree out back, saved the garage, and gave him a holiday citation. We lost the fryer and Mom that day. Father seemed more angry about the fryer.

No, that's not important right now.

What matters is that the night vision goggles show handholds all over the cab roof. It's not that you're supposed to ride an active elevator, but any maintenance man working over the pit needs to keep three points on.

I sink to one knee to preserve my balance and grab a handhold right by the emergency hatch. I don't expect the elevator to wobble, but one slip means plunging to an ignominious death.

Dying's bad enough, but when they found my body Ayaka would laugh till she had to pee. If I get killed, I want her throat in my teeth.

At least we're on the top cab, and don't have another cab looming way too close to our heads.

Deke straddles the mechanical housing. It's not exactly a seat, but it puts the elevator controls at his hands. We're not going to override the elevators, at all. While Sister Silence could make the elevator stop anywhere along the way, Ayaka's probably monitoring elevator activity. A weird stop would alert her people. And everyone would notice an elevator hung between floors. We need to ride the elevator the way it's going, even if the trip takes extra time.

The elevator makes a smooth stop.

Two cabs below the one we're riding, our carefully selected arrival is getting into her cab. When she stops on floor 51, we'll be at floor 53. Hop into the cab and we're out the door.

I relax.

Breathe.

A tiny lurch, and my stomach tries to sink into my guts. We're going up.

A high-speed elevator can twist your innards and make your inner ear demand criminal reparations, and that's if you're inside. On top of a cab, with metal humming all around you and the hot stinking darkness rushing at your face, it's the world's worst amusement park ride. The steel guide rails at each corner of the cab whip past like band saws, promising a lifelong nickname of Miss Stumpy if you get too close, and the counterweight cables hiss and sing in the opposite direction.

In a moment I suddenly feel light and have the sickening feeling I'm going to sail into the air. The cab's easing to a stop. I clench the handhold more tightly. We can't be fifty floors up already?

"Lobby level," Sister Silence murmurs in my earpiece. "Taking on passengers from the Tube."

"You're kidding," I mutter.

"Why?"

"You can't tell me the execs who drive in stop to pick up lobby passengers," I say.

"During the day, the garage elevators are reserved for garage passengers," Sister Silence says. "After nine PM, they save power. Two people in your cab."

I can't help holding a breath.

"Bad news," she says. "They're going to the penthouse. Floor 94."

We can't hop down into the cab halfway through their ride. Maybe Sister Silence can erase us from the cameras, but there's no way she can wipe us from people's minds.

74

Yes, I can't stand wealthy people.

But right now, I especially hate people rich enough to afford a penthouse in the tallest skyscraper in Europe. We have plan to get around them, but it's a lot riskier.

I grow heavy, and the elevator cab swooshes up into the hot stinking darkness.

"How many stops?" Deke says. My night vision goggles show him already grabbing at his utility belt.

"Six," Sister Silence says.

My hands are fumbling at my own utility belt, automatically unclipping a traction pad. Traction pads are electronic suction cups, used by all sorts of specialized government agents who need to get into places they shouldn't be through routes most people can't manage. I've practiced putting them on and off so many times that I really can cinch them in place by touch.

I get my knees padded before the first stop, and the elbows before the second.

Even hotter air gushes down at us. The next elevator over plunges downward in the darkness, nearly close enough to touch.

Our elevator is on the end of the shaft. We're walled on three sides. There's not near enough space between the elevator cab and the wall for me to squeeze. We're going to have to both go off the elevator on the same side, securing ourselves to the wall right above the doors to floor 53 in the few seconds that what's-her-name needs to walk out of the cab below us.

Securing one traction pad to a concrete wall takes a second or two.

We each have four pads.

It doesn't take nearly sixteen seconds for one flunky to get out of an elevator.

Ayaka's pulled in here like a turtle in its shell. She has her own thugs monitoring the building security. Anyone working for Ayaka will be alert, or she'll fire them and dump the ashes in the Thames. Every second Sister Silence delays the elevator increases the odds that one of Ayaka's people notices something weird.

Getting the pads on my knees and elbows and the controller in my hand is quick and easy.

Getting the pads affixed to the wall will be too damn slow.

Every time the elevator rockets into motion, I inch towards the edge of the cab. Even the insensitive rich bastards below us have enough brains to notice booted feet clomping around overhead. I use the handholds, staying well away from the massive steel cables supporting the elevator's core, and move only one hand or foot at any moment.

Each time my stomach even starts to lighten for a stop, I deliberately but silently plant my feet.

By the time we approach the sixth stop, I'm at the edge of the cab. Deke's kneeling right next to me. We've done this before. He'll go low, I'll go high. The concrete wall of the elevator shaft shoots past us, each level marked by the cool square of the floor's side of the doors.

The corner rails of the next elevator over are mounted only a foot or so past the edge of this elevator. We have to reach past that to grab the wall.

"Where's the other elevator?" I say.

"Loading in the lobby," Sister Silence says. "You'll have a minute, maybe a minute and a half, to get in."

"Nothing to it," Deke says.

He's right.

If we get off the elevator before it starts.

The elevator slows again.

"This is your stop," Sister Silence says.

Deke is already sitting on the edge of the cab, right next to the speeding steel of the corner guide rail. I know he knows what he's doing, but I still want to tell him to watch out for those rails. It doesn't matter how dull the metal is; at our speed they'll slice his hand off.

I still that fear.

I trust Deke, and his skills, more than I trust anyone.

Speaking my fear means he'll take attention away from what needs doing and put it on soothing me.

The split second the elevator stops, Deke swings a leg out as far as he can. The knee hits the concrete, and sticks. He follows with an elbow, then the other elbow, then the last knee.

The shaft's a whole bunch quieter when the cab we're on isn't singing with speed. From the cab directly beneath me I hear a laugh and a simultaneous groan.

I grit my teeth and shove down the jealousy. Someone's having a far better night than Deke and I, elevator video cameras or no.

But I only have to wait. Nothing's as fantastic as post-robbery sex.

Deke's clear of the cab but his arms and legs are far too close together, leaving his backside hanging way out from the wall. Hanging far away from the wall puts a horrid strain on the traction pads, but he immediately starts working his knees down to ease the pressure.

I ignore the temptation to throw open the roof hatch and surprise the heck out of the wealthy tryst, instead taking a step to stand where Deke had been half a second ago so I can reach my elbow up and out, as far across the guide rails as I can imagine.

When the elbow pad hits concrete, I tap a button on the controller. The pad instantly adheres to the smooth concrete.

Deke has almost straightened himself out, but isn't anywhere near being able to lower his head. I don't have time to wait for him to get out of the way.

I grab the edge of the guard rail with my free hand and swing the other leg out past his head. I feel the knee hit concrete, and trigger the pad.

"Door closing," Sister Silence says. "I'll hold the elevator."

"No!" I gasp. If Ayaka has her goons watching the security feeds, they'll notice an elevator delay right outside their floor. I only have two traction pads in place, and Deke is still settling into place, but I still have half a breath to finish this.

I swing my leg off the elevator roof and trigger that knee's traction pad almost before it hits.

The cables begin humming.

My knee sticks.

I yank my hand off the elevator guard rail a shaved second before the rising cab takes my fingers.

My heart threatens to beat its way out of my ribcage. I'm sweating like a fiend, and not only from the shaft's appalling heat. My knees are on either side of Deke's head, and my feet dangle past his shoulders. Plus, my backside's sticking into the air even worse than Deke's. My knees and elbows and hips and shoulders are all screaming at me to stop abusing them. In my hand, the pad controller buzzes a warning.

My pack's hanging even farther out.

I can't help imagining the elevator swooping up.

Sideswiping me won't even slow it.

"You know," Deke says through my earpiece, "when I imagine getting between your legs it's not like this at all."

My tension shatters. "Oh? I imagine it exactly like this."

"If you two lovebirds are *quite* finished playing Mirror Universe Nick and Nora Charles," Sister Silence says.

A yard below my dangling feet and off to the side, a slit of actual light appears in the darkness and promptly widens into a gaping, welcoming elevator door.

75

We swing through the open door with thirty seconds to spare.

I want to say I use the very best traction pad technique I know, but the possibility of getting smeared by an oncoming elevator does make me hurry a bit.

The open elevator leads to a great big open floor plan office, dimly lit by every fourth overhead light. I smell fruity cleaner and polishing wax. Mad squiggles in a dozen shades of blue cover the carpet. Nobody has a private desk. The workspaces are thirty-foot tables the color of light wood, with badly padded leather chairs every ten feet. The employees have a set of items at each workstation, photographs and squeezy bottles and mugs, but nothing except open space separates one flunky from another.

The aristocracy is no longer permitted to whip the peasants, but this is close enough.

The carpet sinks beneath my feet, making me wonder how the support staff wheels carts and furniture around. Probably old-fashioned brute force, for the entertainment of their lords.

The entire fifty-third and fifty-fourth floors are rented by Cerus Transactional Solutions. Their website declares them to be global leaders in law, commerce, and intellectual property, but doesn't explicitly list any services or products on offer. That description means they're legally dubious and morally pitch-black.

And the word "Solutions?" That's an extra ten points on the Bring Out The

Guillotines scale.

The company's main entrance is on the fifty-fourth floor, because height means status. This lower floor is where the company hides the necessary employees who are insufficiently pretty to be viewed by the CEO.

While the Thorntree's exterior walls are glass, along the outside of the employee pit I see only doors leading to private offices. Window views are reserved for the important people. Plus, I'm certain whatever business CTS conducts demands closed doors. Telling the peasantry what they really do would only distress everyone, after all.

There's not much call for astrophysics doctorates. If I'd defended my thesis and walked, I probably would have wound up bitterly whoring my mathematics skills to a company like this.

Really, my doctoral advisor trying to kill me was the best thing that could have happened to me. If I could go back in time, I'd thank him before touching those lethal wires.

I'm not going to feel even vaguely guilty about abusing this office.

If we have time, maybe we'll pass through on the way out and blow out Cerus' upper floor. Sow some confusion. Make Scotland Yard wonder who the real target was. Great Britain has a great social safety net for just such situations, after all.

Deke and I had already picked our entry point and used the surveillance system to familiarize us with the route. We circle around to the back of the elevator stack, where the kitchen is tucked safely out of view of the elevators. The soulless industrial kitchen doesn't even have glass walls to baffle sound; anyone trying to make friends over lunch by having a laugh will disturb everyone within hearing.

If we have to blow up this floor, the poor bastards will thank us.

But most likely, we'll leave them with only a mystery.

And a whole stack of cops, sure. But mainly a mystery.

Our main interest is that this kitchen is right over the half-floor Ayaka rents.

Deke slips off his pack as he settles onto the kitchen's intricately cross-hatched ceramic tile floor. I pull my own pack off and hop onto the counter. The office has a suspended ceiling, complete with very nicely patterned rectangular panels. I lift a panel to expose the traditional yellow fiberglass backing and shine a pocket light up into about six feet of plenum. The space seems excessive, but concrete is heavy and cross-laminated wood not that much lighter.

If you want your building to be really tall, and your concrete can only support so much weight, make it mostly hollow.

Beneath me, Deke starts assembling the drill. He can't start cutting until I hang the support line, though.

My flashlight picks out a frame of girders a few feet to one side, supporting the ceiling.

From my bag, I extract a thin line woven from an ultra-flexible metallic alloy and a really tough synthetic fiber. One end is neatly tied around a chunk of brick I picked up by a dumpster. It gives the line enough weight for me to toss it up into the metal girders.

I need three throws before successfully looping it over a strut.

Feeding the line out, I lower the brick until it hits a ceiling tile out over the kitchen floor. I can't reach it from my perch and the fiberglass ceiling tile is dense enough to support that weight, so I hop down and drag one of the cramped tables over to pop the tile and lower the line.

Deke's already dragged all three of the other tables aside. I'm looping the other end of the line around a counter, for traction, when he says, "Hey, they stock bottled water."

"Get me a couple. They're two-inch struts."

Deke tosses me a bottle that's already slick with condensation and sinks to his knees right where our brick plumb line is settling out.

I crack the seal and down pure chilled pleasure while he marks where the plumb line hits, then shifts the drill a couple inches to miss the next strut down. He's already loaded the forty-centimeter bit into its jaws. The bit's marked with a red ring thirty centimeters from the tip.

Drilling through concrete takes a long time. But the Thorntree uses cross-laminated wood floors. It's a fancy way to say "foot-thick plywood." It's a bit lighter than concrete and nearly as strong.

When you're raising a tower to shout "no, *I'm* God!" to the world, every pound matters.

We know the floor's thirty centimeters thick. So long as he doesn't hit a support strut and doesn't jam the bit, minimal sound should reach below.

I finish my water and relieve Deke to get his own drink. The drill's vibration against the chemically hardened wood sets my teeth to vibrating, but it's making steady progress. When Deke reclaims the drill I take a moment to pull off my traction pads and clip them back on my utility belt, then swap my utility belt for the one in my pack, shifting the two handguns from one to the other.

The utility belt adds weight to the pack, but I don't want to abandon it. We plan to leave with the crowd when Security evacuates the Thorntree, but if we need an alternate exit I might need the tractor pads.

My current utility belt is equipped for operations inside Ayaka's lair.

When I take my next turn on the drill, Deke swaps his belt.

After penetrating each inch, we fully extract the bit to clear the plasticized wood shavings from the spiral and to let the bit cool. An overheated bit or too many shavings will jam the shaft. Patience comes easy, now that we're in action.

When we're maybe a quarter inch from finishing, I ready the fiber-optic camera.

Deke nurses the drill for the last fraction of an inch, keeping the bit from plunging when it finally breaks through. He gives it another quarter inch to verify it's through, then slowly extracts it.

We now have a half-inch hole straight down into Ayaka's offices.

According to the original plans, Ayaka's space has a suspended ceiling much like this one. Our hole should open into a great big open dark plenum, the gap between the suspended ceiling and the real ceiling. But she also has enough cash to bribe any underpaid building inspector to approve anything she dang well chooses. Her offices might go all the way up to the true ceiling, or she could have filled her whole space with automated flunky filleters.

We need to peek ahead before we advance.

I uncoil the camera's thin, slick fiber-optic line and feed it down the hole. Deke takes the handheld and offers guidance on the last inch, ensuring we won't leave a white plastic worm dangling down from some office ceiling.

The red mark on the line sinks into the kitchen's ceramic tile when Deke says, "We're in."

I make myself breathe.

His hand swipes across the camera screen, and the unscarred side of his face sweeps up in a smile. "Clear."

I take the screen from his outstretched hand.

The camera's fisheye lens reveals a sprawling gap between the true ceiling and a suspended ceiling beneath. The plenum's pitch-dark, but the infrared lens picks up lines of temperature differential along the truncated tops of interior walls and between square ceiling panels.

I shouldn't be this elated already.

There's still a long time for everything to go horribly wrong.

A little elation is good for the soul, however.

We use a plywood-specific high-viscosity acid to burn a one-meter hole in the floor, carefully measured to minimize seepage below the last layer of laminated wood. As the acid works, we slip an expanding brace down the hole to support the disk we're cutting free and secure the other end of the line around one of the kitchen counters. It should burn a centimeter a minute, giving us half an hour.

I use the time for one last stretch, luxuriatingly aching in the splits on the sawdust-covered ceramic tile and easing the ache out of the joints I abused hanging in the elevator shaft.

Twenty-eight minutes later, there's a crack-pop.

I'm still in the splits, but my spine goes rigid. If the support line doesn't hold, we'll send a great big wooden plug plunging into one of Ayaka's rooms.

The disk of floor drops.

My heart drops with it.

The support line snaps rigid.

The disk vibrates, then stills. The support line holds.

I silently pull myself out of the splits. As of now, sound is failure.

I spray the tile on one side of the hole with high-grade industrial lubricant. As if punching through this kitchen floor wasn't insult enough, this stuff never comes off—but wow, is it slippery.

Deke hoists the wooden plug so I can push it aside. It's heavy, but thanks to the lube I can shove it across the tile in utter silence.

A dark hole looms up at us, expelling warm air from the plenum.

I can't help holding my breath.

If Ayaka knows we're here, someone's going to toss a grenade up the hole.

Five seconds.

Thirty.

Nothing.

Deke gives me a nod.

We've got open access into Ayaka's bolt-hole, and she doesn't know it.

And it's only two minutes past midnight.

This is gonna be a night to remember.

76

Your usual plenum is a vast, dusty space with a so-called floor made of the wrong side of a suspended ceiling, all fiberglass panels and the flimsy aluminum struts barely sturdy enough to hold those panels. It's the lightest possible way to hide the plenum's girders and wiring and dust. They call it the plenum's floor, but there's no way you can stand on it.

Then there's the interior walls. Office walls don't go all the way up to the true ceiling. They end two, maybe three inches above the fiberglass panels. They'll bear your weight, so long as you don't jump or dance or trip. You don't get room to do either, because in your regular office there's maybe four feet between the floor and the true ceiling.

Taken all together, a normal office plenum is a cramped negative maze of the office itself. You travel on the walls, but trying to cross a room sends you crashing down.

Whatever Ayaka's using for her suspended ceiling…isn't that.

The floor is all

dark one-foot squares divided by glittering aluminum struts. Instead of the support occasional wire, entire columns of Vs run up to ceiling. Whatever those tiles are, they're a bunch heavier than fiberglass panels.

Even the lumps of light fixtures are one-foot squares.

It's deliberately designed to make access to—and from—the plenum difficult. Despite all the support, I have no doubt that the floor won't hold my weight. Fortunately, the top of a truncated wall passes only about six feet from our hole.

I reach down, seize the steel beam supporting the plenum's true ceiling, and swing down. My gloves protect my skin, but the edges of each girder still dig into my hands until I can plant my feet on top of a wall and take the weight off. The plenum over Ayaka's office is tall enough that I can stand with only a slouch. If each floor is the same height, her offices must have higher ceilings than Cerus. Keeping my knees bent for balance, I shuffle over to an intersection where two walls meet.

The air's not as hot and thick as the elevator shaft, but it's incredibly arid. I drank three bottles of water right before coming down and pulled a microfiber filter over my mouth and nose, but each stale, dusty breath threatens to pillage every drop of moisture from my lungs.

"You've both gone dark," Sister Silence says in my ear. "No video."

"Thanks." My mutter isn't audible a yard away, but the throat mic picks it up fine.

Deke's legs dangle down the hole. With his big hands and feet he clambers along the overhead girders with more muscle than grace until he swings down where I first perched.

I ache to be closer to him, but the walls are aluminum girders and thin drywall. Our combined weight would break them.

Saturating darkness surrounds the pool of light around the hole. I want to give my eyes a moment to adjust, but the truth is there's not enough light down here to function. Instead, I flip my night vision goggles into place.

The plenum transforms from black to gray, with pale blue and red lines where tiny temperature differences mark the edges of interior walls and the weak grid of tiles across the floor. Anomalous spots of red or blue show where the main office's lights or ventilation shafts are mounted through the plenum floor. In the distance, a patch of mottled reds and blues betrays the extreme warmth and chill of the computer room.

It's like a computer-generated outline image from an Eighties movie, except with feeble and inconsistent colors. A wall top might be outlined in blue on one side and red in the other, only to swap colors where it intersects with another wall. Combined with the stale air and the dust already caking my nose, the overall effect is of a deliberately hostile space. It's not quite uninhabitable, though.

Not yet.

"Go for Nasty Uncle," Deke murmurs.

"Go for Eyes," I say.

Deke starts duck-walking along the wall away from me, knees bent but solidifying his balance with his hands on the ceiling and support girders.

My heart quivers, as it does every time Deke leaves.

I'm told that working a straight job with the one you love is hard. If your work is crime, though, it's even harder. You not only fight about work, you might get shot *at* work.

I have my own task, though.

I crawl rather than duck-walk along the top of the wall. Deke's job demands he hit a bunch of widely separated air ducts, while I need to find the first available chunk of live network wiring—preferably one attached to a camera. Companies always run wiring through the plenum and then down through the walls. Even if the whole office is wireless, which means that some exec chose coolness over the ability to accomplish labor, they'll need to wire the access points.

I should find more cables than I need inside ten seconds.

Instead, I spend nearly two minutes crawling along the painfully narrow wall without finding a one.

Annoyed, I stop and study the wall. Thin drywall rises to meet the aluminum top plate. Below me, the floor's one-foot tiles are wood. Not plywood, either—they look like stained pine. If there's any wiring, I can't see it.

I activate a dim LED light in the front of my goggles. It's not near enough to see with the naked eye, but combined with the goggles it provides something approaching bright moonlight. If I lift my head, though, my dot of light will stand out to anyone who pokes their head into the plenum.

I keep staring down and crawl along the top of the wall.

Where the wall meets another, I find my answer.

An aluminum conduit runs along the side of the wall, a couple inches below the top. From a tiny hole in its top, a cable emerges and immediately disappears into the wall. I could get a blade in to cut the cable, but I specifically want to not sever it. I want to tap it, which means I need a few inches of cable.

It's not tamper-proof. Nothing is tamper-proof.

But it's sure tamper-annoying.

I crawl on until I see what looks like the top side of a standard surveillance camera mounted on the wall but on the other side from the conduit. Access to Ayaka's surveillance would be an ideal start.

I lay prone and hang my head over the side.

There's about six inches of drywall between the flimsy floor and the top of the wall I'm perched on. The aluminum top plate uses up a couple inches off the top of that. There's hardly any space to work.

I grimace, pull my knife, and begin butchering the wall.

The powdered gypsum can't penetrate my microfiber mask, but somehow makes the air feel even more arid.

I burn ten minutes painstakingly carving drywall. Deke's working on Nasty Uncle, and I'm supposed to have the network tap complete already and be preparing quiet entry into the computer room. Our schedule's not blown, but only because we're flexible. Eventually, I expose enough of the wall's interior so I can get both hands in and see what I'm doing. There's my trophy—a gray network wire, stamped in red with CAT 7 SHIELDED and an ISO compliance number.

Splicing an Ethernet tap into a network is painstaking in perfect circumstances. With the cramped space and an inflexible taut wire, it's a nightmare. My head hangs nearly upside down off the edge of the wall, triggering a rising thud in my temples and an occasional painful moment when I bump the night vision goggles into the drywall.

But finally I get a brief green light on the tap.

Raising my head feels heavenly.

My throat tries to cough. I try to swallow instead and concentrate on my breath, willing the cough to pass. When it becomes clear it won't, I sit straight and sip water from my canteen.

It's enough.

"I have signal from tap nine," Sister Silence says. "Processing."

I grunt acknowledgement.

It should take Sister Silence five minutes or so to stealthily penetrate Ayaka's internal surveillance. I settle in to relax and breathe while she works.

Less than thirty seconds later, Sister Silence snarls "Shit."

"What?" Deke says.

"Most of the cameras are off, but I've got a few feeds. The elevator shaft. The crawlspace. Infrared. Both of you are on camera."

My guts plunge. I look wildly about.

My wrist buzzes. The phone remote, my private number.

My night vision goggles amplify the almost invisible message.

THOUGHT THE ELEVATOR HAD YOU. WELCOME TO THE PARTY.

77

Even lying prone on the six-inch-wide aluminum top plate of a severed interior wall, my legs tense in full-on fight-or-flight. I'm breathing too quickly, as if the hot dusty air lacks oxygen, and my pulse throbs painfully against the throat mic.

Ayaka watched our elevator ride.

She watched us pop the hole and crawl into the plenum.

She waited until I hooked into her surveillance cameras, until *we* knew *she* knew, before showing her hand.

"Corrupt surveillance," Deke and I say simultaneously.

"Delivered," Sister Silence says.

So much for stealth.

My wrist buzzes again. RED CARPET IN 10 SECONDS.

My surprise congeals into anger.

She was playing with us. She's *still* playing with us.

Freelancing is entirely about reputation.

Ayaka thinks that Deke and I are poor helpless youngsters that she can brutalize to intimidate others. She probably recorded that call to demonstrate that she'd tried to reach a settlement. She'll distribute photos of our battered corpses to other freelancers with the caption *do not fuck with me.*

If Sister Silence can't corrupt the surveillance system, Ayaka will probably edit the footage into a feature film starring Deke and I and a whole lot of gore.

Maybe Deke and I are decades younger than her.

But we're not helpless youngsters.

"Plan," I murmur.

"Plan," Deke says.

"Surveillance is down," Sister Silence says.

I bare my teeth. Whatever we do, Ayaka can't see us now.

Unless she has a second surveillance system. But if I worry about that I'll worry about the third, and the fourth. Ayaka can't be infinitely prepared.

Only more prepared than Deke and I.

I shove the thought away, leap to my feet, and run towards the far corner of the plenum, where the red and blue smears across the floor betray extreme temperatures beneath.

Maybe this whole floor is a ruse. Maybe the office of Ogden and Scaffold isn't a working office, but a full-on trap built just for Deke and I. If it is, we're dead. I've got to assume that this is a working office, albeit one engineered to frustrate maintenance workers and freelance thieves.

5 SECONDS.

This whole trap is pure self-aggrandizing bullshit.

I'm going to choke Ayaka on her arrogance. And my fist.

Gunfire rips the air.

I instinctively dive, landing with a fierce grunt on the painfully narrow wall header.

But I don't hear bullets passing overhead.

The barrage continues.

Over near the hole we'd cut into the plenum, my night vision goggles show slowly fading heat tracks from the floor up into the true ceiling.

She has gunmen in the office firing up into the plenum?

More heat trails lines appear, and I realize—

I say, "She's *herding* us."

She has a whole line of gunmen shooting upwards.

And the heat trails are getting closer. They gunmen are walking from that wall towards the other side of her suite.

We have to stay ahead of that line. Or we die.

Or we get shoved against the far wall, and discover whatever horrid fate Ayaka's set up for us.

I'm not going to let any of that happen.

"Going down," Deke says.

"Plan," I say as I rise to my feet.

I start running.

The blue-and-red of the computer room is dead ahead, but the shimmering heat trails of the barrage are maybe twenty feet from me and it. The gunmen below are walking slowly, methodically saturating the plenum. The only way I'll make it is sheer speed and sure-footedness.

My exposed ear is beginning to ring, but I don't have time to stuff in an earplug.

All those guns are loud, the curtain of death is only ten feet away and my body armor covers front and back not the soles of my feet, and they're only eight feet away and the datacenter's still too far ahead and even if I make it to the datacenter before the rising rain of bullets I'll drop right in front of gunmen who really want to kill us.

My death would wreck Deke.

So I have to not get killed.

I can't outgun them. I can't outrun them.

I'm going to have to outbrain them.

My every muscle shrieks to flee, but I force myself to slow. To stop.

To study the bullet trails.

Bullets punch up through the air, disappearing into the ceiling and fading along their length in a second or two. Underpowered loads to minimize structural damage explain why the gunfire isn't even louder. The lines aren't straight up, of course; I can trace the fanned-out lines back down to single points below the floor.

Are they concentrating in any one spot? If they're only aiming along the top of the walls—no, they're walking fire all the way back and forth, spraying a tsunami of bullets, I can't escape by hanging onto the framework supporting the next floor up.

Any dead spots for reloading? There's one that stops—but the person next to him fills the gap.

My throat feels too constricted for blood to pass, let alone air. I'm sweating so much under my armor that I feel like a self-steaming crab. There's only a couple feet left between the wall of death and myself, but if I start to retreat there's a good chance my spirit will break and I won't stop running until they pin me up against the far wall.

My wrist buzzes.

More Ayaka taunting. Ignore.

I know how to deal with a wall of gunfire. It's no different than astrophysics.

Look deeper.

Find the pattern in the noise.

Either write a paper on it or exploit it to survive, depending on what field you're in.

The gunman to my right is methodical. He double-taps, shifts a degree, double-taps. The gunman to the left is a little more spray-and-pray, swinging left and right.

The curtain's an arm's length away when Spray-And-Pray swivels away. Mister Methodical punches two bullets right through where my legs would be if I was standing on that part of the wall.

No time to think anymore.

I bend at the waist and dash into the line of fire.

If they both stick to the pattern, Spray-And-Pray will be shooting the other way and the other will shoot over my head—

Something punches me in the gut.

Hard.

78

I'm falling through the plenum's darkness, toppling into the stumpy top of an interior wall or the aluminum-framed floor or even the wires holding that floor or maybe a light because electrocution is all I need, horrid pain in my gut where something punched into me and the force sent me spinning and I'm only pissed that I didn't nail Ayaka but maybe when I bleed out it'll leak through the floor and drip on her head—

The back of my shoulder hits the top of a wall.

My hands flail out, trying to seize my balance before I crash down into the flimsy floor.

Out in the darkness, a foot catches something.

A hand seizes a strand of the floor support wire.

My pulse is louder than the ongoing barrage.

I feel rather than hear the wire's mount snapping overhead, but that impact absorbed enough of my momentum that I can fling my other arm out for balance and shift my weight more onto the top of the wall. That foot is on something solid—a light? Don't use it to support your weight, it'll snap and fall down and they aren't firing enough bullets to blow the infrastructure apart so it'll shriek *put more bullets here* and even if you're already dead you don't want to get shot again. That fucking *hurt*.

But I'm not dead.

Foamed metal is supposed to stop military-grade ammunition. They're using underpowered rounds.

Breathe. Then check yourself.

Drawing a lungful of hot air triggers an ache deep in my gut.

But all my muscles function.

I carefully shift position until my spine is directly over the wall's top plate.

Sometimes, people get shot and don't realize it until they bleed out.

If I'm gonna bleed out, I'll tell Deke good-bye first.

Gingerly, I probe at the impact with my gloved hands.

It's under an armor plate.

The bullet deformed the plate, sinking a divot like the sheet model of a black hole. But the plate's intact.

I slip a finger under the armor and brush it back and forth. My skin protests at my touch, but when I extract the finger the night-vision goggles don't show the warmth of fresh blood.

The bullet bruised me.

I'd watched the two closest gunmen, but someone else had covered their gap. I'm damned lucky to have only a bruise.

But right now, I have an opportunity.

The curtain of rising bullets is receding across the plenum.

I'm on the side the gunmen think they cleared.

Ayaka will send them up to verify, sure, but not until they've finished trying to herd us to whatever nastiness they have on the far wall.

I force myself to my feet. Where the gunmen have passed, the floor is an inverted star field shining up through innumerable bullet holes. Smokeless ammunition or no, you can't fire off that many rounds without adding the stink of gunfire to the heat and the dust. But my night vision goggles still work and I can see the contrasting red-and-blue temperatures of the computer room.

It's even on my side of the line.

"Through the curtain," I mutter.

Even when muttering into a throat mic, Deke's voice carries concern. "You hurt?"

"Bruised. Armor took it." I stagger into motion along the top of the wall. My gut immediately protests, but I grit my teeth and walk slowly until the recurring movement convinces my liver to stop complaining quite so loudly.

Pain is a signal to warn of threats.

I know there's threats.

Ayaka murdered Father.

She's enslaved unknown thousands of people.

I can ignore the pain.

It never quits, but with motion it lessens enough that I can almost trot along the top of the wall to the computer room. Every time I raise my right hand to touch the low ceiling or maneuver around the overhead struts, however, my side feels like it bloats to the size of a melon. I bet I'm really swollen under there. If I take the armor off, I'm not getting it back on.

So leave the armor on. Finish the job.

The truncated walls of the computer room reveal a space maybe ten by fifteen feet. In infrared, the far side of the floor has three bright red rectangles surrounded by glowing blue. They're the right size and shape for three server cabinets and the air conditioning needed to keep them from burning up. I can feel the vibration of the high-power air handlers from here.

In my ear, Deke says "Nasty Uncle ready."

"AC going down," Sister Silence says.

My fingers explore my utility belt until I find my own small nastiness. I hadn't planned on needing to sneak through insanely small squares, but I prepared for tonight to go bloody. It had to.

I'm not above using a shape charge to cut through a vault wall. And I'm not one to carry around good old-fashioned pineapple grenades.

But tiny remote-control explosives can be so useful.

I raise my head to scan the plenum. Deke stands out in red, beyond the rising line of gunfire. He's been pushed to nearly the far wall.

"The AC's still going," Deke says.

"Shit," Sister Silence says. "She's got it hard-wired. I'll kill the whole building's air handlers."

It'll raise alarms, but that's okay. Let the Thorntree's maintenance staff chase digitally-imposed power failures down in the basement. It'll keep them away from the impending bloodbath up here.

I hit the buttons to enable the three little charges, then toss one to the near side of the computer room, away from the machines themselves. I trot backwards, insisting my body keep breathing deeply despite the swelling sensation in my side. The second and third charges I toss out in front of two different groups of gunmen.

At the intersection of two walls, I take advantage of the cross-support to lie down. I can keep my hurt side off the wall, but hanging over the darkness it seems to bloom and bloat. I stuff a heavy-duty plug into my exposed ear. "Ready to blow"

"Ready," Deke says.

I open my mouth to equalize air pressure and touch three keys on my wrist remote.

Three separate giants hammer the world. The ear plug blocks the worst of it.

Three sections of the floor dissolve, each spilling a broad pool of light up into the plenum. I'm sure we trashed all sorts of lamps, but after the plenum's deep darkness that light looks bright as noon in Scottsdale. The night vision goggles suck it all in, switching to light-amplification mode with nearly natural color.

It had been dusty before, but the blasts disturbed every particle of dust and a black haze is rising from, well, everything. The gunfire's gone sporadic, the few bullet trails I can see haphazard through the smoke.

Carefully climbing back up to my feet, I pull the plug from my ear and trot as quick as I can back to the computer room. The night-vision goggles are starting to fade from all the dust and the cloth over my mouth and nose is starting to clog, but I've made us an advantage and I need to take it.

Deke says "Okay."

"Okay," I say. We always check in after something dangerous, like three simultaneous explosions.

"Air down now?" Sister Silence says.

"N—Yes," Deke says. "Going for Nasty Uncle."

I slow my feet long enough to pull the gas mask off my belt and onto my face. The goggles will protect my eyes, but no microfiber mask is gonna handle what Deke's about to unleash.

No, it's not my Nasty Uncle, though Deke has an uncle that can clear a room with his natural gas.

Our gas is unnatural and a lot more nasty.

Mask in place, I run for the computer room.

The little explosives made a noise as loud as a privileged white boy denied the right to oppress his lessers, but totally disintegrated only a square of four tiles. Most of the plenum floor dangles in splinters and shards.

Someone had been sitting at a metal desk right beneath the blast. He's in a ball on the white tile floor, bloody hands clamped to his bloody scalp, coughing and choking and puking and soiling himself after a good lungful of Nasty Uncle. A little .32 automatic lies on the floor behind him.

I loathe shooting helpless, innocent people.

The polo shirt and dress slacks say computer nerd, not gunbunny.

But a regular computer nerd would have run once the gunfire started. And he had a gun.

I pull the silenced .38 from my left-hand holster.

When I climb down into the computer room I try to avoid stepping in the blood, but there's so damned much of it.

79

The computer room was once corporate standard white: drywall painted high-gloss white, wooden ceiling tiles painted the same white, porcelain floor tiles a slightly different shade of white but even more glossy.

The dirt shows up like mad.

And the gun-toting technician's blood, of course.

The pain in my side feels like a weight, dragging down the right side of my body. I try to breathe slow and regular to distract myself from the stabbing sensation, but the gas mask over my mouth and nose makes each breath a little more difficult than usual. There's no way I'm taking a breath of Nasty Uncle, though.

At the far end, beneath a sputtering ceiling light, three tall cabinets with cracked glass fronts contain pristine stacks of computers. Most of the blinking lights are green. Computers without old-fashioned spinning hard drives are fairly resilient to sudden shocks, like explosions.

Small ones, at least.

I study each cabinet, and see no extra wires or other surprises attached to the doors, handles, or locks. It's entirely possible to rig a rack of computers to explode if equipment is mishandled, but you go through an awful lot of nerds that way. The Lock-Release snaps each open.

Swinging my pack off my back, I pull out the biggest sack in it and start yanking out tiny plastic thumb drives.

The high-speed ports used for external drives and keyboards grant unlimited access to the machine's hardware. Own the hardware, own the software. Totally disabling those ports makes routine hardware troubleshooting impossible, and every computer needs the occasional hands-on maintenance.

But I don't have time to fiddle around breaking into these machines.

The air's getting hazy. Maybe the shock didn't kill the systems, but finely ground gypsum and wood and who knows what's in the dust in the plenum will drive a stake through the CPU. AC would clear it, and the gas, out. I hurry to stuff a thumb drive in each port, attach a cable to the drive, and run the cable to a black controller the size of a paperback book.

"Getting signal on first controller," Sister Silence says.

I tuck the black box neatly into the first cabinet and shut the door. If Deke and I go down, a normal-looking cabinet might buy Sister Silence more time to finish her job. On to the second cabinet.

"On the main floor," Deke reports.

Automatic weapons fire echoes down the hole in the ceiling.

"Two down," Deke says.

In less than three minutes, Sister Silence reports she's getting access on all three controllers as I'm shutting the last cabinet.

"Data prepped," I say. Exfiltrating the data is now Sister Silence's monkey.

I've done what I can to help Ayaka's victims.

Now to find Ayaka.

I pull my silenced .38 and slip through the door.

The room beyond is the hands-on computer lab, with workbenches and stripped desktop units and a stack of broken laptops awaiting cannibalization. Most of these places are heaped with busted rubbish that might, someday, possibly be useful, in some incredibly bizarre circumstances, but whoever works this lab is impeccably tidy. A mostly empty desk with a comfy-looking chair is clearly reserved for current projects, and contains only a battered old laptop, a screwdriver set, and a collection of cables hooked up to a modern workstation.

Above the desk, though? Exultant, I say "I found the office wiring diagram."

It's gold.

We had no idea of the layout of this office. We planned to gas everyone insensible before searching the office and tossing Ayaka out a window or whatever. It's not fair, but neither am I.

Another burst of gunfire tells me that not all the gunbunnies went down with the gas. We got some. Not all.

"Two more down," Deke says. "Got you an MP-7."

"Sweetie bear," I say. "The map says there's a big boardroom in the southeast corner."

The walls muffle the sound of gunfire.

"Cat-and-mouse," Deke says. "I'm distraction."

I pull my phone, snap a picture of the wiring map, and send it to Deke and Sister Silence. Deke's going to be too busy to look for a while, but when he gets a moment it'll make him more effective.

I look down from the map, forcing a deep steadying breath through the gas mask.

My breath stops halfway through.

The laptop on the work desk? With all the cables hooking it to the new machine?

It's old enough that the case looks battered. It's the sort of machine you'd expect to see in a fifth-rate flea market, not in a pricey London office.

Most companies don't let employees put stickers on their laptops. If they did, though, who in England would decorate their laptop with Pabst Blue Ribbon and Detroit Lions stickers?

Who would have gotten pissed and scrawled SUCKZ across the Lions sticker with black marker?

Father's stolen laptop.

80

How the hell did Father know what I do for a living? Where did his money go?

The answers might be right there in that aged and abused Lenovo laptop.

Yes, along with a whole bunch of porn. But still.

I swing my bag off my shoulders and stuff the laptop inside. There's lots of space now that I've unloaded Sister Silence's remote hacking kit.

Only then do I remember to report "I got Father's laptop."

"You sure?" Deke says.

"Pretty sure."

"I'll verify it later," Sister Silence says. "Grab and go, girl. How goes that database?"

The database isn't my problem—she must be talking to someone else, and missed flipping her mic off. It happens.

I'm reaching for the computer room door when a familiar voice says, "I'm extracting names now."

I stop. "Nancy?"

"Shit," Sister Silence says.

"Hi Beaks!" Nancy sounds downright gleeful.

Sister Silence says, "Off the line, Nancy."

"What are you doing?" I say. "What is she doing?"

Sister Silence says, "We talked when I had to move them. Turns out Nancy is the best database analyst I've seen in years."

I haven't moved my hand from the door handle. "So you're having her *hack*?"

"She's not a hacker. I hacked in and gave Nancy access. You're keeping me busy enough digging through the rest of this network. We need a big pipe to extract the whole thing."

I huff. "She stays safe."

"Don't worry," Sister Silence says. "She's on another continent. You make with the killing."

More gunfire echoes through the walls. "And you say *we* banter," Deke says.

"Fine!" I don't really have room to argue. Sister Silence needs the help. Nancy has every right to want payback for the way Ayaka's bastards hurt her sister.

But I still don't like it.

Nancy has no idea what kind of world she's touching.

I might not want to read *Nancy Drew Gets Capped*, but I don't want to be involved in *Nancy Drew Learns to Bust A Cap*.

A dull hum ripples through the floor. The hazy air flutters upwards.

"AC is back," I say.

"On it," Sister Silence says.

The hum dies.

Before long, Ayaka's hackers or building security or the power company or someone will block Sister Silence's hacks, restore AC, and purge the gas from the office.

Or Ayaka's goons will gun us down.

Nancy's made her choice, and I've made mine.

I open the door and peer out.

Nobody.

The gunfire's louder now. Deke's drawing fire so I can check the boardroom. He didn't say it, we didn't plan it, so the sooner I get there and bust my own cap in Ayaka's ass or find out she's not there the sooner I can rescue him.

This corridor dead-ends like the map said, the door on one side leading to the computer lab and the other to the janitor closet. I run down the hall, silenced .38 in hand. Each step yanks at the pain in my side, making it feel even more bloated and pressured.

Did the impact rupture something?

No time to guess.

Kill Ayaka. Save Deke. Set off the big alarm, get out.

Then try that lovely National Health Service.

I pass a big glass-walled meeting room with a private balcony. A dimly visible steel box out there contains one of those high-rise escape chutes, but nobody's triggered it yet. It's reserved for conventional emergencies, not this kind of mercenary mayhem.

The next intersection should take me to a big hall that leads straight into the boardroom. I kneel, forcing myself to breathe through that spine-deep bruise. My fingers find the corner-peeker on my utility belt. I turn the screen so I can easily see it and slowly nudge the fiber-optic hook around the corner.

The fisheye lens distorts the view, but the unoccupied hallway and the double doors of etched glass at the end are visible enough. Huge pictures line the walls, interspersed with bronze plaques probably commemorating especially amazing acts of corporate assholery. A red carpet plush enough for royalty covers the last twenty feet of floor before the double doors. According to the map, that wall backs right up on the company lobby.

The floor hums.

"They've fixed the AC power," Sister Silence says. "I have to break back in, it'll be a few minutes."

"Skip it," Deke says. "Focus on exfil."

"On it," Sister Silence says.

Even once the air clears, anyone who got a lungful of that stuff will be down hard for a good day and won't want to eat for a week. And for a few days, as a totally accidental but joyously vindictive side-effect, it'll burn like acid when they pee.

Best. Gas. Ever.

I study the image carefully. No trip wires. No gun ports.

Keep the plan simple. Use an explosive to shatter the doors. Throw another inside, blow it. Rush in, finish the job.

If the blast doesn't kill Ayaka, I'll shoot her the old-fashioned way.

I stuff the plug back into my open ear. "Going into boardroom," I mutter.

"On my way," Deke says.

I'd much rather have Deke with me, but every second I wait is another second for someone to put a bullet in my back.

Silenced .38 in one gloved hand, primed explosive in the other, I pop around the corner and scurry down the hall.

I'm kind of surprised when I'm not instantly shot.

This big hall is meant to impress. There are no doors, only larger-than-life portraits of impressively-dressed black men and women with little plaques beneath them. Of course Ayaka plays up the businesswoman thing; she uses every tool she can get.

The glass doors of the boardroom are so heavily etched in white swirls that I can't see through them, but they're lit from behind and I don't see any movement.

Maybe my gut's wrong and the boardroom's empty.

Gunfire echoes down the hall behind me. I have an impulse to whirl, but it's not right there. Deke's still raising trouble, giving me time.

I'm halfway down the hall when Ayaka says, "Welcome to my trap, young lady." My earplug flattens her voice, but it's still recognizable.

I freeze in half a step, glancing around wildly. Nothing has moved. Nobody's here.

I trigger the gas mask's external speaker. "Not much of a trap."

Ayaka laughs. The sound comes from an intercom mounted in the wall next to me. "This is going to be the YouTube hit of the century."

I say, "Is this the part where you taunt me with your superiority?"

"That was earlier. This is the part where you die."

A series of quick thuds make me spin.

Six of the paintings on the opposite side of the hall have plummeted to the floor. A person in full combat armor, gas mask, and helmet stands behind each.

I'm staring down the barrels of six automatic shotguns.

81

Time halts.

Beneath the haze of smoke and gas, the hallway's a perfect and pristine example of First World Corporate Supremacy. Dark red carpet so deep you could comfortably host an orgy on it. Intricately etched glass doors. Portraits of admired figures.

And the portraits hid massive brutal firepower.

Truly, a perfect example.

It's the last sliver of a second of my life, even past my last breath, and my brain is spending it bitching about the oligarchy.

Figures.

My legs have frozen. Duck one way? The other way? I'm caught, dead center. They can't miss. The body armor will stop the shells, but beat the hell out of me.

Knocked down in the first volley.

Finished in the second.

Ayaka out-prepared me.

Out-experienced me.

Maybe I'm the one who hot-wired the Large Hadron Collider.

But it doesn't help.

Not one bit.

The darkened space behind the gunmen lights up.

A horrific blast hammers my ears. It's not one of my little puppy charges. It's nothing Deke and I brought with us. It's a full-on TNT-filled pineapple or some beast like that.

Time restarts.

I throw myself aside even as men scream and shotguns roar.

Smoke and debris and shotgun blasts rain out of the gun holes.

Someone set off a blast behind the gunmen.

I have about a sneeze to wonder who before hitting the ground.

By some miracle I faceplant into the carpet without getting shot. I start to roll to my feet and run, but the body armor interrupts the roll and I wind up splatting straight on my injured side. Even a touch of weight on that wound triggers a red-hot balloon swelling up inside my gut, pressing all the way up into my chest and throat and down into my groin. My breath rushes out in shock, but I instantly shove myself to roll to the other side and get a foot under me and scramble straight into a run.

Straight towards the boardroom doors.

I've come this far. I'm not running away.

The concussion dissolved the etched glass into a sparkling carpet, revealing a pretentiously massive table and chairs so executive each probably ships with its own butler. I don't see anyone, not even in the dim reflection in the glass wall beyond the table, but nobody's dumb enough to stand right in front of the door when they know I'm coming.

A shotgun blast goads more speed out of me. If I can get into the boardroom and around a corner, I only have to contend with whoever's inside.

Shattered glass crunches under my boots.

I dropped the explosive somewhere. My right hand still clutches the silenced .38. I'd laugh at using a silencer at Explosion Fest, but there's no time.

Another explosion rips the air, this time from the boardroom. I'd rather run towards it than back towards the shotguns. At least I'm wearing earplugs. When they find what's left of my corpse, my eardrums will be okay.

The glass wall beyond the boardroom table dissolves into glitters.

Air pressure blasts the whole wall into the night.

My blocked ears ache furiously, unable to pop. If I can ignore the bloated, growing pain in my side, I can ignore an earache.

I fling myself through the doors and instantly to the side, using the wall to hide from the shotgun-wielding men.

On the other side of the big table, Ayaka faces me.

She's wearing her own foamed metal body armor. Mine is expensive, but hers is pricier still and even covers her neck. Tiny protective goggles obscure her eyes, her features, but she's Ayaka's height and the shape of the cheekbones above the gas mask and the contours of the skull beneath that short-cropped stark white natural hair are distinctly hers.

"Miserable *child*," Ayaka snarls, loud enough to get through my earplug and earpiece.

I wrench my .38 around, squeezing the trigger before I've even aimed.

Ayaka's running. She might be old, but she's fast.

There's no place for her to go, though. She can run around the table, but there's no room to zig or zag and eventually she has to come back towards the door towards me no matter what, then one round will knock her down even if I hit her in that backpack and—

Ayaka flings herself out the window.

I freeze for a quarter second, flabbergasted.

Then run to the edge of the gaping hole.

London lies spread out before me, a glorious panoply of light beneath the gray dome of sky. Churning spots of white and red and blue fill the world, headlights merging and separating from streetlights, business signs flickering on and off all the way to the horizon where they muddle together into a single multicolored haze that surrounds the edges of the world. The Thames is a meandering ribbon of darkness, but even that has scattered lights from tour boats and probably private motorboats.

Ayaka's invisible amidst that chaos.

The darkness blooms below, obscuring a rectangle of light.

A parachute.

I've done exactly that, more than once.

Ayaka murdered my father, then stole my gimmick.

82

I want to shriek in frustrated fury at Ayaka's escape.

My gun hand rises—no.

I can't hit Ayaka from here. It's night, and she's a dark patch against a panoply of lights. The silencer wrecks aim more than a few yards away. And the rectangle of her parachute is already indistinguishable from the churning lights below.

I *can* hit some innocent bastard out for a curry.

"She's escaped," I snarl.

"What?" Deke says.

"Ayaka parachuted out the window," I say. "Sister—cameras. Find her. She's still airborne."

"Which window?" Sister Silence says.

I swap my silenced .38 for the faster, more accurate unsilenced one. Right now, I want the noise. "Boardroom."

"On my way," Deke says.

"Listen," Sister Silence says. "You need to know—"

"Won't be in the boardroom." I'm already running back towards the hallway. I lead with my .38, blindly shooting into the holes in the wall where the gunmen had been lurking with shotguns. I'm not trying to hit anyone, I just want them to keep their heads down as I bolt back. "Going for the balcony."

"Where?" Deke says.

Two shots echo down the corridors.

"Off the hall that crosses the boardroom hall. Big meeting room."

We've knocked Ayaka out of her castle. Parachuting out of a skyscraper into London in the dark isn't an exact science. Maybe she'll come down close to her secondary shelter, and we'll have to blast her out. Perhaps she'll touch down in the middle of East India Dock Road and a semi doing eighty will do us the favor of flattening her. From this height, she can get maybe half a mile out of a parachute.

But when Sister Silence gives us a location, we must have boots on the ground.

"What have we got?" Deke says.

"Escape chute. Out on the balcony."

"Good enough."

I round the corner, glancing left and right, and see what I most want.

Deke, jogging towards me.

He's wearing a gas mask and night vision goggles. There's enough light that we don't need the googles to see, but they're protecting our eyes against Nasty Uncle. The breeze dragging everything towards the blown-out boardroom isn't near enough to clear the gas.

He's limping. There's blood on his arm.

But he's alive and unmaimed.

"No alert yet," Sister Silence says. "But—"

"Later," Deke says, stopping short of me. He's in front of the glass-walled meeting room, yes, but my whole being wants him to run to me instead.

Deke jerks on the meeting room door. It's locked. "Sister, can you open the meeting room door?"

I glance over my shoulder, making sure there's nobody sneaking up behind, and trot quick as I can to join him. The ache in my side has transformed into a constant pressure. I hope I'm not bleeding internally.

If I have a bleed, it's slow. Slow enough. I haven't dropped dead. Yet.

"Hang on…" Sister Silence says. "Quicker to unlock all the doors."

"Do it," Deke says.

A click, and the meeting room door wobbles open an inch. Must be air pressure.

I get to Deke just as he throws the door open. "Got it. Do you have anything on escape chutes?"

"They're not on the building plans," Sister Silence says. "Your floor's a little high for standard chutes—no, wait. You're above the fifteenth-floor rooftop garden. You get down to that and either hop the elevator, or take the fire stairs."

"Stairs," Deke and I say simultaneously as we scuttle out onto the balcony.

Stepping outside feels like entering a new world. Simply leaving Ayaka's offices lightens my spirits. The air feels cleaner on my few scraps of exposed skin. The narrow concrete balcony has no furniture, only the one-yard cube of the escape chute mounted on a scaffold barely high enough to raise it above the four-foot fence.

Deke and I run for it.

"You can go down the stairs, but it'll alarm," Sister Silence says.

"When I get down, we trigger the fire alarm," I say.

"Yes," Deke says.

Right. He's in charge.

"You get the chute," Deke says. "I'll cover."

"On it." I swing two panels on the box. The compressed chute automatically starts spilling out over the balcony towards the distant ground.

"You go first," Deke says. "I'll cover till you're on the ground."

I don't want him to spend another moment up here. "Come right after me."

"The longer I wait," Deke says, "the more chance I get to shoot a goon."

I grimace. We don't want a gunbunny dropping a grenade down the chute either. "Fine."

The chute drops faster and faster, expanding like a weird columnar parachute.

"Get on the ground," Deke says.

"Two things," Sister Silence says. "The cops. They're starting to show up. Those explosions, people heard them. People know what bombs sound like, the parking garage's choked. You go down there dressed like SWAT—"

The escape chute's deployed far enough. I grab the top of the escape chute to pull myself up, wince at my side, and tromp my feet up the ladder instead. "Got it."

Deke says "Sister, once we're in the chute. Any spare time. See if you can spy free wheels." He doesn't mean free free. He means freeable free.

The escape chute's a narrow cloth tube, with snug ring-shaped ridges to slow my fall. I'll have to pull off my utility belt and drag it above me.

But there's no way I can wear my backpack down.

The backpack isn't very large. But I'm a big woman. The chute will already be claustrophobic.

And there's nothing in it I need.

Yes, there's Father's laptop. But I don't *need* that.

I just really, really *want* it.

Unexpectedly finding, and then unexpectedly losing, the knowledge on Father's laptop makes me quiver with frustration. But if it's a choice between avenging him and understanding him, I'm choosing vengeance.

Before I've even decided, though, my body's shrugging out of the backpack.

Guess I already understand him more than I want to.

"Deke," I say.

He doesn't look away from the well-lit meeting room or the hallway beyond. "Yeah, Billie babe?"

"The backpack. Father's laptop's in it."

He nods. "I'll drop it down after you."

Maybe it'll survive. It's survived this long.

But the most delicate and irreplaceable part of a laptop is the hard drive, and Father sure doesn't have one of those indestructible solid state drives in this ancient beast.

But maybe is better than nothing.

"Luck," Deke says.

Looking back at the boardroom, soaking up a last sight of Deke with his shotgun raised, protecting my back, I ease my butt to the edge of the chute. It already feels like being swallowed by a forty-story serpent, and I'm not quite committed.

"The second thing," Sister Silence says. "That explosion—"

Right as I push off, another gunman steps into view in the hall beyond the meeting room.

My brain screams for Deke to shoot.

Gravity sucks me down hard.

Deke's shotgun roars.

The gunman flops down.

Good. Deke's safe.

The chute swallows me, and my brain assembles what I saw.

The gunman had a gas mask that covered his eyes, like something out of a war movie. A M16 with a grenade launcher knocked askew by its single shot. A freaking *bandolier*, dangling more grenades. He wasn't wearing anything I'd call body armor, only a big old bulletproof vest way too small to cover him but belted hard around his bulging gut.

It was Larry the Cable Guy cosplaying Rambo.

Ayaka would never hire that kind of gunbunny.

Oh my god.

It's Will.

My idiot brother followed us across the world.

And my lover just killed him.

83

Using an escape chute feels like riding through a giant snake's colon.

The synthetic fabric squeezes snugly, but not enough to keep gravity from sucking me through as irresistibly as peristalsis. I have my arms above my head, utility belt in a two-handed grip.

Even through my gas mask, the chute stinks of long-stored plastic.

I have about forty stories of slow falling.

A sniper could put me down, easy as tripping Granny.

Fortunately, I'm distracted.

Despite the throat mic I shout, "What the hell! Will?"

"Fuck," Deke says. "What is he—"

"Been trying to tell you since he moved," Sister Silence says.

"You knew about this?" I snarl.

"He paid me," Sister Silence says. "A hacker's gotta eat."

"He's flat broke!" I say.

"He came into some cash a few days ago," Sister Silence says.

"Because I gave it to him!"

Deke raises his own voice in command. "What was your deal? Exactly."

Sister Silence says, "When the FBI figured out their safe house and I moved them, we talked. Said he'd pay to be on hand if you needed help, and to vanish if you didn't."

My brain is reeling. I'm furious with Ayaka, and with Will, and now with Sister Silence and Deke—

How am I mad at Deke?

Because Deke *shot* my brother.

Deke's military-grade shotgun slugs versus that cheap-ass bulletproof vest? No contest.

Will liked donuts. Now he is one.

I flash back to Scottsdale, with Lou shot in the throat and his heart's blood sizzling on scalding concrete.

I'd come home for Father's funeral, and now I'm going to bury my brother.

I'd tried to help Nancy, and she's not in the line of fire but she's sure on the wrong side of the law.

Everyone I touch dies.

Or I corrupt them.

I don't know which is worse.

"I tried to tell you," Sister Silence says.

"You could have said before!" Between the gas mask and the earplugs, my voice booms inside my head.

"That was his deal," she says. "If you hadn't been caught, you'd never know he was there."

"I wasn't caught!"

"What about that 'this is where you die' stuff?" Sister Silence says.

I'm too mad to admit the point. "You were supposed to keep them safe!"

"If I hadn't taken his money," Sister Silence says, "he would have gone looking for a fake passport on his own. He'd be spilling his guts in an FBI holding cell right now. What the hell was I supposed to do?"

"Talk to me!" I say.

"What do you think my handle means?" Sister Silence says. "You've made your feelings about this man clear. If you hadn't been in trouble, I wouldn't have unlocked the lobby door."

I want to scream. Sister Silence had let my useless big brother into the bloodbath. Where he'd shot a pineapple into the back of six men who were about to shoot me.

"He had a goddamn grenade launcher," I say. "Who uses a grenade launcher inside? Who uses it for fucking short-range direct fire? Dead men, that's who, because that's what he is now!"

"Beaks," Deke says.

I stiffen.

He only calls me Beaks when we're with a client. When we're on the job with other people. Or when I need to rein it in.

How can Deke be mad at me?

The chute seems to tighten around me.

Deke carefully enunciates his next words. "Your brother is alive."

He can't be. "But you shot him."

"I did."

"You don't miss."

"I didn't." He's still talking slowly. "That meeting room? Bulletproof glass, both walls. The good stuff. It slowed the slug enough."

A shocking, surprising hope floods through me.

I don't want Will dead.

I don't want to be near him, no.

But there's a part of me that's most comfortable when I'm pissed at him. I like the certainty that he's back home, guzzling beer and ruining T-shirts with his sweat and expanding his gut while I'm out here improving the world one robbery at a time.

Because this job is going to kill me one day.

And if I'm improving the world…who am I improving it for?

Not Will. Not exactly.

Just for people a lot like Will.

I'm still mad.

"But that gear," I say.

"Look," Sister Silence says. "I left him some cash for gear. Told him to get the best he could, hooked him up with Jacoby."

"Jacoby?" I say. "He'd steal milk from a baby."

Deke says, "Do you think Mall would deal with Will?"

I bite back my answer. Of course not.

Jacoby's a bottom-rung arms dealer.

Will probably had to stretch to reach up that high.

The tension in my chest bursts. I'm still not happy. But of anyone, I know what a pain my brother can be. We both got our stubbornness from the same stubborn drunk.

And Will…had saved my life.

I'd given him tens of thousands of dollars, more money than he'd ever seen in his life, and he'd blown it all to cover my back.

The thought of owing Will anything pisses me off almost as much as Will getting himself killed.

"Fine," I say. "How is he."

"Busted ribs," Deke says.

"Good."

"Here's the plan," Deke says. "I'm coming down. Will's taking the laptop, going to the elevator, ditching everything he bought from Jacoby outside the door, and riding down like another innocent victim of whatever's going on here. Silence, when he calls, get him a safe house and make sure he stays there."

"Phone?" I say. "Doesn't he even have an earpiece?"

"He said you'd took his," Sister Silence says.

"And he didn't buy—" I draw a breath. "No. Never mind. Of course he didn't get one from Jacoby. Why use encrypted—"

I bite the rant off.

Not now.

"Going down now," Deke says. "Will says, and I quote, for you to 'fuck her up.'"

"Will do," I say.

84

I feel my feet come free of the escape chute. Before I can react, I immediately splash knee-deep into water. Something flashes and squirms against my calf, and I nearly fall over recoiling.

Gold flashes beneath the water. It's a fish the size of my arm.

A koi.

An entire thousand-pound-a-plate rooftop restaurant, and Ayaka's escape chute dumps into the koi pond.

I swear and, for Deke's benefit, say "Wet landing. Beware the fish."

Fortunately, the restaurant is closed. The Thorntree towers eighty-five stories behind me, but the other three sides of this patio are ringed by a four-foot-high wall to keep drunks from stepping straight down to the pavement fifteen floors below. Four-person round tables impaled on closed giant umbrellas pack most of the open space.

Okay, that's the reason for the water landing. Landing on a table umbrella would make you the restaurant's most unappetizing appetizer.

No, *focus*. Our whole operation's changing now. We lost stealth. Here on this rooftop we'll restore it. Out on the street, we'll keep it.

That means a whole different look.

The gas mask goes first. Cool London night air hits my face like salvation. Ripping off the night vision goggles feels even better. I really want to keep the body armor, but any cop who sees me in it will call for Armed Response Vehicles and *all* the firearms officers.

Unbuckling the chest plate makes my injured gut flare, staggering me. An icy tsunami of clammy London air floods my sweat-soaked T-shirt.

I risk tugging the T-shirt up to assess the damage.

A bruise the size of a dessert plate mars my stomach. It's hot and tender to the touch. Removing the armor's pressure doesn't seem to make it swell any more, though.

I'll need a couple weeks, but it'll heal. Probably.

The water soaked my boots and pants. Nothing I can do about either.

The gloves, throat mic, and earpiece stay. I pull the plug from the other ear, almost wincing at the assault of noise. Car motors and shouting people and a dozen different musics from as many pubs rise fifteen floors, blending into a dull cacophony.

The utility belt is a repurposed tool belt and most of the equipment dangling on it looks innocuous, so I put it back on. I tug pouches over the two .38s so they look like specialized tools—it won't fool a pat-down, but it's dark and if Sister Silence says the streets are chaos then they're chaos.

I'm still not happy with her.

I get why she brought Will over. But I hate it.

I run my gloved fingers through my hair. It's too short to tangle, but it's sweat-soaked where the night vision goggles rode my skull and I need to tidy it before it dries and I look even more like a homeless lunatic or, as they say over here, an American.

I can hear police sirens way up here. This restaurant patio is still way above the surrounding buildings, or I'd probably see the reflections of all the blue lights. Sister Silence understated the police interest, if anything.

The chute wobbles and ripples. There's enough light to see the lump that's Deke undulating his way down. He's passing a floor every couple of seconds.

Weird. My drop was at least ten times that long.

Deke lands on his feet in the pool, raising his own tsunami. He struggles for his balance, waving my little pack over his head like he really doesn't want to get it wet. I left almost nothing in it—why bring it? He doesn't come straight for me, though, instead seizing the end of the chute to find his balance. "Billie! A hand here."

I dash to the edge of the pond, feet squelching in my boots, and grab the chute from him. "What's going on?"

The chute is shaking.

"Bonuses," Deke says. "Aim it over the floor."

I manage to stretch the end of the chute past the edge of the koi pond. Seconds later, dark gleaming metal shoots out of the chute and skitters across the floor, disappearing beneath a table. I hear a thud as it strikes the wall at the patio's edge.

"Will's dropping a few weapons before leaving," Deke says.

I want to be angry that Will dares to actually be helpful. I'm long past that, though. He's here. He's getting out. Accept, move on.

"Ammo's in the backpack," Deke says.

Two more objects come flying out and glide across the patio. One hits the wall. Another bounces off a table or chair leg and ricochets off somewhere. While Deke strips down to something that can pass as civilian wear, I collect two MP-7s from the patio's edge. I search for the third, but it's too dark under all these tables for me to find it before Deke is ready.

All together we have two MP-7s, my two .38s, and Deke's nine mil.

We stuff the machine pistols in the backpack and head for the emergency exit. The stairs grow increasingly crowded with almost panicked late-night cleaners and technicians and a few executives working way too late, but the current carries us inexorably into the street. Police officers herd us towards emergency services, but Deke and I slip out into the gawkers.

We're a block away, catching our breath, when Sister Silence says, "Police report of a parachutist in black coming down in Limehouse, near the waterfront." We persuade an undeserving man in a five-thousand-pound suit to loan us his blue Audi convertible, leaving him his teeth as collateral, and race east.

85

The traffic's terrible going towards the Thorntree, but we're going the other way and our side of the road's all clear and open. A few people make illegal U-turns and force Deke to swing the Audi convertible into the other lane, but I suspect most of them see us screaming towards them like we have a Falcon Heavy booster in the trunk and delay their own lawbreaking in our favor.

Leave crime to the professionals.

Sitting in a car wearing a loaded utility belt is hideously uncomfortable, especially with the way my unsilenced .38 digs at my bruised side. The Audi's passenger seat is clearly designed for people smaller than me. I brace my hands on the dash, more to keep myself from sliding around than from any actual fear. The wind takes some of the dampness from my skin but leaves me chilled. It can't be sixty degrees out—I'm pretty sure the Brits conquered the Empire to escape their own weather.

Fortunately, the heated leather seat warms up really quickly. I turn it off before I get hot.

Sister Silence feeds us instructions, tracking us by our phones and GPS and probably satellite. Turn here. Go straight. Slow down, cop ahead. Yeah, they're not cops here in London, they're bobbies or something, but whatever they're named we don't need any of them.

"Shots fired at Speedboat Tours," Sister Silence says.

"Guide us," I say as Deke says "Where?"

It's not certain that gunshots mean Ayaka, but I'm sure anyone who gets in her way right now dies.

Just as she's in our way.

My Deke insists he knows better drivers than him. But he's damn good. Our Audi hugs the narrow London roads like a miser snuggles freshly minted gold. We don't hit the little old lady. Or the teenage boys. And the four-door sedan we inadvertently transform into a two-door is in a clearly marked "no parking" spot. Totally not our fault.

I'm certain the Audi's owner wanted to repaint his car a color other than Boring Blue anyway.

Sister Silence directs us to stop in front of a long stretch of exposed quay. A giant LED sign proclaims *Speedboat Tours—The Fastest Tour of the Thames!*

The maze of fence to corral the sheep to their fleecing is dark, but the little shed beneath the broad protective awning has a single light on. Even from the road, I can clearly see the backlit shattered window.

Deke parks the Audi and pockets the keys. I snatch the backpack full of firearms and we race for the shed.

I can barely hear a motorboat engine, growing more distant until it melts into London's pervasive background noise. I'm about to speak when Deke says, "Sister. Motorboat that just left here."

"On it," Sister Silence says. "Upstream. It's bright red, big enough for twenty. The cameras aren't good enough for me to pick up the pilot's face, but it's running fast enough to leave a wake and there's only one person on a boat built for twenty."

Should be her.

Probably.

Desperate hope propels me into the shed.

The shed's a combination ticket stand and office. Sprawled against the wall opposite the door, a man tries to hold his face together through all the blood. He's a Sikh, mid-fifties, wearing a blue-black turban and the security uniform and gasping because he's in too much pain to scream. His cheek's slashed open to the teeth and he'll probably lose that eye.

My uncertainty disappears. We're on the right track.

"Keys," Deke says.

The guard doesn't respond.

Deke kneels before him. "I know you're hurt." His voice is soft as if he's speaking to a fragile newborn, though his face has enough fury to ignite fires. "She's gonna hurt more people. We need to catch her right now. We need a boat. Where are the keys?"

"Are the cops coming?" I murmur in my throat mic.

"They've been notified," Sister Silence says. "Dispatch has more attention on the Thorntree."

More loudly I say, "Get an ambulance here. Now. Yesterday."

I don't know if it's the word *ambulance* or Deke's gentle coaxing, but the maimed guard raises two fingers and points to a desk. Deke rises, grabs a metal box, and flips the top open.

We're horribly pressured. Every second that passes means Ayaka gets more distance. And yet Deke's every movement is precise. I want to tremble and scream, and he's in complete control of his body.

As Deke turns with the box, the guard grunts and raises two fingers.

"Two?" Deke says. He pulls a key. "Boat two?"

The guard gives a nod, but the motion makes him groan and sag further.

"Keep holding that wound," I say. "Direct pressure." Where the hell is he supposed to put that pressure? His whole face is slashed deep. "Sit up as much as you can. Help is coming."

I bet he didn't even try to resist.

Ayaka cut him for a moment of glee.

Past the ticket booth, the tourist fencing breaks out into numbered lanes. Lane two leads to an oversized speedboat with four rows of seats. The lights beneath the awning are enough to make out SPEEDBOAT TOURS 2 – VICTORIA in white on the prow.

I don't know why the guard pointed us at this boat. Why it was a big deal.

But when I hop behind the wheel and shove the key into the ignition, the motor roars like it's ready to take its own vengeance.

Deke casts us off, and we hurl down the Thames after Ayaka.

86

Growing up in Detroit, then in Malacaster, I was never far from Lake Huron or Lake Saint Clair or the Detroit River. Father loved to fish. He especially loved to have me pilot a borrowed boat, so he had one hand for the trolling rod and one for a beer.

I know how to run a motorboat.

Powering up the Thames at night in our stolen boat, surrounded by the dark quays and with the city lights reflecting across the angry water, almost none of that skill is useful.

The boats Father got his hands on wallowed through mild chop. This beast has six motors in the back, and they answer the throttle like they're ravenous for river. With all the traffic I don't dare turn the throttle up past an eighth, and at that the boat bounces across the chop and spray spatters my face.

It must be one in the morning. Maybe two. I see a couple of tour boats, but most of the traffic is heavy river freighters grinding their way to their destinations. The Thames was once one of the most important rivers in the world, and London its most vital port. Even today, decades after they surrendered the Empire as too expensive in favor of conquering the world via the BBC, it carries a huge amount of freight. All the city lights thicken the darkness down here, making it impossible for our eyes to adjust. And the Thames doesn't merely meander through London. It twists back and forth like a prize-winning contortionist desperate to outflex Gumby.

Despite our boat's size, the chop batters us from every side.

I'm chilled from my sweaty clothes, pond-soaked pants, and the sixty-degree night.

Plus, this speedboat's mediocre lights might provide enough light for others to see us, but they don't illuminate anything else. I have to navigate by shadows and reflections, staying well away from the quays and freighters alike. As speedboats go this thing is huge, but next to one of those freighters we're petite and crunchy.

And piloting it? The wheel's as responsive as riding a rolling pool table down a steep hill.

I nudge the throttle up. The motor's growl rises through my feet. The boat leaps forward. The throttle's at about one-sixth, and the engines are clamoring to be unleashed.

I don't dare open up. I'm better at boats than Deke, but I'm nowhere near competent to handle this beast, even in daylight.

Hopefully Ayaka isn't either.

Deke's right next to me, crouching for balance so he can pull the MP-7s out of the backpack and get the magazines in place. The motor drowns his voice, but the words "Catch up" arrive via the earpiece.

The water ahead's clear, for a moment. I hold out a hand.

Deke gives me an extra magazine.

I stuff it into my pants pocket and take the wheel. "Can't go too fast. It's called Victoria, but I call it Steers Like Moose. And it'll worry her."

"A little more speed," Deke urges. "I'll watch."

"I think I have her on camera," Sister Silence says. "She's outpacing you."

Shit.

Gritting my teeth, I nudge the throttle higher and aim for the tail end of a freighter heading downstream. Hopefully it will have moved by the time we get that far.

One of these days, I'd like to have a boat chase when it isn't blackest night. At least we're not in a jungle, this time. I don't have to contend with submerged rocks or getting ambushed by the top end of a waterfall, only with where the channel is and all these freighters and probably a dozen police boats lurking in wait.

With any luck, Ayaka doesn't know we're trailing her.

The famous twin towers of Tower Bridge appear, resplendently illuminated. No matter if it's day or night, Britain wants you to see that bridge and know that you're in London, dammit. The top half of the giant wheel of the London Eye looms to our left. I don't have time to enjoy the view, because I'm too busy edging the motor up and trying to aim for clear water.

We'll have to take a nighttime river cruise some time. Preferably with a pilot who knows the Thames.

How do the tours ever have enough open water to open up this engine?

"One o'clock," Deke says. "Another boat like ours."

I shift my perceptions from an all-consuming floodlight and take a single focused glance. Four red lights along the stern of a boat. It's hard to tell distance and size in this dark, but it's a real good guess it's about the size of ours, a couple hundred yards ahead.

I nudge the throttle up a hair more, and turn to ram our bow straight up her backside.

We start to close.

Then the lights of the other boat sink lower in the water.

"She's floored it!" Deke says.

I jam our own throttle forward. Steers Like Moose leaps forward like a cheetah, inertia making me clutch the wheel or be thrown back. "It's called 'full throttle,' dear."

"You can be all boaty at me later. Just catch her."

"Yes, dear."

Sister Silence says, "Has anyone told you two how cute you are when you're working?"

"Shush," Deke and I say together.

The target boat jerks to the side, as if trying to throw us off, then spasms back to its old course rather than plow into a freighter. But we're closing on her.

That's why the security guard said to take this boat. They're both fast. But ours is faster.

I'm gonna find that security guard's hospital room so I can send him a fruit basket and a note that the woman who maimed him has been seen all over London. Pieces of her, at least.

Our boat skips on the water, bouncing and bobbing on the waves. The motor's roar drowns all lesser sounds, but each thud of hull on water grinds my knees and compresses my spine. I have to hold the wheel tight or be knocked aside, but I need to keep one hand raised to protect my eyes from the spray. Some seeps between my lips, and I can't even take the time to spit out the oily bitterness. I started off cold and damp, and thanks to the spray I'm now soaking wet and just short of shivering. Deke has his MP-7 raised, but there's no way he can get a good shot. With us bouncing, Ayaka's boat bouncing, and the water shifting beneath us all, we need to be close enough to spit on her shadow.

The low and flat Westminster Bridge shoots by overhead. Big Ben looms in its perpetual spotlights.

Past the bridge, I glimpse blue lights flashing along the water.

The river police, or whatever the Brits call them.

But we're closing on Ayaka.

Her boat is maybe a third larger than ours. Despite all our jouncing around, I can make out flashes of light rippling across her boat's plastic seats. Maybe it's my imagination, but I think I can even see a dark figure at the wheel.

That flash of light might be her face as she glances back at us.

We come up alongside a long, heavy freighter, riding low in the water with the weight of its burdens. Racing past it probably breaks all sorts of river rules, but Father never taught me any rule except *get me where the fish are*, so whatever.

Deke braces his arm across a rail and raises an MP-7.

We're still a dozen yards away. I wouldn't try to shoot at this distance, but Deke's a better shot than me. If he thinks it's worth trying, I trust him.

I can't do anything about the boat bouncing up and down, but I can hold our course steady.

Deke holds.

Waits.

Our boat bounces off a wave and starts back down.

Deke's shot is barely audible above the roaring motors.

Ayaka's boat doesn't even wobble. He missed.

I blink away spray. Yes, I can see the shape of her shoulders and head now. We're closing fast. We'll run her over in half a minute at this rate.

Ayaka pulls her boat in front of the freighter.

Someone's waving at us from the freighter's bow. Probably shouting something obscene. I choke down an urge to return my own wave and a cheerful smile.

Deke fires again.

That's why we're going to win. Ayaka's alone. I have someone I can count on.

Love trumps death.

Another boat's coming from the opposite direction. But there's plenty of room for me to pull in front of the freighter like a Maserati on the freeway cutting off a tractor-trailer. Curved shapes loom out of the water on the other side, and I barely straighten us out in time to not hit them.

Ayaka's boat slews to the side. It rocks wildly, gunwales sinking to the waterline.

She's turning? Boats can't pivot, they have too much inertia and the water too much drag and most people aren't crazy enough to risk swamping.

She's risking swamping to stop dead, crosswise right across our path.

We're going too fast. I can jerk the wheel and swamp us.

The freighter I just passed? The one that seemed so slow?

If I kill the motor, it'll flatten us.

Dark shapes in the water closer to shore. Docks, or moored ships, or something, something nautical.

To the other side, an oncoming boat.

Maybe love beats death.

But spite? That'll mess you up every time.

I shout "Jump!" but the prow of our boat is already T-boning Ayaka's.

Metal screams and tears. Fiberglass crackles and shatters.

I feel our boat's keel grind up and over, splintering as it mounts and traverses the larger craft. Everything's spinning and crumpling. Overpowered motors bellow as they churn air.

I release the wheel and fling myself towards the gunwale.

Our boat's nose lurches down towards the river.

Deke's got a foot on the gunwale and launches himself towards the water.

There's no time for me to be graceful. Our boat is plowing nose-first into the Thames and if I don't get off right now its wake will drag me down with it.

I fling myself towards the water.

I seem to hang in the air forever, listening to metal scrape against metal.

There's the hollow *pouf-foumph* of marine fuel igniting.

I feel a flash of heat, then plunge into the Thames.

87

I slice through the water's oily surface into pure cold.

Maybe it's summertime, but when I'm already chilled by spray and a fish pond and my own sweat it feels like plunging off the Antarctic ice shelf into the ocean.

Flaring light overhead tells me there's a bunch of heat nearby, if I want to stick my head up and breathe flame.

And the freighter. That freighter's on its way.

I keep my mouth closed and swim like hell.

Pure adrenaline gets me far enough away that the freighter's prow doesn't grind me under. The freighter's motor gets louder and louder. The thought of being chopped up by the propeller's massive blades gives me more strength than I thought I had, and I keep swimming.

The freighter's motor cuts out.

I swim until my lungs are hot concrete and oxygen deprivation fills my head with burning nails, then struggle to the surface.

Breaking water.

Gasping air.

All that swimming, and I'm maybe five feet from the freighter's flank. I'm stroking hard just to stay afloat. About half a powerboat's worth of burning debris floats near the freighter's nose.

I can't keep paddling this hard. The river will have me.

Heavy. I'm too heavy.

I force another deep breath, then kick hard so I can free my hands to fumble with the utility belt. The plastic fibers have swelled with the water and it takes me a long minute to get the buckle undone.

Father Thames swallows my weapons and tools.

Kicking feels like I have a six-year-old stubbornly hanging onto each foot. My boots.

Someone on the freighter shouts "Hello! Is anyone there?"

If I answer, they'll throw a life ring. Pull me out of the water.

I can stop swimming.

I desperately want to quit dragging my booted feet through the water, stop commanding rapidly weakening muscles to obey my will and keep me alive.

But the police are on their way. If I quit now, I'm quitting a whole bunch of things.

Deke would get me out of prison. If he survived.

I cough. "Deke? Sister?"

No answer from the earpiece.

The water fried the earpiece, or the mic, or the phone, or everything. Maybe it took Deke as well.

I shake my head to repel the thought. I survived, so Deke survived. That's just how it is.

And Ayaka probably survived. Maybe she grabbed a life preserver before she dove into the water. I didn't see her jump. I'd love to think of her standing defiant behind that wheel, one fist raised and middle finger extended as I plowed a boat right over the top of her, but it didn't happen.

Ayaka was losing. So she blew up the game.

I have no idea where she is now.

Get out of the water. Find Deke.

It's open war now. Maybe Ayaka toyed with us a little, trying to get a higher grade of blood on her reputation. But she'll go after us silently now. Assassins. Snipers.

We'll have to fight dirtier.

I have assets. Deke has more. Maybe a few million between us.

Ayaka runs a billion-dollar business in human beings.

We'll have to fight smarter. And dirtier.

She has minions. I have a handful of intermittent associates.

And Deke (*he didn't drown didn't drown didn't*).

The battleground was one floor of one office tower. Now it's the whole world.

I'd wanted to hold casualties to a minimum.

An air strike on the Thorntree would have killed fewer people.

If I want to hold the casualties down, though, it's easy. Quit. Change my name. Live a life of quiet obscurity on Mauritius or New Guinea.

Or let the freighter crew pull me from the water. Ayaka won't kill me in prison, but she will pay for a standing rota of abusers.

Or drown. Right now.

A light from the freighter's deck is sweeping towards me.

I pull in a deep breath and stop kicking.

The Thames swallows me.

I unbuckle the boots and swim towards the nearest shore.

88

The Thames is the cleanest industrial river in the world. They don't dump sewage into it anymore, but even the best maintained boat lets out a tiny amount of fuel or oil.

And I'm pretty sure most of that oil wound up in my sinuses.

By the time I drag myself to the quay, my side is shrieking in agony and I'm frozen bitter. How can I ache everywhere if I'm so goddamn cold? I don't know how far the current has carried me. I don't know if I'm even in London proper. I'm not even sure why I'm bothering.

But eventually my hand touches sea-slick concrete. I find enough strength to stay near the wall, letting the current carry me forward, until my chilled fingers hit something I can grab.

A pole.

No, not a pole.

The side of a ladder.

Hauling myself out of the Thames demands more energy than I have. Each foot weighs a ton. I feel oily and waterlogged and yet I don't want to see water ever again.

The concrete on the quay—*warm*.

I flop onto my back and gasp.

I'm reduced to the essentials of life. Breathing. My flank is the only warm part of me, and it's a ball of fire that doesn't shed a drop of warmth to the rest of me. Shivers assault me.

My brain starts to turn over.

The quay still holds a bit of August warmth, but it's not warm. It's only warmer than the Thames.

If Ayaka got to shore, she'll call for help. If she corrupted the FBI, she's got lines into British law enforcement. She'll feed them my name, and Deke's, and blame everything on us.

We've got to move. Get to a phone. Check my message drop to see if Deke got out first. Leave Deke a message if he didn't. Set a rendezvous. Hook up.

Get the hell out of England.

Get ready for war.

All that starts with being upright.

I'm exhausted. Chilled like a chicken breast straight from the fridge. I can smell only the Thames saturating my sinuses.

I need to move anyway.

I'm on a concrete ledge a yard over the Thames. It's probably for mooring a boat, like the two we wrecked. Fortunately, the ladder goes further up.

Climbing is easier this time. Moving my dead limbs demands focusing on what I want my body to do. You—arm! Up. Hand—grab the rung. Hold the rung. Opposite foot. Foot! I'm talking to you. Move.

The ladder's cold metal rungs dig into my waterlogged feet. My gloves, I still have my gloves, and they give my chilled fingers a little protection.

Somehow, I get on the quay. The Thames looms before me, blackest darkness broken only by the reflective metallic darkness of docks and boats.

Start with the basics. Where am I?

Turning around, I see broad stairs leading up to a lighted street. That long dark shape must be a bridge over the Thames, and there—lit windows. Short buildings, facing the river, with a few people still awake. Apartments, maybe?

I wrap my arms around myself and will myself to climb.

Ayaka's a long-term problem. Dawn is long-term.

Right now, I need warmth.

Five stairs or thirty, I don't know. They go on forever, while the light at the top gets brighter. When I finally step onto the road, I stop in surprise.

I'm right by Westminster Station.

Across the road, Big Ben towers above us all. Each time I stand near its base, I'm reminded how the pictures don't do it justice. It's brilliantly lit. The clock face reads three twenty AM. Smaller lights illuminate the sprawling spiky intricacy of Westminster Hall at its feet. Even at three in the morning, a steady stream of vehicles roll past.

Someone speaks. My brain needs a moment to assemble the sounds into meaning.

"Ma'am? You look terrible, can we help?"

It's a college boy. A little tipsy.

Out with friends on a school night.

Because that's what normal people do when they want to get in trouble. They don't trash skyscrapers and blow up boats.

From somewhere deep inside, I dredge up my *do not fuck with me* glare and nail it over my slack jaw and sagging eyes.

The kid steps back, raising his hands.

Too much. I try to relax my expression a touch and lick my battered lips. "I'm okay. I'll be okay. Just…pissed." Wait—wrong country. "Angry. Not pissed."

He still looks worried. "Get you a cab, maybe?"

"I'm okay." To prove my point, I turn and cross the street, heading away from the looming length of the bridge and towards Westminster Station. Behind me, some other boy says something about it being a night for loonies.

You have no idea, kid.

Westminster Station is a long cube of concrete architecture, nicer than any mass transit we'd have in the States but still clearly meant to move as many people as quickly as possible. I don't dare go inside or take the Tube. Tube stations have police. They'll notice people who look like they've swum in the Thames. By now they've all been alerted to watch for anyone who might have jumped off the burning boats.

But I'm freezing. The air is warmer than the water, but not much. The shivers are kicking in hard now. I'm in my sock—one sock, where did the other one go, and wait—what did I step in? Is that puke? Dammit, dammit.

I need water, drinking water. I need warmth.

I need a long hot shower and all the soap.

I shuffle a few more steps.

A sedan glides down the road past me. I don't have strength to steal it.

A red, white, and blue light shines on the station wall ahead of me. I need a few steps before I can get a good enough angle to turn the lights into letters. A Tesco Express.

It's open.

I pat my front pants pocket. Somehow, I still have my wallet.

Coffee. Even bogus coffee from the purple machine. If it's warm I'll drink it straight from the extruder. Overnight clerks won't care what I look like. They've seen worse, and I look like I need coffee with a side of hospital.

The promise of swilling warmth gives me the strength to pick up my pace. The doors slide open for me.

Inside is warmth, and light, and narrowness. Even a small convenience store usually has a couple aisles, but this store opens directly into a single tight hall with coolers close enough to touch on both sides. I'm surrounded by sandwiches. Tesco stocks more types of ready-to-eat sandwiches than anyone else in the world.

But coffee.

I stagger down the aisle. The store's clearly built to service people leaving Westminster in the most efficient manner possible. I get a mental flash of a horde disgorging from the Tube and coming in. Grab your sandwich. There's your fruit. No, no going back, there's more people coming, take it or do without. Microwaveables. Drink.

No coffee.

At least the place widens enough to accommodate three separate registers. The clerk at the lone open register stares at me like she's auditioning for a role as an extra in the remake of *Creature from the Black Lagoon*, and I'm the creature.

Maybe the coffee's around the corner.

I shuffle forward.

Freeze.

Yes, there's a little stand. A freestanding machine of purple plastic promises to extrude coffee-like liquid into a flimsy cup.

The woman standing in front of the machine looks like she's been run through a washing machine with a load of bricks. Her hair's matted to her head and saturated with bits of seaweed. She's a foot shorter than me, and barefoot, wearing combat pants and a soaking wet purple T-shirt with that weird male-female-something symbol and the words PRINCE LIVES.

Ayaka says, "Coffee machine busted."

89

I'm breathing, but time has stopped.

My pulse hammers in my ears.

My side is killing me. My muscles are frozen cold, and my joints ache like I've poured busted-up glass into them. I feel filthy and leprous and hideous.

I haven't been face-to-face with Ayaka in years. I watched her murder my father on video. We had a phone call. She texted me and told me over an intercom that it was time for me to die. I glimpsed her face as she threw herself out a window.

Standing still, facing each other, is different.

I'd forgotten her presence. Even half-drowned and half-burned, Ayaka carries herself like she's ready to tear a body part off of anyone and use it to beat the rest of the crowd to death.

And laugh while she does it.

The Thames carried her to the same general spot as it did me. Maybe the next ladder over.

She got to her feet before me. Not much—a minute. Maybe two.

The boy who'd tried to help me. One of his buds said something about it being loony night.

She'd walked past them.

Walked into the Tesco. For coffee.

We're so close I could reach out and touch her with a fingertip.

She's tired. I'm beyond exhausted.

But if the Thames dragged us both here, Deke might be close behind.

"Probably best." I drag in a breath. "If you'd gotten the last cup, I'd have to fight you for it."

Ayaka has her eyes on my chest, right above my breastbone. Any punch or kick I throw will start from exactly there. Her weight's balanced across her feet, though, so she's not preparing to move.

We're both done in.

But she's breathing deeply. Our bodies run on water and air and food. Facing me, she's not about to get the first or last, so she's oxygenating as much as she can. Just like I'm doing.

And the longer we talk, the longer we can rest.

When one of us feels ready enough? In better shape than the other, even if for a moment? Everything will go bloody.

Or the police will arrive. Or Deke will show. Or Ayaka's spare gunbunnies show, though I suspect she called in everyone local for the building.

"Credit where it's due." Ayaka even sounds worn thin. Her whole diction's shifted, less London and more LA. "You're a pain in my ass, you know that? You and your whole family."

"What did my father ever do to you?" I shift my shoulders, trying to stretch the tightness out of them. Even my shoulder blades ache.

She raises both eyebrows. The fragments of trapped green seaweed make them bushy. I'm sure I look just as bad. "You don't know?"

"We didn't talk."

"It's tragic when families fall apart," Ayaka says.

"How do you get on with your folks?" I say.

"Touché, child."

She's trying to piss me off with that *child* bullshit. I breathe. "What the hell can a drunk night watchman do to you?"

"He made notes," Ayaka says. "Recorded when trains came and went. Watched. He reported our unloading at Star Metals. We had to shift offloading of the in-transit cargo to the switchyard. Made me suspend my Detroit franchise."

"Your rep." Someone troubled her. Reputation is everything.

Ayaka doesn't bother to nod.

We both breathe.

The cashier lets out her own bored huff. "Can I help you?"

"No," Ayaka and I say simultaneously.

I came in chilled. The open coolers make the Tesco almost frigid. The tile underfoot leeches heat from my toes. I don't dare shiver. No weakness. "You're global. And you bothered to show up in Detroit?"

Ayaka smiles. "This not the part where I explain everything."

I give my own smile. "Why not?"

"I'll trade." Ayaka doesn't take her attention from my chest. "You hated your daddy. Why your scrawny ass didn't take my offer?"

I recoil. "There's not enough money."

"You should recognize an opening bid."

"That's not the point."

Ayaka nods, inhaling through her nose. "I miss being that certain. That righteous."

My involuntary snort at her last word interrupts my even breathing. We're playing a game right now, yes, but Ayaka's playing at a level above me. I absolutely *must* control myself.

If I don't recover my strength more quickly than she does, I'm dead.

And rage burns strength. Save it.

"Weren't righteous," Ayaka says, "you would have taken my top offer."

"That wasn't an offer," I say. "That was a trap."

"Oh, no, no, child," Ayaka says. "Yes, my parents protected. But if you'd put a quarter of tonight's effort into it, you'd have them both. You could be using their slow deaths to enhance your reputation."

I move my chin side to side, once.

And that answers my question.

Someone interfered with her. She showed up to put him down.

My chest tightens. I force myself to breathe.

My legs ache from standing.

I shift my weight, triggering a fresh ache in my side.

Ayaka shifts her feet a millimeter in response, like she's aware of my body's every twitch.

I've seen this before. Martial artists who finish sparring matches without even throwing a strike. They watch each other move, then one bows out because they realize they're outclassed by the way their opponent stands.

Buy more time. "My turn." I speak slowly. Like I'm having trouble putting the words together into sentences. "How many lives did you ruin last year?"

She doesn't laugh it off. "A little over fifty thousand. On course to break sixty this year."

"That's my answer," I say. "To your question."

"So righteous." Ayaka swings one foot backwards, switching her stance and increasing the distance between us by a foot or so. "If I let you live, in thirty years you'd be me."

I don't snort. "You'll have to do better than that."

"Everything's easier once you stop believing people have value other than what they bring—"

I don't see the kick. I only feel the pain.

90

Ayaka's heel crashes exactly into my injured side.

The whole time we were talking, she was figuring out where to strike.

We weren't even playing the same game.

I stumble back, crashing hard back-first into a cooler. Metal and glass clatters around me. Pain flares from groin to chin, robbing me of breath and making my eyes bug out, then my head hits the counter and my brain whirls.

The cashier shrieks something about 999.

Ayaka paces calmly towards me, like she has the whole night to deliver this beating and doesn't see any reason to hurry. "And what you can do for me right now? You can end this silly feud."

Die. That's what she means.

I can die.

I try to get a grip on the cooler. Push myself up.

Plastic bottles thud against each other.

"You know the sad thing?" Ayaka says. "About your father?"

I know all the sad things about Father. My chest is too tight. I can't breathe through the pain. My heart shudders hummingbird-quick, squeezed insensible by the horrid pressure bloating my torso.

My brain flashes to Deke. Please come in. Please walk up the aisle right now and plant your size twelve square in Ayaka's ass.

But it's not going to happen.

I'm alone with the woman who's going to kill me.

Unless I save myself.

I flail a foot up.

It stops a good six inches short.

Ayaka's panting. "In all those notes he made about my shipments? Right in the middle of them, with all the notes about fixing the roof and doing something awful to the neighbor's dog?" She raises her fists and sucks in air. "He wrote that you were going to be proud of him."

Ayaka throws herself forward.

Too late, though.

Her words are a seed crystal and my brain's supersaturated with pain and passion and love and hate and every other feeling a grown human being can have so they all crystallize at once into a lattice that's nothing but a perfect fusion of mind and soul and will and body into an absolute, inexorable, inviolate compulsion to kill this evil bitch.

My hand closes on the top of a plastic one-liter bottle.

Her fist's coming for my face.

I swing my arm between us.

The heavy bottle catches her punch, its weight throwing her arm aside and sending her blow straight into the metal edge of a shelf even as it knocks me sideways in the world's worst dodge.

My lungs loosen. Air gushes into my chest again.

Ayaka shrieks in rage.

I jerk a knee up. It's a lousy blow, more of a push than a strike, but it knocks her back enough that I can swing my other arm up towards her face.

I keep just enough fingernail to pry up a corner.

That's just enough fingernail to scratch across an eye.

I miss, but Ayaka reflexively stumbles back.

Bruises and pain or no, I squirm out of the cooler and onto my feet. I've still got that life-saving bottle in my hand, a liter of Tesco-branded sparkling water. That's one soulless megacorporation that's getting all my business from now on.

Ayaka regains her balance a couple yards back. We're both panting. Both of us have our hands up.

I hurt. Do I ever hurt.

Ayaka's right there.

I want her dead even more than I hurt.

I'll use that.

But to do that, I have to stop playing like a child and play like a pro.

She's ready to fight, but she's holding her arm a little off. Even I know that's bad technique. Wound, or feint? Her weight's forward on her feet, and she's shuffling a little, side to side—

That's it.

Ayaka's as worn out as I am.

She saved her strength for one killer shot.

She took it.

She missed.

Now there's blood on the knuckles of her right hand.

I heard her punch the shelf. Felt it through the metal. Knuckles against aluminum? The metal wins.

That hand's got to be bad.

I'm shuffling around with her, hands weaving by my head, trying to will my lethargic body to move.

She throws a left. It's way too slow. I feel like I could eat popcorn watching it come in. My sidestep is as slow, though. The back of her hand brushes against the antenna of my sticky spiky hair before I can get clean and throw my own roundhouse kick.

I kick like I'm striking through tar. Ayaka pivots right out of the way. I twitch to go into a follow-up, but no—I'm about to overbalance. Fatigue has stolen my combinations.

My strikes aren't about her, they're about me.

The real fight is in our brains.

Ayaka uses her left hand to tip a wire rack of chips—crisps, whatever—between us. It buys her half a second, one I use to grab a bottle of Irn-Bru off the shelf and fling it at her head.

I miss. But her dodge steals her momentum.

I half-stagger across a sea of spilled crisp packets while Ayaka gasps. I'm panting. The only sounds are the two of us choking down air and a cashier chanting "God in Heaven" so quickly she sounds like she's a finalist in the First Annual Pray for Rescue Contest.

To quote Father, God ain't nowhere near here.

She launches a front kick and another left like she's throwing through molasses. My sidestep's no faster, but this time I'm lashing out with my own, simultaneous strike.

A friend's been helping me with my knife hand lately.

The pinky edge of my hand is as tense as iron when I crash it into Ayaka's bloody right.

Ayaka shrieks. She hit my wound and now I've returned the favor.

I try to follow up. I really do. But she's already hopping a step back, never taking her eyes off me as she prances towards the praying cashier.

Who, to my shock, promptly hoists a steel flower bucket and cracks the bottom across the back of Ayaka's head.

Ayaka screams.

Both her hands go to her scalp.

I run. Straight at her.

I don't use any technique, just flat-out crash into her and grab her shoulder and arm and bounce off, using the energy of my ricochet to spin into a pivot and push her back towards the cooler she kicked me into.

The cashier's really screaming now. Her bucket has blood on it.

I grab a glass bottle—a fifth of Scotch or wine or whatever—from the shelf.

Ayaka hits the cooler, instantly bouncing back towards me, getting her hands up in front of her face, charging with blood in her hair and my death in her eyes. She's ready to take my makeshift club and stick the whole thing down my throat until I choke or it shatters, either way.

I hold the bottle high.

Take all the strength I have left.

Right as she's coming in.

And throw a fast, low, straight kick right above her groin.

I can almost feel the pop of her pelvis separating.

Ayaka's scream is horrific.

The cashier's isn't louder, but it is higher.

Ayaka hits the coffee machine and falls back, hips too widely spread. Her feet twitch and she clutches at her groin like she can hold her pelvis together.

The clerk's run out of air to scream.

I spare the clerk a glance. "Don't watch this, kid."

"But—"

I tip another wire crisp display over Ayaka. Packets fall everywhere, but more important? It'll lock her hands down for just a second.

Bending over makes me want to faint.

But I stay conscious enough to crash my bottle into the side of her head.

The blow's enough to make Ayaka's head loll to the side.

I drop to a knee and bring the bottle down again.

Again.

Some part of me thinks I should say something about Father. About the people she's enslaved and sold. I'm too tired to think of anything that complicated, though.

I need her dead. Bare hands are too slow.

So I swing the bottle.

On the fourth blow, the glass shatters on her forehead. My gloves save my fingers, but I've slashed the hell out of Ayaka's scalp. The stink of juniper somehow penetrates the gunk in my nose.

But the neck of the bottle's intact enough.

I hate killing helpless people.

But that's the only way to kill Ayaka.

I bring the spiky glass straight down into her exposed neck. Twist.

The stink of blood and gin turns my stomach.

Panting, I look up at the cashier.

"You looked," I say.

"I thought you were the good one," the cashier sobs. "She hit you first."

I shake my head. "Never make that mistake, kid."

Despite everything, I climb to my feet and stagger out the door before the police can arrive.

91

Two mornings later.

I wake up with that special kind of exhaustion you get after sleeping twelve hours without moving. Our bed in the Bayswater safe house has a cloud masquerading as a mattress, plus a really cushy pillow and halfway decent blankets. My arms object to pulling the blankets back. My eyelids consider mutiny, but finally decide to obey orders and grind open.

I don't have sand in my eyes. They're pebbles.

The other side of the bed is only faintly warm. Deke's been up for a while.

The doctor said my side would be fine, though he hadn't seen a bruise that bad since the last time someone got kicked by a horse. He advised I take it easy and avoid exercise for a week. The bruise is the size of a dinner plate, and while the edges are starting to turn green and smear, the middle is concrete-hard and painfully swollen. I managed to stretch a little yesterday, but ouch.

I'm not merely tired. I'm exhausted. I need a month off. On the beach. With a personal waiter to bring me shrimp cocktails and masseuses.

A handful of ibuprofen and a shower later, I stagger out to the safe house's main room. My usual safe houses involve battling the cockroaches to protect my breakfast. I don't know how Sister Silence finds places that belong in Better Homes and Gardens. How do they keep these luxuriant couches and chairs so clean when people might bleed on them?

Maybe it's just me. My reputation might be "Beaks is coming? Quick, hide the silver and spread out a tarp!"

If that's the case, I'll live with it.

Deke's stretched out on the longest couch. His head's on one armrest and his feet dangle over the other. England always feels like home, until you step into one of these doll houses and realize anyone raised on one hundred percent pure drug-boosted American cattle-cartel beef is fifteen percent too big for all the furniture. The mere sight of him eases the soreness around my heart. "Morning, Bear."

Deke's answering smile is always lopsided, but it's too tight. "Billie babe."

Tension ripples up my spine. But if something was really wrong, Deke would be on his feet. Did I do something wrong?

Before I can ask he says, "Look out in the sun room."

Did Sister Silence send us a present? I walk the few feet and open the connecting door.

The sun room is fantastic. It's got northern exposure, but the walls are all glass and it's absolutely filled with pots of lovely green glowing things.

And Will.

My brother is in one of the two rocking chairs.

He's unshaven. He needs a bath.

And Deke closed the door because the stink of whiskey makes me want to gag.

Behind me, Deke says "The Sister called, woke me up. He was makin' too much trouble where she'd stashed him. Driver dropped him off an hour ago."

"Shit." I'm too tired to break a window and throw him into the street. And the reek of whiskey is so bad, I don't want to touch him.

I do the only thing I can do, and close the door. "Anything else?"

"Yeah." Deke groans and sits up.

I'm still tired. I perch on the seat next to him.

His eyes focus entirely on me, full of concern. "You remember what happened when you first sent your pa money?"

"Sure." He'd been mad as hell that I'd sent him a thousand bucks out of my first 'paycheck.'

"You told him to suck it up," Deke says. "You were going to keep sending him money and he was going to like it."

"Damn right I did." Lots of people would say Father wasn't my responsibility. Except I knew he was.

"Sister gave me a message for you," he says.

"I would have called her."

"She knows. But since she dumped Ayaka's data?" Deke smiles. "She and Nancy have work piling up. She's raised her rates four times in the last day."

Reputation again.

Deke says, "She found the money. Wasn't hard, once we quit running her so rough."

I tense. "Do I get to—*have* to throw Will in the Thames?"

Deke shakes his head. "The day you sent your pa the money, he saw a lawyer. Set up a trust. It looks like any transfer from your shell company got routed into that trust. As far as she can tell, he never even checked the balance on it."

I still. "I sent him all that cash, and he—he never touched it?"

"He didn't even use it to pay the lawyer."

That should make me angry. I'm too tired to do more than say, "That fucking asshole."

"You sent him a pile," Deke says.

I sag back in the insidiously comfortable couch. "What the hell is this trust for? The Pabst-Marlboro Community Fund?"

"It's in your name."

For a moment, I can't even think.

Deke says, "Fourteen million and change."

Then I can't help it.

I laugh.

It starts off slow, but quickly expands out of my gut like a geyser.

Deke folds his arms around me. I hug him back.

It's a moment before I can choke out, "I told him fuck you, take it…"

I feel Deke's nod against my head. "And he said fuck you, no."

My father was not a good man.

But the thing that made him impossible to live with is a big part of what made me who I am.

Deke holds me a moment longer and says, "If we don't move, we'll stiffen up even more. Walk in the park?"

Part of the deal with a safe house is you don't go wandering around. But we're leaving today. "Sure."

92

Hyde Park is one of London's miracles. Acres of green grass and trees and immigrant parakeets that masquerade as parrots and will perch on your head to eat slices of apple from your hand. The Serpentine is a placid lake for model boats and gazing at and, in general, people who don't want to go anywhere near the chop of the Thames any time in the foreseeable future. Yes, there's rich bastards, but they get out of our way. There's working-class families taking their children out for a last excursion before school begins and young lovers bravely holding each other's hands.

It's a wholesome world that we don't get to visit very often.

The clouds threaten rain, but the showers won't last long. I hold Deke's arm, smile at children, and treat my love to an ice cream cone from the Rolls-Royce conversion truck.

We don't talk much, just enjoying the fact that we're both alive. It's not until we get onto one of the little trails that meander through the woods that I say, "Ayaka said that she used to be me. That one day, if I lived, I'd be her."

"Oh?" Deke's feet don't slow, but he squeezes my hand between his bicep and his big chest. "How?"

"She said she used to believe in causes." I'm watching the sky between the branches as we walk, not wanting to pay attention to the words coming out of my mouth. "That she used to think people mattered. That she was fighting the good fight. And then she realized that they don't, and she wasn't."

I feel Deke's soft grunt through his ribs.

"There at the end," I say. "When I was…" I need to be circumspect. It doesn't seem like anyone's near us, but there's trees and hills and shotgun mics. "At the end. It wasn't for Father. Or all the other victims. It was just…the way I needed it to be. So I did it."

Deke slips his arm out from mine and wraps it around my shoulders.

I don't dare ask. "Do you think…"

The ring of my phone saves me from having to answer.

It's got to be Sister Silence. Who else could have this new burner number? The caller ID reads all zeroes, but I swipe to answer. "Beaks and Deke's. You stash it, we snatch it."

"Miss Beaks."

It's Very Special Agent Tan. Apparently, the FBI can compete with Sister Silence.

I stop so abruptly I almost rip Deke's arm off. "Agent Tan."

Deke immediately switches from Date to Demolish and starts scanning through the surrounding trees.

"When I gave you that email address," Tan says, "I rather expected you'd contact me when you had a large number of people to take care of. I didn't realize that twenty-two people in a trainyard were beyond your capacity, or I would have phrased things more clearly."

"What did you expect?" I say.

"I *expected* that you would transmit the data on Ayaka's human trafficking ring to me."

Oh. "You can get a copy." I keep my voice light and breezy. "Just download it from the Internet, same as everyone else."

"Do you know of the chaos you've caused?" he says.

"I've been avoiding CNN. And Fox makes my trigger finger itch."

"With that data I could have gathered evidence to prosecute the people responsible." Tan sounds like he's speaking to a child too young to understand right and wrong. "Instead there's boycotts, and protests, and the politicians are demanding we do something, or claiming that the data's a lie. Three of the customers on that list have committed suicide in the last day."

"Oh? Huh. That's sad."

Anger creeps into his voice. "Do you have any idea how much damage you've done?" Tan didn't sound this livid after I lifted his car keys out of his pocket on the way out of the Heisenbug gig. "The chances of us successfully prosecuting any of these people—you've ruined every one of those cases. They will get away with it."

Now I'm getting pissed. "And while you were prosecuting, how many people would have remained slaves?"

"We call them trafficking victi—"

"They've fucking slaves," I snarl. "They are people. And answer the question. How long to prosecute, and how many people? How many wasted lives are you talking about here, so you can get your precious conviction?" Despite my weariness, my rage is starting to quiver my spine. "Tell me how many lives putting one psychopath in jail is worth, and I'll tell you how many bullets I'll spend putting that psychopath down."

"You're one to talk about psychopathy," Tan says.

"Those people *matter*," I hiss.

I yank the phone's battery out, toss it into the trees, and fling the phone itself down onto the asphalt. The phone shatters at my first stomp.

Then I'm storming down the path, almost but not quite trotting. It's not the kind of fury I had for Father, or Will, or even Ayaka. It's a normal human fury. The kind of anger that you get when someone's ethics and principles are so unspeakably alien that you can't tolerate their presence.

Deke's sensitive enough to follow a foot behind. I don't want company. I don't want to abandon him. I want to stomp and scowl until I feel better.

Which takes about a quarter mile.

We walk in silence another quarter mile before I take his arm again.

A few paces later Deke says, "I think you answered your own question."

"Yeah." I squeeze his arm. "I figured that."

As long as I keep caring, I'm not Ayaka.

We come around a curve and back into sight of the Serpentine.

"The real question is," Deke says, "what do we do about your brother."

I'm quiet for a breath. "I owe him."

Deke frowns. "You saved his life at the hotel. Seems pretty even to me."

"He wouldn't have been in that hotel if it hadn't been for us." My lips tighten. "And he spent every penny he had getting to England. Even if it was money I gave him to shut his face."

"He done showed up for you," Deke says.

I give his bad southern charm a hint of a smile. "The truth is, he's destroying himself. I can't stop it. I can't save him. And I can't watch it."

"I know," Deke says. "I couldn't watch it either."

He's not talking about Will now. I squeeze his arm in commiseration.

"He showed up for me," I say. "And yeah, it cost him every penny I gave him. But you know what? Showing up at the big dumb fight is the easy thing. Father taught me to fight. He stood up for us with his fists, all the time. He loved us with his fists." I shake my head. "But with his heart?"

"Some people are just too damaged." Deke's voice is soft.

He's not talking about Will. I take my arm out from his arm and put it around his waist. "You know you can tell me, don't you?"

He wraps his arm around me in turn. "I hope I never have to."

"If we go to your family funeral and you come out with your sister chasing you, I'm saving us all a lot of trouble and shooting her."

He chuckles and squeezes me.

After a few more steps I say, "Truth is, my brother is a jerk."

"Yeah."

"They only one who can save him from that is himself. Maybe he'll hit bottom and know it. I'd pay for rehab."

Deke nods. "Sure we would."

I treasure that *we*. "But I can't..." I chew my words around. "Back in Malacaster. My Aunt Pat. Uncle Carl. They were there for me when it all went bad. They did what could be done. Maybe I'll ask them to keep an eye on him. Give me a call if they think he'll take the help."

"Not a bad idea."

"You don't like it," I say.

"There's no good ideas here," Deke says. "But that's as good as they get."

I stop to hug him. "I should talk to them," I say. "When I do." I swallow. "Would you like to come along?"

Deke's arms grow tighter for a heartbeat. "Sure."

We stand in the middle of the walkway, arms around each other, until the laughter of an approaching child prompts us to break apart.

"So," Deke says. "France. Poissey, was it?"

"France is delightful," I say. "But I'm still kind of worried about my rep."

"I don't think you need to," Deke says. "She did what she did. You answered."

"Still." I glance around. Nobody's close enough to eavesdrop, but I still lower my voice. "We're in London. They have that Big Box of Stolen Treasure, what do they call it…"

"The British Museum," Deke says.

"Yeah!" I snap the fingers of my free hand. "That. Maybe some of it needs stealing back."

Deke laughs. "You know I can never say no to you."

"Then say yes."

"Oh, it's yes. I'm in. But something else you should think about," Deke says.

"This is gonna be good."

"I thought so." He glances at me with merry eyes. "That trust fund. Your pa never paid the taxes on it. With the fines and everything, I figure you owe about seven mil. We need to hire an accountant."

Laughing hurts.

But I do it anyway.

Beaks will return
in

Elephant Crystal Two-Step

Patronizers

My writing of this book was supported by the fine folks on my Patreon. Stefan Johnson, Jeff Marraccini, and Stefan Johnson back me so hard, they get their names in the print versions.

Every one of you Patronizers, named or not, make my ridiculous career less risky. Thank you.

About the Author

https://mwl.io

Never miss another new release!

Sign up for Michael Warren Lucas' mailing list at

http://mwl.io.

Novels:

Immortal Clay

Kipuka Blues

Butterfly Stomp Waltz

Terrapin Sky Tango

Hydrogen Sleets

git commit murder

Nonfiction (as Michael W Lucas):

Relayd and Httpd Mastery – PAM Mastery – FreeBSD Mastery: Advanced ZFS – FreeBSD Mastery: Specialty Filesystems – FreeBSD Mastery: ZFS – Tarsnap Mastery – Networking for Systems Administrators – FreeBSD Mastery: Storage Essentials – Sudo Mastery – DNSSEC Mastery – Absolute OpenBSD – SSH Mastery – Network Flow Analysis – Absolute FreeBSD – Cisco Routers for the Desperate – PGP & GPG –FreeBSD Mastery: Jails –Ed Mastery

See your favorite bookstore for more!

Printed in Germany
by Amazon
Distribution